THE
SUNBEARER
TRIALS

Praise for Aiden Thomas
CEMETERY BOYS

Longlisted for the 2020 National Book Award for Young People's Literature

"This stunning debut novel from Thomas is detailed, heart-rending, and immensely romantic. Don't miss this book."
—Mark Oshiro, author of *Anger Is a Gift*

"Aiden Thomas's debut novel can't help but charm and captivate readers of all ages, though teen readers will invariably identify with and appreciate the high jinks and emotional vulnerability that make each character and scenario deliciously enchanting."
—*Booklist*, starred review

"*Cemetery Boys* is a celebration of culture and identity that will captivate readers with its richly detailed world, earnest romance, and thrilling supernatural mystery. This delightful debut is a must-read for all paranormal romance fans."
—Isabel Sterling, author of *These Witches Don't Burn*

"Thomas marries concept and execution in a romantic mystery as poignant as it is spellbinding, weaved in a mosaic of culture, acceptance, and identity, where intricately crafted characters are the pieces and love—platonic, romantic, familial, and communal—is the glue."
—*Publishers Weekly*, starred review

"*Cemetery Boys* is nothing short of an astonishing work of art. Aiden Thomas masterfully weaves a tale of family, friendships, and love in a heartwarming adventure full of affirmation and being your best self."
—C. B. Lee, author of *Not Your Sidekick*

LOST IN THE NEVER WOODS

"A poignant novel about resilience, the magic of childhood, and the impossible choices that survivors often have to make in order to move forward, this will haunt readers long after they put it down—but will also leave them looking up at the stars."
—*Booklist*, starred review

"Absolutely delightful! *Lost in the Never Woods* is chock-full of suspense, excitement, and nostalgia. Peter Pan is as thrilling and seductive as ever, and Thomas' heartfelt tale feels as ageless as the legend himself."
—Romina Garber, *New York Times*—bestselling author of *Lobizona*

"Thomas's immersive prose and nuanced, trauma-informed perspective add real depth to Barrie's classic characters. Readers of Seanan McGuire's Wayward Children series and Laura E. Weymouth will settle into this emotionally generous update."
—*Publishers Weekly*

"Thomas brilliantly creates a malevolent tone to what should be a safe small town, crafting a feeling that something terrible is just around the bend . . . Characters are well-developed with surprising and emotional story arcs which will leave readers looking at Peter Pan in a whole new light. A captivating mystery that will ensnare those who enjoy retellings and stories with a touch of magic."
—*School Library Journal*

"This spin on a well-known story focuses on childhood trauma, growing up, loss, and letting go . . . An intense, cathartic, bitter-sweet tale."
—*Kirkus Reviews*

THE
SUNBEARER
TRIALS

AIDEN THOMAS

FEIWEL AND FRIENDS

NEW YORK

A Feiwel and Friends Book

An imprint of Macmillan Publishing Group, LLC

120 Broadway, New York, NY 10271 · fiercereads.com

Our books may be purchased in bulk for promotional, educational, or business use. Please contact your local bookseller or the Macmillan Corporate and Premium Sales Department at (800) 221-7945 ext. 5442 or by email at MacmillanSpecialMarkets@macmillan.com.

Library of Congress Cataloging-in-Publication Data is available.

First edition, 2022

Book design by L. Whitt
Interior artwork by Mars Lauderbaugh

Feiwel and Friends logo designed by Filomena Tuosto

Printed in the USA

ISBN 978-1-250-82213-0 (hardcover)
ISBN 978-1-250-88771-9 (special edition)

1   3   5   7   9   10   8   6   4   2

For my friends, my muses, my knights in shining armor:

ALEX

ANDA

AUSTIN

BIRD

EZRAEL

KATIE

MAX

MIK

RAVIV

SAMANTHA

TEDDY

FIRST, THERE WAS ONLY SOL AMONG A SEA OF STARS.

Alone, they formed the world by gathering stardust in their hands.

From the dust pressed between their fingers, mountains grew. From their tears of loneliness, oceans and rivers flowed. From the water, the desolate earth grew lush trees and jungles.

And from the new earth, Tierra was formed, and Sol was not alone.

The world was beautiful and exciting, but the couple was alone in the universe with no one to share it with.

They decided to create a race of godly children.

First, Tierra brought forth gold from deep within the earth, and Sol shaped it into the Golds.

The Golds were powerful but vain. They wanted only to test the limits of their strength, busying themselves with their work instead of spending time with their creators. And so Sol and Tierra tried again.

Next, Tierra brought forth jade from the caverns where the ocean met the shore, and Sol shaped it into the Jades.

The Jades were kind but focused. They were so immersed in finding new ways to bend and channel their powers, that they had no thoughts of their family. And so Sol and Tierra tried again.

Last, Tierra brought forth obsidian from the edges of the earth's hottest flames, and Sol shaped it into the Obsidians.

The Obsidians were passionate but selfish. They sought only destruction, not the development of their home.

Eventually, Sol and Tierra grew tired of shaping gods. Sol went down into the earth and planted their heart deep beneath the ground, to be closer to their beloved. Sol's heartsblood mingled with the humble dirt and, unexpectedly, humans were born.

The small mortals were welcomed, and given a home in Reino del Sol. By nature of their short existence, the humans held more compassion and empathy, loved more fiercely, than any god could through an eternity.

Sol and Tierra loved the humans most of all, so they tasked the gods with caring for the fragile creatures—to provide for them, inspire them, and learn from them.

The Golds, Jades, and Obsidians fought viciously about what aspects of life they would rule over. Sol put an end to the fighting by making a seven-pointed star out of clay and filling it with all the powers the gods could possess.

All the gods took turns hitting it with a stick, but it was a Gold god, Luna, whose blow cracked it open. From the broken clay, stars rained down.

The Golds grabbed the brightest stars, containing the greatest responsibilities. The Jades searched among the smaller stars for the ones most precious to them. The Obsidians snatched their stars from the dust and hid them deep in the earth, where the broiling heat and the pressure of their greed turned their gifts black and brittle.

Agua took stewardship of the oceans and all the life within. Pan Dulce guarded the hearth and gave her name to the mortals' favorite treat, sweet and soft and colorful.

Fauna made all the animals, Guerrero made the great cats in their own image, Quetzal made the birds in hers, and they were all beloved.

The Obsidians—Venganza, Chupacabra, and Caos—grew angry. They were jealous of how Sol loved the humans. Instead of celebrating human life with the other immortals, the Obsidians wanted humans to serve and worship them.

Caos longed for the world before this rigid structure. Chupacabra thirsted for blood. And Venganza crafted a plan to center himself above all others.

They sought out Tierra, who was guarding Sol's heart at the center of the earth. The clever Chupacabra limped and whimpered into Tierra's path, tricking his attention away while Venganza and Caos stole Sol's heart.

Without Sol's heart to warm the earth, the Obsidians turned Sol and Tierra's cherished humans into mindless creatures, who existed only to worship the gods.

In order to save humanity, Sol went to the top of their temple. On a stone slab, they drove a dagger into their own chest. When the last drop of blood drained from Sol's body, they reappeared in the sky as a burning, brilliant star. As the sun, Sol was able to trap the traitor gods in the sky within celestial bindings.

Back on earth, Sol's body turned to lava, burning on the sacrificial slab. While Sol could keep the Obsidians trapped during the day, there was nothing to keep them away during the night.

Tierra stepped forward and took his beloved's molten body into his arms. Even as it burned his skin from his flesh, Tierra formed Sol's skull into the Sol Stone, which shone brightly at the top of the golden temple. He then took the rest of Sol's body and turned it into smaller Sun Stones. Each of the remaining gods took one stone and placed it at the top of their temple to keep the Obsidians from returning to Reino del Sol.

Sol ascended as the sun, watching over the earth and locking the Obsidians within celestial prisons among the constellations.

Every night the betrayer gods try to escape, but the Sun Stones keep them away until Sol rises each morning.

As long as the sun shines and the stones stay lit, the traitorous gods cannot return.

CHAPTER 1

"Careful! We don't want to fuck up and get caught again," Teo whispered as muffled voices bickered inside his backpack. Finally released from his usual stint in detention, Teo was eager to put the plan he'd spent the last two days concocting into action.

Bracing himself, he jogged across the street to where the target of today's prank loomed. The Academy advertisement was unavoidable, plastered on a brick wall of the school. In large gold letters, it read:

Come See the Academy's Best Compete in
THE SUNBEARER TRIALS

Tall figures stood in an arrow formation on the black background of the poster, power posing and smiling for the camera. Teo recognized the woman standing in the center as Brilla, who had been crowned as Sunbearer in the last trials. Flanking Brilla were other past Sunbearers, recognizable by the golden sunburst crowns they wore on their heads.

It made Teo want to barf. He figured since he was forced to see it every day, the least he could do was add his own artistic flair.

Unfortunately, the poster was at least as tall as Teo—who was a proud five foot ten, thank you very much—and well out of his reach. Which was where Peri and Pico came in.

Most people in the city of Quetzlan had a bird, but they were more than just pets, they were companions. It was a lifelong bond between bird and human. But only Teo and his mom—Quetzal, the goddess of birds—could communicate with them directly.

Or, in Teo's case, occasionally team up for some light defacing of school property.

"Coast is clear, come on out you two," Teo said as he unzipped his backpack. Immediately, two birds poked their heads out. "You remember how to use these?" Teo asked, pulling out two of the smallest cans of spray paint he could find at the store.

Of course! Peri chirped.

I love these! Pico said, expertly popping the cap off with his beak.

The two young caiques were Teo's partners in crime and always down to clown. They'd agreed to help Teo before he even offered up the dried mango in his backpack.

What's the plan? Pico asked, tipping his head to stare up at Teo.

"I think they could use some humbling," Teo said, eyeing the Golds. "Maybe some funny faces?" he suggested. "I'm open to your artistic interpretations."

Great idea! they agreed before taking off.

"Try to hurry!" Teo called after them, checking the time on his phone.

You can count on us!

The best part of this prank was by the time anyone found his latest work of art, he'd be long gone to Sol Temple.

The Sunbearer Trials were the biggest out of all the holidays in Reino del Sol—a competition of the very best semidioses that kept the sun fueled and ensured the safety of their world for the next ten years. What had started as a sacred ritual thousands of years ago was now a televised and sponsored event that took over the cities. And Teo and his mom were required to attend.

As a simple Jade, Teo knew there was no chance he'd ever be chosen by the omniscient Sol to compete—something he was constantly reminded of by the posters that had been hung on the sides of buildings and light posts for weeks. They were all over social media, too, making it impossible for Teo to escape.

Like their parents, the kids of Gold gods were stronger and more powerful than Jade demigods. Some could produce and control elements and even move mountains. They went to a fancy academy and had fancy uniforms and got fancy training from the age of seven to be the Heroes of Sol. Whenever there was an emergency or disaster, the Golds were summoned to help.

Meanwhile, Teo and the other Jades weren't deemed powerful enough to attend the Academy, so they got stuck going to public school with mortal kids. Quetzlan High was held together with duct tape and glue, and the only uniform Teo was ever given was awful lime green gym shorts and a gray T-shirt that didn't fit. While Golds traveled around Reino del Sol saving lives, the most interesting responsibility Teo had was judging the yearly Quetzlan bird show.

He was tired of every privilege Golds received getting rubbed in his face.

Pico and Peri used their talons to hook into the advertisement's canvas, giving them something to hold on to while they wielded the cans of spray paint and got to work.

I'm getting good at this! Pico said, repeatedly banging his head on the nozzle as he sprayed light blue paint haphazardly across the beaming faces of the Gold semidioses.

Peri's focus was solely on Brilla. When Teo asked what she was drawing, she proudly announced, *You said to give them funny faces. Nothing's as funny-looking as a cat!*

"That's *very* clever, Peri," Teo agreed.

The graffiti was messy and definitely looked like two birds had done it, but damn was it satisfying to see those smug expressions covered in paint.

"Time for the final touch!" Teo dug into his pocket while Pico and Peri glided down to perch on his shoulders. He unfolded a piece of paper he'd scribbled on during detention. "Can you write this across the top?"

Oh, that's a good one, Son of Quetzal! Pico chuckled before plucking the paper from Teo's hand and taking off.

What does it say? Teo heard Peri whisper as she flew after Pico with her can of spray paint.

I don't know, I can't read!

Peri held the paper while Pico tried his best to re-create the words. What Pico produced was absolute gibberish. Teo laughed behind his hand, not wanting to hurt the bird's feelings.

That's supposed to be a loop, not a squiggle! Peri said.

It is a loop!

Peri huffed. *Will you fly up and show him, Son of Quetzal?* she asked.

Don't ask him that! Pico snapped, nipping at Peri. *You know he's sensitive about his wings!*

Teo pretended he didn't hear them, even as his wings flexed against their bindings beneath his shirt. "It doesn't have to be perfect!" he said. They needed to be in and out before anyone saw.

The spray can hissed, coating Pico's white chest in sticky blue paint. Teo winced. "Not so loud!"

My feathers! Pico squawked, flapping his wings in dismay.

"Teo?"

We've been caught!

Abort, abort!

The spray cans clattered to the ground as Pico and Peri flew off, bickering all the way. As the sound of footfalls approached, Teo scrambled to grab the cans and shove them into his backpack.

Dreading who he'd see, Teo turned toward the voice. Luckily, it was just Yolanda, one of the city's mail carriers, accompanied by a red-lored parrot on her shoulder who delivered letters to residents through their open windows.

Hello, Son of Quetzal! the bird sang with a respectful nod of his head.

"What are you still doing at school?" Yolanda asked.

"Just running to meet Huemac!" he said, securely yanking the zipper of his backpack shut before jogging to meet her.

Yolanda pursed her lips into a knowing look. "No you weren't."

Teo flashed her a toothy, not-at-all-innocent grin. "Well, now I am?"

Yolanda chuckled and waved him off. "Get going, and try to be on your best behavior at the trials. Huemac's not as young as he used to be."

Huemac and the people of Quetzlan had raised Teo. His mortal father had died when he was a baby, and his mom was busy with the responsibilities of being a goddess. So the city had become Teo's family. Even though he was seventeen now, they still looked after him. Sometimes a bit too closely.

"I'm always on my best behavior!" Teo called over his shoulder as he darted to the other side of the street.

"Spoken like a true troublemaker!" Yolanda's voice carried after him.

Every city in Reino del Sol was devoted to a god. The ones in the center were larger, nicer, and devoted to the Gold greater gods like Agua and Tierra. Meanwhile, smaller cities placed on the outskirts were dedicated to Jade lesser gods, like Quetzal.

Teo jogged through jungle trees interspersed among buildings draped with vines. From the outside, Quetzlan looked like a city that had lost its battle with nature and been swallowed by the dense foliage. But though it was a bit run-down, Quetzlan was a proud city lovingly maintained by its people.

The defining characteristic of their city was the abundance of tropical birds that dotted the trees like brightly colored fruit. They were everywhere you turned, living in happy companionship with their human counterparts. Here, people and nature were intimately and inextricably linked.

Teo pushed through the crowd as he crossed a pedestrian causeway that went over one of the many canals where merchants hawked their goods from boats and canoes. As he passed the laundromat, Teo held his backpack over his head to protect himself from the gem-colored hummingbirds dive-bombing passersby who got too close to their streetlamp.

With the Sunbearer Trials officially starting that night, the streets were filled with even more excitement than usual. Signs reading "Watch the Sunbearer Trials here!" hung in the windows of bars and restaurants along pictures of Sol-themed desserts and drinks inspired by the diose. A large group of people loitered outside the electronics store, watching the TVs on display. Clips of Gold Heroes flashed across the screens.

Teo tried to sneak past without being spotted, but almost immediately, a hand caught his backpack.

"Teo!" A round-faced man grinned, dragging him into the group. "Who do you think will be chosen to compete?" Mr. Serrano asked, gesturing to one of the displays.

Some Golds posed and smiled in their crisp uniforms alongside clips of the semidioses saving people from various disasters. Their stats were listed in the corner of the screen.

"The best of the best, I guess," Teo replied, trying to sound polite through a mouthful of resentment. Luckily, everyone present was too busy theorizing to notice.

"Guerrero's kid for sure," Miss Morales replied, scratching the neck of the lilac-crowned amazon resting on her shoulder.

"Agua's boy is far more impressive!"

"Ocelo could squash him in one blow!"

"Sol doesn't only care about strength!"

Teo rolled his eyes and used their arguing as a chance to slip away. He just couldn't escape them. Even kids at school swapped trading cards of the Gold Heroes and placed bets on who would be chosen to compete in the Sunbearer Trials. They peppered Teo with questions to get the inside scoop, as if he cared enough about the Golds to keep tabs.

The light changed and Teo crossed the street, dodging a man pushing his duritos cart and a woman carrying a stack of crates. A bodega sat on the corner, nestled between a bird supply store and a spice shop. It was a short, clementine orange building with windows plastered with flyers and advertisements. Above the front door, the words *El Pájaro* were written in black letters next to a delicately painted mural of a quetzal.

Out front, a man struggled to unload boxes from a small truck.

"Whoa, let me help!" Teo said, sprinting forward to easily take all four boxes in one hand. The ability to carry more boxes than the average middle-aged man was another mostly useless power he had as a Jade.

The man leaned back in surprise. "Careful—!"

When Teo shifted the stack out of his hand, the man's eyes took him in. A wide smile split his face immediately.

"Pajarito!" he greeted warmly, spreading his arms out at his sides.

"Aye, Chavo." Teo grinned. "Need a hand?"

Chavo chuckled. "My back ain't what it used to be," he confessed, slapping Teo on the shoulder. His shirt was cobalt blue and he wore a matching string of tiny blue feathers around his neck. "How's it goin', man?" Before Teo could answer, Chavo's face scrunched up in confusion. "Aren't you supposed to be on your way to Sol Temple?"

Teo shifted another stack of boxes into his other hand. "Just swinging by to pick up my order first."

"Come, come, I've already got it ready!" Chavo said, ushering him toward the bodega. "Huemac's not gonna be happy with you," he said with an amused look.

Teo snorted. "What else is new?" Late was late, and his approximate amount of lateness didn't matter. He'd be getting a lecture either way.

A bell chimed as Chavo pushed through the door.

No cats! an angry voice chirped.

"Hey, Macho," Teo said as he set the boxes down. Macho, the tiny parrotlet, swooped down and landed on the counter.

Oh, it's just you, Son of Quetzal, he said, distractedly dipping his head to look at the door.

"What's got him all worked up?" Teo asked as Chavo went behind the counter.

"Oh, don't mind Macho," Chavo said. "That stray cat's been around again."

Always sneaking in and trying to steal! Macho shouted, blue feathers ruffling as he hopped angrily across the tobacco case. *NO CATS!*

Chavo pulled out a large paper bag that was so packed, it'd had to be stapled shut. "Here you go!"

"You remembered the Chupa Chups, right?"

"Of course!" Chavo said as he rang up the order on his ancient register. "I would never forget those!"

Teo grinned. "Perfect."

"You weren't kidding when you said you were stocking up." Chavo grinned.

"I'm going to need it," Teo told him, fishing out his wallet from his backpack. "Dios Maize doesn't allow 'refined sugar and processed garbage' in Sol Temple."

"Man, what I wouldn't give to go to Sol Temple," Chavo said, sighing wistfully as he stroked his goatee. "I've never seen a Gold diose in person."

Teo couldn't blame Chavo for being fascinated by the Golds. They were rare to come by, especially in Jade cities. They were even bigger celebrities than their semidiose children—famous and untouchable. All of the gods ruled from Sol Temple and only semidioses and priests could make the journey to the island in the center of Reino del Sol.

"I'd like to meet Dios Tormentoso and thank him and Lluvia," Chavo said, glancing back over his shoulder.

Behind Chavo were two altar boxes. The larger nicho was painted in shades of turquoise and jade, with illustrations of birds in devotion to Teo's mother. Bird feathers of every color had been laid inside. The smaller, newer nicho was painted in swirls of light blue and gray with white raindrops and yellow bolts of lightning. Taped inside was a newspaper clipping. Lluvia, the eldest daughter of the weather god, Dios Tormentoso, stood in the center of the black-and-white picture, hands on her hips and beaming.

Three years ago, a hurricane had hit the western coast of Reino del Sol. Even though hurricanes were common in September, this one tore through the western Jade cities, requiring the demigods of Tormentoso to be summoned. Lluvia arrived in Quetzlan and managed to tame the angry storm enough to save civilians from the flooded streets— including Chavo and his wife.

"I'll put in a good word if I run into them," Teo lied as he handed over his debit card.

"Are you nervous?" Chavo asked, eyebrows pinching.

Teo frowned, confused. "About what?"

"You know, getting selected for the trials."

"Oh, that? No way." Teo snorted as he took his card and receipt and shoved them into the pocket of his jeans. "I'm just there as a formality."

Teo had only been seven years old during the last trials, so he didn't remember much. What he did know was that Jade semidioses were almost never chosen to compete. The last Jade had been chosen 130 years ago, and they hadn't made it out alive.

"All I'm gonna do is explore the Gold cities, eat as much food as I can, and blow all my money on souvenirs." He grinned, the impending sights and travels sending his heart racing.

But when he looked up, Chavo still looked worried.

"Hey—only the most powerful and honorable semidioses get chosen, remember?" Teo said, bumping his fist against Chavo's shoulder in an attempt to reassure him. "I'm just a Jade."

That seemed to ease the tension in Chavo's expression. He was back to his apple-cheeked smile. "Hey, it don't matter if you're a Gold or not. You're still our Hero, patrón."

Teo snatched the bag and shoved it into his already full backpack. "All right, okay, I'm outta here before I freaking barf."

Chavo laughed as Teo slapped his palm one last time. "You should stop by the panadería!" Chavo called after him as Teo bolted for the exit. "Veronica made some green concha especially for Diosa Quetzal!"

"Oh man, you know I can't pass those up," Teo said with a grin.

"See you in a couple weeks!" Chavo called.

"I'll literally be counting down the days!" Teo said as he slipped out the door. The bell rang behind him.

NO CATS! Macho's voice followed.

Teo could smell his destination before he even made it around the block.

The street was crowded and filled with restaurants, food carts, and taco trucks. The sizzling scent of al pastor hung heavy in the air, tickling his nose along with the sweet smell of elote and the spicy zing of chamoy. Teo was so distracted by his growling stomach that he didn't notice anything was wrong until movement rippled through the crowd—turned heads and raised voices.

The hairs on the back of Teo's neck stood on end, and a moment later, a flock of birds tore down the street. Their screeches filled the air, making everyone stop and stare upward as their colorful feathers streaked across the sky. Teo tried to make out what they were saying, but they were all shouting at once, panicked cries tumbling over one another.

A crowd of bodies surged into him, nearly knocking Teo over. That was when the sharp smell of smoke hit his nose.

Teo tried to get on his tiptoes for a better look. Down the street, thick, black plumes billowed from where the panadería sat. All at once, the birds' voices became clear.

FIRE! FIRE!

Human shouts crashed with the birds' cries. The crowd surged forward again, a wave of bodies trying to get to safety. Teo had to latch on to a light pole to keep himself from being swept away.

"Where's María?" a girl wailed.

Teo searched and found a little girl crying in the middle of the street. He pushed his way through the crowd and crouched down in front of her.

"Who's María?" Teo asked as calmly as possible with adrenaline slamming through his body. "Your sister?"

"My doll!"

For Sol's *sake.*

"I need you to do something very scary right now, okay?" he asked, squeezing her small shoulders to get her to focus on him. "You need to get somewhere safe, find someone you know, and I'll look for María, okay? Can you do that?"

The sound of cracking stone split the air. The large windows of the warehouse where the panadería was located exploded into shards.

Teo tugged the girl to his chest and crouched over her. Tiny bits of glass rained down around them.

After that, she didn't need more encouragement and took off.

Teo stared up at the building engulfed in flames. His heart thudded in his chest, his breaths sharp and shaky. Most of the food carts in the alley ran off propane. If the fire from the panadería got out of control, it'd be a street full of bombs ready to go off. How fast could the whole block burn down? Had anyone summoned help?

An anguished scream cut through the air.

Through the curtain of smoke, Teo spotted a pair of arms desperately waving for help.

The frantic thoughts in Teo's brain cleared in a snap. Only one thought remained: Someone needed help.

While everyone else fled from the growing flames, Teo ran toward them.

CHAPTER 2

Teo sprinted to the front of the panadería. Thick, black smoke billowed into the air, blotting out the sun, while flames licked the now-empty window frames of the third floor.

Something swooped down from above, knocking into Teo's head.

She's still inside! She's still inside! The masked tityra zoomed back and forth, frantically beating his wings. Streaks of soot darkened his silvery feathers.

"Who's inside?!" Teo asked, but the bird was inconsolable.

I left her! I can't believe I left her!

Out of impatience, Teo caught the bird between his hands. "Who?"

My human! I left my human! Teo could feel the poor thing's racing heart. *Veronica!*

Teo's stomach dropped. "Where is she?"

The second floor!

"Show me!"

Teo released the bird and he darted to a broken window on the second floor. *Here, she's here! Please help her, please!* the tityra begged.

Every fiber of Teo's being told him to go in. There was a fire escape that led right to the window, but he didn't know what he was doing. Teo didn't know jack shit about fires. It wasn't like fire science was an elective at Quetzlan High.

But this was *his* city, *his* panadería, the green concha waiting for *his* mom. If any of his people were in danger, he sure as hell wasn't going to sit by and watch. If he didn't do something, Veronica could die.

Without a plan or a single coherent thought in his head, Teo ran for the fire escape.

"*Shit, shit, shit*," he hissed to himself as he tore up the rickety steps.

Teo tumbled through the window and was immediately choked by thick, acrid smoke. Teo coughed, his eyes stinging as he dropped to a crouch, trying to stay below the smoke line.

He tried to call out for Veronica, but more burning smoke filled his lungs.

Teo looked frantically around the room. It was by sheer luck that he spotted the crown of someone's head peeking out from behind a counter. He ran over and found Veronica slumped on her side, unconscious but still alive.

A loud crack cut through the air and the floor beneath Teo's feet trembled moments before part of the ceiling caved in. Smoldering roof beams crashed down, sending sparks swirling in the air and blocking off the window he'd just used. Ropes of fire chewed at the wood and crept across the floor. The paint on the walls bubbled as the temperature in the room skyrocketed.

Teo knew you weren't supposed to move someone who was unconscious, but now seemed like a pretty good time to make an exception.

Teo scooped Veronica easily into his arms, but when he tried to squeeze past fallen rafters to the window, his arm scraped against the burning embers. He jerked back as jade-colored blood bloomed on his singed skin. It wasn't like he could put the fire out or just slam through a wall to make a new exit. The best he could do was find somewhere for them to get away from the fire, but the options were limited.

Thinking quickly, Teo pulled Veronica into the open walk-in freezer, seconds before a beam crashed through where she'd been lying. Inside the cooler, the plastic containers started to melt, but it would at least buy them some time.

"It's Marino!" someone shouted from outside.

If Marino was here, that meant the Golds had arrived. Relief and dread twisted in Teo's stomach. That meant Aurelio and Auristela were here, too.

Another window shattered as water poured inside. Scalding steam billowed. Teo tried to call out, but his throat was so raw he could only cough, and even that sound was drowned out by the rush of Marino's water spray.

He had to block himself and Veronica from the steam. Teo grabbed the stainless steel door and tugged it closed to act like a shield. He pulled Veronica as deep into the walk-in freezer as he could, but the fire was moving fast. He could hear the hissing steam and jets of water, but flames were already licking under the door, reaching for them.

"*Help!*" Teo finally managed to shout.

Suddenly, the flames under the door disappeared, like they'd been sucked away. Voices spoke from inside the warehouse, muffled by the steel door.

"*We're in here!*" Teo shouted, his voice strained.

"Oh, shit!" he heard Marino, Son of Agua, say. "I think there's people in there!"

Three sets of footsteps came pounding toward them. The door was ripped off its hinges. Teo collapsed into a heap. Through the steamy haze, three figures stepped forward.

"Dios, are you all right?" a boy with strong bone structure and a thick build asked, quickly stepping into the freezer. Marino's cool umber skin hadn't even broken a sweat.

Teo could only nod as his chest heaved against his binder and he desperately tried to gulp down fresh air.

A girl pushed past Marino. Her ember-colored eyes flicked to Veronica before landing on Teo, narrowing sharply. "Is she alive?" Auristela, Daughter of Lumbre, demanded, like he'd been purposely keeping the unconscious baker captive or something.

Teo nodded again.

She moved in, lifted Veronica into a fireman's carry, and promptly made for the exit.

Veronica would be okay. The relief crashing through Teo made him shake. His eyes burned so badly from the smoke, he could barely see through his tears and singed lashes.

"You're okay," Marino said, kneeling down next to Teo. He cupped his hands and conjured two gentle spouts in his palms, like a makeshift eyewash. "That was either a very smart move or a very stupid move, Bird Boy."

"I like to toe the line," Teo replied, his voice barely more than a wheeze, before he bent over to rinse his eyes. The cool water both stung and soothed.

"Is he all right?" a third voice asked. One that made Teo's chest clench painfully.

"He will be," said Marino, thumping Teo on the back a little too hard.

He sat up and wiped the water from his face. A pair of strong hands pulled him to his feet. Teo blinked the droplets from his eyes to find a pair of copper-brown ones staring back at him. Aurelio, Son of Lumbre, frowned at him.

While Auristela's features were softer, and Aurelio's nose was broader, the two were unmistakably twins. They wore the same hairstyle—an undercut with their hair knotted at the back of their heads—and even their form-fitting crop top uniforms were similar, except for the gold bands Aurelio wore around his forearms and the flint-tipped gloves that covered his thumb and pointer finger.

"Are you okay?" he asked.

"I'm fine," Teo snapped, but he was wobbly at best, and his arms trembled in Aurelio's warm iron grip. He tried to yank himself free, but Aurelio held firm.

Aurelio was the last person he wanted to see right now, especially when he was in such a sorry state. Teo hadn't spoken to Aurelio in years and he wasn't interested in starting now.

"You're shaking," Aurelio replied, his voice as cool and calculating as ever. "You might be in shock."

Teo attempted a sarcastic laugh. "You're being dramatic."

"Can you walk?"

"Of course I can." Teo took a step, but his knees immediately buckled.

Aurelio caught him easily. He slung Teo's arm over his shoulder and hooked his arm around Teo's waist. The sudden proximity sent a shock through Teo's body; his breath hitched in his throat, only making him more annoyed.

"I don't need your help," Teo snapped, even as Aurelio led him out of the freezer.

"Yes, you do," Aurelio said.

Teo would've preferred sarcasm, annoyance, or even anger instead of his infuriatingly placid response. It was bad enough that the Golds had to show up, but worse was knowing Aurelio was right: He needed their help.

As they walked around the smoldering debris, Teo's foot landed on something soft. Under his shoe was a rag doll with ribboned hair, a hand-woven blouse, and a colorful skirt.

"Wait—" Teo planted his feet, pulling Aurelio to a stop.

His heavy brow furrowed. "What are you doing?"

Teo ignored him and bent down to scoop up the doll. It was a bit soggy and would need a good wash but was overall still intact.

Aurelio frowned at him disapprovingly.

Heat flushed Teo's cheeks. "I told a little girl I'd get it for her."

Aurelio shook his head, like he didn't understand. "It's a doll. It doesn't matter."

Maybe he was right, but Teo would never give him the satisfaction.

"To *you* it doesn't, but to her it does," he shot back.

"It's just a toy—"

Teo let out a sharp laugh. "I wouldn't expect *you* to understand."

Teo was ready to argue—wanted to, in fact—but Aurelio only stared at him for a moment before shaking his head and looking away. He practically carried Teo down the fire escape and back to the street, where fire trucks and camera crews had gathered.

Great. Now there was photographic evidence that he'd needed to be rescued by *Aurelio*. Teo wished he had been swallowed up by the flames.

Veronica was wheeled into an ambulance, her tityra companion pacing anxiously across her legs. Aurelio didn't release Teo until the paramedics hefted him away. Aurelio took his simmering body heat with him, leaving Teo shivering as the paramedics tended to him. Luckily, semidioses healed quickly thanks to their godly blood.

A group of concerned citizens crowded around Teo.

"Thank goodness you're all right, Teo," someone said.

"Your mother will be so worried!"

"That was dangerous, you should've waited for the Heroes!"

Teo didn't have the energy to respond. Instead, he watched discreetly as Aurelio rejoined Auristela and Marino. The other two smiled for the cameras and frenzied reporters who swarmed like bees, but Aurelio hung back, gingerly massaging his thumb into his palm.

An odd mix of anger, spite, and something more electric that he couldn't place buzzed through Teo's whole body. When Aurelio glanced in his direction, Teo quickly turned away, jaw clenching as the sensation danced across his skin.

Teo searched the crowd lining the street and spotted the little girl, her face all but buried in her mother's skirts as she tried to reassure her daughter. Teo walked over and dropped to a knee before her.

"Is this María?" Teo asked gently with a tired grin.

The girl looked up and tentatively took the doll from him. In a blink, a wide smile brightened her tearstained face.

"You saved her!" The girl crashed into Teo, throwing her arms around his neck.

A surprised laugh bucked in Teo's chest.

"Our hero!" the girl's mother said with a relieved sigh.

The bitter twist of his mouth was hidden by the girl's curls. Hero. Yeah, right.

After convincing the paramedics and everyone else that he was fine, Teo made to head home. At this point, he was doomed to a lecture to rival all lectures from Huemac.

Every temple in Reino del Sol was U-shaped with a large set of exterior steps that led to an observatory where the main altar stood. They looked different, depending on the god and the city, but each housed a Sun Stone—the piece of Sol that provided light and protection from the dangers locked away among the stars. At night, the beams from the Sun Stones could be seen from several miles away.

At the moment, it was a glaring reminder that the Sunbearer Trials began in a handful of hours, and Teo was *very* late.

The Quetzal Temple was in the middle of the city and could be seen from nearly anywhere. It was painted a bright, warm yellow, with many archways so birds could come and go as they pleased. He normally loved looking at the larger-than-life mosaics of tropical birds, painstakingly crafted with colorful tiles, but today they seemed to loom over him as he hurried toward the courtyard.

The fluttering of wings echoed and birdsong rang out, welcoming

Teo home as they flew between the canopy of trees overhead. In a matter of moments, he was swarmed. Gem-colored hummingbirds zipped past his ears while a pair of toucans bounced happily at his feet, singing their greetings.

"It's good to see you, too." Teo chuckled, trying not to wince and accidentally hurt the feelings of the peachy-pink parrot squawking joyfully from his shoulder. "Ouch!" he hissed, ducking as a rose-bellied bunting expressed his love by tugging out a small chunk of Teo's dark hair.

"Shoo, shoo, leave him be!" Claudia's voice rang out.

In a flash of feathers, his friends dispersed. "They act like I was gone for days. Thanks for saving me," he said with an amused grin to the woman in the turquoise robes of Quetzlan priests.

"Don't thank me," Claudia huffed with a stern look, sharpened by a tight hair bun nestled on her head. "You look a mess, and Huemac has been looking for you! You're *very* late—don't keep your mother waiting!" Claudia gave his shoulder a smack.

"I'm going, I'm going!" Teo grinned, not even attempting a straight face as he danced out of her reach. He sprinted across the wet floor, his dirty sneakers leaving black footprints while a priest mopped the old stone.

"Ugh, Teo!" the priest lamented.

"Sorry!" he called with a guilty dip of his head, narrowly avoiding another priest carrying a large platter filled with fruit, seeds, and bugs. A quetzal waited patiently on the priest's shoulder while a toucan made himself at home on a pile of passion fruit and hummingbirds fought noisily overhead.

Teo passed tiny waterfalls that spilled over volcanic rocks into crystal-clear pools filled with water lilies. Birds splashed around, droplets sparkling in the sunlight on their multicolored feathers.

He rounded a corner and found Huemac waiting for him with folded arms. He stood on the large stone steps that led to the observatory, surrounded by a group of priests. His quetzal companion, Cielo, sat perched on his shoulder.

"Huemac!" Teo greeted, his arms held wide at his sides as he put on an even wider smile. "You haven't welcomed me home from school since I was a little kid! Aren't there more important things you should be doing?" he asked with as much innocence as he could muster.

"Yes, there are," Huemac agreed with a withering look, his thin lips pressed into a line.

Huemac was tall and angular with sun-wrinkled skin and a perpetually exasperated expression that seemed to deepen whenever Teo entered the room. He wore emerald green robes that marked him as the head priest of Quetzlan. A jade rod was pierced through his septum, and one of Cielo's tail feathers hung down to his shoulder from a jade plug in his left ear.

"Been catching up with the stars?" Teo guessed. He always found the head priest bent over his telescope.

"Planets," Huemac corrected, adjusting the chunk of jade engraved with the Quetzal glyph that hung around his neck.

"And what do the planets have to say today?"

"That you're late."

"You need a telescope to tell you that? Most people use a watch."

"And that you nearly got yourself killed," he added, looking Teo up and down.

"The planets knew about the fire?" Teo asked, impressed.

"You're also covered in soot," Huemac added.

Teo clicked his tongue and pointed finger guns at the annoyed priest. "You got me there!"

"This isn't a joke, Teo," Huemac said, his voice suddenly sharp.

Teo's grin faded. "I know it's not."

A deep crease settled between the older man's eyebrows. "You could've gotten yourself hurt, or worse, put others' lives in danger."

Teo scoffed. "What was I supposed to do, stand by and watch while—?"

Huemac cut him off. "You are *not* a Hero, Teo."

Teo's mouth snapped shut.

It was true, he wasn't a Hero. But it wasn't like anyone had given him a chance to be. He was destined for a dull life of serving his mother like a glorified priest. The very thought was enough to send his pulse thudding, trapped under his skin. He didn't want to be cooped up in Quetzlan for the rest of his life—never getting the chance to see the rest of the world or find something he was actually good at.

Huemac closed his eyes and pinched the bridge of his nose before taking a deep, long-suffering breath. "It is the responsibility of the Heroes to protect the people of Reino del Sol," he explained. "And it is *my* responsibility to protect *you*, troublemaker."

A responsibility that Huemac undoubtedly loathed.

"Go up and greet your mother, and don't make her wait any longer than she's already had to," Huemac said in a tired voice. "We'll meet you there with your regalia." With that, he went back into the temple, leaving Teo feeling like a scolded child.

He took a deep breath before hitching his backpack higher on his shoulder and starting the long ascent to the observatory. Teo had tried to talk Huemac into installing an escalator but the head priest had just sniffed indignantly and cited tradition, the sanctity of the ancient temple, and blah blah blah.

When he finally reached the top and entered the gold-framed glass observatory, Teo could see all of Quetzlan far below. A gray smudge lingered in the air where the fire had broken out. The observatory housed Huemac's beloved quetzals, the pride and joy of Quetzlan. The electric green-and-blue birds perched on ancient astronomy tools like tarnished armillary spheres and jade sundials. They cleaned their ruby chest feathers from the tops of telescopes and ate from golden bowls with their short yellow beaks.

The main altar was set in the middle of the observatory. It was surrounded by candles of different shapes and sizes in tall gold holders. His mother's glyph stood in the very center. The ten-foot square slab of pristine jade was carved to resemble a quetzal midflight—its wings spread and long tail feathers curled in while its small pointed beak tipped skyward.

Hovering above the glyph was the Sun Stone, slowly spinning in midair. It was too bright to look at it directly, but before Teo burned his retinas, he could catch a glimpse of the smooth surface that seemed to undulate with light, giving off tiny flares. It beamed a radiant blaze of light up into the sky, disappearing somewhere beyond the clouds.

He passed a young boy with a blessing from Teo's mother—a scarlet macaw feather—gripped tightly in his hand. Jade gods were the only ones who gave out their blessings in person. The Gold gods were too busy and passed off dealing with mortals to their priests.

Teo awkwardly lingered off to the side, not wanting to interrupt as his mom gave an older woman a long shimmering green feather. Quetzal cupped the woman's cheek with her hand and spoke softly as the woman smiled up at her with watery eyes.

As a priestess escorted the woman out, Quetzal turned. Upon seeing her son, a bright smile broke across her luminous face. "There you are!" she said, relief in her singsong voice.

"Hey, Mom," he said, guilt settling on him like a weight.

Quetzal was a vision of beauty, as vibrant as the birds surrounding her. Instead of hair, long feathers framed her oval face. Shades of brilliant blue and green at the crown of her head faded to rich brown as the feathers trailed down her back. A choker made of gold-plated feathers spread from the base of her jaw to fan out across her clavicle. Earrings made of tiny magenta, purple, and ruby red hummingbird feathers hung from her ears.

"You're late!" she added, sweeping her son into an embrace and giving him a tight squeeze, towering over him. The gods all stood well over seven feet tall and his mother was no exception.

"Sorry," Teo said, returning the hug, her feathers tickling his nose. "I got held up."

The bodice of Quetzal's dress was adorned with scarlet macaw feathers and the rest was made of bright green, cyan, and sapphire blue plumage. The plunging back put her huge wings on full display. While Teo's were unwieldy and knocked into everything if they weren't bound, his mother's folded prettily against her back and never got in the way.

"They told me there was a fire," the diosa said, stepping back to look him over. "Your arm!" she gasped, delicate fingers running over a burn on his elbow.

Teo tried to tug his sleeve down over it. "It's not a big deal—it's already starting to heal."

Quetzal sighed but smiled. "Well, thank Sol for that." Her skin was warm brown just like Teo's, and he'd also inherited her large, dark eyes. "Huemac and I were *very* worried."

Teo seriously doubted the former was true. "Sorry."

Quetzal affectionately pushed Teo's wild hair out of his face. "I'm just glad you're safe," she said, smiling. "Thank goodness Marino, Auristela, and your friend Aurelio got there in time."

"He's *not* my friend," Teo said, harsher than he'd meant but unable to reel in his anger at the mere mention of Aurelio.

His mom gave him a disappointed look, but, luckily, Huemac and the other priests showed up at just the right time.

"Undress. Let's get you changed," Huemac said, and a flurry of movement engulfed them. Quetzal stepped out of the way as a standing mirror was brought in along with a clothing rack.

"Right down to business, huh?" Teo muttered. A younger priest took the opportunity to take Teo's backpack from his shoulders. "Careful, I've got important stuff in there!" Teo said.

Huemac raised an eyebrow.

Teo cleared his throat. "Y'know, homework. And stuff. I need it while we're traveling— Can I at least take a shower?" he asked before Huemac could question him further.

In return, he was presented with a large silver bowl filled with water and a face cloth.

Teo scowled. "This is it?"

"If you had been on time, you could've taken a shower," Huemac told him as he calmly clasped his hands and waited by Quetzal's side.

Teo dipped the cloth into the basin and immediately hissed between his teeth. "The water is *freezing*!"

"If you had been on time—"

"Yeah, yeah, I get it. I can do this part on my own, thank you!" he added, flapping his hand as a priest tried to assist him. "Any chance I could get some privacy?" he asked the audience as he undid his belt.

On cue, a priestess brought forward a screen for him to change behind. He made quick work of scrubbing the soot from his cheeks and arms.

Usually, he could attend the various holidays and celebrations wearing a nice shirt with slacks. But, since the Sunbearer Trials was their most important ceremony and only happened once every decade, things were a bit more involved.

"I don't see why I have to dress up," Teo grumbled as he pulled on bright blue-green charro pants with gold feathers embroidered down the outer seams.

"Because you are a semidiós and there to represent Diosa Quetzal and all of Quetzlan," came Huemac's gruff voice.

Teo grunted.

"You'll be able to hang out with Niya for a whole week and a half!" his mom called.

Aside from visiting cities, that *was* the only perk. But Niya was a Gold, and a powerful one at that, so there was a good chance she'd be chosen to compete in the trials, in which case he wouldn't be able to spend any time with her at all. Being chosen to compete in the trials was a great honor, of course, but it was also incredibly dangerous.

And always deadly.

Teo did his best to ignore the twisting in his stomach at the thought of his best friend competing. He struggled out of his shirt and attempted to readjust his binder before stepping out from behind the screen.

While Quetzal did her best to keep smiling, Teo didn't miss the softening of her expression or the way her eyes darted to his chest for a fraction of a second.

Teo tensed. Two years ago, when he was fifteen, Teo realized he was a boy. He'd started hormone replacement therapy and gotten top surgery, which helped him feel more at home in his own body. He even liked his top surgery scars—they looked badass. The binders he wore were for the set of wings he'd been born with. When he was little, he hadn't thought much about them, but that changed when he'd started school. His classmates were always staring, and they laughed whenever he accidentally knocked into something. But the worst part was the *touching*.

The kids in his class could never keep their hands to themselves. Even his teachers were mesmerized, going as far as to touch his feathers and comment on how they felt. He hated the attention and the way it made him feel like the lone animal in a petting zoo.

As if that weren't bad enough, his wings were also the source of Teo's first experiences with dysphoria. They weren't the brilliant blue and green of male quetzals, but grayish-brown with hints of green like the females' plumage. At nearly the same time Teo realized he was a boy, his wings started molting.

With help from some of the priests, Teo made binders for his wings so he could keep them hidden, tucked against his back with crisscrossed bands of black spandex. The more he tried to restrain them, the more they seemed to fight back. He only let them free when he slept or took a shower, doing his best not to look at the dull feathers and huge bald patches.

"Are you sure you don't want to take that off?" Quetzal asked gently.

"Mom," Teo said, his voice tight. He did not want to have this discussion again, especially in front of Huemac, who at least had the manners to busy himself with applying a salve to the burn on Teo's arm.

"Doesn't it hurt?" Quetzal asked, softly smoothing her fingers down a section of exposed feathers between their bindings.

"No," Teo lied, shifting out of her reach.

The truth was, it did hurt. It was like having a second set of arms hand-cuffed behind his back, but that was nothing compared to the cloying dysphoria that choked him whenever he saw his wings.

Huemac handed over a red, sleeveless tunic that a priest helped Teo pull down over his binder. Clearly having anticipated Teo's refusal to have his wings out, Huemac draped a cape made of the same blue-and-green feathers as his mother's dress over his shoulders.

The most substantial piece was the pectoral. The centerpiece of the collared necklace was Quetzal's glyph painted in gold onto a huge chunk of jade adorned with smaller bits of jade, turquoise, and gold beads. The weight of it made Teo sway as Huemac secured it in place.

Lastly, Huemac pulled out a circlet made of gleaming quetzal tail feathers.

"Oh, Huemac, it's beautiful!" Quetzal beamed, hands collapsed to her chest.

Huemac was usually a very reserved man who prided himself on being humble, but Teo didn't miss the way the corner of his lips twitched or the faint hint of red that tinged his cheeks at the compliment. "Thank you, Diosa," he said, positioning the circlet on Teo's head.

But as soon as Huemac stepped back, it slipped down Teo's forehead.

"A little big, don't you think?" Teo asked, trying to push it back out of his eyes.

Huemac's pleased expression wiped clear.

"If you'd shown up on time, we could've altered it," he replied.

"You look so *handsome*, Teo!" Quetzal sang as she fluttered around her son, making tiny adjustments.

Teo inspected himself in the mirror and tried to flatten down his curly dark brown hair. He didn't look *bad*; it was just . . . so *much*. But he was a semidiós, and ceremonial finery came with the territory. He didn't want to hurt his mom's feelings and, as much as he enjoyed teasing Huemac, he knew how much this meant to both of them.

So Teo smiled and thumped the priest on the back of his shoulder. "It looks great."

Huemac gave a slight bow of his head, which was the closest thing to a smile Teo ever got from him, so he took it as a win.

"It's getting late," Quetzal said, still fussing with the feathers of Teo's cape. "I should get back to Sol Temple."

"We'll leave now and meet you there, Diosa," Huemac reassured her.

Quetzal smiled. "Thank you, Huemac." She caught Teo's chin and gave him a kiss on the cheek.

"Ugh, Mom," Teo groaned, wiping it off with the back of his hand.

"I will see you all soon!" she said. In a flash of light, she vanished.

"Wait—what about my stuff?" Teo asked as the priests carted out the rack and mirror.

"We already packed for you. The boat is ready," Huemac replied curtly, following the other priests toward the stairs.

"Don't forget my backpack!" Teo said.

Huemac picked up the beat-up bag from the floor, weighing it in his hand. "Homework?" he asked, side-eyeing Teo.

Teo nodded vigorously. The circlet slid down to his brow. "Lots of homework," he agreed, pushing the feathers out of his eyes.

Huemac sighed deeply. "The trials are the single most important event you will ever attend. Don't cause me trouble, boy."

Teo blinked his large, dark eyes at Huemac. "Me?" His voice broke around the word. "I would never!"

With a disgruntled grumble, Huemac turned away.

"Is this because of what happened during Día de Muertos? Because that was an accident! I apologized to Dios Maize!" Teo called after him. When he didn't stop, Teo chased Huemac down the steps. "Hair grows back!"

CHAPTER 3

Thousands of waterways connected the cities of Reino del Sol. Wide rivers allowed for large cargo and transport ships to ferry goods and people between communities, while smaller canals provided local drainage, irrigation, and water supply. Even with access to cars and public transport, boat travel was still the only way to reach Sol Temple.

The Quetzlan entourage of Teo and the priests was small enough to fit in only one trajinera, a flat-bottomed boat about twenty-five feet long and six feet wide. It was made of wood and painted with intricate designs in Quetzlan's distinctive vibrant colors, with a curved roof that would protect them from the blistering sun and errant downpours as they traveled through the microclimates of Reino del Sol.

A priest in the back of the boat pushed against the eroded slate bottoms of Quetzlan's canals with a long pole. Since Quetzlan was located on the western edge of Sol, their journey inland along the Río Agua cut through other Jade cities. Save for some of Quetzlan's neighbors, Teo had seen little of Reino del Sol. For years he had only caught glimpses in this pilgrimage to the sun god's island.

There was Maizelan, with its meticulous patchwork quilt of farms and orchards. The Maizelan temple towered in the distance: Dark vines dotted with crimson tomatoes and chili peppers of all shapes and sizes glinted like jewels. They went through Médicali next, with its tall glass buildings, where Diosa Médica's temple served as a teaching hospital.

The only Gold city they crossed was the lavish Puerto Cascadas. The canals were wide and filled with large boats and watermills that were used as renewable energy sources. Diosa Agua's temple—difficult to glimpse among the shiny glass skyscrapers—was made of slick stone covered in moss, with waterfalls cascading down every side.

The waterway opened up and dozens of trajineras spread out before them in the massive lake set in the heart of Reino del Sol. Crowds gathered on white, cable-stayed bridges that looked downright futuristic compared to the stone arches they had in Quetzlan. Cheers swelled as each patron's children passed by, dipping significantly when the tiny Quetzal trajinera followed suit.

Sol Temple was on an island in the lake, surrounded by an unnatural ring of jagged mountains that acted as a wall. The highest point in all of Sol, the temple was easily three times the size of Quetzlan's and made entirely of gold. The Sol Stone was housed in the open-air observatory at the top, giving off a powerful ray of light.

Their progress slowed as trajineras crowded together, lining up at one of the many waterfalls cascading down the mountains.

"Any chance I can fake sick and skip the opening ceremony?" Teo asked, dread sinking into his stomach as the mountains towered before them.

Huemac considered Teo for a moment, just long enough for him to get his hopes up. What he didn't expect him to say was, "Niya will be fine, Teo. You don't have to worry about her."

Teo blinked. Was Huemac a mind-reader now?

Each Gold semidiose had a specialization of their godly parent's powers that they harnessed while training at the Academy. As the semidiosa of the earth god, Niya could manipulate metal and rock with nothing more than a thought. She was also obscenely strong, even by Gold standards.

"I'm not worried about her," he lied, quickly trying to recover.

Huemac looked like he didn't believe him, but at least had the decency not to say it. "No, you cannot skip the ceremony."

Teo huffed, blowing his drooping circlet higher on his forehead. "Worth a shot."

Finally, it was their turn. Even though he'd gone through the enchanted barrier to Sol Temple hundreds of times before, it still took his breath away. Right before the front of the boat was doused, the thunderous waterfall slowly split open just wide enough for them to pass through. When he was little, Teo liked to shout and hear his voice echo, but he hadn't done that since a particularly messy bat incident after which Huemac grounded him for a week.

Once they made it through, the island came into full view. Sol Temple was ancient, never having been renovated or industrialized like the outside cities, but still pristine. The golden temple was covered in intricate carvings of the sun, planets, and various constellations.

When it was time to disembark, the priests, in their clean white robes embroidered with the sun glyph of Sol, came on board to help them unload and to take their things to their housing for the night.

They filed down the main road, merging with the large crowd. As Teo craned his head in search of Niya, Huemac kept catching his cape and dragging him back in line.

More priests greeted them as they approached the courtyard. Through the doors of the temple, a grand staircase led down into the main hall. A large statue stood in the center—a huge golden sun with constellations etched into its smooth surface. Crowds of semidioses and temple priests gathered around standing tables, a sea of colorful robes and outfits. Laughter, music, and the smell of food floated through the air.

As people milled around chatting, Dios Mariachi's children performed at the base of the steps. Half were dressed in black suits and matching wide-brimmed hats, stomping their boots in heavy, percussive steps. The other half danced and waved their ruffled skirts like colorful trompos spinning in circles. Small flashes of lightning danced in Dios Tormentoso's curly gray hair and beard as he laughed at something Dios Mariachi said.

Surrounded by Jades and Golds, Teo felt like he'd been shoved in a cage. Jade semidioses were sequestered in their own cities and didn't mingle much. Without Niya, the humiliating truth was that Teo didn't have any other friends to search out, so he stuck to Huemac's side.

Meanwhile, it was like the Golds were all in a secret club, flocking to one another in packs. Niya had told him how the highest-ranked Gold semidioses were their own clique, never associating with the lower-ranked students. Even now, Teo watched Xochi, the daughter of Primavera, and Atzi, the daughter of Tormentoso, pass by, laughing with their arms linked.

Both wore exquisite dresses. Xochi's black off-the-shoulder outfit had rows of flounces made entirely of real flowers, while Atzi's light blue ensemble featured a high collar and ruffled skirt trimmed with silver ribbons that formed a star around her hips when she spread the hem apart. Her box braids were adorned with silver string, gold cuffs, and tiny seeds that mimicked the sound of falling rain when she moved.

Everyone seemed to have their own social circles and hierarchies, and Teo was squarely outside of them. Well, almost.

Suddenly, the scent of sweet apples, copal incense, and must tickled Teo's nose. It was subtle enough that the average person probably wouldn't have noticed, but Teo had been expecting it. He turned, and it took a moment to spot the figure, dressed in black, waiting in the shadows.

"Fantasma," he said with a wide smile. The diosa looked like a young girl, maybe a couple of years younger than Teo—though age, of course, meant nothing to a god. As she stepped closer, light sparked in the golden embroidered stars and suns on her robes and lace mantle. Her butterfly companions rested on her clothes like tawny orange brooches. One sat at her temple, holding back her dark wavy hair and showing off the bright marigold blooms that hung from her ears.

Fantasma was a Jade goddess who served Muerte, the Gold goddess of death. Muerte's power was second only to that of Sol, two sides of the same coin. The Giver of Life, and the Taker. While Muerte was the harbinger of death, Fantasma was the gentle caretaker of the dead.

As Teo approached, the petite goddess lifted a hand in greeting with a hesitant smile.

"I've got something for you!" Teo said, digging his hand into the tight pocket of his pants.

Fantasma's eyebrows lifted and she leaned forward.

Teo pulled out a strawberry cream Chupa Chup. "It's your favorite!"

A wide smile brightened the goddess's face. Her cold fingers brushed against Teo's as she took the lollipop and gently cradled it in her hands like it was a tiny bird. Her gray eyes, the color of stone after rain, drank in the pink-and-white wrapper.

Teo grinned. Even though he could never get Fantasma to laugh, he was proud of the many smiles he'd collected.

When Teo was little, he'd found Fantasma sitting at the base of the Sun statue in the Sol Temple courtyard. Thinking she was lonely and in need of a friend, Teo had given Fantasma a Chupa Chup he had in his pocket. She looked a little confused but smiled and accepted his offering. In return, a skeleton hand popped out from the ground between them, which admittedly should've been terrifying, but held between its bony fingers was the most perfectly round and vibrant marigold Teo had ever laid eyes on.

The two had fallen into a ritual of gift-giving ever since.

While Teo always gave Fantasma a Chupa Chup, Fantasma's gifts were . . . more of a surprise. A skeletal hand popped right through the stone floor, presenting Teo with a mouse skull.

Teo took the tiny skull and smiled. "Thanks!" he said, now left with the problem of figuring out where to put it.

"There you are!"

Teo heard his mom's happy, singsong voice a second before she swept him into a hug as if she hadn't seen him a few hours ago. "And Fantasma!" Quetzal added with a warm smile.

Fantasma meekly waved, the Chupa Chup in the iron grip of her free hand.

Teo was about to ask his mom if she'd seen Niya yet when his ears began to ring. At the same time, the palm of his left hand started to itch, which only meant one thing—

"Teo and Quetzal, two of my favorite people!" came the booming voice of Dios Mala Suerte.

Teo immediately bit his tongue and stuffed his hand into his pocket to stave off any bad luck before forcing a smile. He knew better than to go against the old superstitions in the presence of Mala Suerte. Priests and semidioses alike quickly stepped out of the Jade god's way, muttering prayers under their breath.

Tall and thin as a rail, the god of bad luck wore black slacks and a matching guayabera with round eyes stitched in purple thread running down either side. His hair was oily black and always slicked back out of his face. Teo thought his grin showed too many teeth and never seemed to reach his eyes. But the really unsettling part of his ensemble was the strings of teeth he wore about his neck and wrists.

"Always so good to see you—and how tall you've gotten!" Dios Mala Suerte chuckled, thumping the back of Teo's shoulder. "They must be feeding you well in Quetzlan! And you look so much like your beautiful mother."

Teo did his best to smile, tongue still pressed between his teeth. Mala Suerte was like a weird, annoying uncle, but Teo knew better than to risk insulting him.

"Are you enjoying your night?" Quetzal asked, taking over the conversation.

"Very much so," Mala Suerte said. "It's always nice to get quality time with the kids."

The kids consisted of a large group of semidioses following the god. Some were older, in what Teo guessed were their early thirties, the youngest a toddler in the arms of a teenage girl. They were a rambunctious group of about ten, but they moved so much—laughing, shoving, and teasing one another—that it was hard to keep track.

There was one boy Teo recognized, however, who stood behind his dad, anxiously looking around the temple. Xio was thirteen, which Teo only knew because he'd recently attended Xio's gender confirmation ceremony.

"Dani and Renata are eligible this time, as is Xio," Mala Suerte said. Xio seemed to hate being the center of attention, shifting awkwardly and wringing his hands. Mala Suerte placed his large hand on top of Xio's head. Unlike his siblings' sleek black hair, Xio had a curly mop that fell into his eyes. "My little troublemaker," Mala Suerte said affectionately.

Teo felt bad for Xio. He clearly didn't want to be here, and Teo could relate.

Since the itching had faded, it was safe to finally speak. "Hey," he said, giving the younger boy a nod.

Xio returned it with a tight-lipped smile, fidgeting with his father's eye glyph that hung around his neck on layered strings of teeth. Teo didn't want to know where they came from.

"I suppose us Jades are just here as a formality," Mala Suerte said, scratching his stubble with black painted fingernails.

"Not necessarily a bad thing," Quetzal said with a tired smile.

Mala Suerte flashed another toothy grin. "I would have to agree."

"Sorry to interrupt."

Everyone turned to see that Verdad had joined them.

"I'm writing a piece on the Lumbre twins," Verdad said, notebook and pen poised at the ready. She had short hair, longer on the top and always swept across her forehead, and a monotone voice that Teo found difficult to pay attention to. "Teo, I was wondering if I could ask you a couple of questions about the fire in Quetzlan earlier today?"

There was literally nothing Teo would like to talk about less. "There was a fire, and they put it out," he said in a not-exactly-friendly tone.

A small crease formed between Verdad's eyebrows. She was dressed in a pinstripe suit that perfectly reflected her brand of no-nonsense investigative journalism. "I've never been able to interview a semidiose survivor of a rescue like this," she said, tapping her pen. "I'd love to hear about what it was like to be saved by your peers."

"They're not my peers."

Verdad glanced up. "Why do you say that?"

It took concentrated effort to keep his tone even. "Ask the Academy."

"Told you he'd be useless."

Chisme approached the group, high-heeled shoes clicking across the stone floor and his photographers not far behind. The only thing more alarming than being the focus of Chisme's attention was his plastic, red-tinted smile.

Chisme and Verdad were the adult children of Diosa Comunión, and while they both served as Reino del Sol's leading journalists, they had very different approaches to their craft. Chisme was the tabloid mogul known for getting the inside scoop before anyone else while Verdad preferred heavy-hitting reporting that focused on politics and current events.

A bright flash burned Teo's eyes, making him flinch and throw his arms up in defense.

"Don't waste the film," Chisme scolded before turning to Teo. "How's about something more interesting—do you think your friend Niya has what it takes to make it into the trials?"

"Don't give this viper a sound bite," Mala Suerte growled, his lip curling with distaste.

Teo smirked. "He's just mad we ruined his outfit last summer—"

"*My rare anaconda-print suit,*" Chisme hissed. "Listen, Bird Boy—"

"It's Teo," he snapped. "And don't you remember what it was like being a lowly Jade close to a potential Sunbearer? Or has no one ever wanted to get close to you?"

"*Teo,*" his mom gasped, but Teo refused to be sorry.

"So, you agree!" Chisme brought a small recorder close to his mouth. "Teo, Son of Quetzal, believes his closest friend, Niya, Daughter of Tierra, is a likely Sunbearer."

Verdad rolled her eyes at her brother, flipped her notebook closed, and strode away without a word to any of them.

"At what point does journalism become harassment?" Mala Suerte drawled.

Chisme smiled serenely. "I haven't found out." He turned back to his photographers. "We can at least get a picture of all the Jade rejects in a dark corner."

Quetzal managed a patient if tired smile, but poor Fantasma seized up entirely, her eyes growing wide as she stepped back into the shadows and disappeared.

"I wouldn't recommend it," Mala Suerte said, casually lifting an upturned palm. "Shame if all today's negatives were overexposed."

Chisme's mechanical grin twitched. "Fine. We have actual celebrities to interview, anyway." He turned on his heels and stalked away, the photographers scrambling after.

Quetzal gave Teo's hand a quick squeeze. "I'm going to say hello to some old friends. I'll see you at the ceremony?"

Teo nodded. "Okay." As he watched his mom leave, he heard a

metallic clatter, quickly followed by the shattering of what must've been a camera lens.

Chisme's angry voice cut through the murmurings of the crowd. "Fool!"

Deep chuckles rumbled in Mala Suerte's chest. When Teo looked over, the god shrugged. "Whoops," he said with a wicked grin.

This time, Teo couldn't help returning it.

CHAPTER 4

T eo!" a familiar voice called from the crowd.

Huemac took a large step to the side a split second before Teo felt like he was hit by a bus. Teo let out a strangled yelp as he was scooped off his feet in a viselike hug. The force made his wing joints pop.

"Hey, Niya," he greeted her with a weak smile.

At well over six feet tall, Niya had to look down as she beamed happily at Teo. In addition to her height, Niya was incredibly muscular, with broad shoulders and huge biceps. She had a heart-shaped face and prominent chin, with deep brown hair that was tied into two long braids.

"Aye, Teo, you're so short! It was hard for me to find you!" she scolded affectionately as her hazel eyes, the color of palm fronds and wet earth, danced with amusement.

"I'm not short!" He scowled. "And I think you bruised my ribs," he added, gingerly pressing a hand against them.

She laughed, loud and unabashed. "Sorry!"

It was hard to stay mad at someone who was so warm and happy to see him. That, along with how little she understood personal space, made Niya a lot like a puppy. If said puppy were the size of a bull and able to break you in half with no effort.

"Wait a second—" Niya leaned into Teo again and sniffed his hair before jerking back. "You stink like smoke!" she said, waving her hand in front of her nose. "The heck happened?!"

Teo tried to shove her but Niya barely budged. "Long story short: There was a fire in Quetzlan. I got a bit too close."

"Oh no," Niya groaned dramatically. "Did the twins show up?"

Teo nodded. She didn't need to know all the humiliating details.

"That explains it—you smell just like them," Niya said with a smirk.

Teo attempted to cover his hair with his hands. "No I don't!"

"Well, I'm glad you didn't get roasted!" she told him in typical Niya fashion. "I like this!" she added, switching topics at breakneck pace as she petted the feathers of Teo's cape.

"I feel like I've been tarred and feathered," Teo grumbled, pushing his circlet back into place. "Yours is . . ." He hesitated as he took in what Niya was wearing.

Barefoot as usual, she wore a white wrap skirt that ended high on her absolutely massive thighs. Gold pendants the size of Teo's hand hung around her waist from a belt, engraved with the same glyph as the gold pectoral sitting on her chest. As the daughter of Tierra, the god of earth, the glyph bore the likeness of three jagged mountains with the sun peeking from behind them. Matching discs adorned her ears and gold bands sat above her thick biceps.

"Dios, how are you not freezing?" Teo asked, laughter jumping in his throat.

Niya cocked her hip and tossed a braid over her shoulder. "Listen, I'm *shredded*—it's not right to cover it up! It's bad enough they make me wear this." Scowling, she tugged on her white bandeau top. "I don't see why my brothers can have their titties out but I can't. Theirs are even bigger than mine!" she announced loudly, throwing her hands up and getting looks from a group of nearby priests. There was no filter between Niya's head and her mouth. She just thought thoughts and said words.

"Huemac!" she exclaimed, eyes landing on the priest at Teo's side. "I missed you!"

When she spread her arms, Huemac's back went rigid.

"Niya." It was supposed to be a hello but it sounded more like a warning.

When Teo and Niya became friends, Huemac took on the role of guardian for both of them whenever they were at Sol Temple. Niya had her own priests to look after her, of course, but Huemac seemed to be the only one she'd listen to.

"I'm going to make my rounds," Huemac announced. "You two—" He eyed Teo and Niya suspiciously. "For the love of Sol, please be on your best behavior."

Niya's arms fell to her sides, bottom lip jutting. "Is he still mad about Día de Muertos?" she asked Teo, eyes following Huemac's retreating back.

Teo shrugged. "Probably."

"Come on, let's eat and you can catch me up on all things Teo and Quetzlan—I want to know everything!" she said, grabbing Teo's hand and dragging him to the food tables.

He couldn't help smiling. It was good to have his best friend back.

Long tables piled high with steaming tamales and arepas lined the outer edges of the cavernous event hall. As they joined the buffet line, Teo eyed some yellow tortillas next to lines of juicy carne asada and spiced carnitas. Dios Maize, the god of the harvest, and Diosa Pan Dulce, the sweet goddess of the hearth, had really outdone themselves. By the time Teo and Niya were ready to find their seats, he was struggling to balance the heaping tower of food on his plate.

The Golds took up the larger tables around the main statue while Jades squeezed into smaller ones around the outer edge. Teo couldn't help observing how the seating arrangements mirrored the placement of the cities across Reino del Sol. Niya didn't even hesitate to follow Teo to a small, rickety table on the outskirts. They passed Marino, who was dressed in a tunic accented with pastel coral, pink seashells, and polished sea glass in every shade of blue imaginable. His mother, Diosa Agua, stood next to him. Her black skin glowed like the ocean under moonlight, her gray eyes glinting like abalone shells. The side of her head was shaved and her blue hair tumbled over her shoulder like a waterfall.

Teo filled Niya in on everything he'd been up to that they hadn't covered over late-night texts. Niya had lived at the Academy since she was seven, so he couldn't go visit her, and when she got days off, she spent them with her dads back home.

"Other than the fire, Quetzlan has been pretty boring, honestly," Teo confessed as he sipped on fresh mango juice. "Unless you count talking a flock of flamingos into relocating from the fountain in front of city hall."

"That sounds like fun to me!" Niya said, but her enthusiasm dimmed when her gaze shifted past Teo's shoulder. "Ugh, great, here come the twins," she grumbled, angrily taking a big bite of steak.

Teo glanced back. Tension pinched his shoulders.

Aurelio and Auristela descended the stairs side by side, in matching black pants and sleeveless tunics with gold-and-red embroidery that imitated flames, closely followed by their mother. Large pectoral adornments made of real burning coals covered Aurelio and Auristela's chests.

Chatter immediately broke out. In the world of half gods, Aurelio and Auristela were basically royalty. Diosa Lumbre was the head of the Academy and had a long line of semidioses who were not only famous Heroes but *Sunbearers*.

Lumbre scanned the crowd, silently observing the priests and semidioses with eyes that smoldered with liquid fire. Every angle of her face was severe. Teo had never seen the goddess smile a day in her life. Diosa Lumbre was intimidating, sure, but Teo's loathing for her was so strong, it canceled out any possible fear.

Aurelio and Auristela moved through the crowd, greeting people as they passed. Chisme and Verdad pushed to the front, their photographers rapidly snapping pictures. Auristela smiled and posed like some celebrity walking down the red carpet, talking animatedly with Chisme.

Meanwhile, Aurelio stood by her side, looking stoic and maybe even a touch uncomfortable as lights flashed in his face. He adjusted his pectoral. Thin chains arched across the curve of his biceps from his signature golden armbands to small loops hanging from the golden neckpiece.

There was always something about Aurelio—the glow of his skin, the burning intensity of his eyes—that made Teo wonder if he was favored by Sol. They were all half gods, but it was like Aurelio had been touched by the sun itself. Like if Teo looked at him for too long, he'd burn up from the inside out.

Someone called Aurelio's name, and as he scanned the room, his eyes caught Teo's.

It was only a second, long enough for recognition to flash across Aurelio's face and heat to burn in Teo's chest, before he quickly looked away. It was bad enough that Aurelio had just saved Teo's sorry ass from burning up in a fire, now Teo had to watch him bask in all his golden glory at the trials, too.

When Teo stole another glance, Aurelio had already turned, swept up in a conversation with his sister.

Teo turned back to Niya, desperate for a change of subject. "How's the Academy?"

"Rough. They've really been kicking our asses," Niya said between bites of food. "With the trials coming up, they've amped up training. We're doing drills *constantly*," she groaned, practically slumping on the table. "They'll summon us during dinner or even in the middle of the night to run different disaster scenarios and rescues."

Niya scrunched her face up into a scowl and imitated Diosa Lumbre's sharp, bossy voice. "'If you want to be in the trials, you need to train harder! Move faster! Get stronger! Only the best of the best will be chosen!'"

When she put it like that, it was easier for him not to feel like he was missing out. "Sounds like a pain in the ass, if you ask me," Teo replied.

She sighed deeply. "It is, but"—Niya gave him a sheepish smile—"I still love helping people."

"And competition," Teo added.

She sat up straighter and grinned. "I'm fourth in the class right now!"

Teo forced a smile, ignoring the heavy weight that dropped into his stomach. "I'm really happy for you, Niya." He *was* proud of how well she was doing at the Academy, but he was also scared.

If she was ranked fourth in the class, it seemed inevitable that she would be chosen for the trials. This worry had turned into a recurring nightmare for Teo, and with the opening ceremony only a handful of hours away, he couldn't help feeling like his greatest fear was about to come true.

"Niya," Teo said carefully, "do you . . . *want* to be chosen for the trials?"

Niya bit her lip. "I *know* they're just more stupid Gold showboating, but they're also—I don't know, important? I mean, it's an honor, right?"

"To risk your life for this?" Teo asked, gesturing around the room. *This* meaning the pomp and circumstance of it all, the *Gold*.

"No, not for *this*," Niya said, shaking her head. "For our people. To uphold Sol's sacrifice and keep Reino del Sol safe."

Teo held his tongue. The worst possible scenario consumed his thoughts—his best friend laid on the altar at the end of the trials, and Teo unable to do anything but watch.

"Aye, look, the triad of douchebaggery is complete," Niya said, pulling him back to the present.

Teo turned around to look at the latest semidiose to enter the hall—the twins' terrible sidekick, Ocelo. As they walked down the stairs, Ocelo's thickly muscled arms swung back and forth, like they were some kind of cartoon villain. Diose Guerrero trailed behind their child. With their jaguar head, yellow eyes, and battle-scarred face, Teo found Diose Guerrero the most intimidating of the gods.

Aurelio and Auristela were pompous elitists, yes, but Ocelo was an obnoxious narcissist. They were shorter than Teo—probably somewhere around five foot five, which was short for a demigod—but held themself like they were seven feet tall. They wore a red cape knotted on their left shoulder, draped diagonally across their body so as to display the glyph of a jaguar head. Their hair was always buzzed short and they'd decided to dye it like jaguar spots for the special occasion. Ocelo was the only semidiose whose physique came anywhere near rivaling Niya's.

A small group of Jade demigods chatted in a group, blocking Ocelo from where Chisme and Verdad were fawning over Aurelio and Auristela.

Instead of asking them to move, or just going around them like a normal person, Ocelo shouldered their way right through, sending the semidioses stumbling out of their way.

Teo clenched his jaw, frustrated that Ocelo was able to get away with such blatant disrespect.

But then he got an idea.

Teo nudged Niya. "You thinking what I'm thinking?" he asked under his breath.

"No!" she whispered back. "But whatever it is, I'm game!"

Teo pulled Niya with him, dodging people as they slunk to the edge of the stairs. Ocelo was nearly at the bottom when they crouched into position behind an unused table.

Teo pinched Niya's elbow and pointed to where gold fasteners accented Ocelo's leather sandals. "Wanna send them on a little trip down the stairs?"

A wicked grin curled Niya's lips.

Niya clenched her hand into a fist and the pieces of gold shuddered. Quickly, she tugged, and the fasteners, along with the shoes and feet inside them, jerked.

Ocelo stumbled, pitching forward and tumbling head over heels down the stairs. They landed in a heap at the foot of the steps, red cape flipped over their head.

Gasps rose from the crowd and the photographers swarmed, cameras flashing wildly. Ocelo thrashed until they freed themself from their cape and leapt to their feet. They spun around, seething as their yellow-green eyes searched for the culprit.

Teo and Niya dropped below their table, dissolving into fits of laughter.

"Oh my gods, I can't breathe!" Niya said, arms wrapped around her stomach as she cackled. "Did you see their face?"

"Pure gold!" Teo agreed, wiping a tear from his eye. There was something so satisfying about seeing an asshole get what they deserved.

Above, someone cleared their throat.

Teo and Niya's laughter died as they looked up to find Huemac standing over them. He stared down at them, an exasperated expression on his face.

The pair quickly jumped to their feet. "Not very graceful for a cat, huh, Huemac?" Teo said with a solemn shake of his head.

One of Huemac's bushy eyebrows arched. "They could have gotten hurt."

"They didn't, though, see!" Niya said, gesturing at Ocelo, who was red-faced and stomping away.

"Yeah, nothing but their ego," Teo added, trying to hold back a laugh.

Niya nodded. "Probably why they fell over in the first place."

"Big head," Teo agreed. "*Very* top-heavy."

"Actions have more than your intended consequences," Huemac said.

"Tell that to Ocelo and their whole"—Teo gestured vaguely—"everything."

"*Ocelo* is not my responsibility," Huemac said tersely. "Or obliged to follow my rules. I don't think either of your parents would be happy about this."

Niya was immediately shamefaced, but Teo was just frustrated. Ocelo never got in trouble for being a dick—how was that fair? Luckily, before Huemac could dole out any sort of punishment, crowds started moving toward the stairs.

"Looks like it's time to head up for the ceremony," Huemac said, scanning the room.

"Finally!" Niya said, grinning from ear to ear as she grabbed Teo's arm and gave it an excited shake.

Teo's stomach rolled. He stuck to Niya's side, following Huemac and the rest of the crowd as they started the long trek up the steps to the top of the temple where Diosa Luna waited for them at Sol's altar.

"If you'd all gather around, we'll get the ceremony started," Luna announced.

Diosa Luna had coily dark hair streaked with silvery gray, an hourglass figure, and dark, cool brown skin. Crow's feet sat at the corners of her eyes, wrinkling as she smiled at everyone gathered. The dress she wore had a plunging neckline that started out midnight blue at her shoulders and faded to a starry silver where it pooled at her sandaled feet. It was covered in tiny pinpricks of silver that mirrored the stars and constellations in the night sky.

The rays of her sunburst necklace stretched out across her shoulders and clavicles, marking her as the high priestess of Sol Temple. Luna was the diosa of the moon, giving her the power to reflect the voice of Sol.

Niya went off to be with her dad, and Teo went to his mom, standing with some of the other Jade gods.

"This way, Teo," Quetzal said, waving him forward, but before he could follow, Mala Suerte stepped into his path.

"Good luck, Teo." He grinned, giving Teo's arm a squeeze before wandering off, his brood in tow and Xio sticking close to his side.

"I can never tell if he's messing with me or not," Teo said to his mom as they joined the crowd gathering around the altar.

"I think most of it is just for show," Quetzal agreed with a sad sort of sigh. "If people treat you like you're bad for long enough, I imagine you start believing it. Or, as I think might be the case with Suerte, playing it up for fun."

As they got into position, Teo craned his neck in search of Niya. He found her on the other side of the room, bouncing on the balls of her feet, practically vibrating with excitement. Tierra stood behind her with her older brothers, Monte and Mino, who flanked him like sentinels.

Dios Tierra wore a black suit with gold-embroidered accents that reflected his glyph, and a crimson tie. Leather gloves and a simple gold mask that cast his eyes in shadow covered his skinless flesh.

"The last person you need to worry about is Niya," Quetzal told Teo, smoothing her hand down his covered wings. "She will do just fine."

"I know," Teo said as he watched his best friend greet her family.

Niya said something to Monte, who grinned and bounced his pecs in turn. Niya punched his arm while Mino threw his head back with a barklike laugh.

"Dioses and semidioses," Luna said, her voice carrying over the crowd, which immediately hushed. A younger Sol priest stood next to her, interpreting what she said in sign language. "Diose Sol and I welcome you to Sol Temple to celebrate the end of this decade and the start of the next." She lifted her hands to the Sol Stone, which silently churned and glowed with golden light.

Luna smiled and pressed her palms together. "This is a time to give thanks to Sol for the good fortune they have brought us, and to remember all they have given so that we may live.

"Every ten years, the sun's power must be replenished so that Sol can continue their path through the sky, keeping our world safe from the Obsidians and monsters that have been locked in their celestial bindings," Luna explained. "Ten eligible semidioses between the ages of thirteen and eighteen are selected as the worthiest to compete in the Sunbearer Trials. The winner will be chosen by Sol as this decade's Sunbearer and join the distinguished ranks of our past champions."

Luna gestured to where a line of semidioses stood, all wearing golden sunburst crowns. They were all Golds, of course, and Diosa Lumbre's glyph was the most common hanging around their necks. They ranged in age from the youngest, Brilla, who was twenty-seven, to Arnau, a semidiós of Diose Guerrero who was one hundred and forty-eight.

"Our Sunbearer will travel through Reino del Sol and refuel the Sun Stones at each city's temple." Luna paused long enough to let her gaze travel around the open-air observatory. "But it is the semidiose who becomes the sacrifice who has the greatest honor of all."

Teo shifted uneasily next to his mother. He'd heard this story enough times to know what came next. What had kept him up late at night these past weeks leading up to the Sunbearer Trials. What made him terrified of Niya being chosen to compete.

"To be sacrificed to Sol and have their body melted into the elixir that will refuel the Sun Stones, so they can continue to provide safety and protection to all of us for the next ten years."

Diosa Luna approached the altar and stood next to the cloth-covered rectangle. In one swift movement, she unveiled what was underneath.

The sacrificial stone slab was covered in intricate engravings of the sun and webs of constellations. It rested on top of a stack of golden skulls—they all belonged to past semidioses who had died in sacrifice to keep the Sun Stones burning. After Tierra melted their bodies, he saved their skulls, plated them in gold, and engraved their names in thin script across the forehead.

Teo looked back to the line of former Sunbearers. They did not turn to face the skulls of the dead.

"Just as we honor Sol, we owe our lives to the semidioses who sacrifice themselves—to remind us what they gave so that all of us may live," Luna said. "Without this sacrifice, Reino del Sol would fall to inevitable destruction."

Teo clenched his hands into fists, willing his knees not to shake. It sounded so noble, but Teo didn't want his best friend to end up among the pile of skulls.

Someone had to keep the world from ending, just not Niya.

"Dioses," Luna said, looking out into the crowd. "Please present your children for Sol's selection."

As everyone around him started to move, Teo froze.

"Don't worry, Pajarito," his mom said, her soft feathers brushing his cheek as she kissed the top of his head. "You'll be fine."

He knew she was right, but it wasn't his fate he was worried about. Teo's movements were mechanical as he followed the other semidioses, forming a ring around the Sol Stone floating above their heads.

Teo desperately searched for Niya and spotted her across the way. She smiled and gave Teo a small wink.

All he could do was stand there between two other Jades—Cacti, child of the goddess of agave, and Juanita, daughter of the god of lost things—rooted to the floor. Sweat prickled his brow and ran down the middle of his back under his binder. He tried to steady his breathing, to avoid fainting right there in front of everyone.

Silence hung thick as they all waited.

Gradually, a hum filled the air and the Sol Stone grew brighter, pulsing in time with Teo's thundering heartbeat.

A flash of light sparked to Teo's left. A sunburst crown appeared on Ocelo's buzzed head. A wicked grin cut their features as they basked in the honor of being the first one selected by Sol. Diose Guerrero beamed proudly, their fangs glinting.

With another flash of light, a crown appeared on Marino's head. The water semidiós let out a breath, shoulders slumping in relief. A third flash and a crown appeared on Auristela's head. She sucked in a gasp, nearly jumping with excitement before she seemed to remember herself and returned to standing with her arms held straight at her sides. Still, Teo saw the corners of her mouth twitch in a suppressed grin.

Beside her, Aurelio didn't so much as flinch. His expression remained unreadable as he stared up at the Sun Stone, waiting. For a moment, Teo wondered if Aurelio was jealous of his sister, but then there was another flare of light.

A gleaming crown appeared on Aurelio's head. His eyelids fluttered in relief. Auristela latched on to her brother's wrist, doing her best to trap her grin between her teeth.

The crowd broke out into hushed chatter. Even Teo's lips parted in surprise. A set of siblings, let alone twins, had never been selected to compete in the trials in the same year, as far as he knew. The confused and surprised expressions around the room confirmed his suspicion. Diosa Lumbre, however, didn't seem at all shocked. In fact, she stood motionless, almost bored.

A strange feeling that Teo couldn't define churned in his stomach as he watched Aurelio. He hadn't let himself think of it before tonight, but here it was, impossible to look away from: Aurelio would be competing in the Sunbearer Trials.

Teo shook his head at himself. Now was not the time to worry over Aurelio's fate.

Teo pushed his feather circlet up out of his eyes only to realize his hands were trembling.

One by one, three more Gold semidioses were selected. When Atzi, the thirteen-year-old rain semidiosa, was chosen, Teo could hear the approving rumble of thunder from her father, Tormentoso. Next was Xochi, the semidiosa of spring, dressed in flowers. Her mother, Primavera, excitedly hugged her diosa sisters. The Estaciones, the goddesses of the seasons, were a tight-knit group of tías who absolutely fawned over Xochi. Dezi, the son of Diosa Amor, was also selected. Teo didn't know much about him other than that he was astoundingly gorgeous. In the center of his tunic he bore his mother's glyph—an anatomical heart on fire.

There were only three spots left.

For a moment, Teo let himself hope. Maybe Niya wouldn't be chosen, and then they'd get to spend the next ten days together, watching the trials and getting sick on candy.

Not Niya. Not Niya. Not Niya.

But that hope was short-lived.

In a flash of light, a sunburst crown sparked from Niya's head.

Teo's heart clenched.

A huge smile lit up Niya's face, and she immediately turned to her brothers, who clapped and whooped, ignoring the customary silence. Meanwhile, Tierra's gloved hands gripped his tie.

The back of Teo's throat burned as he tried to swallow. He couldn't panic, not while he was standing in a room full of people. It wasn't a guaranteed death sentence, he tried to remind himself. This was *Niya*. She didn't lose anything, especially not the trials. She'd be okay, she just needed to get through it and not come in last place. She just—

A flash of light, far too close, snapped Teo from his thoughts.

This time, surprised voices erupted from the crowd. Heads swiveled.

The newly selected semidiós was only two people down from his left and it was—

A jolt shot through him.

The large crown sitting atop Xio's curly hair made him look so small compared to the Golds.

Xio.

Xio? But he was a Jade.

The world beneath Teo's feet seemed to lurch. He turned back to his mom to find her looking as shocked as he felt, her brows pinched in confusion.

Another flash. Too close. Too bright and disorienting.

Teo squinted. Across the circle, Niya stared at him, alarmed.

For some reason, he sought out Aurelio. The boy's lips were softly parted, eyes wide and looking right at him—the most emotion Teo had seen on Aurelio's face in years.

Over the growing noise of the crowd, Teo heard his mom gasp but he didn't know why. He turned to her but felt a sudden shift of weight on his head.

He went to push his feather circlet back into place, but when Teo reached up, his fingers touched the cold rays of a sunburst crown.

CHAPTER 5

Teo's feet moved under him but he had no idea where he was going. Camera flashes exploded in his vision as people passed in a blur, murmuring and stepping out of the way while someone guided him through the observatory and down the main steps. There was a groan of wooden doors opening and then closing again behind him. All other sounds were muffled except for the thunderous pounding of his pulse.

"Teo?"

His mom's face materialized before him. Her hands were on his shoulders. She'd never squeezed him so hard.

"Teo," Quetzal repeated, voice tight. Deep creases puckered the smooth skin between her delicate brows. Teo didn't want to see it.

Just past her shoulder stood an astronomical clock. The main dial represented the position of the sun, moon, and planets—nearly in alignment now—in the sky. A calendar dial with medallions representing the months was encircled by another that displayed the gods' glyphs.

A deep, hollow ticking sounded from deep within.

"You need to take a deep breath, Pajarito."

Tick, tock. Tick, tock.

The crushing weight of reality dropped onto him.

"Wait, no—!" He jerked back from his mom, suddenly—acutely—aware of his heart hammering in his chest. "I'm not—this is impossible!

I can't compete in the trials!" he said, a strangled laugh catching in his throat.

This couldn't be real. It was a fever dream or maybe some kind of sick joke.

Searing heat clawed up Teo's throat. His lungs fought against his binder, but it tightened around his ribs like a giant fist.

"Focus on your breathing, Teo," Quetzal said, her voice infuriatingly calm as she slowly moved a step closer.

Teo shook his head fiercely. "I can't, there's no way!" The circlet of feathers slipped down his forehead. The sunburst crown tilted to the side.

He ripped the crown off his head and hurled it across the room. Metal clattered over stone as it skidded across the floor before hitting the base of the clock. In a blink, it disappeared.

The heavy weight dropped back onto his head.

Teo yanked it off again and held it out in front of him. The gold glinted dully. The cold, pointy rays dug into his clutching fingers. Teo's head swam, the room gently swaying around him. "I don't want this!" he insisted, looking to his mom for help.

She only stared at him, delicate hands pressed over her mouth as her black eyes glistened.

Behind them, the doors groaned open.

Luna walked in. Instead of being outraged or confused, she only watched Teo, still and silent.

How could she be so calm when the world was ending?

"This is some kind of mistake!" Teo said to the goddess, desperate for some sort of reaction. "I'm just a Jade!" Another wild laugh shook through him. "I can't compete in the Sunbearer Trials!"

"Sol chose you," Luna said, voice steady. Her dark eyes shone with tiny pinpricks of silver, like stars. "You must compete in the trials."

"How am I supposed to compete with the Golds? I'm not a Hero!

They have been training their whole lives for this and—I'm not even allowed to go to the same school!" Teo shouted, clutching the sunburst crown in trembling hands. "I don't want to be the Sunbearer!"

Not when someone had to die.

Luna's expression remained placid, but Quetzal flinched. Teo spun to face his mom.

"Mom, tell her!"

Teo's mother pressed her lips between her teeth for a moment. Teo could see her throat dip in a swallow before she spoke slowly and carefully. "I know you're scared, Teo…"

He waited for her to tell him that it was going to be okay—that this was all a huge mistake, that they could go home right now, that he was going to be all right.

But as he stood there, waiting, no reassurances came. She could only stare at him, at a complete loss for words.

A shiver dragged down Teo's spine. Why wouldn't she tell him it'd be okay?

In the heavy silence, the clock continued to tick.

Tick, tock. Tick, tock.

"Mom—?" It was little more than a croak before the doors banged open again.

A high-pitched ringing made all three flinch and clamp their hands over their ears.

"LUNA!" Mala Suerte bellowed. The dios radiated dark energy, trembling around his edges like smoke.

Teo stumbled back into his mom but Luna straightened, wincing but not budging as the dios charged toward her.

"You tell Sol they cannot have Xio for their games!" Mala Suerte's voice rumbled through every bone in Teo's body, a terrible, thundering sound.

Mala Suerte towered over Luna, but she didn't back down.

"Sol has chosen Xio to compete in the trials," Luna said, her voice steady and unwavering.

An ugly snarl curled Mala Suerte's mouth, pulling back to reveal sharp, growing teeth. "*Sol is wrong!*"

"*Suerte,*" Quetzal warned.

The earsplitting ringing grew louder with the god's rage. Teo bit his tongue and resisted the urge to scratch the itching palm of his left hand. It was then that Teo noticed Xio.

He stood behind his father, so small in comparison. He covered his ears with his hands, squinting up at his dad. The sunburst crown still sat crooked on his mop of curls.

"Sol is not wrong," Luna said, lifting her chin. "And they do not make mistakes. Xio was chosen for a reason."

The whites of Mala Suerte's eyes turned bloodred as his form shook violently. A third eye peeled open on his forehead, its pupil a startling blue as the god grew larger until he was hunched over Luna. The room trembled and, for a moment, Teo feared Mala Suerte's shoulders would burst through the ceiling.

"I WOULD TEAR THIS CITY TO THE GROUND BEFORE I'D LET YOU TAKE HIM FROM ME."

Mala Suerte's skin glowed scarlet, washing the room in red.

With a sudden jerk, Quetzal grabbed Teo. Her wings enveloped him, blocking Teo and covering his eyes from seeing the enraged god. Teo tried to not let his legs give out from under him. He'd heard stories of how if a dios lost their temper, the sheer force of their wrath could melt anyone less than a god who was standing too close.

"Stop this before you do something you regret," Luna said, sternly.

"XIO IS MY SON!" Mala Suerte roared.

Teo squeezed his eyes shut as the ringing cut through his head. His mom tightened her arms around him. The itching was unbearable, like ants burrowing under his skin.

"Dad, *stop.*" The quiet voice somehow cut through all the noise.

The ringing in Teo's ears slowly ebbed. Hesitantly, his mom loosened her grip.

"We both know there's nothing you can do."

Carefully, Teo peeked out from behind his mother's wing. Mala Suerte, still giant and terrifying, looked down at his son.

"I just want to get it over with," the young boy said, chin lowered and cheeks red. "Don't make this harder than it needs to be."

Because Mala Suerte's back was to him, Teo couldn't see his face.

"Please?" Xio asked.

The ringing in Teo's ears and the itching of his palm faded away.

With a long, low sigh, the god of bad luck shrank until he was back to his usual size. Mala Suerte's shoulders bowed over his chest, arms falling to his sides. Xio stepped closer and Mala Suerte placed his large hand on the back of his son's head, behind the sunburst crown.

"Wait here," Quetzal told Teo.

He watched as his mom and Diosa Luna spoke in hushed tones to Xio and Mala Suerte.

Compared to Xio, Teo's situation didn't seem nearly as dire. Xio had only just turned thirteen a couple months ago. He hadn't even hit a growth spurt yet and still had round baby cheeks. Xio was only a Jade, and the son of Mala Suerte, at that.

What awful luck.

Would Sol really select both of them only to be decimated in the competition?

Teo averted his gaze, a lump forming in his throat. He looked around the room, taking in their surroundings. They were below the observatory. Across from the clock was a desk that, judging by the star charts and astronomical instruments, must belong to Luna. A map of Reino del Sol had been engraved into the surface, the different cities noted by small figurines of each god's glyph carved from pieces of gold and jade.

Around the room, murals with faceless figures and brightly colored scenes were painted on the walls. Teo realized they told the story of Reino del Sol.

There was the creation of the world and the breaking of the seven-pointed star. Dark celestial figures fighting the Gold and Jade dioses illustrated the war with the Obsidians. The final mural showed the people of Reino del Sol living happily under the golden sunburst, but it was the scene just before it that Teo approached for a closer look.

The gods stood in a circle, holding the Sun Stones in their outstretched hands. Teo spotted his mom with her blue-and-green wings right away. In the center, Tierra was on his knees, surrounded with swirls of red-and-orange fire.

Sol lay dying in his arms. Their body was painted in metallic gold, a dagger in their chest and crimson rivulets of blood spilling around them.

On the wall, the clock ticked away.

Tick, tock. Tick, tock.

Luna led Teo and Xio inside Sol Temple, leaving their parents behind. His mom had told him that the gods weren't allowed to visit their children during the trials to avoid cheating, but that she would be there to watch every event. When the rankings were displayed at the end of each trial, they could steal a moment together, and then there would be a final banquet with their families the night before the last trial.

As he followed Luna through the opulent halls, Teo's mind spun, trying to think his way out of this mess. If he snuck out of the temple, he'd have to steal a boat. If he made it that far, he'd have to pass through the waterfalls, which were operated by the Sol priests. And even if he somehow got through them, what would he do?

He couldn't go home to Quetzlan, so at best, he'd be on the run for the rest of his life, and at worst—well, he wasn't sure what the punishment was for deserting the trials, but given what happened during the closing ceremony, it was probably nothing good.

The only thing he could do was not get himself killed.

If he could stay high enough in the rankings to not come in last, he could survive this.

Teo stole a glance over at Xio. The younger boy followed the moon goddess silently, eyes downcast. His expression was blank, like he'd already resigned himself to his fate. Teo hated it.

There was the distant sound of chatter before they rounded a corner and found the Golds. They were in a group, talking among themselves—except for Niya, who was off to the side pacing back and forth.

As they approached, the talking stopped and everyone turned.

Atzi was braiding Xochi's hair on an emerald green velvet couch while Marino and Dezi leaned against the arms. Ocelo smirked, looking Teo up and down while Auristela shook her head, an amused quirk to her lips as she whispered to Ocelo.

And there was Aurelio. He frowned at Teo, staring at him almost calculatingly as the coals smoldered around his neck.

Teo's face burned with heat.

"Dude!" Niya shoved him and he stumbled. "The fuck?!"

"I have no idea," he replied, trying to keep his voice down.

"This is wild!"

"I know—"

Niya yanked him into a hug, lifting him off his feet. "We're gonna have so much fun together!"

A surprised laugh jumped in Teo's throat. Leave it to Niya to see the silver lining of his probable death sentence.

"You always talk about how you wish you could see the other cities!" she said, setting him back down.

"Yeah, but not like this," Teo hissed under his breath. "I was supposed to be in the stands, *watching* the Sunbearer Trials, not *competing in them*."

But Niya didn't seem to get it. "We can hang out, stay up late talking and playing games," she rattled off happily. "I could even teach you how to fight!"

Teo blinked at her. Was she serious? A terrible scene played out in his mind's eye—Niya, the Sunbearer, standing over his lifeless sacrificial corpse.

Thankfully, he didn't need to come up with a response because Luna called them all to attention.

"Congratulations, competitors, on being chosen for the Sunbearer Trials," Diosa Luna said. "I think we've all had a long day, so if you'll follow me, I'll show you to your rooms for the night," she said, signing as she spoke. "This way."

The Golds fell into step behind the diosa, excitedly murmuring to one another. Xio followed them at a safe distance, and Teo and Niya lingered at the very back.

"Why is she signing?" Teo asked Niya.

"Dezi's deaf," she said with a shrug.

Dezi was tall and had deep, warm black skin and a high fade with sponge curls. He was objectively beautiful but not in a chiseled, supermodel kind of way. He had soft features, kind eyes, and the sweet sort of smile that made your legs feel like Jell-O. Dezi followed Luna, watching her hands attentively as she led them down the hall.

"He's, like, a *total* badass, we all knew he'd get picked," Niya went on. "He's *really* strong, super smart, and the powers he got from his mom?" Niya let out a low whistle.

"What are his powers?" Teo asked, but they were interrupted before Niya could answer.

"You'll be staying here tonight, but tomorrow we will be boarding the boat to travel to the first host city after breakfast," Diosa Luna announced as they walked. "This is the beginning of a very long journey for all of you, so I suggest getting as much sleep as you can."

"Can we check out the rest of the temple?" Xochi asked, a hopeful lift in her voice.

Luna smiled. "No, you may not." She addressed the group. "You are only allowed to see your parents at the beginning and the end of each trial, and communicating with any of your priests is considered a conflict of interest."

"Cheating," Marino said and signed to his friends.

"However, there will be Sol priests available twenty-four seven throughout the competition. If you need something, just ask them," Luna continued. A pair of Sol priests stood on either side of the next doorway, smiling as they passed through. Teo wasn't sure if they were actually there to assist or guard.

Niya gave Teo's arm a nudge and nodded toward Xio. "How's he taking it?" she whispered.

The younger boy stood off to the side, nervously twisting a bracelet on his wrist.

Teo winced. "Better than his dad, I guess."

"This door leads to the dining room and kitchen," Luna went on. "Diosa Pan Dulce and Dios Maize kindly volunteered their services for the duration of the trials. They'll cater all your meals during our travels and if you need something in between, you may ask them."

"What happened?" Niya whispered.

Teo quietly filled her in on how Mala Suerte completely lost his shit.

Niya frowned. "Huh."

"What?"

Niya shrugged. "I'm surprised, is all. Mala Suerte always seemed kind of…" She tipped her head from side to side.

"Aloof?"

"Does that mean 'full of himself and acts like he isn't bothered by anything'?"

"Yes."

"Then yes."

"I really don't think Xio has anybody else, even outside of the trials. He seems like kind of a loner," Teo said. His chest was tight as he watched Xio look around the room, giving Aurelio and the others a wide berth. *My little troublemaker*, Mala Suerte had said. Teo turned to Niya. "We should try to look out for him."

Niya's eyebrows lifted. "Yeah?"

"Yeah, I mean, he's a defenseless little thirteen-year-old. And he's a Jade," he added. "We haven't been trained for any of this shit. It's like Sol chose us *just* to be an easy sacrifice."

Niya finally looked worried. "I didn't think about that ..."

"And outcasts need to stick together, right?" Teo asked, nudging her with his elbow.

"Right!" Niya replied, already convinced.

Around another corner, Luna showed them to their sleeping quarters. A long hallway stretched out before them, lined with doors, each of which had a dios's glyph on the front.

"Your priests already brought up your belongings. This is where I leave you," Luna said. "I need to go reconvene with the other dioses."

For some reason, her starry gaze lingered on Teo.

"I would suggest turning in early and getting a good night's rest. Tomorrow we will begin our journey."

Teo's room was at the very end of the hall, right across from Xio's. He thought he should say something to the younger Jade, offer him some kind of reassurance, but Xio ducked into his room without so much as pausing, the door snapping shut behind him.

Inside, Teo's first thought was to wonder whether or not his contraband had made it, but that was quickly replaced with shock over how big his room was. He had his own living quarters back at Quetzal Temple, but he just had the same lumpy twin bed and cheap furniture that he'd had since he was a toddler.

This place was so *fancy*. For such an old temple, they really hadn't skimped on interior renovations. There was a large window with expensive-looking drapes, gold furniture, and a door that he assumed led to the bathroom.

When he turned to inspect the massive bed, Teo nearly jumped out of his skin to find someone waiting next to it.

"Huemac!" Teo gasped, clutching a hand over his chest. "You scared the *shit* outta me—"

"I can't stay for long," Huemac interrupted in a hushed tone, crossing the room so quickly it made Teo stumble back.

Huemac's dark eyes locked on Teo, his posture rigid.

Teo had known Huemac his entire life and not once had he ever seen the head priest of Quetzlan break a single rule. "What are you—?"

Huemac gripped his shoulders and squeezed them tight. "Be quick on your feet around Xochi, and steer clear of water or else Marino and Atzi will use it against you."

He spoke so quickly, Teo struggled to keep up.

"*Don't* get near Dezi during competition. You can outsmart Ocelo—they may have brute strength but they lack tactical strategy. You're clever and you're fast, use it to your advantage. And, Teo—"

He blinked up at Huemac, at a total loss for words.

Huemac leveled him a hard stare. "Stay out of Aurelio and Auristela's way."

Teo jumped as the door behind him creaked.

Niya stood there, having already changed into a loose white crop top and a pair of spandex shorts. When she saw Teo and Huemac, she froze.

Huemac released Teo and stood up straight. "I have to go now," he said. "I put your backpack in the armoire," he added, giving Teo a pointed look before swiftly exiting the room.

Niya looked back and forth between Teo and the empty hallway. "I thought we weren't allowed to talk to our priests?" she said, face screwed up in confusion.

"We're not," Teo said, rubbing his shoulder where Huemac's fingers had gripped him.

"Then what was he doing here?"

"Giving me advice, I think," Teo murmured. It was so unlike Huemac to do anything against protocol. It was unsettling. Did he really think Teo was in that deep of trouble? "He told me how to deal with the Golds during the trials."

Niya gasped and quickly closed the door behind her. "Huemac was *cheating*?" she hissed under her breath. "I'm impressed!" Niya laughed. "What did he say about me?"

"Nothing."

Niya scoffed.

Teo rolled his eyes. "What's up?"

"Oh!" Niya said, as if just remembering. "I was gonna see if you wanted to raid the kitchen!"

An amused grin tugged the corner of Teo's mouth. In all the chaos, at least he could rely on Niya's insatiable appetite. "I'm down," he said as he took off the circlet and sunburst crown, tossing them onto the bed. This time, the crown stayed put. "I think we should invite Xio, too."

"Aw, we're gonna have our own little misfit gang!" Niya grinned as she leaned against the closed door, crossing her arms over her chest.

Teo removed his heavy feathered cape and then hesitated. "Uh …" He glanced around the room. "Where's the armoire?"

"*What's* an armoire?"

"I was hoping you'd know."

Teo and Niya exchanged a look before breaking into laughter. It felt good and released some of the tension from his shoulders. If he had to face the trials, at least he had Niya to face them with. At least he wasn't alone.

CHAPTER 6

Teo swapped his regalia for comfy sweatpants and a tee. "Try not to freak him out, okay?" he told Niya as they crossed the hall.

"What do you mean?" she asked with a frown, stopping outside of Xio's door.

"I mean, I think he's pretty nervous and you can come on a little, y'know…" He gestured at her full six-foot-something height and built frame.

But apparently Niya *didn't* get it because she just tipped her head to the side.

"Strong," Teo clarified with a chuckle.

"What's wrong with *strong*?" she demanded, propping her hands on her hips.

"And scary," he added.

"I'm not scary!" Niya barked, to which Teo cocked an eyebrow. She scowled. "Shut up, I am very friendly and totally not scary!"

Before Teo could stop her, she turned and banged her fist on the door. Unfortunately, it hadn't been closed all the way, so it flew open and slammed into the wall.

Inside, Xio had been sitting on his bed, head lowered, but when Niya nearly broke down his door, he jumped, hands going up to shield himself.

"*Dios*," Teo groaned under his breath.

Niya smiled brightly. "Hey!"

Xio looked back and forth between the two of them, alarmed. "Hi?"

"Ah, sorry." Teo cringed. "We were going to check out the kitchen— do you wanna come? Have you had enough to eat?"

"Oh … Are you sure?" Xio said, surprised. With him in it, the bed looked massive, or maybe it just made him look extra small. "People usually avoid me," Xio explained with a half-hearted shrug. "Y'know … because I'm 'bad luck.'"

Ouch. Poor kid. Teo thought he had it bad as a Jade, but what must it be like to be a Jade *and* a child of Mala Suerte when everyone thought your mere presence would bring bad luck?

Xio reached to gather up the large binder and cards on his bed. "I thought I'd make things easier by staying in my room—"

"What's all this?" Niya interrupted, plopping herself down on the bed.

"Oh—uh—it's nothing—" Xio tried to grab the open binder, but he wasn't quick enough for Niya.

She snatched it up and flipped through the pages. "Dude, nice collection!"

"It's nothing, really," Xio said, trying to cover up the scattered cards, but it was too late.

Teo realized what they were immediately. Hero trading cards were popular at school and constantly passed around by collectors. There were nearly a dozen spread across Xio's bed and even more in the binder. Each one had a picture of a Hero with their basic stats listed.

"Damn," Teo said, impressed as he picked up a few. There were professional Heroes like Marino's older sister Marea, but also Golds who were still training in the Academy that Teo had never even heard of. "Do you have *every* trading card?"

"Nearly," Xio admitted, his hands twitching like it took everything in him not to snatch them back.

Niya gasped. *"Where's mine?"* she shouted, flipping wildly through the pages.

"That's really cool," Teo said.

Xio blinked up at him. His rigid shoulders relaxed just a touch. "They do a lot of reprints and updates, though," he explained tentatively. "It can be hard to keep up."

Teo picked a random card and flipped it over, only to be met with Aurelio's fiery eyes staring back at him. Aurelio stood in the center of the card with his arms crossed over his chest, his expression hard and maybe a little annoyed. Diosa Lumbre's fire glyph in the upper right-hand corner indicated who his godly parent was, in case the gold foil flames around the edges weren't obvious enough.

Teo had never seriously collected the cards himself. It was too weird, knowing his mom would never have one even with everything she did for their city, and Teo would never get one, either. It was easy to end up with them, though, as birthday presents or school raffle prizes, and he had kept a little stash—until three years ago, when Aurelio's first card was released and found its way into a pack at Teo's favorite bodega.

That afternoon he had given his box to little Edgar next door, along with every pack he ended up with from then on, unopened.

"Wow, they have *everything* listed now—strengths, weaknesses, special moves," Teo murmured as he fanned through a few.

"Look how awesome my thighs are in this one!" Niya demanded, shoving the binder in Teo's face so he could see the special-edition card where she was kicking a boulder clean in half.

Teo leaned around Niya and gave Xio a teasing grin. "You're kind of a Hero nerd, huh?"

Red bloomed in Xio's cheeks. "Yeah, I guess," he admitted.

"This will come in handy for the trials," Teo pointed out. "Lucky you brought them with you." With this sort of encyclopedic knowledge, maybe Xio wasn't as hopeless as he'd originally thought.

"I just remembered I'm still hungry!" Niya announced, handing the binder back to Xio and jumping to her feet.

"You should come with us," Teo insisted while Xio gathered up his cards. "Everyone else is probably in bed already, and Niya and I are already black sheep, anyway."

"It's true!" Niya agreed cheerily.

Teo half expected Xio to turn them down, but then the smallest glimpse of a smile curled his lips. "Yeah, okay," he said, pushing his hair out of his face.

Niya beamed proudly and gave Teo a look that said, *Told you so*, which he ignored.

Xio struggled to climb out of bed, the plush blanket attempting to swallow him up. He was wearing a pair of checkered pajama pants and an old gray long-sleeved shirt. They were way too big on him, which made Teo think they may be hand-me-downs.

"Cool bracelet!" Niya said.

Around Xio's wrist was a cord bracelet that had red coral, jade eyes, and matte beads of jet. A shiny black charm in the shape of a fist with a protruding index finger knuckle dangled from it.

"Thanks," he murmured, quickly tugging his sleeve down over it.

"That's an azabache bracelet, right?" Teo asked.

"Yeah." Xio's face turned red. "It's my dad's."

"It's cool," Teo said, not wanting him to feel self-conscious about it. He'd only ever seen babies wear azabache bracelets for good luck back home. He supposed it made sense that Xio wore one. If you were the son of Mala Suerte, would you need good luck? Or was bad luck part of your whole deal?

Didn't seem like a good trait to have while competing in the Sunbearer

Trials. More important, Xio probably missed his dad, which was exactly why he needed a distraction.

Teo had been expecting a setup like his school cafeteria, with round tables and linoleum tile. Instead, the dining room they walked into was just as fancy as the rest of the temple. A long table with high-backed chairs was laden with bowls of fresh fruit. Overhead hung a large golden chandelier in the shape of the sun.

"Whoa," Xio said quietly, taking everything in.

"Seriously," Teo agreed.

"What?" Niya asked, looking around.

"This place is fancy as hell," he told her.

"Is it?"

Xio gave Niya a wary glance.

Teo threw his elbow into her arm. "Not all of us are from Gold cities," he reminded her. "She's not a douche, I swear," he added to Xio.

"Not on purpose," Niya clarified, unfazed.

Xio let out a small, surprised laugh.

Two people walked in from the kitchen. Or, not people, Teo realized, but gods.

The diosa spotted them first and her face lit up immediately. "Hello!"

"Dulce!" Niya cheered, bounding across the room while Teo followed and Xio kept a safe distance behind.

With a warm smile and sticky-sweet personality, Diosa Pan Dulce was one of Teo's favorite people. She was short with soft curves and wore her hair in braided spirals on either side of her head like novia sweet bread.

Her counterpart, Dios Maize, was less excited to see them.

"Sol help me," he groaned, coming to an abrupt stop. For the god of harvest, the tall and lanky dios didn't look like he ate much. He had a long face, a wide nose, earth-rich black skin, and eyes the color of tobacco leaves that were currently glaring at Teo and Niya.

Maize and Dulce were both Jades, and as such weren't as revered as the greater Gold gods, but everyone acknowledged that they were the backbone of any event. They were the best chefs in all of Sol and very dedicated to their art. Though Maize took it a bit more seriously than Dulce.

"I like the new haircut," Teo said.

Before the Incident, Maize had had shiny cornrows that fell to the middle of his back. Now his hair was styled into glossy 360 waves.

Maize glowered at him, the edge of his right eyebrow still missing. "What do you want?"

"We'll get to that," Teo said, brushing aside the question. "First, how are you?"

"Very busy," Maize huffed.

"Do you need something?" Dulce asked, tightening an apron around her waist.

"We were hoping for a late-night snack," Niya said, sitting on one of the stools and swiveling back and forth. "Do you think you could make us some hot chocolate?"

"And pan, if you've got any?" Teo added.

"Please?" they both said in unison, flashing matching smiles.

Dulce beamed and moved to go back into the kitchen. "Of course—!"

"*No!*" Maize snapped, stopping her in her tracks.

Teo dramatically flopped over the counter. "But we need sugar!"

Dulce looked to Maize, but he wasn't falling for it. "If you want to be Sunbearer, you need *protein* and *vegetables*," he said.

But the joke was on Maize—Teo had no desire to win the trials, just to get through them as quickly as possible.

"But Dios Maize!" Niya whined.

From the corner of his eye, Teo caught Xio grinning.

"No! I'm done cooking for tonight!" Maize huffed, wiping his hands on a dish towel before stomping across the room. "If you need a snack, there's plenty of fruit on the table. You shouldn't be filling yourselves up anyway. It's bad to sleep on a full stomach!"

At the door, he stopped and turned. "*Good night.*" And with that, Dios Maize was gone.

"I'm sorry, you three," Dulce said with an apologetic smile. "He's had a very long day, and he *does* have your best interest at heart."

Niya slumped, her bottom lip jutting out in a pout. "We know."

Teo propped his chin in his hand. "The Quetzlan priests always made me hot chocolate when I couldn't sleep. We're just feeling a bit homesick, is all." He lifted his shoulder in a shrug and sighed theatrically.

Dulce's eyebrows tipped with concern and she clasped her hands.

"Aren't we?" He turned to give Niya and Xio a pointed look.

"Oh yes, very homesick," Niya agreed, bobbing her head enthusiastically.

It took Xio a moment to catch on, but then he nodded, too.

The poor diosa looked between the three of them, stricken. Her face went on a journey, mouth twisting as she anxiously looked to where Maize had left.

"Okay, okay, just a *little* treat!" she whispered before hurrying into the kitchen.

"Maize is a stickler," Niya told Xio. "Also, we kinda fucked up his hair and he's still not over it. Long story."

"Dulce is way softer," Teo agreed.

He'd barely finished his sentence before Dulce burst back into the room, holding a huge tray with three steaming clay cups of hot chocolate—topped with whipped cream and canela sticks—and a small mountain of baked goods in all shapes and sizes.

Xio's eyes bulged as Dulce set the tray down on the island. "*Whoa.*"

"Thank you, Dulce!" Niya sang, pulling the goddess into a tight hug.

"Oh!" She giggled, a blush blooming on her apple cheeks.

"You're the best!" Teo agreed, immediately taking a cup and a pig-shaped puerquito.

"Don't let Maize catch you!" she said, brushing off her apron after Niya released her. "And if he does, you didn't get it from me!"

"We won't tell a soul!" Niya promised with a full mouth, already halfway through an oreja.

"Thanks," Xio said meekly with a shy smile, his hands cupping a hot chocolate.

Pan Dulce beamed and handed them all napkins before retiring for the night.

They took their hot chocolate and pan into the common area. Teo put the tray on a coffee table and they sprawled out on some of the plush armchairs. The hot chocolate was amazing—frothy, velvety smooth, and with just the right amount of spice. The pan was perfect, as only Dulce could make it, but Teo had to tap out after his second concha.

"I'm in a food coma," Xio groaned, pink crumbs at the corner of his mouth.

"Someone's gonna have to roll me to the first trial," Teo agreed.

"You're both *weak*!" Niya said, taking another large bite of bigote before washing it down with a swig of hot chocolate. She swallowed, thumped her fist against her chest, and released a belch so loud, Xio jumped.

The three of them dissolved into laughter. Teo was in that funny stage of being too wired to be tired, crackling at the edges from the influx of sugar.

Suddenly, voices approached from down the hall.

"Wait—*shh!*" Teo hissed. "*Someone's coming!*" He quickly shoved the nearly empty tray under the table while Xio and Niya sank low in their chairs.

The murmuring grew louder until Teo could finally make out who it was.

"They shouldn't be here," Aurelio said, his voice low and gruff. "It's not right—they're *Jades*."

The words hit Teo like a punch to the chest.

"At least we don't have to worry about one of our own losing," came Auristela's voice, loud and clear as they passed by the door. "It'd suck if the sacrifice was one of us."

Niya moved to get up, but Teo threw out his hand and shook his head. Judging by the determined glower on her face, he thought Niya was going to ignore him and stomp into the hall after them anyway. But then she gritted her teeth and sank back down, fingers digging into the arms of her chair.

"Yeah, it'll be easy for us to keep them at the bottom." That time it was Ocelo. "We can just focus on winning!"

Across from him, Xio's chin dipped to his chest.

"That's not—" Aurelio started, but Teo had heard enough.

"Don't listen to them, Xio," he said, speaking over the voices as they receded down the hall.

Xio nodded but didn't look up, toying with his father's bracelet.

Teo's jaw clenched. Just when they'd gotten Xio to break out of his shell, the Golds had to come along and fuck it up.

"You should've let me go after them," Niya growled.

"And let them know they got to us? No way," Teo said, crossing his arms and trying to ignore the flush spreading up the back of his neck. "We can get them back later, I promise you that," he added to Xio.

Niya seemed satisfied with that answer, though Xio didn't look quite as sure.

"It's totally fucked," Teo said. "On TV, they're always portrayed as these selfless Heroes protecting all us lowly civilians, but it's all for show, isn't it?" Teo said, seething. "No offense, Niya."

"It's true for *them*," Niya agreed. "I don't bother getting to know the others, but Auristela and Ocelo are cutthroat as hell. And Aurelio?" She laughed and shook her head. "The guy just sits there in class like a robot, like he's been *programmed*. Sorry," she added, seeing Teo's face. "I know you were friends."

"You're friends with Aurelio?" Xio asked, finally speaking.

"*Were*," Teo emphasized, sitting up straighter. "That was a long time ago."

Xio's brow puckered. "What happened?"

Teo really didn't feel like rehashing ancient history. He'd given Niya the broad strokes and she didn't push for more. But if commiserating made Xio feel better…

"We were friends when we were super little," Teo said, ripping a concha into tiny pieces as he spoke. "Aurelio and Auristela were mostly raised by their mortal dad. I've never met him but everyone says he's really nice—totally different from Diosa Lumbre. I mean, you've seen her, she's not exactly the *nurturing type*," he pointed out.

Xio and Niya nodded in agreement.

"I was really outgoing and Aurelio was super shy," Teo explained. The first time he ever saw Aurelio, he'd looked so small in a group of black-robed priests. Ocelo and Auristela were glued at the hip, but Aurelio was always attached to a priest, warily looking around like he was on the verge of tears.

"When I first saw him at some random ceremony…he looked like he could use a friend."

Teo thought Aurelio was lonely, which was a sentiment he could relate to, so, with determination, he decided the two of them should be less lonely, together. Aurelio broke out of his shell a bit and during every ceremony that brought all the dioses and semidioses together at Sol Temple, they were inseparable. Aurelio and Teo were looked after by Quetzal most of the time, playing tag and hide-and-seek around her large wings.

"Even when we got older, he didn't talk much, except when the Academy was brought up," Teo said. The elite training school for Golds was run by Diosa Lumbre in her home city, San Fuego. When she wasn't ruling with the other gods from Sol Temple, she was there instructing.

Aurelio always talked about starting at the Academy, how he'd become a proper Hero and finally be able to spend time with his mom. For a long while, Teo had assumed he would go to the Academy, too. He and Aurelio would run around the temple, pretending to fight off monsters and rescue civilians. Teo even made homemade trading cards for him and Aurelio.

Then his mom told him that only Golds went to the Academy, not Jades.

Aurelio started at the Academy the year after the last Sunbearer Trials. Teo had been heartbroken, but Aurelio promised that he'd tell Teo *everything* about it. New Years was the first time they saw each other after that. Teo spotted Aurelio across the room, standing with Auristela and Ocelo. He ran up to Aurelio, wanting to hear all about the Academy.

Instead of a warm reunion like they had every year, Aurelio was cold and unresponsive. Teo tried to ask him questions, but Aurelio only gave short answers and wouldn't even look at him. He kept his eyes on the floor as Diosa Lumbre stood by, watching.

What's wrong? Teo had tried to ask.

Stop bugging him! Auristela cut in, tugging on her brother's arm.

Golds only hang out with other Golds, Ocelo scoffed.

Yeah, no Jades, Auristela agreed.

Teo had tried to catch Aurelio's eye, but the other boy turned away.

He remembered how humiliating it had felt, how his heart thudded dully in his chest as Ocelo and Auristela laughed and Aurelio refused to acknowledge him. Huemac found him some time later, hiding under the sun statue in the courtyard and crying.

But he left that part out of the story.

"He started classes at the Academy, and I haven't had a real conversation with him since," Teo finished, doing his best to ignore the burning at the back of his throat.

"And then you upgraded to *me*!" Niya said, beaming.

Teo exhaled a relieved laugh. "I sure did."

"They call Auristela, Aurelio, and Ocelo the Golden Trio because they're the top-ranked students at the Academy, but they're just a bunch of assholes. All they care about is becoming Sunbearer, and only one of them can win. They'll probably start eating one another alive during the trials. You'll see, they'll get what's coming to them," Niya said with a pleased smile.

"I hope you're right."

"I used to get teased by these girls at school a lot," Xio said suddenly in a small voice.

"Seriously?" Teo asked. Who had the balls to pick on a child of Mala Suerte?

"I used to have really long hair and they'd always come up to me and say how much they liked the curls and how *pretty* they were." Xio's expression soured as he said the word.

Irritation simmered under Teo's skin. He understood all too well.

"Even after I came out as trans and cut it short, they kept touching it and calling my hair pretty. I hated it." Xio frowned, absently tugging on a lock of his hair. "Then one day, all three of them got lice. Like, *really bad* to the point they had to shave their heads."

"Oh my *dios*," Niya said, fist pressed to her mouth, barely able to hold in a laugh.

Xio's shoulders lifted in a small shrug. "Bad luck, I guess."

"That's what they get," Teo agreed with a huff. "I like your hair a lot," he added. "I see guys on social media getting perms to get theirs to look like yours and it's nowhere near as cool."

"*Very* handsome," Niya agreed with an enthusiastic nod.

For the first time that night, Xio smiled.

Teo grinned back. It was nice to meet someone who had been through the same kind of bullshit as him. Niya was his best friend, but as a cisgender girl and a Gold, there was a lot about his life and experiences she just wouldn't get.

But Xio could.

Teo sat upright. "You know what? We should team up."

"Team up?" Niya repeated, sweeping her finger on the inside of her mug to get the last drops of melted chocolate.

"Yeah, I mean, if those three have it out for us, why don't we work together to tear them down? We could be the Jade Trio—or, well, Niya's a Gold, but you get the idea."

Niya's eyes lit up. "We can be the Kickass Trio, 'cause we're gonna kick their asses! Ooh, or the *Great*-Ass Trio, 'cause we got great asses! Or at least I do. Xio, how's your butt?" she asked, peeking over at him. "Toned? We can start a squat regimen."

Xio hesitated, his hand frozen midreach for another pastry.

"I don't give a shit about becoming Sunbearer," Teo said. "I just want to get through the trials in one piece, and we're stronger if we work together, right?" He turned to Xio. "With everything you know about the Golds, we can *definitely* outsmart them. We don't have to do this alone. We can show them they're wrong."

He could watch out for Xio. This didn't have to be a death sentence.

"I don't know," Xio said meekly, rubbing the back of his neck. "I don't want to drag you guys down ..."

"You won't," Teo insisted.

"I've always hated those fools anyway—so obsessed with hierarchies and pedigree," Niya said, rolling her eyes. "You know gold is like *the* most useless metal, right?" She flicked her wrist and one of her gold bangles leapt into her hand. "It's way too soft, good for nothing but looking pretty." She closed her fist, turning the gold lump into mangled bits. "Jade was actually way more valuable, back in the day."

Teo grinned, adrenaline coursing through his veins. "We can look out for one another and make sure none of us becomes the sacrifice. That'll really show them." Already he was drunk on the idea of seeing Aurelio's, Auristela's, and Ocelo's faces at the idea of a Gold coming in last. "What do you say?"

"I am *so* in," Niya agreed, leaning forward to rub her hands together.

For a long moment, Xio chewed on the inside of his cheek, but then he finally nodded, his curls bouncing against his forehead. "Okay."

A sudden lightness made Teo feel giddy. "Then it's us against them."

Now, being in the trials didn't feel like a death sentence. Now, they had the chance to really prove something. Not just to the Golds, but to everyone.

CHAPTER 7

That night, Teo slept like shit. He'd thought the fancy bed would be like sleeping on a cloud, but it was too soft, too different. He spent hours tossing and turning, trying to get comfortable. The room was also way too quiet. He was used to the constant hum of Quetzlan drifting in through his open window every night. Here, the silence pressed against his ears.

Too soon, a light rapping on the door woke him from his fitful sleep. A Sol priest stuck his head in, informing him that breakfast was ready. Teo spent a long time in the shower, letting the hot water relax the tension in his wings. In a bleary-eyed haze, he put on his binder and stumbled down the hall.

When Teo walked into the dining room, he found Niya sitting at the long table, swiping the last bit of egg yolk from one of her two finished plates with a torn-off piece of tortilla.

"Good morning!" she said, jumping up from her chair.

"Is there coffee?" Teo asked, squinting at the buffet Maize and Pan Dulce had laid out.

"Loads! And Dulce snuck us out some sugar to add," Niya said, crossing to Teo with a few long strides. She stopped and gave him a once-over. "Wait—why aren't you in your gear?"

Teo rubbed his fist against his eyes. "What gear?"

He realized Niya was dressed already. Her dark hair was in her usual braids, but her outfit made him pause.

It was like some high-tech, futuristic athletic wear you'd see in a magazine. She had on tight leggings and a compression sports bra. The material was black, but Teo could make out a subtle honeycomb pattern to it. Panels of gold material and mesh crossed her thighs and accented her top. Sol's sunburst was embroidered with gold thread on Niya's upper left chest, and the mountain glyph of her home city, La Cumbre, was stitched inside the sun.

"What are you wearing?" Teo asked, suddenly much more awake.

Niya's expression shifted from amused confusion to dreadful realization. "These are our training uniforms from the Academy."

Our? Teo looked past Niya to find Xochi, Atzi, Marino, and Dezi sitting at the table eating. They all wore clothes similar to Niya's with slight variations.

Meanwhile, Teo was standing there in his pajamas.

Someone laughed and Teo turned to see Ocelo, Aurelio, and Auristela walk in. Ocelo had a wide, mean smirk on their face. Auristela laughed behind her hand and nudged her brother, but Aurelio didn't react. Silently, he looked Teo up and down, scowling.

The war semidiose stood between the twins—comically short in comparison—in a training uniform that left their arms and legs bare. Aurelio and Auristela were in the same matching outfits they'd been wearing at the fire in Quetzlan—leggings, shorts, and sleeveless tops that left their midriffs bare.

Aurelio's gold cuffs were still locked around his forearms, the strange three-fingered gloves on his hands. The thin material of his uniform clung to his chest and thighs, hugging every muscular curve and leaving very little to the imagination.

It was fucked up that he was such a jerk and still looked *that* hot in just training clothes.

"Where are your clothes?" Aurelio suddenly asked, that damn frown back on his face.

Teo was about to ask what the hell *that* meant when Ocelo let out an ugly laugh. "Yeah, are you really going to compete in sweats?"

Teo's hands clenched into fists, embarrassment a hot slap on the back of his neck.

Without warning, Niya lurched toward Ocelo. They stumbled back, startled.

Niya exhaled through her nose and crossed her arms. "Yeah, that's what I thought."

Now it was Teo's turn to laugh. He looked back to Aurelio but he was glaring down at the breakfast table like he was about to light it on fire.

Ocelo's stunned expression quickly contorted into a snarl.

"What's all this?"

Diosa Luna had walked into the dining room from the kitchen. Her dark eyes cut among them. "Is there a problem?" she asked, even and calm.

Teo straightened and cleared his throat while the other four also gathered themselves to look as innocent as possible.

"No, Diosa," Ocelo said gruffly, like it physically pained them to hold their tongue.

They all knew good and well not to evoke the wrath of Luna.

After another moment of scrutiny, she nodded.

"Teo, come with me. We have your uniform waiting for you," Luna said, motioning for him to follow her. "Xio just finished his own fitting."

Teo followed her back into the hall, making a point to keep his chin held high.

Diosa Luna brought him into a room where a small group of Sol priests was waiting. A circular dais was in the center with a set of three mirrors and a rack of clothes.

"We've made you a uniform like the students at the Academy receive. We didn't know your preferences, and we were a bit crunched for time, so we had to use our best judgment," Luna said, pulling a shirt off a hanger and giving it to Teo.

Teo ran his fingers over the short-sleeved shirt, getting a closer look at the honeycomb pattern in the light. Instead of gold accents like Niya's, these accent panels were jade green. "This seems really fancy," he murmured, noting the Quetzlan glyph stitched into the sun with matching green thread.

"It's the latest in performance wear," Luna agreed. "Moisture-wicking and tear resistant. These will hold up to damage even better than your semidiós skin."

"Damage?" Teo repeated, cutting Luna a nervous glance.

She gave him a patient smile. "These *are* the Sunbearer Trials."

Teo did his best to ignore the heavy weight that dropped into his stomach. He didn't want to think about what possible outfit-tearing scenarios lay ahead of him. While running his hand over the back of the shirt, he found two vertical slits.

"What are these for?" he asked, sliding his fingers through the gaps.

"Each uniform has special accommodations depending on the semidiose's talents. Some are flame retardant, others have extra stretch," she explained. "Those are for your wings."

"My wings?" Teo shook his head and tried to hand the shirt back. "I don't use my wings."

Luna's eyebrows pinched. "You'll need them for the trials—"

"No, I won't," Teo insisted. "I can do it without them." Luna gave him a look that rivaled Huemac's long-suffering exasperation, but Teo wouldn't back down.

"Then don't use them, but you still need to wear the uniform," she said, ignoring Teo's outstretched hand. "The material has enough give that they should fit fine underneath."

Teo was tempted to argue that he needed a whole new shirt, but he didn't want to press his luck with the diosa.

"Fine," he agreed, albeit tersely.

With some help from the priests, Teo changed and managed to

wrangle his wings under the shirt with the help of his binder. He stood in front of the mirrors, examining himself and feeling absolutely ridiculous.

The clothes were so *tight*, he felt completely exposed. They'd given him a pair of shorts, thank Sol, but they were tiny, and every time he tried to pull them down toward his knee, they sprang back up to the middle of his thigh.

The doors flew open and in strode Chisme and Verdad.

"Who's up next?" Chisme asked as his two assistants filed in behind him. When they spotted Teo, they hefted their large cameras and started snapping pictures.

Teo threw his hands up, cringing as lights danced in front of his eyes. "What's he doing here?" he asked Luna, scowling. The last thing he wanted right now was an audience.

"We need promotional photos of all the competitors in their uniforms," Luna explained.

"We just finished up with your creepy little friend," Chisme said through a smile. Today he'd exchanged his red outfit for an obnoxiously bright orange one and matching lipstick.

"Another Jade," Verdad said, jotting down notes while wearing a practical pantsuit. "*Two* Jade competitors for the very first time." She glanced up at Teo through her glasses. "I'd love a first-person perspective on what that might mean."

Teo ignored both of them. "I don't want my picture taken."

"Teenagers, always so self-conscious," Chisme mused.

"You're not used to being in the spotlight, are you?" Verdad asked.

To Luna's credit, she did at least seem sympathetic to Teo's pleading look, but it was no use. "I'm afraid it's part of the gig," she said.

Teo groaned and tipped his head back. "*Fine.*" He stepped back onto the dais and scowled at Chisme. "I just want to get it over with."

"The feeling is quite mutual," Chisme reassured him.

Verdad stepped forward. "*I* would love to sit down with you, Teo. Maybe we could—"

"*No*," Teo snapped.

He stood there while Chisme barked orders and his assistants took rapid-fire pictures. He didn't know what to do or how to stand. He couldn't even figure out where to put his hands before Chisme said they were finished.

"I think that's the best we're going to get," he said as he checked the camera roll. He waved Teo off without even looking up. "You can go back to being angry with the world now."

"Teo, really," Verdad tried again, "If you—"

Teo stomped out of the room, hoping he'd never have to see those pictures for himself.

When he got back to the dining room, most of the Golds were sitting at one end of the table and talking, not even bothering to look up when he entered. Aurelio watched as Teo took the seat on the other side of Niya from Xio, and Teo did his best to ignore him.

The younger boy had on a similar uniform to his, but he had a light-weight jacket on top.

"Lookin' sharp!" Niya grinned as Teo plopped into the seat next to her.

"I feel ridiculous," he grumbled, tugging on the high collar of the shirt. "How did you get a jacket?"

Xio shrugged as he chewed on a pineapple spear dusted with Tajín. "I asked for one. Felt kinda naked otherwise."

Teo huffed. "Well, shit, why didn't I think of that?"

Niya laughed and thumped him hard on the back. "You'll get used to it! Now eat up, we've got some ass to kick!"

Xio pushed his plate away. "Are you nervous?" he asked Teo in a small voice.

"Hey, we'll be fine—we just gotta get through it without being in last place," he said, giving Xio's arm an encouraging shake. "You've got your bracelet, right?"

Xio nodded, tugging back his sleeve to reveal it safely on his wrist.

A couple of seats away, Aurelio stared at it. "Why do you have an azabache bracelet?" Aurelio asked, sounding more curious than anything, but the last thing Teo wanted was for Xio to be put on the spot by the Golden Boy of the trials.

"It's for good luck," Teo snapped, but Aurelio didn't even glance in his direction.

"Why do you need a bracelet to ward off bad luck if your dad is Mala Suerte?"

"Why, are you scared of me?" Xio asked, a hint of challenge in his voice.

Aurelio said nothing. The two watched each other for a moment, but then Aurelio shook his head and turned away.

A surprised laugh jumped in Teo's chest.

"Damn, I knew I liked you for a reason," Niya said with an approving nod.

"Yeah, I really don't think we need to worry about you holding your own," Teo agreed, bumping shoulders with Xio, who ducked his head and smiled.

"I trust you're all ready to travel to your first host city?" Luna asked as she entered the dining room.

Immediately, excited murmurs passed between the Golds. Even Niya was grinning ear to ear. Meanwhile, Teo tried to fight off the sinking feeling in his stomach.

"The day after each trial, you will have some time to explore the host city—"

For the first time, a thrill of excitement shot through Teo. *Finally*, he'd be able to see what other cities were like.

"And the hosting dios will throw us a farewell banquet that night, before we board the boat again to travel to the next city. Your belongings have already been gathered," Luna continued, motioning for them to get up. "So, if you'll all follow me, we can begin our journey."

"Where are we going?" Atzi asked, practically buzzing on the edge of her seat.

Luna smiled. "The host city for the first trial will be La Cumbre."

"*YES!*" Niya shouted, punching a fist in the air.

Teo relaxed a little. He wasn't exactly *relieved*, but going to Niya's home city seemed less terrifying than any other option.

Auristela scoffed and crossed her arms over her chest.

"That's not fair!" Ocelo said, their face all scrunched up and angry.

"Oh shut it," Niya snapped.

"Her dad is going to cheat to make it easier on her!" Ocelo argued.

"Already making up excuses for why you'll come in last, huh?" Teo quipped. Ocelo's angry snarl was a satisfying sight.

"The host cities were decided on and designed by the gods long before the selection took place," Luna explained. Ocelo opened their mouth, but when Luna cut them a hard stare, they snapped it shut.

"Can you give us a hint at what the first trial will be?" Xochi asked and signed with a sweet voice, batting her eyelashes.

"Is there going to be lava?" Atzi asked.

"I hope not!" Marino choked.

"Wouldn't that put Aurelio and Auristela at an unfair advantage?" Xio asked Teo, worry pinching his eyebrows. Before Teo could reassure him, Auristela cut in.

"Sucks to suck," she said with a sarcastic smile from across the table, not loud enough for Luna to overhear.

A quiet *tink*ing noise turned Teo's attention to Aurelio, who was tapping his fingers rhythmically on one of his golden armbands, his head turned toward the windows. Real useful.

Teo rolled his eyes and ignored both of the twins. "I'm sure it'll be fine," he told Xio, though he didn't quite believe it himself.

"There won't be any clues given out," Luna said, speaking over the wave of excited chattering. "Tierra being the one to host and organize the trial is a hint in and of itself. You're all smart and capable—"

"Debatable," Teo grumbled under his breath. Xio covered his smile with his hand.

"I'm sure you can think up some scenarios on your own. It will be an even playing field for all competitors," Luna said, looking at everyone in turn. "Understood?"

Teo held back a sarcastic snort. *Even playing field.* Sure. All he could do was try his best and take care of his friends. He just had to stay focused on that.

And maybe fuck with some Golds along the way.

Teo had seen cruise ships on TV before and plenty of commuter boats in person, but the boat they'd be using to travel through Reino del Sol was on a whole other level.

Somewhere between a yacht and a ferry, it was sleek and tall with three levels of massive windows. The boat itself was white, but the hull was painted with churning waves in shades of cornflower, cobalt, and navy blue. The pattern looked familiar but Teo couldn't quite place it, until he noticed the flags at the stern and the bow. The one at the back was white and had Sol's glyph stitched in golden thread, and the one at the front displayed Diosa Agua's tumbling waves. There were also banners displaying each of the competitor's glyphs. The jade green eye of Mala Suerte and bird of Quetzal were the only pops of color among the gold pennants.

The Golds, including Niya, walked right up the ramp like they did this all the time. Only Teo and Xio hung back.

"Whoa," Xio whispered, and Teo was glad he wasn't the only one. "This thing is bigger than my entire school."

Teo grinned. "Damn, and I thought Quetzlan High was the smallest in all of Sol," he teased with a nudge. When they reached the deck, Sol priests handed them thin crystal glasses with something clear and bubbly inside.

"This is way too fancy for me," Xio murmured before tentatively taking a sip.

Niya laughed. "Being a Hero does have its perks!"

"Salud!" Teo took a big swig and his tongue was immediately assaulted by bitterness and sharp bubbles. He coughed and choked, shooting the liquid out his nose.

"Oh my gods!" Teo spluttered, frantically wiping at his burning nose as his eyes watered. "What the hell was that?"

"It's mineral water!" Niya said while Xio dissolved in a fit of laughter.

"It's *rancid*!" he coughed. "Why does it taste like that?!"

A haughty scoff caught their attention. "Amateur," Ocelo said with a mean smirk.

"*Poor*," Auristela corrected, studying her fingernails.

Before Teo could think of a smart-ass retort, Aurelio thrust a napkin in his face.

"You have snot on your chin," he said plainly.

Everyone burst into a fresh peel of laughter.

Teo pushed Aurelio's hand away and quickly wiped at his face. "Yeah, got it, *thanks*," he said gruffly, turning away.

Xio at least had the decency to hide his mouth behind his fist. Meanwhile, Niya cackled.

So Teo wiped his hand off on her arm.

But she only shrugged. "I've got two older brothers. I've had grosser stuff wiped on me."

Luna led them into a huge room filled with plush furniture and wide windows. Everything was polished wood, shiny bronze, or white upholstery. More Sol priests awaited them, along with a crew of people in crisp white uniforms. Teo immediately recognized the one in front with the pixie cut and sharp gray eyes as Marino's older sister Marea.

"This will be your new home during the trials," Luna said, coming to a stop next to Marea. "I'm sure some of you know our captain."

Marino grinned and his sister threw him a wink.

"Marea has taken time off from leading the search-and-rescue fleet to transport us to the host cities."

"Pleasure to have you on board," Marea said, her voice sharp and clear. "Let's have a little tour and we'll be off shortly."

"This is the common area," Luna said, gesturing around them.

It was filled with chairs, couches, and books. A large television that was currently showing the news sat on the back wall. Oddly enough, it was footage of the boat they were currently on, shot from the docks. If it weren't for the tinted glass, Teo could have waved and seen himself on the screen. There was also a large wooden table with cushioned chairs and a shelf loaded with games like El Gocho and dominoes.

"Feel free to spend time here between the trials and get to know one another better," Luna said before leading them back outside.

"Not likely," Teo said to Niya under his breath.

"This is the main deck," Marea said, leading them out onto the main deck. "As you know, we'll be headed for La Cumbre first and should be arriving by late afternoon."

The deck had a large, semicircular white couch set into the shiny wood floor so you had to step down into it. A glass table in the middle already held bottles of water and juice on ice along with fresh fruit. The boat shifted as it pulled away from the dock.

As the boat picked up speed, the group rushed to the bow to look over the edge. Niya stepped up onto the railing and leaned her entire upper body over. She threw her arms into the air and crowed happily.

"How's this big thing going to get through?" Xio asked.

Teo turned to see that they were pointed at the wall of mountains that surrounded Sol Temple, heading straight for one of the waterfall passages, but there was no way the boat could possibly fit. Marea was deep in conversation with Luna, neither of them the least bit bothered.

As they neared the wall of jagged rock, the small waterfall stretched, growing taller and wider until finally the water split open. The boat easily passed through, a light cascade of water raining down around them as they were plunged into the darkness of the cave.

"I guess that answers your question," Teo said to Xio.

The Golds spoke animatedly with one another and Niya threw herself onto the white cushions of the couch. "Man, I could get used to this," she sighed. Teo thought if Niya won the Sunbearer Trials, she would adjust quite nicely to the life of a celebrity.

The only people who didn't seem excited were Aurelio and Auristela. They hung back by the entrance of the common room, their usual air of grandiosity now a matching set of soft frowns, eyeing the errant water that dripped onto the deck. Then Teo realized—as a pair of fire demigods, being trapped on a boat surrounded by water was probably their worst nightmare.

Not that he cared, obviously.

As they made their way through the caves, Luna called them back inside. On the other end of the common room, double glass doors opened up to another deck.

"This is the aftdeck. Dios Maize and Diosa Pan Dulce's meals will be served here," Marea said, showing them a dining table dressed with white linens.

Teo's heart sank. "Every meal?"

"Yes, every meal," Luna said.

"I thought we were going to the cities?" Teo pressed. "You know, travel Reino del Sol, see the sights, *eat the food*?"

"You will have designated time when you are allowed off the boat to be shown around as a group," Luna explained coolly.

Teo groaned. "A *group*?" This was turning into a glorified field trip.

Luna went on like she hadn't heard him. "But aside from the host city banquets, you will have your meals here, *also* as a group."

Maybe those were the rules, but what Luna didn't know wouldn't hurt her. As they continued their tour, Teo kept an eye out for potential escape routes.

Marea led the way up a set of spiral stairs to the next floor. To their left was a corridor and to the right, a single door. "This is the main cabin," Marea explained. "Above us is the bridge where my crew and I will be running this operation. And your cabins are this way."

As they entered the hallway, Teo saw that their glyphs were once again displayed on each door.

"Each of you will have your own cabin with a private bathroom," Marea said. She opened the door to the first room, marked as Auristela's. It was a bit smaller than the ones in Sol Temple but just as luxurious. Large portholes looked out above the water line.

As everyone rushed to find their rooms, Teo hung back. With all the opulence and excess, it was easy to get distracted from the real reason they were there. But Teo didn't forget. It was like he was staying at some really fucked-up sleepaway camp where instead of giving out super-latives, someone got stabbed at the end of the summer.

When they were done scoping things out, Marea gestured toward the other end of the hall. "The training room is that way—"

Excited chatter broke out among the Golds. Even Niya's face lit up as she followed everyone into the room.

Teo rolled his eyes and glanced at Xio. "Jocks."

"Should we follow them?" Xio wondered, casting an uncertain look to Marea and Luna, the only ones left in the hall, who were deep in their own conversation.

Teo sighed. "Yeah, I guess," he grumbled. There was no way he'd give anyone else the satisfaction of thinking he wasn't up for the challenge.

Walking into the training room was like walking through a portal to a dystopian world dominated by the fitness industry—there was a climbing wall with different colored flags for some reason, huge racks of metal weights, and a bunch of machines that looked like torture devices.

The Golds were already putting the equipment to use. Some of them tried out the obstacle courses that had been set up, Auristela shadow-boxed with balletlike precision, and Ocelo stomped around lifting literally anything heavy-looking that wasn't bolted to the ground.

"Do you know how any of this stuff works?" Xio asked as they lingered by the door.

"I usually ditch PE," Teo confessed with a shrug. They could've asked Niya for pointers, but she was already halfway up the rock wall. "If those meatheads can figure it out, it can't be that complicated, right?" Teo said, confidently walking up to a barbell loaded with weights, one of the few things he actually recognized.

What could he lift? Two hundred pounds, at least, right? He didn't know what the milk-crates-to-kilograms conversion was. He bent forward and curled his fingers around the bar.

"That's not how you do a deadlift," Aurelio said, so close to Teo that he felt the heat radiating from all his bare skin.

When he looked up, the other boy was standing in front of him, again with that disapproving look on his face.

Aurelio's words from last night burned in Teo's chest. *They shouldn't be here.*

"You're going to hurt yourself," Aurelio went on.

"Let him," Auristela said with a disdainful laugh, not even a glint of sweat on her brow.

Teo glared. "I think I know how to *pick something up*," he said. "It's not rocket science."

Aurelio gave a small shake of his head. He moved to step closer. "You need to hold the weight close to your body and use your legs—"

"Why do you care?" Teo suddenly snapped. He didn't need Aurelio giving him pointers, or saving him, or making fun of him. And he certainly didn't need more unwanted attention from everyone else in the room.

He didn't need Aurelio. Period.

Aurelio opened his mouth to respond, but Auristela's voice cut in.

"Yeah, why *do* you care?" She stared at her brother, waiting for his response.

For a moment, Aurelio stood there, looking between Teo and his sister like he couldn't decide what to do.

Teo glared back, the only act of defiance he could manage when trapped under those flinty eyes.

"*Relio*," Auristela insisted.

Finally, Aurelio exhaled through pursed lips, then turned and walked away.

Never one to back down, Teo scoffed and bent forward again. He grabbed the bar and wrenched. The good news was he was easily able to lift the weight.

The bad news was that pain immediately exploded in his lower back, shooting up his spine.

The weights dropped with such force, even Dezi looked over. Teo had to clench his jaw to keep from yelping when Aurelio glanced back. He stood up, back rigid, and quickly turned away so Aurelio couldn't see his pained expression, but found Xio watching him with a concerned look.

"Are you okay?"

"We gotta go," Teo managed between his teeth.

Xio looked like he was trying not to smile. "You need help?"

Teo nodded quickly and hobbled out of the training room. He needed to lie down.

CHAPTER 8

Teo found his new cabin and took a long, hot shower, per Luna's suggestion. Luckily, his back wasn't completely destroyed, and with his accelerated healing and the soothing heat, Teo felt substantially better by the time he got out of the shower.

Now his ego just needed time to recover.

Teo wiped the steam from the mirror and stared at his reflection. He shook out the water from his wings—they were impossible to reach with a towel—and stretched them out. He groaned. They were always so sore from being bound all day.

Teo turned side to side, trying to get a look at them in the mirror. A part of him hoped that they'd miraculously change one day, but no such luck. His feathers were still dull and brown. Feminine.

His wings were a part of him—his identity and his heritage—given to him by his mom, but they never felt *right*, as though they belonged to someone else or he'd been given the wrong ones. Teo had to work harder than a lot of guys to get the body he was meant to have, and most of the time that didn't bother him. Testosterone was testosterone however it got into his body.

But his wings refused to get with the program. Why wouldn't they be what they were supposed to be? Why couldn't they just be *his*?

Frustrated, Teo took out a clean uniform and retrieved his backpack. Sitting on his bed, he fished out his small bottle of testosterone and a fresh syringe. The amber liquid moved like oil as he flicked the syringe to remove any air bubbles, tipped it upside down, and inserted the needle into his thigh. Giving himself his weekly dose of T was quick and easy after doing it for so many years.

When he was finished, Teo slapped on a Band-Aid and went to go find his friends. Niya had saved them a spot on some lounge chairs out on the deck. Teo listened while she and Xio sat together, flipping through the binder of trading cards with a look of intense concentration.

As a major Gold city, La Cumbre wasn't far from the entrance to Sol City, but it was taking them forever to get there. He suspected the slow speeds were for show. As they coasted down the river, people stood along the banks, causeways, and bridges, waving and cheering like it was some kind of parade.

Teo would have thought that Auristela and Aurelio would've been eating up the attention, but instead they were lying out on the large, sunken couch, soaking up the sun. Auristela's eyes were closed, her foot bouncing to whatever music she was listening to on her phone while Aurelio watched something on his.

It was actually Ocelo who raced back and forth along the railing, waving at their audience. Whenever they triumphantly raised their hands over their head, the cheering swelled.

Atzi, Xochi, and Dezi ran around the bow of the boat, trying to evade Marino as he sprayed them with jets of water he pulled from the river. Atzi used a fancy gold tray to protect her hair while Xochi danced out of Marino's reach. They laughed, shouted, and chased each other, seemingly without a care in the world.

Were they all so confident about the trials that none of them were the least bit worried? The dread in his stomach kept getting heavier the farther they got from Sol Temple. It made him feel like he was walking through mud by the time they went to the upper deck for lunch. Everyone else was wide awake and hyper, talking animatedly and laughing.

The only other person who seemed rightfully worried was Xio. He plopped into the seat next to Teo and stared intently at his plate of food but didn't touch a thing. Teo wanted to reassure him, but right now he couldn't even reassure himself. Soon, they'd be competing in their first trial, and Teo was starting to worry whether he could make it through one, let alone all five.

He couldn't even lift a weight without fucking up—how was he supposed to compete with elite Golds who had the advantage of training for the trials with professional Heroes?

Teo was pulled from his catastrophizing when an errant stream of water meant for Dezi hit Aurelio and Auristela. Aurelio flinched but Auristela gasped loudly and leapt to her feet.

Atzi, Xochi, Dezi, and Marino all froze, realizing their grave mistake.

Auristela turned on them, her pristine ponytail now a sopping mess. She bared her teeth and clenched her hands into fists. The water on her skin sizzled and evaporated into wisps of steam.

Dezi clamped his hands over his mouth, eyes wide with alarm.

"Scatter!" Marino shouted and signed.

"She can't kill all of us!" Xochi followed up before grabbing Atzi's small hand and making a run for it.

"*Watch me!*" Auristela roared.

As the other four scrambled to get away, Aurelio shook the water out from the speakers of his phone. When it seemed to be working, he sat back and watched Auristela terrorize the others.

Aurelio had a pinched and unsure expression on his face. It was one Teo had seen many times when they were little kids and Aurelio wanted to play with the others but didn't know how to start.

Back then, Teo would've just grabbed his arm and pulled him into whatever game it was. Watching him now, he wondered if Aurelio and Auristela's tendency to keep to themselves was by design or if, despite his celebrity status, Aurelio hadn't changed as much as he thought.

"What are you watching?" Teo asked him from across the deck, surprising both Niya and Xio.

Aurelio blinked. "Me?"

"No, the guy behind you."

Aurelio turned.

"Yes, *you!*"

"Baking videos," Aurelio replied, wiping the screen dry on his shirt.

Teo squinted at him, unable to tell if he was being sarcastic.

Aurelio responded with an arched eyebrow.

Teo huffed. "Fine, don't tell me." That was what he got for trying to make small talk.

Around them, the terrain grew hillier as the mountains in the distance gradually got closer.

"Are we there yet?" Xio asked Niya, who nodded enthusiastically, a wide smile brightening her face.

"Nearly!"

"We'll be disembarking soon," Luna said, appearing at the door.

Auristela stood with her fists on her hips, both Marino and Dezi pinned under her foot. Xochi and Atzi peeked out from behind a lounge chair where they had taken refuge.

Luna squinted at them but decided not to ask.

"Please head back to your rooms to make yourselves presentable," she said.

Teo's stomach clenched.

"Once we disembark, we are heading straight to the first trial."

Tucked into the northwestern mountain range of Reino del Sol, La Cumbre was gorgeous and unlike any city Teo had ever seen. Its name referred to the large, dormant volcano the city was built against, at the top of which sat Tierra's temple.

Teo had never seen mountains so big and up close. The buildings were tucked into the mountainside, carved into the stone, and there were a lot fewer trees than he'd imagined. The city shone, gold plating and silver trimmings glittering in the waning sunlight. Small paths zigzagged their way up the steep mountainside. The roads themselves weren't paved but were made of soft, packed dirt.

The Golds chatted among themselves up ahead, placing their bets on what the first trial would be. Meanwhile, Niya and Teo hung back, Xio walking between them.

"I hope it's a race," said Xochi, readjusting the flowers that she'd taken from a bouquet in the kitchen and put in her hair.

"I bet it's hand-to-hand combat" was Auristela's enthusiastic guess.

"I want to fight a dios!" Ocelo announced, punching their fist into their palm.

"They're not going to do that after what happened ninety years ago," Aurelio said, voice edged with annoyance.

Teo shot Niya a concerned look over Xio's head. "What happened ninety years ago?"

"Oh, competitors had to fight Diosa Culebra but she got a little over-excited," Niya explained with a shrug, as if it were common knowledge. "Ended up constricting three competitors and breaking their spines"— she snapped her fingers—"right in half."

"*Dios*," Teo hissed under his breath. "I've never heard about that!"

"Part of the curriculum at the Academy is learning about all the past trials," Niya explained. "We use them as practice exercises!"

Great. Just another Gold advantage.

"Bummer, though." Niya sighed. "It'd be pretty cool to be able to say I fought a dios."

Teo gave her a bewildered look. "You Golds are out of control."

Xio remained silent at his side, staring straight ahead and not blinking in a way that made Teo nervous he might pass out before they got to their destination. He needed not to let his own nerves get the better of him, for Xio's sake. If he started panicking then Xio would too, and that wouldn't do either of them any good walking into the first trial.

He'd have to keep his expressions in check and push his worries down deep, where they could later manifest as a stomach ulcer or something.

"Don't be scared," Teo said quietly so the Golds wouldn't overhear.

"I'm not." But Xio's voice was tight as he continued to stare ahead.

Teo and Niya exchanged worried glances.

The streets of the city were full of spectators lined up to watch them arrive. Tierra's glyph—three mountains with the sun rising behind them—adorned lampposts, and altars to the god of earth were set outside businesses. Niya was clearly the crowd favorite. She had a huge smile plastered across her face as she waved, practically bouncing with excitement. Larger-than-life posters of Niya hung in shop windows and massive murals were painted onto the sides of buildings.

Apparently Chisme worked faster than Teo had realized, because when they rounded a corner, he was horrified to find a line of all ten competitor portraits taped up in the large windows of a grocery store.

The Golds looked like professional athletes who modeled all the time—posed, smiling, and powerful. Even Xio looked great, if a bit uncomfortable. His chin was raised and he stared right into the camera with a fierce look of determination.

Meanwhile, Teo's poster on the far left was downright painful to look at. The uniform seemed even tighter on him than in the mirror and his face was pinched into a weird grimace, his hands in tight fists at his sides.

A humiliated blush burned Teo's cheeks and he tried to duck behind Niya, hoping no one would recognize him.

"We are about to enter the arena," Diosa Luna announced and signed as they walked up to a huge circular stadium. "Get into a single-file line and follow me inside. Your parents will be waiting for you—please join them and I'll go over the rules before we get started," she said with a smile.

Teo took one last shaky breath before following the others through the looming arches.

They entered a long tunnel. What felt like thousands of voices bounced against the stone walls. When they stepped out into the arena, cheers from the crowd exploded.

The space was as massive as it was ancient. Weathered stone stadium seating surrounded the outer edge of the arena. Scattered amid the La Cumbre residents waving posters of Niya were pockets of other priests and semidioses proudly representing their home cities, everyone grouped with colorful robes and banners.

White flags rippled throughout the stands, mostly displaying Tierra's glyph, but Teo could see the other Gold competitors all had supporters as well. Among the sea of white, there wasn't a single jade flag. Teo wasn't surprised, but it still stung. The only spot of blue and purple was in the far upper corner, where Quetzal and Mala Suerte's priests sat.

A huge screen dominated the stands displaying Chisme in a chair on the right, while Verdad was on the left. Chisme was decked out in a white cotton outfit with an excessive amount of gold jewelry, including large hoop earrings, but Verdad wore the same boring black-and-white suit. Verdad's expression was serious while Chisme's was overly animated, but Teo couldn't hear what he was saying over the noise of the crowd.

The promotional images of the competitors swiped across the screen one at a time. Normally, having a thirty-foot-tall, painfully awkward image of himself on display in front of tens of thousands of people would've been enough to send him spiraling, but there was something even more dire.

Rising up from a body of water in the center of the stadium was a craggy mountain. Steeply pitched, it was covered in lush tropical plants and trees. Tiny cascades of water fell in intervals, cutting through switchbacks that led up the steep face of the mountain. At the very top, a boulder-sized slab of gold carved with Sol's glyph sat gleaming in the sunlight.

The full stands and towering peak were dizzying. Teo did his best to keep walking forward as vertigo sent his legs wobbling. Xio followed Niya with determined steps.

Aurelio and Auristela had already turned on the charm as they walked out into the stadium. Auristela smiled and waved while her brother lifted one hand, his mouth arranged in a smile, his eyes sharp and focused. The crowd welcomed the competitors with cheers as Luna led them to a platform where the dioses waited.

Aurelio and Auristela took their places on either side of their mother, as if standing guard, while Dezi ran the last few steps to his mom. Amor, the beautiful and full-figured goddess of love and community, swept him into a hug. When they broke apart, they signed animatedly to each other with matching apple-cheeked smiles.

As everyone split off to join their parents, Teo focused on his breathing as he crossed over to his mom. He felt outside of his own body, like it was on autopilot and he was just along for the ride. He'd thought seeing her would calm him down, but she looked just as anxious as he felt.

"Are you okay?" she asked, hugging him tight.

"Yes," Teo lied. When she released him, he stood close to her side, looking anywhere but at the overwhelming crowd. His throat was tight, the neck of his uniform suffocating.

To his left, Xio was with his dad. Mala Suerte's expression was stony and unfriendly as he stood still as a statue, his hand on Xio's shoulder.

"Welcome to the Tepetl!" Luna called in a magnified voice as she stepped forward. The roaring cheers dulled to a low hum. Dios

Mariachi—smiling in his white suit with brass cornet in hand—stood to her right and a familiar figure stood to her left.

It was strange seeing Fantasma out in broad daylight. Usually she didn't show up to events until nightfall, and then she spent most of the time as a wallflower, hanging out in the shadows. It was obvious to Teo that this wasn't in her comfort zone, either. Her hands fidgeted as nervously as the butterflies around her.

But for Teo, seeing her was a relief—a friend in an otherwise unfriendly place, even if Fantasma was a morbid reminder of the trials' stakes. Teo smiled at her and she wiggled her fingers in a tiny wave with the slightest quirk of her lips.

"She's so *creepy.*"

Auristela stared at Fantasma, her mouth twisted in disgust.

"Why does she never talk?"

Ocelo snorted. "I heard she doesn't have a tongue."

"Probably eaten by maggots," Auristela replied.

Aurelio glanced over at his sister. He frowned, a deep crease between his eyebrows, and for a second Teo thought he might actually grow a pair and say something—but no. Instead he looked away, his attention focused back on Luna as he tapped his armband again.

Angry heat flushed through Teo. He clenched his hands into fists, nostrils flared as he tried to focus on what Luna was saying instead of picking a fight.

"The object of this trial is to race to the top of the mountain," Diosa Luna explained and signed, her voice amplified by a mic. "Along the way, there will be ten markers with your city's glyph, including the final one at the top. You must activate them by touch, one at a time, as you race to the finish. Each competitor has a separate but identical path with obstacles along the way. If you don't reach the top in time, or if you step into another competitor's path, it will negatively affect your ranking," Luna warned.

"I smell a loophole," Auristela murmured to Ocelo. Teo rolled his eyes.

"Competitors have ten minutes to reach the top of the mountain," Luna explained as a Sol priestess handed each of them a black rubber watch. When Teo put his on his wrist, it buzzed and the face flashed his mother's glyph. "There is a barrier at the finish point. When you cross it, you lock in your position and will not be able to leave until the trial is over."

Ten minutes? The mountain looked about as tall as the Quetzlan Temple, which he easily climbed every day, but this was a *mountain* with *obstacles*, whatever the hell that meant.

Teo's mind raced to come up with a strategy. The mountain looked like one of his favorite reality shows, *Secrets of the Lost Temple*. Competitors attempted to complete a series of obstacle courses of increasing difficulty up a fake mountain. Teo used to be obsessed with it when he was little.

When he thought about it like that, the trial was a little less scary. It was basically the same thing, except it was an actual mountain, and instead of foam and padded edges, it ended in steep cliffs and rugged terrain.

Teo swallowed hard. How difficult could it be?

They crossed a bridge to the base of the mountain, where each competitor's glyph was on the ground equidistant from one another. It was easy to make out the switchbacks of his own path up the side. The first glyph to activate sat at the entrance—a carved piece of jade about the size and shape of a headstone.

A little too on the nose, if you asked Teo.

He couldn't see Niya but to his left, Ocelo separated him and Xio, and to his right, Atzi stood poised on the balls of her feet with Auristela on her other side.

So much for teaming up with his friends.

Teo tried to mirror Atzi's starting position, as if that would give him some kind of edge, and shook out his arms. He just needed to stay on his path, activate all of his glyphs, and get to the top without getting disqualified.

"On your marks!" Luna's amplified voice echoed.

Teo's jade glyph pulsed with light, and his watch buzzed with the same beat.

"Get set!"

Mariachi's cornet trumpeted.

The Quetzal glyph flashed at the same time the watch made a long buzz.

Teo ran.

As soon as he hit the first glyph, it glowed with bright, jade green light and his watch gave a short vibration. The terrain of the mountain alternated between rocky and lush. A waterfall started somewhere far up above and ran perpendicular to his path. Teo sloshed through the water on each switchback, the stream growing stronger the higher he went.

Teo ran as quickly as he could, but by the time he got to the second switchback and slapped the next glyph, his lungs burned. He wasn't a runner. It didn't agree with his binder, and he didn't know a damn thing about maintaining his pace.

A loud noise jolted Teo out of his focus.

Higher on the mountain, Atzi and Auristela duked it out from their respective sections. Auristela kept lobbing balls of fire at Atzi, who deflected by conjuring up thick sheets of rain with a swipe of her arm. The water sizzled and steamed on impact. When she had an opening, a crackling bolt of lightning materialized in Atzi's hand, electric and shuddering, before she threw it at Auristela like a spear.

Auristela narrowly avoided the bolt. It crashed into a tree with a thundering crack, splitting it in half.

Teo was so hilariously, terrifyingly out of his league. The Golds had *real* powers and strength. Even small Atzi could easily kick his ass if she wanted to. She could hurl *lightning bolts* with her *hands*, for Sol's sake. At least they were keeping one another busy.

On the third switchback, Teo hit his first obstacle. The path suddenly ended and Teo, distracted by the battle overhead, almost went right over the edge.

He skidded to a stop, arms pinwheeling, and threw himself against the craggy side of the mountain. Sharp stones dug into his wings. A sheer cliff separated him from the next glyph, his foot mere inches from a steep drop. The stream of the waterfall trailed down the open space to the switchback far below.

"*Shit,*" he hissed, gulping down air. How was he supposed to get across?

Precious moments ticked away as he tried to come up with a plan. He couldn't fly—he hadn't used his wings since he was little and now was *not* the time to experiment. He sure as shit wasn't going to attempt to jump it, semidiós or not.

Frantically, he looked around for something to help him.

There were plenty of trees, but going straight up wouldn't do him any good because he still needed to activate the glyph on the other side of the gap. But there *was* a thick branch that extended out with a thick vine hanging from it, just in reach.

Teo grabbed hold and gave it three sharp yanks to be sure it would take his weight. He'd used rope swings along the banks of the canals in summertime. It couldn't be much more difficult than that, right?

Before he could second-guess himself, Teo held on for dear life and, with a running leap, swung out across the drop. He clenched his teeth, holding back a shout, and released the vine when he was over solid ground. Gracelessly, he landed on his butt, but he *didn't* fall to his death, so he'd take the bruises.

"YES!" he shouted, punching his fists into the air. He hit the next glyph and his watch gave him another short buzz.

There was a gust of air as something large flew right over his head.

A boulder smashed into the tree he'd just swung from. Branch, vine, and stone crumbled down the side of the mountain.

Teo swung around in time to see another flying right for his head. Quickly, he dropped to the ground. The boulder smashed into the cliff face, rubble showering down around him. Teo choked on dirt and grime, pushing himself up onto his knees. Through a gap in the trees, he could see Ocelo standing menacingly, hefting a large rock in their burly arms.

"You missed!" Teo shouted, fueled by spite.

Ocelo chucked the rock. Teo threw himself between two large boulders, narrowly avoiding the projectile.

Teo poked his head out from his hiding spot and smirked. He'd have thought a Gold would have better aim. "Are you angry because you're so short?" he called out.

Ocelo bared their teeth.

Teo did what he knew every bully hated to be on the receiving end of—he laughed, short and sharp.

Ocelo slammed their fist into a tree, splintering its trunk. They drew in a deep breath, their chest swelling, growing, *changing*. They tipped their head back and released a bellow.

No, not a bellow but a roar.

Ocelo's body changed, their muscles growing and rippling under their skin, hulking out like some kind of luchador. Their nails morphed into claws and four heavy canines protruded from their mouth. When Ocelo bared their teeth, their amber eyes bulged.

Teo immediately regretted everything. How could he compete with *this*?!

Overhead, Mariachi's cornet rang out and Teo's watch gave two short buzzes, announcing someone had reached the finish.

"Seriously?!" Teo craned his neck but the top of the mountain was still far out of sight. How had someone made it already?

Apparently having the same thought, Ocelo gave him one last snarl before rushing off.

Teo needed to hurry.

The higher he went, the steeper the terrain became. Not long after the fourth glyph, the waterfall crashed over the path. Even in his fancy new shoes, Teo's feet slid on the slick stones and moss as he crossed to the next glyph and activated it.

Buzz.

On the next switchback, the path was gone, replaced instead by jagged rocks protruding straight up into the air. It looked like the tops had been sliced off so they could act as stepping stones, but they weren't close enough to step from one to the other. If Teo was going to cross, he'd have to jump between them, but they were barely larger than his foot and wet from the waterfall.

Adrenaline was working against him, making it hard for Teo to focus. On top of that, he was short of breath and his legs were dangerously unsteady.

Two short trumpets of the cornet cut through the air. *Buzz, buzz.*

He didn't have time to think, he just needed to *go*. Teo ran and leapt for the first stone.

His foot hit true. There was no time to hesitate—if he slowed down, he could lose his balance. So Teo used the momentum and jumped to the next stone, one leg at a time.

He was nearly to the other side when the cornet startled him. *Buzz, buzz.*

Teo's foot slipped as he launched himself from the final stone. He sucked in a breath. His body pitched forward.

Teo stretched out his arms, desperately trying to reach for the outcropping.

His chest slammed into the edge, crushing the air from his lungs. His ribs exploded with pain. Legs dangling over the jagged rocks down below, Teo started to slip.

Panic squeezed his heart in an icy grip. He scrambled, desperately clawing his way to stable ground, but the mud slipped between his fingers. A strangled shout caught in his throat as his chin dragged painfully over rock. He kicked his legs wildly, trying to get leverage.

Finally, his foot caught on protruding rock. With all his might, Teo pushed off.

The rock crumbled under his foot, but he was able to throw himself forward. Kicking and crawling on his arms, Teo got himself back on solid ground. Covered in mud, he collapsed onto his back, staring up into the lush canopy. His heart thudded painfully as he gulped down air.

But the cornet trumpeted again. *Buzz, buzz.*

Teo smacked his sixth glyph—*buzz*—and pressed on to activate the seventh. *Buzz.*

Then he reached the apex of the waterfall. It flowed from an unknown source within the mountain and spilled out from a hollow space between jutting rocks, thundering down onto the path below. This time the glyph was nestled within the waterfall in a small cave. Teo could barely glimpse the jade stone through the frothy cascade.

Carefully, Teo edged closer. Water sprayed his face, stinging his skin and obscuring his vision. The rush was unrelenting. When he stepped too close, the force of it nearly shoved his foot out from underneath him.

Teo turned and pressed his body against the cliff face. With his right hand, he wedged his fingers deep into the nearest crevice. Pressing his cheek into the wet stone, he leaned out, blindly reaching with his left hand. The second he tried to reach through it, the water violently shoved his arm out of the way with such force it nearly tossed him off the ledge.

Gritting his teeth, Teo tried again. This time, he pressed his palm flat against the mountainside, sliding it behind the waterfall so it wouldn't knock him away again. He stretched as far as he could and finally, his fingers touched the smooth surface of jade. Behind the water, the eighth glyph lit up. *Buzz.*

The path ended at the waterfall, so he needed to find another way up the rest of the mountain. With only one glyph before the final at the top, it was now so steep, he'd essentially have to climb. Teo tried to catch his breath as he scoped out the best path, cold water dripping from his hair and down the back of his neck.

It was mostly boulders and sharp outcroppings. He could see the ninth glyph sitting on a flat sheet of rock. Above it was another fifteen feet or so of rocky cliff face before the summit of the mountain. There were distant voices and Teo could even see the top of Sol's glyph undulating with golden light.

He was almost there. He still had time. He needed to keep pushing forward.

With trembling hands and shaky breath, Teo climbed. Sharp stone bit his fingertips, drawing beads of jade blood as he grasped for handholds, wedging his foot between some rocks. The heavy, humid air did little to cool him down and the smell of earthy moss filled his lungs. Dragging his chest over unyielding stone, he pulled himself higher up the cliff face.

The ninth glyph was nearly in reach now, the jade just a few inches away. If he stretched, he could probably hit it. Desperately, Teo pushed off with his foot, but the rock supporting him gave way.

A yelp lodged in Teo's throat. Choking on dirt, he held on for dear life as gravel shifted and slid.

Overhead, he heard Niya's voice call out, "Teo!"

He looked up.

Ocelo had made it to the top of the mountain. Instead of crossing the barrier that marked the finish, they stood on the very edge of the platform, a large piece of slate hefted in their arms.

Teo's heart stopped. Ocelo grinned, their eyes black as pits. They chucked the slate and Teo flinched, but Ocelo didn't throw the chunk of rock at him.

Instead, it crashed into the section to Ocelo's right.

Xio's path.

Teo saw him, curled up in a small ball and wedged between two boulders, covering his head as rocks shifted and clattered down around him. The rock face splintered and crumbled under Xio's hands and he fought to keep a grip.

Fear and anger warred inside Teo. Ocelo was ruthless and so strong, there was nothing Xio could do to defend himself. Instead of just finishing the trial, Ocelo wanted to fuck with him.

Teo needed to *do* something and not helplessly cling to the cliffside. He couldn't cross over to Xio's section to help him because then they'd both get their scores docked, but if he did *nothing*, Ocelo was going to crush Xio under a rockslide.

If he wanted to help Xio, he'd have to stop Ocelo. Ocelo, the half-jaguar Gold demigod who could hurl whole boulders the size of donkeys.

There was no way to even the playing field. He couldn't beat Ocelo hand to hand, but maybe he could outsmart him. Teo had a secret weapon, if he was willing to use them.

They were the only leg up he had in these trials, especially this one. It was practically made for a flying competitor to dominate.

As Ocelo hefted another slab of stone, Teo's anger and determination won out.

I really hope this works, Teo thought as he summoned every ounce of strength he had left. Teo strained his wings as hard as he could. His binder ripped and popped as they broke free and extended. With no time to second-guess himself, Teo flapped his wings down forcefully and propelled himself to the next outcropping.

He overshot it a little, crashing into the cliff and sliding down to where he'd been trying to land. His neglected muscles screamed and seared with white-hot pain, but Teo pushed through it, beating his wings once, twice. By the third, he was up in the air, flying up the side of the mountain.

Ocelo froze with the boulder held over their head. Shock flashed across their face. They shook their head roughly, as if clearing their vision, and when they looked back up, Ocelo's yellow-green eyes were wide and confused.

As Teo shot past them, he twisted his hips and struck Ocelo's head with the inside of his foot like it was an ugly soccer ball. Ocelo fell back, which was good, but the sudden shift sent Teo tumbling through the air.

Desperately, Teo tried to regain his balance, pinwheeling his arms and trying to flap his wings. He managed to right himself, and when he looked back, Ocelo was sitting in the dirt, dazed, as a line of gold blood slid down the corner of his mouth.

He did it! He'd stopped Ocelo and he was *flying*!

Teo hadn't done this since he was little. Huemac and his mom were always worried about him getting hurt, which made sense because he had had so little control over his wings when he was small. He could only ever get a few feet off the ground, but that was before he had fully matured. Teo had given up on using his wings when his body started to change.

He had no idea how *good* it would feel to stretch his wings out and fly. For a moment, he just breathed, relishing the air rushing over him. The sensation of flying filled his chest with euphoria, so much so that Teo found himself laughing.

But now he needed to focus; he was still in the middle of the trial and needed to make sure Xio was okay—

"HOLY SHIT, TEO!"

Niya shouted at him from the top of the mountain, a huge smile plastered across her face. She was standing next to Sol's glyph behind a shimmering barrier that must've been the finish point. Xochi, Auristela, and Aurelio stood next to her. They seemed stunned. The ever-stoic Aurelio's lips were actually parted as he stared up at Teo.

"What?!" Teo shouted back through strained huffs. He was quickly running out of breath, his body feeling heavier with every beat of his wings.

"*Look at your wings!*" Niya screamed, jumping up and down.

In the thrill of flying, for once Teo hadn't thought about what his wings looked like. He spent so much time trying to avoid the sight in his periphery and mirrors. Now he hesitantly glanced over his shoulder and let out a surprised yelp.

His wings were no longer the familiar sight he'd spent every morning hiding. They weren't brown and patchy.

Now, brilliant ultramarine, iridescent blue, and electric green feathers sprang from his back.

The feathers of a proper male quetzal.

CHAPTER 9

Fully extended, the brilliant feathers fluttered as Teo kept himself in the air, far above the water down below. He felt like his heart was going to burst out of his chest. Teo whooped and punched his fist into the air, but that sent him toppling again. This time, he quickly recovered.

It was like suddenly having a second set of arms. He knew how wings worked, but he'd never bothered to learn how to properly fly. He was already exhausted and losing all the momentum the adrenaline had given him. How the hell was he going to get himself down?

He didn't get long to figure it out.

There was a sudden explosion of white light. A crashing boom. A jolting, excruciating pain exploded in Teo's body. Every muscle seized. He couldn't move. He couldn't breathe.

Down, down, down he fell, crashing into the freezing water below.

Cold, dripping wet, and humiliated, Teo stood next to his mother as they waited for Sol's rankings. To the side, Niya flashed him a thumbs-up, her grin wild and excited.

After Atzi had zapped him out of the sky with a lightning bolt, Diosa Agua had been kind enough to scoop him out of the water so he didn't drown. Though he could've done without the goddess's amused laugh as she dumped him back on the platform in front of the huge crowd.

At least Atzi had the decency to give him an apologetic shrug.

"Just *look* at them, Teo!" his mother cooed, running her fingers across his new wings. They shuddered and shook themselves out, tickled by the touch and spraying anyone close with water.

"*Mom*," he pleaded, but he couldn't stop smiling. The embarrassment of getting eliminated in front of a crowd of tens of thousands of people was at war with his excitement over his changed wings, but there were still bigger issues at hand.

Teo tried to get a good look at Xio, but Mala Suerte stood in the way, talking to his son and probably offering reassurances. Already, Teo felt like he was failing the younger boy.

Ocelo seemed quite pleased with themself, smugly eyeing Teo after exchanging affectionate headbutts with Diose Guerrero. And while Xochi seemed to be actively ignoring Teo as her mother fussed over regrowing the flowers in her hair, the way Dezi openly smiled at his wings made Teo blush.

Dezi signed something and Teo was about to apologize because he didn't know sign language, when someone said, "They're very handsome."

Aurelio stood behind Teo with his head tipped to the side, studying his wings, while Auristela was distracted talking to their mom.

Teo's breath hitched. "What?"

Aurelio's attention snapped to his eyes. He stood up straighter. "That's what Dezi said."

Teo's stomach dropped. "Oh." He turned away from Aurelio, not wanting him to see the flush creeping across his cheeks. To Dezi, he signed, *Thank you*. It was the only sign he knew.

"Stubborn things, aren't they?" Quetzal mused and signed before trailing her fingers down the bright feathers. "Not unlike yourself," she added with a teasing smile.

"Took them long enough," Teo grumbled. His left wing twitched and whacked him across the face. He spluttered through his feathers. "*Hey!*"

"I suspect they refused to change until you properly accepted they were a part of you," his mom reasoned with a knowing look. "That you *needed* them."

Teo glanced at Aurelio again, but he had already gone back to his sister.

Auristela stood next to her mom, hands on her hips and looking smug. Her makeup was still perfectly in place. The light sheen on her forehead somehow made her look even prettier.

Diosa Lumbre had that same half-bored, half-annoyed look on her face. Her back was to Aurelio as he inspected his soot-covered hands. He flexed his gloved fingers and massaged his thumb into his palm. He looked perplexed, like he was trying to solve some complicated math problem in his head, but something wasn't adding up right. Then someone called to Aurelio from the crowd and he looked up, his reserved smile back in place as he waved.

Teo didn't know how the others had ranked, but it'd be a miracle if Sol didn't put him in dead last. Not only had he not completed the trial, but he'd failed in an epic fashion. Chisme was going to have a field day with the footage.

Diosa Luna gathered everyone's attention. "Sol has determined the rankings," she announced, gesturing at two priests who rolled out a large stone slate. On its face, Sol's symbol was engraved and filled with gold paint. Along the bottom, each of the ten competitors' glyphs sat in a horizontal line—eight made of gold and two made of jade. There were two Lumbre glyphs, one with an *O* in the flames for Aurelio, and the other with an *A* for Auristela.

For a moment nothing happened, but then the glyphs moved, positioning themselves in a vertical ranking in the center of the sun.

Auristela shrieked, her composure flying out the window when she saw she'd come in first. She tried to recover, but the grin on her face was insuppressible. With a soft smile, Aurelio reached over and gave his sister's hand a gentle squeeze. In the most affectionate act Teo had ever seen from the goddess, Diosa Lumbre nodded her approval.

"Congratulations, Auristela," Luna said.

"If you'd come with us," Verdad said, appearing out of nowhere with Chisme at her side. "We'd love to get a few words."

"An *exclusive* interview with our first top-ranked competitor!" Chisme sang, draping his arms across Auristela's shoulders as he led her to a group of awaiting cameras and reporters.

But Teo couldn't care less who came in first. He quickly skimmed the list as thundering cheers broke out from the stands, not at all surprised by Auristela, Aurelio, and Niya being so high.

Xochi and Diosa Primavera held hands and screeched with excitement. Looking smug, Dios Tormentoso nudged a very angry Guerrero.

Teo expected to be at the very bottom, but to his surprise—

"Eighth?" Teo breathed.

Beside him, Quetzal exhaled a sigh of relief, her hand pressing to her chest. "Thank Sol."

Xio was right beneath him, in ninth. Teo leaned around his mom to see that Xio was covered in dirt but otherwise unharmed. As he stared up at the rankings, his lips pressed into a line.

Behind him, Mala Suerte squeezed Xio's shoulders and gave him a small shake. The dios's expression was unreadable, but Teo could see his skin looked even paler than usual and the sweat on his brow probably had little to do with the sun overhead.

If Xio was in ninth, that meant his run must have been even more of a disaster than Teo's, but at least neither of them was last. In tenth place was—

Ocelo fumed.

"Marino, Teo, and Xio didn't reach the top within the allotted time," Diosa Luna explained.

"So why am I last?" Ocelo demanded.

Teo's eyes nearly bulged out of his skull. Murmurs floated through the crowd. Teo knew good and well that Luna was the last diosa you'd want to piss off.

"*Ocelo*," Guerrero hissed. The jaguar-headed god looked just as outraged as Ocelo, but at least they had the brain to scold their child for speaking so brazenly to Diosa Luna.

Luna gave them a smile completely void of warmth. "Are you questioning Sol's ranking?" she asked, her voice resonating more loudly as the crowd grew silent.

Ocelo seemed to immediately regret their decision. "I—I don't—"

"You intentionally used rocks to destroy another semidiós's glyphs, making it impossible for them to complete the trial. Then you caused a rockslide—which fairly impacted your competitors, yes, but also put the priests acting as spotters at the base of the mountain in grave danger. The dioses had to step in to protect them."

Ocelo's eyes cut to the mountain where dust still swirled in the air like fog.

Teo hated to think what would've happened to him if it weren't for his wings. He was a demigod, yes, but he didn't think that would've saved him from being splattered under a bunch of boulders.

"I would remind you, Ocelo," Luna said slowly, deliberately, "that as a semidiose, it is both your honor and your duty to protect the people of Reino del Sol, not harm them. Your behavior in this trial proved that you have much to learn about your position in the world. Be careful. This trial is complete," Diosa Luna addressed the crowd, leaving Ocelo red-faced, his head lowered.

Niya looked like Luna had just brought her a platter of pan dulce. Teo wanted to enjoy this moment, too, but he couldn't. He and Xio managed to stay out of last place, but only due to Ocelo badly fucking up. Something told Teo they wouldn't be so lucky in the next trial.

If Teo wasn't careful, one of them was going to end up dead.

"No hetero, but damn, Teo, your wings!" Niya circled Teo back on the boat. "Does this make me a furry?"

"Shut up!" Teo swatted at her, turning to get his wings out of her reach. After taking a shower and nursing his bruised ego, he'd met up with Niya and Xio in the common room.

"What?" Niya said, laughing. "I'm just saying, they look *really* good!"

Teo did his best to look annoyed even though, secretly, the compliments left him feeling warm and buzzing. When they folded up, the top of his wings hit his shoulders and the long primary feathers ended at the small of his back. But with their new freedom, they didn't want to cooperate. Instead, they ruffled and stretched like they couldn't stand staying still.

"They *are* really cool," Xio agreed from his perch in an armchair.

"And your hair looks great, too," Niya added.

"My hair?" Teo reached up. It was still wet from his shower but didn't feel any different.

"You didn't see?!" Niya grabbed Teo and pushed him over to a circular, gold-framed mirror hanging on the wall. Instead of a dull brown, his hair had turned a deep, iridescent black.

"What the …"

Luminous hints of blue and green caught in the light when he turned his head.

"Folks pay good money to try to dye their hair like that," Niya said.

"How did you not notice?" Xio asked.

"Guess I was too distracted by my wings," he murmured, tugging on a lock of his hair.

Taking a shower with his wings had been nothing short of a struggle. They had knocked over every single bottle of fancy toiletries. He'd tried to wrangle them into one of his binders, but now it was like they had a mind of their own, with zero intention of letting Teo restrain them again.

"You should let them be free!" Niya said, moving to lounge on the arm of Xio's chair. "They're badass, and if you learn how to actually *use* them, they'll give you an edge in the trials. No offense but, uh, you could use it."

Teo glared, but he knew she was right. Today had been a catastrophic failure he couldn't afford to repeat.

"*And* they saved your life," Xio added in a voice that immediately made Teo feel guilty for taking up all the attention.

"Are you okay?" he asked Xio, turning away from the mirror.

Xio blinked his dark eyes slowly at Teo, offering him a wry smile.

"Er, all things considered, I guess?" Teo added.

"Well, I didn't get squished under a landslide, so I guess that was lucky," he mused with a small shrug.

"The hell even happened?" Teo asked.

Always the chismosa, Niya jumped right in.

"Okay, so, I was next to Aurelio and Xochi," she said, talking a mile a minute and gesturing wildly. "Aurelio? Couldn't be bothered. He basically did a speed run to the top and that was that. Marino tried to use the waterfall to slow him down, but he wasn't quick enough. I was doing *awesome—totally* killing it," she said, cutting her hand across her neck for emphasis, "But then *Xochi* did, like, a drive-by vining! One second I was scaling the mountain, looking awesome, then BAM!" Niya punched the back of the chair, nearly toppling Xio over.

"It was like BDSM, which is hot, but without consent, which is *not* hot."

Xio's eyes bulged. Teo let out a surprised laugh.

"But, y'know, I just whipped up some silver blades and *shing shing*!" Niya slashed her hands through the air. "I was back on my game!

"By the time I got to the top, Auristela, Aurelio, and Xochi were already there and I could pretty much only see folks as they finished. But then fucking *Ocelo* showed up—" Niya's voice raised, a scowl firmly in place. "They were about to cross the barrier to finish, but then they just *stopped.* Auristela even tried to get them to finish, and they usually do whatever she says, but they got this weird look and decided to fuck with the rest of y'all!"

Anger simmered under Teo's skin. So it wasn't enough for them to finish on time, Ocelo had to make it harder on everyone else for no good reason. "What a douche," Teo growled.

"A *massive* douche," Niya agreed.

"Did Ocelo really destroy your glyphs?" he asked Xio, who nodded and sank lower in his chair.

Niya huffed. "I mean, as established, Ocelo is a douche—"

"Right."

"But that's *extra* douchey, even for them!" Teo gave her a skeptical look, but she went on. "Even Aurelio tried to tell them to stop right before they caused the rockslide—"

"He did?" Teo cut in, surprised. Since when did Aurelio go against Ocelo?

"Yeah, but it was like Ocelo couldn't even hear him!" Niya continued. "Usually, the others follow whatever the twins want."

"Then they caused the rockslide," Xio said, fiddling with his bracelet. "I wedged myself into a spot between two boulders and waited for it to be over."

"Well, at least you didn't get smashed into a pulp," Niya offered, trying to sound optimistic.

"You don't have any semidiós powers that can help you out in the trials?" Teo asked, feeling a bit desperate for some kind of solution.

Xio shook his head. "Nothing useful like magic weapons or wings."

Teo rubbed his hand over his face, hit with a fresh wave of exhaustion. What was he going to do? He had barely been able to keep himself alive in the first trial, so how was he going to help Xio? The odds were not in his favor.

It was like Xio was set up for failure.

CHAPTER 10

When Teo went back to his room, some new clothes had been laid out on his bed. Soft sweatpants, gym shorts, and a couple of cotton T-shirts. They all had the golden sun with the Quetzal glyph in the middle, always in jade thread, a constant reminder of how he didn't belong. Did Golds have all their clothes picked out for them at the Academy?

Teo swung by Xio's and Niya's rooms to gather them for dinner. They were the last ones to arrive. A nice breeze rolled through the open deck. The long table was covered in food, and Maize was explaining what everything was, like they were diners at some fancy restaurant and not just a group of hungry teenagers.

Maize cut the three of them an annoyed look, probably because they were late, but Pan Dulce gave them a cheery wave.

Niya collapsed into a chair at the foot of the table and Xio took the one next to Auristela, the lesser of two evils considering Teo had to be next to Ocelo. He scooted closer to Niya and did his best to fold his wings neatly against his back, but they kept twitching. Teo pushed them against the back of his chair to try to keep them in place.

When Maize and Pan Dulce left, they dug into the impressive spread. Everyone seemed tired and agitated after the trial. Dressed down and exhausted, the Gold Heroes of Reino del Sol seemed almost normal.

Auristela seemed to be the only one in good spirits. She kept taking selfies with her phone and tugging Aurelio into the frame.

"Ugh, stop yawning, you're ruining the pictures!" she chided, throwing her elbow into his arm.

Aurelio replied with another large yawn. When his sister was done using him as a prop, he sat with his head bowed over his plate, eyes heavy-lidded.

Dezi kept nodding off at the other end of the table, his chin dropping to his chest after every other bite. Marino and Xochi sat on either side of him, the former cutting angry looks to Ocelo. Ocelo, surly even by their standards, stabbed their fork into their food as they ate.

When Teo leaned forward to get another helping of delicious blackened fish and rice, one of his wings escaped. It shot out, whacking Ocelo in the face.

"Watch it—your stupid feathers went up my nose!" they barked.

"I can't help it!" Teo snapped back, trying to flex the right combination of muscles that would pull his wing back in place.

Glass clattered and Auristela gasped.

"Can someone come fetch their toddler?" she seethed, the front of her shirt covered in water. She snatched the napkin Aurelio offered. "He's getting his bad luck all over me!"

"That wasn't my fault," Xio said, voice small but expression fierce as his cheeks bloomed bright red.

Anger burned Teo's vision. "Lay off."

Auristela let out a sharp laugh. "You two shouldn't even be here!" she said, holding Teo's eye like a challenge. "You're just background noise."

"Stela," Aurelio said, short and surprised as he stared at his sister.

Shame made Teo's face tingle. He didn't need Aurelio defending his honor.

"It's really a competition between us Golds," Ocelo agreed. "You two are the default sacrifices."

"Guys, chill—" Atzi tried to pipe in, but the damage was done.

"Oh, and you think one of *you* three is going to win?" Niya demanded, pointing between Ocelo, Auristela, and Aurelio before laughing.

"Hate to say it," Teo said, emboldened by Niya's refusal to back down. "But you guys are gonna need backup plans for convincing your parents to love you."

Auristela fumed. Her ember eyes blazed. Teo basked in it. "You're pretty smug for eighth place, huh Bird Boy? Ocelo, what's that saying I like so much? About the cat with a canary?"

Ocelo flashed their fangs at Teo.

"Sol can see right through your bullshit," Niya delivered with a smile.

"Oh, because you're so much better than us?" Ocelo sniped. "You're only here because your dad is Sol's disgraced ex-boyfriend."

Teo sucked in a breath.

The table jumped. Plates rattled. Niya and Ocelo were both on their feet.

Teo jerked back, avoiding the long obsidian blade that had materialized in Niya's hand, the tip directed at Ocelo's throat.

"Say it again," Niya said, her voice deadly low. "I dare you."

Ocelo snarled. Auristela's pretty face twisted into an ugly sneer. Aurelio shifted and Teo instinctively grabbed the edge of a plate, ready to—

Thwack-thwack-thwack-thwack-thwack!

Something smacked the backside of Teo's head, throwing his head forward and snapping him out of his rage.

"*Ouch!*" he hissed. The others rubbed their heads, looking around dazed.

"That's quite enough."

Luna stood with her silver sandal in hand. "I thought you'd have more energy after such an auspicious day, but you're all acting like overtired children, so—" She clucked her tongue. Her tone was teasing with acid boiling underneath. "Time for bed. Dinner is over."

"But we didn't even do anything!" Marino argued. Luna shot him a look and he immediately shrank back. Slowly they filed out, Marino stuffing some bread into his sweats on the way.

Teo knew this fight was far from over, but Luna had put it off for now.

As Ocelo and Auristela stormed off with Aurelio in tow, Niya blew them a kiss.

※

"*Assholes,*" Teo hissed when they got to Xio's room. Xio sat on the end of his bed while Niya flopped onto her back next to him.

"Now you get to see what I have to deal with all the time," Niya grumbled, twisting her bangles around her wrist. "Though usually it's not *this* heated."

Teo rubbed his forehead. He couldn't speak to the rest of them, but usually he had a pretty good grip on his own anger. Being here seemed to be wearing his patience thin.

"Maybe we're all just tired and getting on each other's nerves," he said, pacing.

"It's my fault they hate us." Xio's face was twisted in frustration. "This always happens! And now they brought your dad into it, Niya, that was *so* messed up . . ."

Niya sat up and balled her fists into the clean white comforter.

"It is *not* your fault, dude," Teo reassured him. "They've always hated us."

Xio's expression shifted from anger to defeat. "They called us default sacrifices . . ."

Teo's blood ran hot again. "*Assholes,*" he repeated. "None of them deserve to be Sunbearer! If they do, I swear I'll rip my own wings off!" Teo spun to face his friends. "We *can't* let them win, no matter what," he announced.

"Shouldn't we be more focused on not dying?" Xio asked.

"I mean, *yeah*," Teo agreed. "But we also need to beat their asses! Think of how humiliating it'd be if Ocelo, Auristela, and Aurelio *lost*!"

"It's not like we can stop them," Xio said miserably.

"It's not enough that we just get through this, we need to take down those three, too," Teo pressed. Xio gave him a skeptical look, so he went on. "What better way to get back at them for all their bullshit elitism than to have one of the misfits win? Niya's the one with the best chance, obviously."

"It *would* piss them off to no end," Niya mused. "And I'd *really* love to see Diosa Lumbre's face if neither of her kids became Sunbearer. All she cares about is the Academy and making sure Aurelio and Auristela are always on top—she would totally lose her shit!"

"Even better!" Teo agreed.

"You think we could pull it off?" Xio asked with an uncertain look.

Teo gave his shoulder a small shrug. "Sure we could! I mean, I know the first trial didn't go great—"

"Bit of an understatement—"

"But that was only a dry run. We've got four more trials to get through, right? Plenty of chances for us to take down the trio and get Niya to the top of the rankings," Teo said. "*And* keep us from being in last place."

Xio scratched the back of his neck and looked up at Teo from the fringe of his curls. "Not gonna be easy."

"No," he agreed. "But we've got a secret weapon."

"My killer bod?" Niya guessed, picking at her teeth.

"No—Xio!"

The younger boy looked alarmed. "*Me?*"

"Yes!" Teo plopped down onto the bed next to him. "You and your encyclopedic knowledge of all the competitors!" he said, tapping Xio's forehead.

Niya sat up straighter, her eyes wide. "*Ooh!*"

But Xio still looked less than convinced.

"Where's your binder?" Teo asked.

Xio gave him a confused look, his hand automatically moving to his chest.

"No, I mean with the trading cards and stuff," Teo corrected.

"Oh!" Xio pulled it out from where he'd hid it under his pillow.

"Give us the rundown on Aurelio, Auristela and Ocelo," Teo said. "If we know their strengths and weaknesses, we can use that against them during the trials."

Niya scooted in on Xio's other side. "That's an awesome idea!"

"Well, every semidiós has general strength and stamina boosts over mortal humans," Xio said as he flipped through his binder. It was full of small, clear pockets that held nine trading cards per page in alphabetical order. Some people only had one card while others had many, and some were plain while others were holographic or lenticular. Xio even had a few that were made out of solid gold.

"By default, Golds are stronger than Jades, but every semidiós has their natural inherited powers from their parents, like you and your wings," Xio continued. "And Niya's ability to manipulate earth."

Teo nodded. "And what about special powers?"

"Golds have their natural powers but when they go to the Academy, they hone in on one and turn it into a specialization."

"Mine is how I can turn earth minerals and rocks into weapons," Niya said. To demonstrate, she turned a titanium bangle into a shield in her left hand, and a silver one into a very painful-looking mace in her right.

Xio turned to Aurelio and Auristela, whose trading cards took up two whole pages, front and back. "Trading cards list those specializations along with strengths and weaknesses," Xio said, pointing them out. He pulled out one each of Aurelio's and Auristela's to compare. "Aurelio is a Manipulator and Auristela is an Ignitor."

"What does that mean?" Teo asked.

"Aurelio can easily manipulate fire to make it bigger, smaller, or put it out completely," Niya supplied. "Auristela can create fire. That's why Aurelio wears those dorky finger gloves. The flint tips let him spark a fire."

"Aurelio's a defensive Hero, Auristela's an offensive one," Xio added.

"Why did they summon both Aurelio and Auristela to the fire in Quetzlan, then?" Teo asked. "Wouldn't Auristela just make things worse?"

"All of Diosa Lumbre's semidioses are fireproof," Niya said, like everyone knew that.

Xio nodded. "So she can still assist by rescuing people."

Teo supposed that made sense.

"These radar charts show a semidiose's general strengths and weaknesses."

Teo furrowed his brow. "What kinda charts?"

"Radar charts—they show multivariate data by giving each variable an axis and plotting the data as a polygonal shape over all axes," he explained, pointing to a type of graph Teo had never seen before in his life.

Teo stared blankly at Xio.

"Can't believe I'm finally smarter than Teo, but here we go," Niya muttered to herself as she sat up straighter. "They show how good or bad someone is at different things and they make cute little shapes!" she supplied.

"Oh." He examined the amorphous blobs. "I think that makes sense . . ."

"There's six plot points on three axes," Xio went on. "Power and strategy, speed and stamina, and then offense and defense. Typically, a more top-heavy graph means the semidiós is more of a powerhouse, and a bottom-heavy graph means they're more strategic, but ideally you want to have a balance of all six. So, the more your chart looks like a hexagon, the more balanced you are."

"Wait, where do these statistics even come from?"

"Our grades at the Academy," Niya explained.

"So basically, your report cards are public knowledge?"

She shrugged. "I guess."

"Sheesh." Teo looked between Aurelio's and Auristela's radar graphs. "Theirs are practically identical."

"Almost, except Aurelio is more strategic and Auristela is more powerful," Xio said, pointing them out.

"Their powers kind of go hand in hand, don't they?"

Xio nodded. "They're very complementary, yeah."

"That's why they train together all the time, like a team instead of individuals," Niya explained, an annoyed edge to her voice. "I think this is the first time they've ever been split up and actually competing against each other."

"Doubt that'll keep them from teaming up when they get the chance, though," Teo grumbled. It made the most sense and was a good strategy.

Teo knew Auristela was powerful as hell and used it to her advantage, but he hadn't considered that Aurelio was more on the defensive side. It was so easy for him to think of them as the same person. But Teo had seen them disagree, like whenever Aurelio made that crumpled-up expression at something mean Auristela said.

"This is where their specific weaknesses are listed," Xio said, pointing below the graph.

"Water and cold," Teo read aloud.

"Oh yeah, we had a training camp where they dropped us in the mountains during winter," Niya said with a smug look. "It rained and was freezing cold. By the time we were done, both Aurelio and Auristela were really sick and had to stay the night in the infirmary."

"I'm not sure how easy it'll be to use water or cold against them," Teo said, irritated that there wasn't an easy solution.

"It depends on the trial," Xio said.

"And we don't know what the trial is until it's time to start." Teo huffed. "It'd be easier if we could see them in action. I barely caught a glimpse of Auristela in the first trial and Aurelio was on the opposite side from us."

"It's been all over the news," Xio said, pulling out his phone, an older model with a chunky protective case. "I bet they're still showing clips." In a matter of seconds, Xio had a livestream of the news pulled up that, indeed, was playing reruns from the first trial.

"Never thought I'd see the day I was thankful for Chisme," Teo grumbled as he took the phone. Conveniently, they were showing Aurelio and Marino racing up their side of the mountain, locked in battle. They lobbed fire and water back and forth, each trying to outmaneuver and outrun the other while still staying in their own section.

"See how careful he is around water?" Xio said, pointing to Aurelio as he dove behind an outcropping of rocks, narrowly avoiding a pressurized stream of water.

"Yeah," Teo murmured to himself. "What are the odds the next trial takes place underwater?" he said with a wry grin.

"I've always wondered how they, like, *bathe* if water fucks them up so bad," Niya said, toying with one of her messy braids.

"Probably can't take baths," Teo mused.

"Maybe they just hose themselves off *really fast*," Niya suggested with a grin.

The idea of Aurelio quickly jumping into a shower and back out again made him laugh.

But the laughing stopped when the clip changed to another one of Teo hovering midair with his new wings—just to be struck by a bolt of lightning.

"What's Atzi's weakness?" Teo asked. "I'd like to avoid getting electrocuted out of midair in front of thousands of people again."

Xio flipped back a couple of pages. "'Rapid energy depletion.'"

Teo frowned. "What's that mean?"

"She gets tired easily," Niya explained. "It takes a lot of Atzi's physical energy to create bolts of lightning. Those rings she wears are conduits, which help her out, but she's still only thirteen—no offense, Xio—so if she's going too hard, she can exhaust herself."

"Sounds like a rechargeable battery," Teo mused.

"Or one of those defibrillator things," Xio added.

Teo remembered the explosion of electricity that had shot through his body as the clip kept looping. Teo tossed Xio's phone back to him. "I think I'm done watching the news."

"Oh yeah, that clip went viral on TicTac!" Niya said enthusiastically.

Teo's heart stopped. "*What?*"

"Yeah!" Clearly she hadn't caught the dread in his voice. "People reenacting it and stuff like that. There's even this girl who turned it into a dubstep song by mixing the weird shout you made and the crowd gasping!"

Teo ground his teeth. This was *not* what he wanted to be remembered for during the trials. "I take back what I said about Chisme."

"Hey, it's not all bad!" Niya said, pinching his elbow. "You could make bank by leaning into it!"

"You could probably get a bunch of followers and start monetizing your content," Xio suggested with a grimace, trying to make Teo feel better, but it didn't work.

"I'm good, thanks."

"Auristela has a huge following on Instagrafía," Niya prattled on. "Did you know she's sponsored by that sketchy MLM smoothie company?" she asked, sitting up and pulling out her own phone. In a couple of seconds, she had Auristela's Instagrafía account pulled up on her very cracked phone screen. "If I have to see her holding up a puke green smoothie on my feed one more time, I swear I'll blow chunks."

There were several pictures of Auristela power posing in a gym or somewhere pretty, always with her high ponytail and some kind of product in hand.

"What about Aurelio?" Xio asked, leaning over Teo's shoulder.

Teo shook his head. "He doesn't have his own account."

Niya narrowed her eyes at him. "How do *you* know Aurelio doesn't have his own account?"

It took all of Teo's willpower to keep a straight face. "How do you know *Auristela* is sponsored?"

"I—what!" she spluttered before scowling. "Give me my phone back!"

"Let's move on to Ocelo," Xio said, holding back laughter.

Ocelo had three cards. Xio pulled out the most recent—a lenticular trading card that switched back and forth between Ocelo's normal form and their powered-up form.

"Ocelo is a transformation semidiose," he said. "That means their powers let them change their body properties temporarily, and since they're a child of Diose Guerrero, that means jaguar characteristics."

"Their radar graph is super top-heavy," Teo noticed.

"Ugh, yeah, Ocelo is a total meathead—nothing but strength and brute force," Niya said with a roll of her eyes.

"Sounds like you," Teo teased.

"Aye, I am *way* smarter than Ocelo!" Niya insisted. She sat up to compare the chart on one of her trading cards. "See?!"

"Weaknesses: intelligence and problem-solving," Xio read from Ocelo's.

A laugh burst from Teo. "Wow, that absolutely checks out."

"Where are you guys' cards?" Niya asked, moving to flip through the pages again.

"We don't have any," Xio said.

"We're just lowly Jades, remember?" It was supposed to be a joke, but Teo's voice was a bit too gruff to pull it off.

"Oh yeah," Niya gave a sheepish smile and handed her cards back to Xio. "Sorry, I forget sometimes."

"What are your powers, Xio?" Teo asked, pivoting the conversation, but Xio just shrugged.

"I don't have any," he said in a quiet voice, staring down at his binder. "Not any useful ones, anyway. Not sure 'being unlucky' is much of a power."

"That sucks, bud," Niya said, not very tactful but still sympathetic.

"Being able to *inflict* bad luck on other people would be a cool power," Teo mused.

"It would, yeah," Xio agreed, short and curt like he didn't want to talk about it. Teo wasn't going to press him.

"The last Jade to compete was a hundred and thirty years ago, right?" Teo asked.

"Yeah, we learned about that in history class," Niya agreed. "But that's like all I remember."

"Do you have anything on them, Xio?"

"No, they only started producing trading cards about fifty years ago, give or take," he said. "They made retro cards but they're really hard to come by. There's bound to be something online, though," he said, pulling up the app on his phone.

In a matter of moments, Xio had a video pulled up. The footage was black-and-white and grainy, making it difficult to tell what was going on. The camera focused and Teo could immediately tell that this was a clip from the Sunbearer ceremony.

The winner, some Lumbre semidiós with a terrible haircut, stood proudly under the Sol Stone, beaming at the gathered crowd. Fantasma stood between them, and on her other side was the Jade semidiosa.

The camera was zoomed in tight on her face. It was hard to tell with the old footage—everything was blurry and nondescript—but she looked terrified, her lips pressed into a tight line.

"What's her name?" Niya asked, squinting at the screen.

Xio flipped to the back of his binder where several pages listed the winners and losers of every Sunbearer Trials to date. "Paloma," he said, reading from the page. "She's—" Xio cut himself off.

Niya leaned in. "What?"

The camera zoomed out, showing a wider shot of Sol's altar and the semidioses.

"What's that?" Teo wondered out loud, pointing at two smudges behind her shoulders.

Paloma turned to approach the sacrificial table.

It was like someone punched the air out of Teo's lungs.

"They're wings!" he breathed. "She has wings!" He turned to Xio and Niya. "Why does she have wings?!"

Niya's eyes were wide, her fist pressed against her mouth.

Hesitantly, Xio held out his list and pointed. "Paloma, daughter of Quetzal," he read.

Teo's heart pounded in his head, his rushing pulse making his whole body feel tingly and numb. His sweaty hands gripped the phone, trembling as he watched the girl—his half sister—lie on the stone table. Her wings splayed out behind her across it, long and elegant.

"Why didn't you tell me?" Teo asked, watching as the footage continued to roll.

"I didn't know!" Niya said hurriedly. "History class is *really* boring and right after lunch—I fall asleep, like, *all the time.*"

"Your mom never told you?" Xio's quiet voice asked near his shoulder.

Teo shook his head. She'd never spoken a word about Paloma to him before.

"Why wouldn't she have told you about her?" Niya wondered.

On the screen, the Sunbearer approached the table, a black dagger in his hand. When he stood over her, the dagger raised above his head, Paloma closed her eyes.

And the video ended.

Why *hadn't* his mom told him? Maybe she didn't want him to be frightened, or maybe she simply couldn't bear bringing her up.

Memories flashed through his mind. How she'd shielded Teo from watching the sacrifice ten years ago. How terrified she'd looked when Sol selected him to compete. Her iron grip and the relief in her voice when he passed the first trial.

His mom had been carrying this on her own, alone in a city where she was the only immortal, where none of her people knew, or even remembered, her fallen daughter.

"Your poor mom," Xio said, his voice small and sad.

Teo felt sick. She'd already been through watching her daughter compete and fail in the trials. Now she was reliving it all over again.

And if he didn't do something, she'd lose him, too.

CHAPTER 11

True to her bearlike nature, Niya decided she was too full from dinner to do anything else and went to bed. Teo was too anxious to sleep, so he and Xio went to the common room only to find Auristela and Ocelo had claimed the massive TV and turned on the news. Xio expressed interest in a puzzle, but when Auristela and Ocelo started ugly laughing over clips of Teo getting zapped from the sky on repeat, Teo decided he needed a task to work out his aggression.

When he told Xio his plan to go to the training room, the younger boy agreed to accompany him, but only for moral support.

"Good luck," Xio said, patting Teo on the back before slumping into a pile of mats with his hood pulled up and binder of trading cards open in his lap.

Teo exhaled a puff of air as he looked at all the fancy equipment he had no idea how to use. He contemplated stomping back to Niya's room and dragging her out of bed to help him.

Well, if his wings refused to be bound anymore, then it was probably a good idea to learn to use them. He was the only competitor with the ability to fly, and that was his biggest advantage over the Golds.

But where the hell was he supposed to start?

Most birds learned how to fly when they were babies and their mothers helped them jump from their nests. But Teo didn't have his mom or a high enough point to jump from, so he'd have to wing it until he figured out something that worked.

The floor was padded, so it seemed like a safe enough space to try. First, he practiced taking off. When he managed to get into the air, he was extremely tippy and couldn't get a good rhythm going to flap his wings. It was like he didn't have enough brain power to focus on moving his wings while also staying balanced. Keeping track of an extra set of limbs was no easy task and resulted in several attempts of getting about three feet off the ground before falling very gracelessly to the floor.

With the slightest shift in his weight, he'd try to compensate with his wings, but then he'd overcorrect and end up on his ass. It was impossible to land on his feet when he had his arms and wings knocking him off-balance.

But he kept getting up and kept trying again because even if he was a fool, he was a stubborn fool who was determined to get *something* right.

After the thirtieth or so fall, Teo realized Xio had dozed off on his nest of mats, so at least he didn't have an audience.

Sitting on the floor with sweat running down his face, Teo was losing his patience. "Would you just *cooperate*?!" he growled, throwing his elbow back into his wing.

The other one flung itself around and whacked him in the face.

Scowling, Teo spat tiny blue-and-green feathers from his mouth.

Maybe the problem was the wings weren't strong enough yet. After being bound for so long, perhaps they'd lost the muscles required for balanced flight. Maybe he needed to strengthen his shoulders or whatever to gain some control.

For extra safety, Teo dragged over one of the mats, careful to not wake Xio in the process. Next, he got the chalk stuff on his hands because he saw gym bros do it on TV and approached one of the weight racks.

The weights were circular discs, the shape and size of shields. After eyeballing the selection for all of five seconds, he went to get a fifty-pound weight. He remembered what Aurelio had said, to hold the weight close and use his legs.

When it didn't budge, he downgraded to forty-five pounds.

And then thirty pounds.

Teo rolled the weight on its edge over to the area he'd set up. After some struggling, he hefted it up, holding it to his chest with crossed arms. This was bound to get his wings stronger.

He started moving his wings in wide, forceful flaps. Sweat prickled his forehead by the time he finally managed to lift himself off the floor. The added weight seemed to at least steady the tipping, but it took concerted effort to keep his wings going.

So much, in fact, that he squeezed his eyes into a grimace, and when he opened them again, he was ten feet in the air.

A triumphant laugh bubbled in his throat, throwing off his concentration. He dropped a couple of inches and rushed to catch himself, struggling to find the steady rhythm again.

That was when the door opened and Aurelio walked in.

He was dressed in the Academy-provided workout gear—black shorts and a tank top that covered very little of his well-built frame. He took a few steps before noticing Teo.

Teo cursed under his breath. Of course *he* would show up right here, right now. He always seemed to get a front-row look at Teo in his worst possible moments. Teo did his best to ignore Aurelio, but the excessive sweat on his hands was turning the chalk dust into a paste, and the rubbery coating of the weight slipped in his fingers.

Teo attempted to heft it higher onto his chest while still keeping aloft, but the sudden shift made him drop another foot.

Aurelio stopped, crossed his arms over his chest, and watched.

If he had a free hand, Teo would've flipped him the bird.

Panting hard, Teo gritted his teeth and tried to push through it, determined to not fail in front of Aurelio.

But his arms burned and a stitch stabbed into his side. He could feel the muscles in his back and wings trembling. He tried to hold on to the weight, but he was losing his grip.

When he made one last desperate attempt to hoist the weight, his right wing cramped and gave out.

Teo let out a strangled shout as he tipped back and fell from the air.

He landed on his back, hard, the single flimsy mat doing nothing to break his fall. A split second later, the weight crashed down on top of him.

"*OOF!*"

The weight crushed all the air from his lungs. Spots dotted his vision. He tried to push it off, but his arms were too weak from holding it up for so long.

Teo gave up and collapsed back onto the mat, wings splayed and arms flopped uselessly at his sides. He closed his eyes and wished for Aurelio to leave him to sit in his humiliation, or for Sol to just let him pass out and escape embarrassment.

But, of course, neither would make things that easy for him.

"Do you need help?"

Teo opened his eyes to find Aurelio standing over him, looking down with a placid expression. His soot-soft black hair was pulled back from his face in its usual knot and his thick eyebrows were furrowed with concern over his clay-colored eyes. A faint scent of smoke followed him around. It wasn't strong, more like the way Teo's hoodie still smelled faintly of smoke weeks after he'd worn it to a bonfire.

When Teo didn't respond, Aurelio added, "Or is this some new work-out routine I'm not familiar with?"

Teo mustered all the energy he had left to glare. "Either help me, or be an ass," Teo wheezed. "*Not both.*"

The corner of Aurelio's lips twitched into an almost-smile. He stooped down and lifted the weight with frustrating ease, setting it on the mat next to Teo.

Teo sucked in a deep breath, rubbing his aching chest. He watched as Aurelio wandered over to the water cooler.

The smart thing would probably be to take the L and go to bed, but Teo rarely ever did what was smart and he wasn't about to start now. He got to his feet and started flapping again.

"You're not fully extending your wings."

Teo turned just in time as Aurelio tossed him a water bottle.

He scrambled and managed to catch it. "Yes, I am." To prove his point, he stood upright and unfurled his large wings.

Teo smirked, but Aurelio gave him an exasperated look.

"Roll your shoulders down and back," he said, going through the motions himself. His rounded shoulders sank, pulling his shirt taut across his well-toned chest. "Open up your chest."

Teo scowled, a flush creeping across his cheeks. Was he showing off? "Since when are you an expert in wings?"

Aurelio shook his head and moved to what looked like a jungle gym with a bunch of weights and pulleys.

It went against all of his instincts to do what Aurelio told him to, but he could at least give it a try, just to prove him wrong. Teo waited until Aurelio was focused on repositioning a piece of equipment and then he tried rolling his shoulders down and back.

Automatically, his wings extended out, locking into place a good two feet wider than he'd ever managed before. "Whoa," Teo breathed, examining his feathers as they gleamed under the lights.

"Told you," Aurelio said, not looking up from what he was doing, but he wore a small, pleased grin.

The only thing Teo hated more than being wrong was Aurelio being right.

"There's some stretches—"

"No thanks."

"It'll help your wingspan."

"You just want me to die of boredom," Teo grumbled as he stomped back to the weight rack. Maybe if he tried a lighter one—

"If you push yourself too hard, you'll either hurt yourself or be too sore to compete," Aurelio said, leaning against the rack.

Teo dug his fingers into the weight. "I'm not a child," he said, stubbornly meeting Aurelio's sharp gaze.

"That wasn't a personal attack," Aurelio said slowly, evenly. It was hard to get into a fight with someone when they refused to raise their voice.

Teo decided to take that as a challenge. "Oh, so you're just offering advice out of the kindness of your heart? I thought you wanted to *win* this thing."

Aurelio steeled himself.

"I do," he said, maybe more to himself than to Teo. "I do, but I don't want to be Sunbearer just because you—" He cut himself off.

What was that about? "Just because I'm what? Just because I'm Jade? Just because I'm weak enough not to be worth playing against?" His voice wavered.

"This isn't a game," Aurelio said, frowning.

Teo's chest tightened. "*I* know that."

"Then why do you act like it is?" Aurelio asked, expression deadly serious. Teo thought maybe he really wanted an answer, that he wasn't just trying to get under Teo's skin.

Teo froze, not knowing how to respond.

From the corner of his eye, he noticed some movement. Back on the stack of mats, Xio had woken up. He sat up, watching Teo and Aurelio, a small crease between his brows.

Frustration clouded Teo's mind and dug under his skin. "I'm taking it seriously! What's twisted is how excited you and your friends are to become a murderer."

Aurelio straightened. "Without the sacrifice, the world would end," he reminded him.

"Yeah, well, if getting *killed* is such an honor," he grunted, trying to move the weight, "Then it's the *winner* who should be sacrificed."

For a moment, Teo thought he'd won because Aurelio didn't say anything, but then he finally spoke—his voice terse.

"It's not a fair fight," Aurelio said.

Teo shoved the weight back onto the rack with a *clang* before turning on Aurelio. "Why?" he snapped. "Because I'm not a *Gold*?"

Aurelio jerked back, surprised, but quickly recovered. "Yes," he said, as if it were obvious. "The Academy has been training us for this since we were children. You have no idea what you're doing—"

Teo let out a sharp, bitter laugh, shaking his head. "Wow, you are *so* full of yourself—"

The muscle in Aurelio's jaw jumped, his nostrils flared. "If you'd trained half as long as the rest of us have, you'd actually do pretty well."

"You take shit *way* too seriously—"

Finally, Aurelio snapped. "And you don't take things seriously *enough!*"

Every ugly feeling Teo kept closed off and pushed away was dragged to the surface. Every time he felt not godly enough to be a Gold, or too godly to be a boy. Every cruel look from Auristela and every terrible laugh from Ocelo.

Every time Aurelio turned his back on him.

It twisted and churned and leapt from his mouth.

"You Golds run around *pretending* to be Heroes when you're just bullies with a god complex!" he spat. "I'm trying to keep me and my friends alive—all *you* care about are the rankings and making Mommy proud!"

Aurelio's coppery eyes flashed.

Teo waited for Aurelio to get angry, to yell and rage, because he *wanted* to fight. He wanted to make Aurelio feel small. He wanted Aurelio to see what it was like.

But, of course, Aurelio would never give him what he wanted.

Aurelio straightened his back, his cool facade in place even though Teo could see how his hands clenched into fists at his sides. "You're going to get yourself killed."

He said it simply, plainly, before turning and leaving the training room, the door clattering shut behind him.

In his wake, Teo was left breathless on shaky legs. He wanted Aurelio to leave, but it still hurt when he walked away.

Quietly, Xio walked up to him. "That was weird," he said, looking to where Aurelio had left before giving Teo a nervous glance. "You okay?"

"I'm fine," he said. He sniffed and wiped the sweat from his brow. He wouldn't let Aurelio get under his skin. This was all just some machismo power play and Teo wasn't going to fall for it. More important, he wasn't going to let Aurelio win, and there was only one way to stop that from happening.

If Teo wanted to take down the Golds, then he was going to have to act like a Gold.

CHAPTER 12

The next morning, Teo was so sore he could barely get out of bed. Every muscle in his upper body—from his shoulders to his wings, and even down to his fingers—ached and screamed in protest as he showered and changed into his uniform.

The worst part was that Aurelio had been right, but Teo would rather suffer than let him know it. It took all of his concentration not to wince and let on how much pain he was in, but it didn't matter because Aurelio didn't pay him any attention during breakfast.

None of the Golds did, in fact. They talked among themselves, predicting with genuine excitement what terrible thing was awaiting them at the next trial. Teo, Xio, and Niya were back to being background noise, just like Auristela had said.

While Xio and Niya talked, Teo could barely pay attention. He was too distracted trying to catch Aurelio's eye. Usually Aurelio at least glanced in his direction, but not today.

It was almost like he was purposely not looking at Teo. Probably just to piss Teo off. It took a lot of restraint for Teo to not slam his fist on the table and *make* Aurelio look at him.

"He eats a banana like a *serial killer*," Teo grumbled to his friends as he watched Aurelio slice one up and eat the pieces with a fork. "Don't you think—"

He turned to Niya to find her biting into a stack of pancakes like a hamburger. She blinked at him.

"Wha'?" she asked through a mouthful of pancake. "I'm carbo loading!"

Teo sighed and shook his head.

Xio dissolved into a fit of laughter and immediately choked on the guava juice he was drinking, spraying it out of his nose and onto the table.

"Oh my gods, I need new friends!" Teo announced as he grabbed a stack of napkins and handed them to Xio.

"Look, I don't know why you're staring at Aurelio so hard but it's making me uncomfortable," Niya said, shoving Teo's shoulder as Xio mopped up his mess.

"*Ssh!*" Teo hissed, shoving her back, which did nothing. "I'm not staring!" He was, but he didn't need her drawing attention to it.

"You're definitely staring," Xio confirmed, nodding.

"Ogling, even. It's *creepy*, Teo." Niya squinted suspiciously at him. "Are you trying to undress him with your eyes or what—?"

"Shut up!" Teo barked, which made everyone else look at him— except for Aurelio, which just made his not-looking more suspicious. Auristela leaned forward to give him a dirty look.

Embarrassed, Teo slid down in his seat and scrubbed his hands over his face. "I'm glaring at him with *disdain*, I'm not ogling!" he said, much quieter this time, but he knew he wasn't convincing anyone after that display.

Niya laughed. Xio at least had the decency to try to cover his chuckle with a cough.

Teo groaned, but when he looked up at Aurelio again, he could've sworn he saw Aurelio glance away, the corners of his lips twitching up.

"Your clothes for today are already waiting for you to change into," Luna announced as the Sol priests cleared away breakfast.

"Change?" Teo asked. "Again?"

Luna stopped and shot Teo a look.

He snapped his mouth shut.

As she spoke, her signs were sharp and emphatic. "Dios Tierra has kindly arranged for you all to spend the day at the La Cumbre hot springs—"

An excited ripple ran down the table.

"*Yes*," Teo hissed under his breath, his mood instantly improved. Finally, he'd be able to see what a real Gold city was like!

"—before welcoming us to his temple tonight for dinner," Luna continued. "And I won't have you all running around in your training attire." Her dark gaze swept across all the competitors. "I expect everyone to be respectful and courteous while we are there. I will not accept anything less. Is that understood?"

Everyone nodded and mumbled their agreement.

Luna gave a curt nod. "Good. Now go—you have one hour before we leave for the hot springs."

Niya immediately leapt to her feet and sprinted back inside.

"What do you think they're going to make us wear?" Xio wondered with a look of dread.

"Can't be any worse than these uniforms," Teo said.

It wasn't *worse*, but the La Cumbre outfit presented its own set of challenges. Teo's tight athletic wear had been swapped out for soft, white cotton. The sleeveless tunic was nice in the warm weather and Teo's wings fit seamlessly through the slits on the back, but the bottoms were the bigger issue.

Teo had never worn a hip cloth before. They were traditional in a few cities, but Quetzlan wasn't one of them. The best he could manage was wrapping it around his waist like a towel. When Niya met Teo in his room, she laughed and snatched it off him, leaving him in his boxer briefs before she tied it the correct way.

All the competitors wore the same white cotton garments with their glyph embroidered onto the upper left chest. They were also given a selection of swimwear and a white drawstring backpack to carry it in.

As they filed off the boat, Teo self-consciously tugged at the hem of his hip cloth. "I'm paranoid I'm gonna accidentally flash someone," he grumbled. Another issue was the complete lack of shoes. He knew Niya never wore them, but he thought that was just a Niya thing, not a La Cumbre thing.

Niya waved off his worries. "I doubt anyone would notice," she said, dressed in an outfit nearly identical to the regalia she had worn in the opening ceremony, minus the ornamentals. "People walk around half naked and full naked all the time!"

Teo and Xio exchanged looks, too shocked to ask *why*.

A lot of his questions were answered as they headed up the main road.

"It kind of tickles," Xio said with an amused smile as he wiggled his toes in the soft, almost ashy dirt. Under the breezy white tunic, Teo could see Xio was wearing a white binder.

"It makes us feel more connected to the earth and La Cumbre," Niya explained. "She talks a lot, so feeling her rumbles through the soles of our feet keeps us connected." Niya spoke of the volcano affectionately, like the people in Quetzal spoke of their bird companions. It made Teo smile.

So, of course, Auristela had to ruin it.

"Gross," she scoffed. Ever since they'd stepped foot off the boat, she'd had a mildly disgusted look on her otherwise pretty face.

"No one asked you!" Niya snapped.

"I like it," Teo said, completely ignoring Auristela.

Auristela rolled her eyes and turned away, her high ponytail whipping.

Teo was worried they'd have to walk up the huge mountain to get to the temple, but luckily Luna led them to an aerial tram station. They were loaded onto what looked like a silver bean with glass windows on all sides. When it lifted into the air, Teo white-knuckled the railing as it ascended up the cables.

Seeing La Cumbre from above was even more incredible. As they made their journey, everyone pressed close to the glass and Niya pointed out the landmarks below.

Dozens of crystal blue mineral baths and hot springs cascaded over the mountainside. Grottos housed altars and steaming pools of blue water.

As they neared the top, the strange smell of rotten eggs tickled Teo's nose.

"What's that stink?" Auristela asked, crinkling her nose.

Dezi nudged Marino.

Marino shoved him back. "*It wasn't me!*"

Dezi laughed.

"It's sulfur," Niya told Teo, pointing as they went over another ridge and a caldera came into view. "Everything is warmed by the geothermal heat of La Cumbre!"

As the tram crossed the crater, Teo could see volcanic vents spewing yellow, sulfurous fumes. Before the tram dipped down, he was able to get a glimpse of Tierra's temple. Unlike Queztlan's simple slab of jade, this altar was a huge chunk of gold carved with the three mountains and rising sun of the dios's glyph.

They were greeted by more crowds as soon as they stepped off the tram. People waved and cheered, snapping pictures as the competitors were led down the path to the hot springs. Tierra priests lined the way, politely holding the spectators back. Everyone clamored for Niya's attention, which was sweet, especially since it seemed to annoy Auristela and Ocelo to no end.

The entire hot spring, including the hotel and pool, was carved into the side of the volcano. The buildings were all made of the same soft, beige stone they walked upon. Inside the lobby, the floor had been polished until it sparkled. Loads of plush seating added to the atmosphere of comfort and luxury.

"Where is everyone?" Teo asked as priests led them to the changing rooms.

Niya frowned at him. "What do you mean?"

"Isn't this place, like, really popular?" he asked, gesturing around. His voice echoed through the empty halls. Aside from the priests escorting them, the lobby and café were completely empty. "Where are all the people?"

"Oh, you mean mortals?" Niya laughed and waved him off. "They always close down places to the public when we visit."

Teo frowned. "All the time?"

Niya gave him an unsure smile. "Yeah!"

"Why?"

She blinked, like she didn't understand. "I don't know." She shrugged. "Just how it is!"

It was a weird concept. The Gold semidioses seemed to live completely separately from the mortals they protected. Teo wondered if it was because they were famous, or because of their half-Gold status. The answer was probably both. Teo couldn't relate in the slightest. There was no such separation between Jades and mortals. Teo went to school, went grocery shopping, even went to the movies among the mortal citizens of Quetzlan. The detachment between Golds and the mortals they devoted their lives to protecting seemed unnecessary and a bit backward.

They entered the locker rooms and changed into matching bathing suits, which were, again, all white. Unfortunately, the swim bottoms were also hip cloths but smaller and made out of a more water-friendly material. Teo opted to go bare chested, but Xio went with an oversized tunic. The other option was a bandeau top.

When Teo and Xio stepped out into the main area of the hot springs,

Teo couldn't believe how fancy and beautiful everything was. The view from the tram really couldn't do it justice. Built into the side of the volcano were at least a dozen tiered pools filled with steaming turquoise water. Lush canopies protected them from the harsh sun, and waterfalls tumbled down the rocky cliffs and fed into the hot springs.

"This place is *really* fancy," Xio said, large eyes taking everything in.

"Yeah," Teo agreed, unable to keep himself from grinning. Maybe he didn't agree with all the special attention Golds got, but he also wasn't going to turn it down while he had it. "The closest thing we've got to a spa in Quetzlan is this guy Rico who hangs around outside the market and will pay *you* five bucks to let him rub your feet."

Xio let out a startled laugh.

Before Teo could even put his stuff down, he heard Marino whoop. Teo turned to watch as Marino sprinted forward and cannonballed into one of the pools. Niya took off after him, landing with an impossibly bigger splash.

Teo and Xio grabbed glasses of ice-cold mango juice from a table laden with drinks, fresh fruit, and nuts as everyone else filed out of the locker rooms.

"Aw man, you know where they have the *best* mango juice?" Teo asked, just as Auristela and Aurelio stepped into view.

Teo's brain stuttered to a stop.

It wasn't like he hadn't seen their skin before. The twins' uniforms were basically fancy crop tops, but Aurelio was entirely shirtless now, standing there like some *actual* god. Aurelio reached up and adjusted the knot of his hair, sunlight glistening on his warm brown skin.

Had someone oiled him up? And how the hell did he get those side abs on his ribs?

"Teo?"

He jumped, mango juice sloshing in his hand as he quickly turned back to Xio. "What?"

"Where's the best mango juice?" Xio repeated.

"Oh, uh." Teo cleared his throat.

The younger boy squinted up at him.

Teo couldn't remember what the hell he'd even been talking about. "I don't remember."

Xio glanced to where Aurelio and Auristela had entered a pool surrounded by warning signs: DANGER, EXTREMELY HOT! Maybe they could handle water as long as it was boiling.

He arched an eyebrow. "Uh-huh."

Teo shoved him. "Shut up and pick a hot spring."

They decided on one of the mineral-rich pools. With the help of his water-repellent wings, Teo could float on his back without even trying. Niya set up camp at the food table while Dezi and Xochi lounged in a mineral bath with mud masks on their faces. Atzi and Marino kept going underwater to see who could hold their breath the longest and Ocelo dozed off on a lounge chair in a puddle of sunshine.

Niya brought Teo and Xio over to a waterfall. When they stood under it, the water thundered over their heads, swallowing up their laughter as it hammered on their backs. The pounding warmth was amazing on his sore wings. Teo suggested they play a game where the person who was It had to close their eyes and listen for the others in order to tag them. Xio was *really* good at it and somehow managed to sneak around in the water without being heard, but Niya was way too loud and splashy and kept getting caught.

On her third time being It, Teo noticed Aurelio and Auristela had only spent a few minutes in the hottest pool before Auristela left to take selfies against the gorgeous scenery.

Alone for once, Aurelio disappeared into what looked like a cave cut into the side of the mountain, shielded by a trickling waterfall.

While Niya splashed around with her eyes closed and Xio followed her around, silently laughing, Teo took the opportunity to sneak off after Aurelio.

Cold water tickled his back as he stepped through, only to be hit with a wave of heat. The inside was a small grotto with lush ferns growing out of cracks in the craggy walls. There was a pit of black stones in the middle of the floor billowing with steam, making the air hot and humid.

Aurelio sat on a bench that had been carved into the stone wall of the makeshift sauna. Blue sunlight filtering in through the waterfall and red firelight from the torches danced across Aurelio's skin. His eyes were closed, head tilted back in a way that made Teo think he might be asleep. Teo stepped forward, and one of Aurelio's coppery eyes peeked open.

"Mind if I take a seat?" Teo asked, pointing to the bench.

Aurelio shook his head and sat up a bit straighter.

Teo confidently walked over and took a seat a safe distance away, his wings tucked behind his back. Aurelio leaned forward and picked up a large ladle from a bucket of water. He poured a spoonful over the hot stones, sending a fresh wave of steam into the air.

It was way too hot; Teo didn't know how Aurelio could stand it. He was just sitting there, all peaceful and relaxed while sweat beaded on his bare thighs and chest, a small trickle running down—

"You okay?"

Teo jolted. "Yes, I'm fine," he lied, sweat trickling down the back of his neck.

A crease formed on Aurelio's brow. "You look a little red."

"Yeah, well, it's hot in here," he replied. The truth was, he was sweltering and the steam in the air was so thick, he felt like he couldn't take a proper breath. But it wasn't like he could leave *now*. "I'm *relaxing*," he added, stretching his arms and wings out for emphasis.

He wasn't used to having his wings out and had no real perception of how wide they were, so when he did, his feathers touched Aurelio's shoulder.

The other boy's eyes darted to where they'd brushed his skin, Teo quickly retracted them again, choking on an apology he refused to give.

"You sure you're not too hot?" Aurelio asked again.

Teo rolled his eyes, secretly wishing he could fan himself off right now. "What are you, my mom?"

"Has anyone ever told you you're very stubborn?"

"Pretty much daily. Huemac always says I'll stubborn myself to death."

"I'm starting to think he's right." Aurelio leaned down and picked up a water bottle. "Here," he said, handing it over.

For a moment, Teo hesitated.

Aurelio sighed and blinked slowly at him.

Teo huffed. "Fine." He snatched the bottle from Aurelio's hand. "But not because I'm overheated."

"Right."

"I'm a normal amount of thirsty."

Aurelio nodded. "Sure."

Teo felt his cheeks grow impossibly warmer. "Thirsty as in—like, *hydrated*, not—" He sputtered, trying to regain some semblance of composure.

"You know being thirsty means you're *de*hydrated, right?"

Aurelio still didn't know how to keep up a joke. At least that was one thing that hadn't changed since they were kids. He opened his mouth, ready with a snappy comeback to tease him, when—

"What would you do," Aurelio suddenly asked, "if you were Sunbearer?"

Teo let out an explosive laugh, more out of surprise than humor. "I honestly haven't even considered it, dude. Not like it's a real possibility."

"It is. Sol didn't choose you just to—"

"To be killed?" Teo guessed. "By one of the *real* contenders?"

Aurelio took a deep breath. "I've been thinking about what you said—"

Teo really didn't want to talk about this anymore and something in his face must have made Aurelio realize that. His mouth snapped shut.

Awkward silence fell between the two of them. Teo felt like a fool for even following Aurelio here in the first place. What *had* he been expecting? Maybe to get a glimpse of the Aurelio he'd seen the other night. The Aurelio that didn't seem so untouchable.

"I think I'm done with the sauna," Teo said, getting up onto his very wobbly legs. "But *not* because it's too hot."

An amused look danced across Aurelio's face. "Are you sure? Because you look pretty hot."

Teo tripped on his way across the cave. "Thanks!" he yelped.

Thanks?! What was wrong with him?

Teo stepped through the waterfall and was immediately relieved by fresh air on his sweltering skin. When he saw Niya and Xio standing there staring at him, he skidded to a stop.

"Hey there," Xio greeted him with a smile that was far from innocent.

Teo squeezed the water bottle in his hands. "Hi."

"We were wondering where you went," Xio said, arms crossed over his chest.

"I was just—uh—" He jerked his head toward the grotto. "You know, checking stuff out."

"I'm sure you were," Niya said, shaking her head.

"I—what's that supposed to mean?!"

"No fraternizing with the enemy, Teo," Xio teased.

"I wasn't!"

"*Two bros chillin' in a sauna, five feet apart cuz they're not*—" Niya sang, but Teo twisted off the cap of the bottle and splashed the cool water in her face.

Niya gasped, mouth hanging open. The look on her face made Teo burst out laughing.

"Oh, you think that's funny?!" Niya demanded, charging toward him.

"No, don't!" Teo tried to run but it was too late.

Niya grabbed him and tossed him into one of the pools like a rag doll before diving in after him. Teo, still laughing, choked on water as he used his wings to push huge waves at his best friend.

"Try not to drown each other!" Xio called from the edge of the pool.

✳

After they showered and changed back into their clothes, it was a short walk to the La Cumbre temple. It sat at the highest point of the volcano on the opposite side of the caldera from the spa. The temple itself was made out of reddish clay. The only pop of color was a basin made of raw amethyst crystals that cradled the La Cumbre Sun Stone. Its beam shone steadily into the dusk-colored sky.

There were gold accents, mostly around the windows and main outer steps that led to the altar up top, but other than that, the temple was quite plain compared to what Teo had expected from a Gold city. Tierra priests in earth brown robes welcomed them as they approached.

"What do you think?" Niya asked, tugging on Teo's arm as they walked through the courtyard. It was simple as well, with a couple of cloudy blue hot springs surrounding a golden statue of Tierra.

"It's awesome!" Teo said, not wanting to hurt her feelings, but it was also—

"A little stinky," Xio added. Not unkindly, just an observation.

"I know!" Niya practically shouted as she looked around her home. "Isn't it great?"

Teo found himself grinning. He knew she didn't get to go home very often because of her training. He'd probably be more fond of Quetzlan if he was stuck at the Academy all the time, too. Though he was quickly getting acquainted with the previously foreign feeling of homesickness.

"I thought it'd be more ... elaborate," Teo admitted.

"Wait till you see inside," Niya said with a smirk.

Before he could ask what she meant, they were ushered into the temple and it became abundantly clear.

Tierra's temple was like a geode. While the outside of the temple was plain, the inside had tall, cavernous ceilings, and every surface was covered in gemstones. Blazing fire opals, red jasper, and crystals in every color imaginable jutted out from the walls in jagged, irregular angles and glittered in the torchlight. The kaleidoscopic colors and sheer size of the gemstones were dizzying.

Teo would've liked to wander the hall, but the sharp look Luna gave him when he drifted toward another corridor kept him in line.

They were brought into a dining hall where a large stone table was set for them. Massive, honey-colored citrine crystals bigger than Teo hung from the tall ceiling like a chandelier.

Four people stood at the head of the table to greet them. Dressed in his usual suit and golden mask, Dios Tierra lifted a gloved hand in greeting. The earth god was tall, but his slender frame made him seem small compared to the bulky men at his sides.

Monte and Mino were dressed in matching white hip cloths and tunics. An older man Teo had not met before stood at Tierra's side. His brown hair was graying at the temples and he was built like a mountain. When he smiled, it was identical to Niya and her brothers', pressing deep lines into his face and crinkling the skin around his eyes.

"DAD!"

Niya sprinted forward, breaking formation to throw herself onto her mortal father. Chuckling, he wrapped his arms around Niya in a tight hug as he picked her up and spun her around.

Gods weren't limited to mortal means of reproduction or childbirth, so having two biological fathers wasn't uncommon among demigods.

"Tierra, Andres, thank you for having us," Luna said, smiling as she approached.

Andres wrapped his arm around Tierra and pulled the god closer to plant a kiss on his cheek. If Tierra had skin, Teo guessed he would've been blushing.

Teo lingered toward the back of the group, suddenly feeling a bit out of place. The weight in Teo's stomach was heavy enough to pull him toward the back of the group. Among the gods and demigods, his mom was all the blood family he had, and that was enough. But seeing Niya at home with her family made Teo painfully aware of how different they were.

"We're so thrilled to have you!" Andres announced, welcoming the rest of the group. He had a deep, booming voice that echoed in the large room. "Please, have a seat," he said, gesturing to the open chairs. "We've got quite the spread—the priests have really outdone themselves!"

Teo moved to take a seat at the far end of the table, Xio right on his heels like a shadow, but Niya grabbed their arms. Everyone stared as she dragged them to chairs next to hers near the head by her dad and brothers. Two Jades sitting among some of the most powerful Golds in Reino del Sol. Warmth flooded Teo's body and he couldn't hold back a smile.

As they fell into easy conversation, Tierra priests started bringing out food and drinks for dinner. They drank from clay jarritos and the plates were made of polished agate.

There were roasted root vegetables in more colors than Teo even knew existed. Andres explained that the steak had been vacuum-sealed and cooked in the hot springs until it was soft as butter, falling apart as soon as Teo stuck his fork in it. He avoided the chicken, but helped himself to fish that had been grilled in the kitchens using La Cumbre's geothermal heat. Even the rebocado had been slow cooked underground in clay pots.

"Eat up!" Andres instructed when everyone seemed hesitant to start. "You need protein for your next trial tomorrow!"

Dezi turned to Luna and signed something.

"The second trial will be hosted by Diosa Fauna," Luna explained and signed back. "We'll leave for El Valle when we board the boat tonight and should arrive by midday."

Immediately, the group broke out into excited chatter. Teo didn't eat much after that. The later it got, the more his stomach churned and a tightness settled into his chest.

When it was time to leave, Niya and her family exchanged backbreaking hugs. Teo was ready to console his friend, but instead of being sad, the time with her family seemed to have given her a burst of renewed energy.

Everyone's hypothesizing didn't stop when they left the temple and rode the tram back down the mountain. At night, the zigzagging paths of the city down below were illuminated by torches.

"Sleep tight, La Cumbre!" Niya shouted back up the mountain as they approached the docks.

Teo could've sworn he felt the volcano rumble under his feet in response.

CHAPTER 13

The next morning, Teo, Niya and Xio went onto the foredeck to watch their progress. They'd left the mountains far behind and were making their way east through the span of tropical forest between La Cumbre and El Valle.

"I wonder what kind of trial Fauna set up," Xio murmured to himself as he fiddled with his bracelet.

"Probably something to do with animals," Niya said, leaning back against the railing.

"Seeing as Fauna is the goddess of animals, I'd say that's an astute observation," Teo grumbled, leaning against the railing as he stared out into the thick tangle of trees along the riverbank.

"Somebody woke up on the wrong side of the nest today," Niya teased, petting his wing.

It flicked her hand away, agitated.

"You okay?" Xio asked, which made Teo feel like an ass because Xio was the one who was really screwed over in all of this.

"I'm fine. I just didn't sleep well." It was only half a lie. He had tossed and turned all night worrying about the upcoming trial. He was very much not fine. "I'm just..."

"Cranky?" Niya guessed.

Teo scowled. "No!"

"Anxious?" Xio asked, like he understood all too well.

"Something like that," he admitted. He was nervous about the next trial, and all night he'd dreamt about Paloma.

Over on the large couch, Ocelo was sprawled out in a puddle of sun, taking a cat nap.

"Meanwhile they're over there sleeping like a baby," he grumbled.

"The self-confidence is really something," Xio agreed with a roll of his eyes.

"Hey," said Niya, nudging him. "Maybe they'll keep it up and *stay* in last place."

As they rounded a corner, familiar chatter caught Teo's ear. Grouped together on a long, hanging branch at the river's edge were a trio of toucans.

Teo saw an opportunity and took it.

He cupped his hands around his mouth and called out, "Hey there!"

The toucans paused, looking at one another curiously and then back at Teo before taking flight.

"Whoa." Xio laughed, stepping back as Teo was swarmed.

You've got wings! one said, landing on the railing to stare up at him in complete shock.

Another rested on his shoulder, tail feathers sticking up in the air as she leaned down to inspect his feathers. *Never seen a boy with wings before!* she said, patting them tentatively with her foot.

The third made himself comfortable on top of Teo's head. Before he could introduce himself, the bird tugged at a lock of his hair.

"Ouch!"

Blech! The toucan shook out his feathers. *Only strange human feathers up here, though!*

"I'm Quetzal's son—"

QUETZAL'S SON! the one on his head squawked.

All three birds took flight and perched on the railing. They devolved into excited chatter, hopping around excitedly on their blue feet.

Quetzal's son?!

QUETZAL'S son!

You're Quetzal's fledgling?!

They bobbed their heads up and down in funny little bows.

Hello, Son of Quetzal!

So good to meet you!

It made Teo smile. The birds in Quetzlan were used to seeing him, so he rarely got this sort of enthusiastic introduction.

"What are they saying?" Niya asked, giving Teo's arm a shake.

"They're excited to meet me because of my mom," he said.

"Aw!" Niya beamed. "You're bird famous! Like their little bird prince!"

Teo rolled his eyes. "I wouldn't say that." He turned back to the toucans, who were still bowing and bumping into each other. "I was hoping you three could lend me a hand."

Haven't got hands, one said, gravely apologetic.

Got six wings between us, though! rushed another, giving them a flap.

The third tipped his large beak in the air and chattered a laugh. *That was funny!*

Thank you!

"You see them sleeping over there?" Teo asked, pointing to where Ocelo was still out cold.

Smells like a cat.

Don't like cats!

"That's Diose Guerrero's fledgling," Teo explained.

One of them shuddered. *Like that even less!*

"They're a jerk," Teo agreed. "And very rude to me and my friends—"

WHAT! one gasped.

NO! squawked the other, stomping her foot.

To Son of Quetzal?!

Teo nodded, trying to keep his expression solemn. "I was wondering if you wouldn't mind giving them a rude wake-up for me?"

For Son of Quetzal! one announced. Into the air they shot.

"What are they doing?" Xio asked, confused.

But his question was quickly answered.

FOR SON OF QUETZAL! they sang in unison before all three dive-bombed Ocelo.

Ocelo woke with such a violent jerk, they toppled off the couch entirely, disappearing from sight. Teo, Niya, and Xio burst into laughter as they watched the helpful toucans take turns going after Ocelo.

Bad cat!

That's our boy!

Ocelo's startled yelps cut through the air, making Niya double over with laughter while Xio had to grip the railing to keep his giggles from toppling him.

Silly cat doesn't even have claws! a toucan said.

With surprising speed, Ocelo leapt to their feet, a snarl contorting their face. They threw out their hand and sharp claws unsheathed like switchblades.

CLAWS!

The toucans tumbled midair to avoid Ocelo's swipe and took off back to shore. Safe and sound, Teo's new friends hopped up and down on a branch.

We avenged you, Son of Quetzal!

Teo waved his thanks, still laughing too hard to shout back.

Ocelo rubbed their head, bleary-eyed and confused as they looked around.

"*Hurry!*" Xio hissed. All three ran down the side of the boat and out of sight before Ocelo could spot them.

"That was *amazing*!" Niya laughed once the coast was clear. "I'm so jealous, all I can do is make stupid weapons!"

"I guess being a lowly Jade isn't all bad," said Teo, unable to keep the grin off his face.

"Next time you should see if they'll poop on his head." Xio grinned, his small shoulders shaking with laughter.

Niya grabbed Xio by the arms and shook him, practically lifting him off his feet. "OH MY GODS, YES!"

Teo smiled, his tension from the morning finally fading away.

As they got closer to El Valle, the scenery shifted. The dense trees faded to rolling hills and grassy plains. The valley was circled by the mountains in the far-off distance and Teo was pretty sure he could see a large lake farther north that connected to the river through a series of canals. On the outskirts of town, there were wide open spaces and the occasional grass-roofed ranch, but the closer they got to Fauna's temple, the more urban it became.

All too soon, they were instructed to change into their uniforms. This time, Teo let his wings be free. They kept ruffling and shaking themselves as they lined up, betraying his escalating anxiety. When it was finally time to leave, Luna led the way. As soon as they stepped out onto the dock, the waiting crowd roared with excitement.

They proceeded through the streets of El Valle with full fanfare. They were escorted by the eight Fauna jinetes on horseback. Each rider wore the same matching outfits in white with gold accents—lace trousers embellished with ribbons, elaborate dresses with three layers of ruffles and traditional embroidery in the shapes of different animals. They wore boots, tied belts, hair bows, and sombreros.

Flanking the competitors, the riders performed a carefully crafted choreography while riding sidesaddle on their steeds. The spins and backward steps were perfectly synchronized; it was like watching a ballet on horseback.

Chisme's camera crews were also on scene, snapping pictures and recording video that was displayed on large screens throughout the city for people around Reino del Sol to watch live. Teo did his best to look confident as they walked down the main road, lifting his hand every now and then even though he knew good and well that no one was cheering for him.

Unlike the outer areas of El Valle, the heart of the city resembled any other flashy Gold metropolis he'd seen on TV but with added adjustments made with wildlife in mind. Modern buildings had animal-sized doors and there were feed troughs outside of shops visited by donkeys and cows. Teo marveled at large communal birdhouses that towered over him, several stories high and nearly the same size as the apartment buildings. Dense thickets of trees stood between high-rises, giving workers views of monkeys swinging along outside their windows or jungle cats napping on branches.

Larger roadways had grassy overpasses to allow animals to cross undisturbed. Dispersed between chrome buildings were functional sculptures that provided roosts for slumbering bats. Some of the ground floors were designated dens and burrows with windows where Teo spied a pile of sleeping agoutis. Herds of coatis roamed open parks, disappearing up trees and into the secure houses tucked under branches, while capybaras soaked in a pond.

Xio pointed out a large herd of goats trimming the front lawn of a school and Teo nearly walked right into a hutch on the sidewalk that housed a group of napping rabbits.

"How is it so clean?" Teo wondered aloud. "With all the animals, you'd think everything would stink." Instead, he only smelled dirt, hay, and fresh-cut grass.

"It's a working ecosystem," Xio explained, pointing to a group of people in jumpsuits who were hosing down a sidewalk and carting some bins. "They collect animal waste to compost and turn into manure which gets exported to cities like Maizelan where they have a lot of agriculture."

They continued their procession through the city until they found themselves at the arena. Teo's footing faltered.

It was completely different from the first trial. Unlike the elaborate mountain Tierra had constructed, this arena was almost barren. It was flat dirt with large rocks of varying shapes and sizes. In the center stood a ring of tall jungle trees, densely packed together, side by side.

As they approached the platform where their parents waited, a deep growl sounded from the trees. The canopies trembled with the rustling of leaves as birds fled into the air.

Teo shivered. "What kind of trial is this?"

A pleased grin curled Niya's lips. "Sounds like a monster brawl to me."

Dead weight dropped into the pit of Teo's stomach as Luna ushered them forward. When Teo saw his mom, standing with her hands clasped anxiously in front of her and a strained smile on her face, the back of his throat burned. He jogged the last few steps and threw himself against her, wrapping his arms tight around his towering mother.

Her surprised laugh tickled his ear. "What a lovely hello."

For a moment, Teo didn't say anything but pressed his face into the crook of her arm. He squeezed his eyes shut, trying to push out the roar of the crowd to pretend, just for a second, that they were back home in their own temple.

"Pajarito?" His mother's delicate fingers pushed through his hair.

The small touch and his nickname made his heart ache. Teo reached back, catching her soft feathers between his fingers. "Mom?"

Quetzal's black eyes searched his face. "Are you all right?" she asked.

"I found out about . . ." He swallowed hard. "Xio was showing me and Niya some footage from the past trials because we wanted to see what other Jades had competed and . . ." Teo faltered, unable to find the right words.

His mother's face pinched as she braced herself, like she could tell what was coming.

Teo took a deep breath. "Paloma."

Quetzal let out a long breath. "Paloma," she repeated with such love in her voice it made Teo's chest ache. Her eyes glistened as her lips pulled into a soft smile. "It's been so long since I've heard her name..."

"What was she like?" Teo asked, desperate to know more about her. The world around him shrank down to nothing but him and his mom. The cheering of the crowd, the press of bodies around them, the sound of his friends talking nearby—all of it faded away as he watched his mother recall a lifetime of moments with his sister.

"She was like you, Pajarito," Quetzal said at last, a sad little chuckle caught in her throat. "A troublemaker. She was brave, too, and feisty. Always giving the priests plenty of grief..."

Teo imagined his own childhood. Had Paloma had her own Huemac? Had she been friends with the mortal residents of Quetzlan, too? Did they have the same bedroom back at the temple?

"She gave the trials her all." Quetzal's tone took on an edge. "And she was strong. She—"

Teo reacted on instinct, pulling his mother down into a hug before the break in her voice turned into full-on tears. Though his mother was a Diosa, looming larger than life, in that moment *Teo* felt like the bigger one, like his mother was a small, delicate thing he needed to protect. "I'm sorry, Mom. You don't have to talk about it if you don't want..."

"For so long, I was afraid," Quetzal continued, the words tearing out of her with a ferocity Teo had never heard. "To have another child, to love someone that much, only for them to..." She pulled away, taking Teo's face in her hands.

"I won't let it happen again," Teo vowed. It was a big promise to make, but he meant every word. He wouldn't let his mother lose another child, not to the trials.

"That day, I wished so hard I could have taken her place." Quetzal's eyes cleared, coming back into the present. She gazed down at him, and for a split second, Teo thought she might start preening his feathers and his hair, the same way she'd done when he was small.

But instead, she took a deep breath and stepped away. "It's time for you to line up," she said, forcing a smile. "I love you. Good luck."

Teo turned to face Luna, avoiding the stands because he knew he'd find no supporters there. Next to Luna stood Fantasma.

The small goddess had been waiting for him to catch her eye, and when he did, she smiled shyly and waved. At least he had one friendly face there to cheer him on.

Luna stood in the middle of the platform, Mariachi on her left and Fantasma on her right. Standing by was Diosa Fauna. She was dressed in a simple long-sleeved dress and had an angular face with high cheekbones. She had the large, entirely dark brown eyes of a capybara and long chestnut brown horse hair that cascaded down her shoulders. Her nose was pointy and blush pink. Her most striking feature, of course, was her large deer antlers on which a lace mantle was draped. It gave Teo a headache just imagining what it'd be like to balance those huge things on his head 24/7.

Teo was confused to see that the Estaciones were also present. The goddesses of the seasons—Verano, Otoño, and Invierno—looked perfectly pleased with themselves, basking in the attention of the cameras as they stood side by side in dresses adorned with flowers befitting their titles. The only one missing was Primavera, who stood dutifully next to Xochi.

"Semidioses," Luna began, voice amplified for the spectators in the stands. "For your second trial, you must retrieve a baby alebrije from a nest."

Low murmuring spread through the crowd. Teo's heartbeat raced. Most of the alebrijes had intricate patterns, but some of the strange hybrid animals were so fluorescent, they practically glowed. It was impossible to tell by looking at them if the bright colors were harmless or a warning sign of having venomous skin, fire breath, or even electric barbs.

"To obtain your alebrije," Luna continued, "you must get past the mother."

Luna nodded to the Estaciones. In a coordinated motion, Diosas Primavera, Verano, Otoño, and Invierno twisted their hands. The tall trees in the arena shuddered and then shrank down until they were little more than spindly saplings, revealing what was inside.

A nest made of dried foliage and moss-covered logs was in the center of the arena. Among the dull leaves and sticks, Teo spied tiny colorful dots that must have been their targets. He wasn't sure how they could look so small when their mother was so big.

Pacing back and forth in front of the nest was what looked like a jaguar the size of a box truck. Her fur was black and her spots were kaleidoscopic colors that shifted and changed as she moved. She had a long iguana tail with acid green spines and large, leathery bat wings the color of wine. Large, yellowing fangs that must've been the size of Teo's forearms protruded from her open maw as she stalked back and forth.

"Aw, Ocelo," Niya deadpanned, "you didn't tell us your mom was coming."

"*Jealous,*" Ocelo shot back.

Teo was going to pass out. Or barf. Or maybe both at the same time.

The other semidioses surveyed their new challenge with varying degrees of interest, but Xio was the only one with enough sense to look terrified. Auristela was already whispering to Aurelio, Marino's face was screwed up like he was running math problems in his head, and Dezi appeared far too confident. And then there was Niya, who looked like she'd just been given an early birthday present.

"You have ten minutes to safely bring an alebrije back to the finish,"

Luna announced. With that, Mariachi trumpeted his cornet and Teo's watch vibrated, initiating the trial.

Teo jogged across the bridge with Xio and Niya at his side, watching warily as the other semidioses sprinted headfirst into danger.

"We need a strategy," he said, idly noting how much easier it was to run without his lungs straining against a binder. "There's no way we can take that alebrije down."

"I can!" Niya shot back, offended.

"I know *you* can, I'm talking about *us*!" he said, gesturing to himself and Xio. "Teamwork, remember?"

"Oh yeah." Niya laughed. "I forgot."

Up ahead, Auristela and Aurelio met the mother alebrije at the end of the bridge. With a flick of his flint-tipped gloves, fire ignited in Aurelio's hands. Auristela took the lead, lobbing fireballs at the alebrije's paws. The mother roared as they tried to push her back, dodging her claws and snapping teeth.

"What if I brought back the mom instead?" Niya asked as they reached the island.

Aurelio and Auristela threw up a trembling wall of fire, keeping the mother alebrije corralled and allowing them—and the rest of the competitors—to get onto the island.

"Diosa Luna said a *baby* alebrije," Xio said, keeping as much distance between himself and the fire as he could without falling into the water.

Niya made a disgruntled noise at the back of her throat.

As if on cue, the alebrije leapt into the air and over the fire, claws extended and ready to fight.

"Watch it!" Teo caught the back of Xio's and Niya's shirts, dragging them down just as Ocelo lobbed a boulder at the hybrid jaguar. But she leapt out of the way and quickly pounced on them in retaliation, pinning Ocelo to the ground with her massive paws.

Ocelo transformed, their snarl turning into an actual growl as their muscles grew and fangs elongated. They gripped each of the alebrije's fangs in their fists. Ocelo's brute strength was the only thing keeping her from sinking her teeth into the flesh of their shoulder.

Niya, Xio, and Teo had to sprint forward to avoid getting squashed as Ocelo and the alebrije wrestled for dominance.

"You still want her now?" Xio asked, winded and puffing as they ran.

All three ducked under the huge iguana tail as it slashed through the air.

"Yeah, okay, I see your point!" Niya conceded.

"We just need to get to the nest and back to the platform," Teo reminded them as they ran. "How hard can it be?"

As it turned out, very.

Aurelio and Auristela had already made it to the nest while the others were closing in. The two of them split off, running to the opposite sides of the nest. When she was nearly in reach, Auristela pulled a wild move in which she jumped and swept her leg through the air, shooting an arc of fire from her foot directly at the nest.

It was one of the most needlessly extra things Teo had ever seen. He didn't realize it was possible to loathe her more, but Auristela always managed to be full of surprises.

Her fire sent the little alebrijes running to the other side of the nest where Aurelio was waiting. He snatched up a very angry bright blue gecko alebrije by its tail. Teo heard its tiny, angry growls as it thrashed and spat fire at Aurelio.

Meanwhile, a fluorescent green coati with the armor of an armadillo had rolled up into a ball, quivering like a frightened soccer ball. Auristela scooped it up and tucked it under her arm. Without so much as a pause, the twins turned back to the bridge.

And that was when things really started to go south. Unattended, the fire Auristela had flung at the nest spread. Some of the alebrijes scrambled out, fleeing in a panicked frenzy. A black-and-green jaguarundi anaconda that was basically a slinky with claws slashed at Ocelo's ankles. An orange jackrabbit roadrunner chased circles around anyone who tried to reach for it, causing Atzi and Xochi to collide right into each other.

Panic gripped Teo's spine, urging him to run faster. To hell with getting an alebrije first, he just wanted to make sure they weren't going to be roasted. As Teo ran toward the nest, he spotted Auristela heading for the bridge, with Aurelio right behind her. In the split second they passed, Auristela's eyes locked on to his.

Her lips quirked into a smirk, and before she was gone, one ember eye winked closed.

Teo simmered with anger. His goal flickered out of focus. All he wanted now was to take them down a notch. He threw his body sideways, flinging his wing downward in an attempt to take out Aurelio at the shins.

But the golden boy of Reino del Sol leapt straight in the air like it was nothing. Teo cursed under his breath, but before he could try anything else, the ground shuddered, knocking both of them off-balance.

The jaguar had abandoned Ocelo and returned to her nest. The tiny alebrijes screeched and wailed from inside. Hackles raised, she crouched and tried to swat at the flames. Singed fur stung Teo's nose as she let out a pained yowl.

Teo's heart lodged in his throat, snapping him out of his rage. To his surprise, Aurelio was still there.

Aurelio's copper brown eyes widened, the gecko still swinging from his hand.

"Relio, hurry!" Auristela shouted.

Aurelio's weight shifted, like he meant to chase after his sister, but his feet stayed planted.

He looked worriedly at Teo. "I—" He cut himself off.

Anger boiled Teo's blood. Aurelio just *stood there*, not willing to give up his chance at victory. Teo refused to stand by. Brain buzzing with adrenaline, he ran toward the fire and did the first thing he could think of.

Shoulders back and chest open, he extended his wings and used all his strength to flap his wings in an attempt to put out the fire. Unfortunately, the extra oxygen only stoked the embers, breathing new life into the flames. With a *whoosh*, a wall of heat grazed Teo's face. He threw his arms up and squeezed his eyes shut, waiting for the blaze to devour him.

But it didn't.

When he opened his eyes, Aurelio stood in front of him, arms held out and fingers splayed. Flames licked his arms and along his neck, trying to get to Teo, but Aurelio didn't let it. He held back the wall of fire and with a large heave, shoved it back.

But there was no one to protect the jaguar. The mother alebrije let out a deep, guttural cry.

"*No!*" The word came out strangled as Teo stood there, fear rooting him to the spot.

Suddenly, inexplicably, Marino was next to them. He made a sweeping, pulling motion with his arms and a large wave splashed across the nest, extinguishing the flames and knocking Teo right off his feet. He scrambled, frantically trying to stop himself from being pulled into the water at the edge of the arena, when a large hand grabbed him and pulled him out of the current.

"Sorry about that—you good?"

Teo blinked the water out of his eyes to see it was Marino. He managed to nod and the taller boy smiled. "Good." With that, he ran back into the action.

The charred nest dripped and the alebrije mother was drenched but seemingly unharmed as she snuffled in the remains. All but one baby had fled the flames and into the forest. A bright blue-and-green toucanet with a snake tail popped its head up and looked around. It squawked up at its mom, its chameleon eyes spinning in independent directions.

Relief crashed over Teo upon seeing the alebrije was unharmed.

"Holy shit!" Niya stood on the other side of the nest, gaping at Teo. "Are you okay?!"

"I think so," Teo said, patting himself down, chest heaving. "I think Marino just saved me from getting knocked out of the arena." But why? Weren't they enemies?

When he looked for Aurelio, all he saw was his retreating back, pausing only to pick up the gecko again before tearing off after his sister across the bridge.

With the fire out, the jaguar tore off after the twins.

"Did you see how big that wave was?" Niya asked, grinning ear to ear. "That was *wild*!"

"Focus, Niya!" Teo snapped. The three of them needed to find alebrijes that wouldn't horribly maim them.

The toucanet! But he'd been distracted too long. When he looked back, the alibrije mother was alone, staring at him coolly.

Their options for finishing this trial were quickly dwindling. "Where's Xio?"

Niya jerked her head to where Xio was crouched against a boulder, curled up in a ball with his arms over his head.

Something small and absolutely *pissed* shot through the air, angrily chirping. It wasn't until Teo ran closer that he realized it was a small mouse with the beak and wings of a hummingbird relentlessly dive-bombing Xio.

When he got to Xio, Teo threw one of his wings over him, causing the hummingbird mouse to prick him with his sharp beak. "*Ouch!* You had to try to pick the smallest, angriest one to go after?" Teo demanded as he attempted to shoo the tiny alebrije away.

"I wasn't trying to!" Xio huffed, peeking out from under Teo's wing to scowl.

"Smallest and angriest." Niya chuckled. "Just like Xio!"

"There's no time for jokes, Niya!" Teo barked.

Niya shook her head at herself. "Right—there's no *time*, Niya!" she repeated.

Two sharp bursts from Mariachi's cornet. *Buzz, buzz. Buzz, buzz.* Auristela and Aurelio had returned to the platform with their alebrijes.

"Both of you grab an alebrije before all the easy ones get picked!" Teo shouted and they split up.

It was pure chaos. Teo lunged after the jackrabbit roadrunner, but Ocelo beat him to it. When they picked it up by the scruff of its neck, the alebrije rapidly kicked Ocelo in the face until they dropped it and it bounded away.

Teo barely managed to jump out of the way as Marino slid across the ground, having been knocked on his ass by a wily teal goat with butterfly wings. It bounded and kicked, its tiny wings, fluttering with all their might but too small to lift it more than a few inches into the air.

Without Aurelio and Auristela, the mother alebrije's attention had zeroed in on Atzi. Sweat on her brow, Atzi threw as many bolts of lightning at the jaguar as quickly as she could, but even Teo could see that they were getting smaller and weaker. Probably from all the effort she was putting into dodging gnashing teeth and swiping claws.

Off to the side, Dezi squared off with a scrawny green rooster with the long horns of a bull. The rooster scratched at the ground with his taloned feet before letting out a mighty crow.

"*Kikiriki!*" It lowered its head and ran at Dezi.

For some reason, Dezi didn't seem at all worried. In fact, he grinned as the angry bird charged. Teo wanted to call out and warn him, but that was, of course, useless. Quick on his feet, Dezi sidestepped the rooster just in time and touched his fingers to its back, like they were playing a game of tag.

Instantly, the rooster skidded to a stop, kicking up a cloud of dust. It turned to face Dezi, cocking its head as it considered him for a moment before letting out a confused cluck. Dezi held out his hand and, much to Teo's astonishment, the rooster walked right up to him. With zero retaliation, Dezi scooped up the rooster and tucked it carefully under his arm. The once-angry creature contentedly murmured as Dezi raced with it back toward the bridge.

"Freaking Dezi," Niya grumbled.

"How the hell did he do that?" Teo asked, bewildered.

"He's the son of Amor," Niya said, like that explained everything. "Every child of Amor can manipulate affection," she added when Teo gave her a lost look. "Dezi's specialization is 'addictive contentment'—if he touches you, he can make it so you feel *so good* being near him, you never want to leave. Some folks at school say he can make it so strong that you'll, like, die 'cause you can't bear to live without him, but that's pretty dramatic, if you ask me."

Suddenly, Huemac's warning not to get near Dezi made much more sense, but right now there were more important things to worry about. Niya gasped and Teo spun around to find a scarlet red alebrije with the body of a javelina and the head of a rhinoceros beetle digging its tiny hooves into the dirt.

"Holy shit, look at that thing!" Teo yelped, backing out of its way.

"He's beautiful!" Niya beamed. When it lowered its head and charged, Niya raced forward. "Dibs!"

Teo gladly let her have it. The teal goat with butterfly wings bounded across Teo's path, but when he tried to grab it, it kicked out its tiny hooves, ready to take out his shins. In a flash, vines suddenly ensnared the creature, knocking it on its side and tying its legs together. Xochi tugged the vines back and caught the alebrije's bound legs like it was a purse.

She gave Teo a smug grin before running back toward the bridge, the alebrije bleating angrily in her arms.

"You know, it'd be a lot easier to hate her if she wasn't so hot," Niya huffed.

"You say that," Teo panted, "about everyone."

"It's not my fault we're all *really hot*, Teo!"

Another semidiós with an alebrije wasn't a good thing, but as the jaguar raced to intercept Xochi, Teo thought at least it would buy them some more time.

"We need to hurry!" Teo called to his friends. Frantically, he looked around for an alebrije.

"Squonk!"

The strange noise made Teo jump. The tiny toucanet alebrije stood at his feet. It cocked its head to the side, peering up at Teo with strange, googly chameleon eyes. When Teo only blinked in response—surprised and also very confused—it impatiently made the same sound again. It was much more of a honk than any bird call he'd heard before.

Teo hesitated for a moment, unsure if this was some sort of trick, before kneeling down.

"Squonk, squonk!" The toucanet bounced on its tiny feet, wings flapping and snake tail swishing before it waddled up to Teo.

He extended his hand to the strange little creature, but then a terrible, piercing yowl rang out. Xio had stepped on the tail of a midnight blue kitten with a neon yellow turtle shell. It hissed and spat, batting at Xio's leg while the hummingbird mouse continued to dive-bomb him.

"I didn't mean to!" Xio cried. But the damage was already done.

Swooping down on its massive wings, the mother alebrije landed in front of them. A roar echoed from her gaping maw. Teo grabbed Xio and jumped into the air, using every bit of strength he had in his wings to get them out of the way. They barely cleared the jaguar as she barreled through. They landed hard on the ground, a sprawled tangle of limbs.

Niya threw herself between them and the mom and conjured up a large steel shield. "Stay behind me!" she shouted as the silver bangle on her wrist melted and re-formed into a spiked club in her fist.

The jaguar snarled, its large head lowered as it stalked toward them. Teo knew she was strong, but he didn't think even Niya could take on an angry mother alebrije.

In the distance, the cornet sounded Xochi's safe return. *Buzz, buzz.*

That was when Teo noticed the small ball of bright green and blue between the jaguar's two front legs.

It was the toucanet, waddling after Teo and squawking insistently.

"What's it doing?" Niya asked.

Teo shook his head. "I have *no* idea."

"Ask it!"

"I can't ask it! It's not a bird, it's an alebrije!" Teo shot back.

The trumpet of the cornet cut through the air as his watch vibrated again.

Teo thought back to Dezi. How the rooster had willingly gone with him. How he hadn't used any violence or brute force.

Now that he thought of it, the mother had gone after every other semidiós who'd taken one of her brood, but he couldn't remember her chasing after Dezi. An idea struck Teo with a jolt. It was a very bad, impossibly dangerous idea that would maybe get him killed, but if he didn't try *something*, all three of them were dead anyway.

"What are you doing?" Niya hissed as Teo stepped out from behind her shield.

"This is either gonna help us a little, or hurt me a lot," he murmured as he slowly moved closer. His heart rammed painfully against his ribs.

The jaguar's black lips pulled back from her teeth as she let out a low growl. Teo's knees shook violently. Every fiber of his being screamed at him to turn and run, but he refused.

Instead, he focused on the toucanet and kneeled. His breaths shook in his lungs as he slowly, *slowly*, extended his hand.

The big alebrije paused. Her teeth were less than a foot from his neck, hot breath washing over his skin, but she didn't attack.

The tiny toucanet hobbled out from under its mother and climbed right into Teo's palm. It tipped its head back and let out a terrible warbling sound that made Teo wince, but it bounced happily in hand before scaling his arm.

The jaguar watched as the toucanet hopped onto Teo's shoulder. When he glanced back, Teo realized the toucanet's vibrant feathers matched his almost perfectly.

The small bird nestled into Teo's scapular feathers where his wing met his shoulder and squawked its ugly little song again. It clicked its banana-shaped beak, which was pretty cute until it started happily plucking Teo's feathers. He cursed under his breath, but if it made the little alebrije happy, then so be it.

But Teo wasn't going to count his chickens before they hatched.

The mother considered Teo, her golden eyes bearing into his for what felt like forever. But then she huffed, the puff of air from her nostrils ruffling Teo's hair.

A familiar yowling cut through the air. Atzi was struggling to get a hold on the turtle cat, carrying it by the scruff of the neck as it slashed its paws through the air.

The jaguar's pupils dilated and she left Teo to chase after Atzi. Teo staggered, the relief dizzying. Finally, he had an alebrije, and a willing one at that. Niya and Xio gaped at him.

"Damn, when did you get bigger balls than me?" Niya asked before breaking into delighted laughter.

Xio continued to stare, so shocked that he didn't even swat at the hummingbird mouse that continued to attack him. But now was not the time for celebrating. The trial wasn't over.

As a reminder, the cornet trumpeted again as Marino crossed the finish. *Buzz, buzz.*

"We gotta go!" Teo urged. "*Now!*"

"Well what the heck are we supposed to do?!" Niya said, throwing her arms into the air. "We're not alebrije whisperers like you and Dezi!"

"Then just be *fast*, while the mom is still distracted!" Teo said. "Give me your jacket!" he told Xio, growing impatient as the younger boy struggled to pull it off over his head.

As the hummingbird mouse swooped in for another attack, Teo used the jacket to catch it out of the air. It chirped angrily and flitted around, stabbing its sharp beak into the material.

"Take this, and be careful!" Teo said, pushing the bundle into Xio's arms.

Maybe they couldn't coax the alebrijes into submission, but they could at least be more careful with them.

Catching on, Niya used her bangles to form what looked like a large metal mixing bowl and used it to scoop up the beetle-headed rhinoceros javelina. It bucked and thrashed and tried to get out, but its hooves slid uselessly against the tall, smooth edges.

Atzi and Ocelo were left. Ocelo grabbed the jaguarundi anaconda and like an angry fire hose, it wrapped itself around their arms and gnawed relentlessly on their shoulder, drawing smudges of golden blood as they started to run for the bridge.

In order to stay out of the bottom of the rankings, the three of them needed to get back before the others.

"Let's go!" Teo shouted, and he ran for the bridge, Xio and Niya on either side.

They got to the bridge first, but Teo could hear Ocelo's heavy footfalls right behind them.

Ocelo was strong, but the three of them were faster. They crossed the bridge, made it back to the platform and dove across the finish barrier—Teo, Niya, and then Xio.

Three short trumpets burst from Mariachi's cornet, and Teo's watch shook in time with them.

But before Ocelo could cross, the cornet trilled. *Buzzzz.*

Ocelo slammed into the barrier and bounced right off, sending them flying back.

Time was up. The trial was over.

CHAPTER 14

Disheveled and exhausted, the semidioses gathered with their parents on the platform in the order in which they had finished. After congratulating him on a job well done, Teo's mother was entirely distracted by his new friend.

"What a sweet little thing," Quetzal cooed, gently scratching the back of the alebrije's neck as it sat on Teo's shoulder.

In return, it made soft and happy *mrrr*-ing sounds in Teo's ears, its chameleon eyes closing in contentment. But Teo was distracted. Back on the island, the mother alebrije paced at the bridge. Some of the other dioses guarded it, making sure she didn't cross. She let out a low moan and guilt churned Teo's stomach.

"Please present your alebrijes," Luna instructed.

Diosa Lumbre stood between her son and daughter, stoic and cool as always, but her features softened the slightest bit, nearly impossible to catch, as Auristela presented her alebrije. The poor coati armadillo was still rolled up in a tight purple ball and trembling as it was presented to Luna and the crowd. Auristela grinned smugly, basking in the fact that she had completed the trial first.

Meanwhile, Aurelio's camera-ready smile was missing. His face was taut with concentration as he attempted to wrangle his alebrije. The blue gecko growled angrily and kept running across his hands. Aurelio struggled to not drop it. When the gecko spat fire, Aurelio hissed, jerking his hand back.

Good, that was what he got for being an ass.

But Teo's vindication didn't last long when he saw the way Diosa Lumbre's burning eyes slid to her son. Teo looked for the slightest bit of warmth in her expression as she gazed down at her golden boy, but found only coldness. Teo couldn't imagine anything that would impress, excite, or please her. It actually made him feel sorry for Aurelio.

Dezi proudly held his green rooster in his arms and it nuzzled him, staring up at him with an expression as close to "adoring" as a bird's face could get. Xochi's goat was still tied up but had been placated by the bundle of vines Xochi fed him. Marino nearly dropped the orange jackrabbit roadrunner as it kicked furiously. Niya's rhinoceros beetle javelina was still pissed and letting everyone know from inside the makeshift bowl.

Teo was happy Niya had finished, but he was even more relieved that he and Xio had managed not to be last. He was feeling pretty good when it was the younger boy's turn to present his alebrije.

Carefully, Xio unfolded his jacket.

The first hint that something was wrong was that there was no angry chirping. Xio frowned as he carefully opened the jacket, checked the sleeves and then the pockets. Finally, Xio carefully shook it out, but there was no trace of the hummingbird mouse.

Teo's heart dropped into his stomach.

"Where's the alebrije, mijo?" Mala Suerte asked, his voice uncharacteristically soft but his dark eyes sharp with urgency.

Xio shook his head. "I don't know." His cheeks turned splotchy red as he looked up at his dad.

Mala Suerte took the jacket and desperately checked all the folds of the material again.

"It must've escaped while we were running back," Xio said miserably.

The empty jacket fell to the ground. Xio's chin dipped, his mass of curls hiding his face. Mala Suerte wrapped his arm around his son's shoulder, pulling him close to his side. The dios didn't say anything and the look on his face silently warned others to keep quiet as well.

Teo hung his head, feeling horrible. It was *his* idea to catch the alebrije in the jacket. He should've come up with something better. He wanted to give Xio his toucan instead, but he knew Diosa Luna—and more important, Sol—wouldn't allow it.

Because of him, Xio was bound to get a low rank.

"Teo," Quetzal said, gently giving his arm a squeeze.

Everyone was watching and waiting for him.

Swallowing the lump in his throat, he carefully scooped the baby toucanet in his hand and held it out for Luna to see. It purred and affectionately nipped at his thumb with its large beak.

Luna nodded and moved down the line.

Teo kept his head down, shoulders hunched up to his ears.

While Ocelo had caught an alebrije, they hadn't gotten back in time. Atzi—looking haggard and worse for wear—was entirely empty-handed.

Luna took a moment to reflect before she announced, "Sol has determined the rankings." She gestured toward the stone slate. The gold and jade glyphs took an unbearably slow moment to rearrange themselves.

Teo held his breath.

Niya screamed and punched the air before grabbing her dad and lifting him off his feet. His arms pinwheeled as she hopped up and down, squeezing him tight. Teo was thrilled for her and wanted to celebrate, but he was distracted trying to make sense of the rankings as hushed whispers broke out among the spectators in the stands.

Auristela was *seething*. Even though Niya had finished way later, she'd somehow been ranked first. Marino had also jumped up in the rankings, right under Aurelio.

Perhaps the wildest of all was that Teo had come in *fifth*.

"What the fuck," Teo said under his breath as his mom gave him a tight hug. Even Xio had gone up—not by much, but at least neither of them was in last. He turned to Xio who looked just as stunned as he felt. "What the *fuck*?"

Xio shook his head, like he couldn't believe it, either.

He glanced around, trying to gauge the others' reactions. Surprisingly, Aurelio didn't look upset. Instead, it was like he was studying the rankings, trying to figure out the puzzle that everyone was so confused by.

Auristela's anger was snuffed out by Ocelo's barely contained rage. They were breathing so loud that Teo thought they were going to completely lose their shit, but apparently Ocelo had learned their lesson from last time. Or maybe Diose Guerrero was talking Ocelo down, speaking quietly into their ear.

Sensing the confusion, Luna addressed the group. "Now is a good time to remind you all that rankings aren't determined simply by the order in which you complete the trials," she said with a calm smile as Verdad and Chisme led a very happy Niya over to the reporters. "They update based on *Sol's evaluation* of how you perform throughout the competition."

Relief, joy, and frustration all warred inside Teo. How was he supposed to game the system if there weren't any clear-cut rules?

"You may release your alebrijes," Diosa Luna instructed.

The colorful animals scampered back across the bridge to their mother. When Dezi put his bull-horned rooster down, it shook itself out, like it had just woken up, and scurried away fast. Teo's little toucanet had fallen asleep in his palm, beak nestled under its wing and snake tail curled around it like a cat.

"You gotta go back," Teo said, nudging it with his thumb. "You can't stay with me."

The toucanet just turned away from him and curled up again. It was pretty cute, but Teo had his hands full taking care of himself. He was not qualified to be responsible for a baby alebrije.

From the island, the mother called again, a low-pitched moan.

The toucanet poked its head up and looked to where its family waited, then up at Teo again.

"Go on, then."

The alebrije let out another tiny squawk before clumsily flying back to its mother.

"What a sweet creature," Diosa Quetzal said with a smile, the feathers of her hair glistening in the afternoon sun. "I think he might enjoy Quetzlan. What do you think?" she asked Teo, smoothing her hand down his wings in a gesture that made Teo's tense shoulders relax.

"Maybe." Teo shrugged, giving her a hug before he fell into line behind Luna, making the trek back to the boat.

He didn't want to think about home right now. Not when there was still a chance he'd never see it again.

Niya rejoined them as they headed back to the boat. "I can't believe I came in first!" she squealed, bouncing as they walked. She grabbed Teo's shoulders and shook him. "And you came in fifth! *Fifth!*" she emphasized. "You beat out *four* Golds, Teo!"

"I know!" Teo laughed and shook his head. It was true. He didn't know how, but he had. Suddenly, their plan to beat all the other Golds didn't seem so far-fetched. "Holy shit, we might actually be able to pull this off!"

Xio, however, was dead silent, refusing to look up from his feet as they walked.

"Hey, it'll be okay!" Teo said, giving his shoulder a squeeze.

"Yeah, that was just one bit of bad luck!" Niya added.

"We've still got three more trials to get through," Teo told him. "There's plenty of time to get you higher in the ranks."

"Yeah," Xio mumbled, his eyes hidden behind his dark curls. "I guess."

Teo and Niya exchanged worried looks. It was true, they *did* have time, but not much. It was almost like the universe was hell-bent on Xio messing up. They had prevented him from being last so far, but how long would the three of them be enough to keep that up?

"I think we all need a good meal," Teo said.

"And a shower," Niya added. "I definitely reek."

"We could—"

"Hey, rejects!"

All three stopped and turned to see Auristela quickly coming up behind them, chin lifted and fists at her sides.

Niya groaned.

"What do you want?" Teo snapped, moving to put himself between Xio and Auristela's scorching glare. He was not in the mood to deal with her on top of everything else. "Don't you have some baby animals to torment or something?"

"Let me give you some advice for surviving the trials," she said, coming to a stop before them. Auristela's eyes burned into Teo's. "First, watch the way you talk to me."

Teo scoffed but she continued without pause.

"And second, stay out of me and Aurelio's way."

"How is that going to help me survive the trials?" Teo shot back.

Auristela took a step closer. It took everything in Teo to not instinctively step back. When she spoke again, her voice was low, deadly, and even.

"Fuck around and find out, Bird Boy."

With that, she pushed her way between Teo and Niya and strode confidently to where Aurelio was waiting for her at the exit from the arena.

Xio gulped. "That was terrifying."

"Hate to admit it, but yeah," Teo agreed, exhaling.

Niya stared after Auristela, a pained look on her face. "Why does someone so hot have to be so mean?"

After dinner, the Golds were a lot less braggy and sure of themselves. Instead, they spoke quietly to one another, any joke met with a half-hearted smile. The reality of the situation—that this wasn't all fun and games—finally seemed to be setting in. Two of their own were currently in the bottom ranks, and while Teo enjoyed seeing them sweat, it was still too close for comfort.

Xio was silent the rest of the night, head down and only responding in hums and single-syllable words. Teo and Niya tried talking him into hanging out and gorging on candy, but Xio said he wanted to be alone and went to bed early. Niya wanted to force Xio to spend time with them, but Teo held her back. The least he could do was to make sure Xio had his space.

In the middle of theorizing what the next trial could be, Niya fell asleep at the foot of Teo's bed, surrounded by candy wrappers. Sleep didn't come to Teo so readily. He was exhausted but restless. Instead of disturbing Niya, Teo changed into gym clothes and left her gently snoring in his room.

He needed something to distract himself, so he figured the training room would fit the bill.

As luck would have it, someone else had the same idea. When he pushed through the door, Teo came to an abrupt stop.

Aurelio was already there, lying on a bench and pressing weights that were probably five times heavier than Teo. He let the door shut with a loud clatter behind him.

Aurelio set the bar on the rack and glanced up, catching Teo's reflection in the mirror. He dropped his hands and straddled the bench, looking at Teo expectantly as sweat dripped down the side of his face.

Teo pointedly turned away and marched toward—

Crap, what was he going to do? What did he even know *how* to do?

A black boxing bag hung in the corner of the room. Boxing didn't sound that hard and it seemed unlikely to result in self-injury. Teo closed his hands into fists and started punching the bag like he'd seen people on TV do. He threw a punch, checking to see how much the bag moved. It hardly budged. It didn't help that Aurelio was staring at him the whole time.

He shot Aurelio a glare from over his shoulder. "What?" he demanded, bracing himself for hostility. He was not in the mood to be made fun of. Teo threw another few punches that just barely nudged the bag.

"You're doing it wrong." Aurelio stood and, with one hand, pulled the bottom hem of his shirt upward to wipe his brow. The gesture was quick, but it was enough to expose almost all of Aurelio's torso, the peaks and valleys of muscle beneath warm brown skin. When Aurelio's hand fell from his face, Teo made sure he was looking away.

Teo scowled. What the *fuck*. Aurelio looked like an ad for a high-end sportswear company.

"That's not how you use a heavy bag," Aurelio repeated. He spoke calmly and evenly, leveling Teo a vaguely annoyed look.

"It's a bag full of sand, and you punch it," Teo said, pulling back his right arm. "I think I can manage."

"You're supposed to wear gloves or wrap your hands," Aurelio explained like he was giving a lesson, but Teo wasn't interested.

He rolled his eyes and threw his right fist into the bag as hard as he could.

Pain exploded down his thumb.

"Son of a—!"

"And never tuck in your thumb," Aurelio added.

Teo hissed between his teeth and shook out his throbbing hand.

Aurelio sighed and crossed the room. "I tried to tell you—"

"You think you're *sooo* great, huh?" Teo spun to face Aurelio, stopping him dead in his tracks. "Golden Boy Aurelio, son of Diosa Lumbre," he said, feigning awe as he wiggled his fingers.

Aurelio's posture went rigid, eyebrows bunching. Aurelio was way closer than Teo had expected. He took a moment to recalibrate in the face of all that *skin*, sweaty and right there and smelling faintly of campfire smoke and cinnamon.

Teo shook his head to clear it and puffed up his chest, refusing to let himself feel small. "I bet I could take you one-on-one."

Aurelio exhaled, a short snort, like he couldn't tell if Teo was being serious or not.

"Come on," Teo coaxed, raising his fists in what he hoped looked like a boxing stance as he bounced back and forth on the balls of his feet. "I may not be a Gold, but I *am* scrappy."

Aurelio gave him a withering look. "You'd rather fight me than let me help you?"

"Yup," Teo confirmed, popping the *P*.

Was he stronger than Aurelio? No. Was he a good fighter? Also no.

But was he still gonna irritate Aurelio into a fight anyway? Absolutely.

Teo flashed a sarcastic smile. "I bet you'd love to get your hands on me."

Aurelio only hummed in response.

"Let's go, Golden Boy, I—" Teo didn't get to finish his sentence.

In a flash, Aurelio swept his legs out from under him—the same move Teo had tried to pull on him during the second trial. Teo landed hard on his back, knocking the wind out of him. His wings did very little to cushion the blow and ached under the force of his weight. Teo let out a groan as he struggled to get back on his feet.

"That looked like it hurt," Aurelio said, extending his hand to help Teo up.

"That's because it *did* hurt," Teo shot back, knocking Aurelio's hand out of the way as he scrambled to stand up on his own. "Do you ever take those stupid things off?" Teo said, motioning to the gold bands locked around Aurelio's forearms.

Aurelio stood straighter. "No."

Teo winced as he reached back to rub his very sore wings. "That committed to the aesthetic, huh?" A strangled yelp shot out of Teo's throat as he was knocked down again.

Aurelio had dropped onto one knee, the material of Teo's shirt bunched in his fists as he pinned Teo's shoulders to the ground. Teo grappled for the armbands. The gold was cool against his fingers, but heat radiated from Aurelio's skin.

Teo's chest heaved up and down, breath audible. Aurelio wasn't even winded. His russet brown eyes stared down at Teo, a hint of a smile hidden behind them.

Teo pressed his lips together, his pulse thudding in his neck.

Just as quickly as he'd knocked Teo down, Aurelio got back on his feet. "You're not very good at this," he said, frowning down at Teo where he laid sprawled out on the mat.

"I'm just warming up!" Teo scrambled back to his feet. "Luring you into a false sense of security!"

Aurelio sighed. "Do you have to make *everything* into a competition?"

Teo let out a sharp laugh. "Look who's talking! I can't tell if this is your strange way of trying to be helpful, or if you're just a douche. The haircut doesn't help," he added.

Aurelio jerked back like Teo had struck him. "This is the traditional warrior knot that Heroes of Diosa Lumbre have worn for *centuries*—"

"It's literally a man bun, my guy."

Teo had never seen Aurelio look so disgruntled. It was incredibly gratifying.

"Did I hit a soft spot? Are you mad?" Teo tipped his head to the side and stuck his bottom lip out. "You look mad."

Aurelio huffed. "Shut up."

Teo grinned. "*Make me.*"

In a flash, Teo was thrown backward off his feet once again. But this time, when he hit the floor, he let out a pained cry. "*Agh!*"

Poor, unsuspecting Aurelio rushed forward, reaching down to help him up. "Are you—?"

Teo grabbed Aurelio's arm as he bent down, using the momentum to tug him off-balance. Using all this strength, he flipped Aurelio over and pinned him onto his back.

Aurelio sucked in a breath, surprise etched into his features.

Teo smirked triumphantly down at him. "Told you I was scrappy."

Aurelio swallowed hard before asking, "Scrappy enough to get through the trials?"

For a second, he'd been able to pretend that they were kids again. That they were still friends. That Aurelio wasn't basically a stranger to him now.

That they weren't in the trials.

Teo's heart sank.

He pushed away from Aurelio and got back on his feet. "You Golds are really obsessed with becoming Sunbearer, huh?" he said gruffly, stretching out his wings before folding them against his back again. He frowned at Aurelio as the other boy slowly got back up to his feet.

"I mean, seems pretty stupid to me—blindly following orders, putting yourself in danger just because your mom told you to."

Aurelio's expression shuttered. It was a subtle shift in his posture, one that Teo couldn't name if he had to, but Aurelio was back to performing. "Sol chose us for a reason," he said. "I would gladly give my own life to maintain peace and prosperity in Reino del Sol."

"Really? That's funny," Teo challenged, taking a step forward. He heard the venom in his own voice. "That's not how I remember the last Sunbearer ceremony."

The muscles in Aurelio's shoulders tightened.

Teo clenched his hands into fists at his sides. "I still remember how scared you were."

When they were seven, Teo and Aurelio had watched the Sunbearer Trials together. Huemac had volunteered to look after them, which mostly meant managing Teo's mischief. He hadn't understood what the trials were, not really, but he knew they meant playing tag with Aurelio far away in the stands where his mom had sent them, and Huemac bribing them with candied pecans if they could just sit still for five minutes.

When they were paying attention, both he and Aurelio thought the trials were cool and exciting. The competitors seemed so big, strong, and grown-up. Nowhere else could they see so many semidioses flexing all their powers at once. It was awe-inspiring, seeing what Teo thought he would become when he got older.

But when the trials were finished and it was time for the Sunbearer ceremony, Teo's mom kept him away. As they stood around the Sol Stone, waiting for the ceremony to be completed, Quetzal circled her wings around Teo like a cocoon.

When it ended, Teo wanted to find Aurelio so they could go play on the steps of the temple, but his mom held steadfast to his hand.

Confused, Teo looked around.

Brave Niya stood stick-straight, eyes wide and lips pressed into a tight line. Her tiny fist was balled up in her dad's pant leg, holding on for dear life as he led her back into the temple.

When Teo spotted Aurelio, he was crying uncontrollably, empty hands rubbing his eyes as tears spilled down his cheeks. Teo tried to go to Aurelio and ask what was wrong, but Diosa Lumbre flicked her wrist dismissively and a priestess ushered Aurelio away—just a small boy in a circle of towering priests in black robes.

Teo didn't understand. He tried to look back at the altar, to see what had happened, but his mom's huge wings blocked his view, gently sweeping him toward the temple with promises of Pan Dulce's hot chocolate before bed.

It was strange to see the same boy before him now. Someone Teo had known for so long, who meant *so much* to him then but was a complete stranger today. Familiar but unrecognizable. Their friendship was now the ghost of a memory that left nothing but a dull ache in his chest.

"So, what changed between then and now?" Teo asked.

The delicate skin around Aurelio's flinty eyes bunched in a pained stare. His shoulders lifted in a defeated shrug. "Everything."

Looking back, *that* had been the beginning of the end. It was the first glimpse of the future that was awaiting them. They went their separate ways for good when Aurelio started the Academy—he had become untouchable and Teo had become, well, just Teo.

And now they were here, trapped in the trials together.

"I was only a child back then," Aurelio tried to explain. "I didn't understand the importance of the trials."

Teo rolled his eyes.

"It's an honor to win or lose—"

"It's an honor to let yourself get *murdered*?" Teo heard himself shout, his fists trembling at his sides.

"It's an honor to die in order to keep my people *safe*," Aurelio shot back.

Teo recoiled a step. He'd never actually heard Aurelio raise his voice in anger before. The back of Teo's throat burned and his eyes stung traitorously. It'd been so easy to keep it together during the trials and in the face of Ocelo and Auristela, but now Teo felt himself crumbling.

Aurelio closed his eyes and took a slow, deep breath. "I'm just trying to help you," he said slowly, evenly.

Teo shook his head. "Why?"

Aurelio gave him a tired look. "Because it's not a fair fight."

Teo remembered what he'd said the other night—how Jades shouldn't compete in the trials. Aurelio didn't want an easy win. He wanted Teo to up his game, to even the playing field.

"A fair fight," Teo repeated, thoughtful. As much as he didn't want Aurelio's pity, Teo also knew that his friends were relying on him. He'd promised to look after Xio and keep him from the bottom of the ranks, and so far he'd done a real shitty job of it.

"Okay," he said after a moment.

"Okay?" Aurelio said it like he thought it was another one of Teo's pranks.

"Okay," he repeated, lifting his chin. "Just don't cry when suddenly I'm kicking your ass in the trials."

A surprised laugh jumped in Aurelio's chest, a small, relieved sound. "Come on," he said, waving him back toward the heavy bag. "I'll show you how to throw a punch without breaking your thumb."

"Oh, he's got jokes now!" Teo grinned, falling into step next to Aurelio. "Here I thought they made you hand over your personality when you started at the Academy."

Aurelio rolled his eyes, but the hint of a smile tugged at the corner of his lips. "Don't make me embarrass you again."

CHAPTER 15

The two of them trained late into the night and early the next morning. Teo was even more sore than yesterday, but Aurelio's encouragement made him feel energized and ready for the next trial. Instead of dragging his feet in the shower, Teo was up and ready before Xio and Niya.

"You're in a good mood," Xio said, watching him from across the table. The younger boy had deep purple bags under his dark eyes. Teo wondered how much sleep he'd gotten in the last three days. Not much, by the looks of it.

A pang of guilt twinged in Teo's chest. He flattened his smile out between his teeth. "I guess so," he said with a casual shrug.

Niya jolted. "Why? Did I miss out on something fun last night?" she demanded, voice raising through a mouth full of rice, eggs, beans, and potatoes.

"You didn't!" Teo reassured her before she got too worked up. "I was just practicing with my wings and stuff."

Niya choked, sending bits of food shooting from her mouth. "You were *what*?!" she choked out. "You, Teo, were *working out*?"

Teo leveled her with a flat expression. "Niya."

"Did someone force you against your will?!"

"You're not funny!"

She shrugged. "Xio's laughing."

Teo took the drag in order to keep her from asking more questions.

Aurelio was still their competition and he didn't want Xio and Niya to think he was a traitor.

He waited until Xio went back to poking at his plate of food with a fork and Niya was off on a tangent about the dream she had last night to steal a glance down the table at Aurelio. Auristela had her elbow on the table and chin propped in her hand as she spoke to her brother. Aurelio listened, head bobbing in agreement to whatever scheme she was probably plotting for the next trial. His gaze shifted past her shoulder, catching Teo's eye.

Teo held his breath, but the glance was fleeting. Which was fine, really. It wasn't like Teo expected their secret training session would change anything. Even if he wasn't completely awful, Aurelio was different now—as was Teo—and one night wasn't going to change that, no matter how much he wished it had.

They each had their own agenda—Teo would use Aurelio's advice to perform better in the trials so he could help himself and Xio. And he was only doing it to help satiate whatever moral reasoning he needed to feel like his success in the trials was earned.

It wasn't a big deal. Teo wouldn't let himself read into it; it was just a way to help him get ahead.

Another city meant another outfit change. They had been invited to tour the alebrije sanctuary, one of the many El Valle was famous for, before going to Fauna's temple for dinner. All ten competitors were given simple brown suits and chaquetillas. Teo's had been altered to allow his wings through, which he did willingly. The trousers had auburn silhouettes of all kinds of animals running down the sides in suede fretwork. The only pop of color was the Quetzal glyph embroidered onto Teo's lapel.

Even though he felt incredibly fancy dressed up in such a fine suit, it was *far* from Teo's favorite look. With the heavy fabric, silk mono tie, and sombrero, it was absolutely sweltering.

"I think I'm going to sweat to death," Teo complained as they lined up in the common room. He could already hear the crowd of people cheering their arrival.

"I think mine's too big," Xio said, pushing his sombrero off his forehead only for it to slip back down over his eyebrows again.

"How does anyone get anything done in these?" Niya growled, tugging at her clothes like some feral cat. "The ladies need to *breathe*!"

"Which ladies?" Teo asked, looking back at her as he tried to loosen his tie.

"These!" Niya flexed her biceps. The muscles strained against the fabric of the jacket. "The tiddies aren't doing great, either, though," she said, glancing down at her chest. "I can't tell you how much underboob sweat I've got right now."

The other Golds weren't faring much better. Xochi was struggling to find a way to incorporate flowers into her outfit, and Ocelo's hat was too small for his big head. Aurelio's sleeves wouldn't fit over his golden armbands so he had them unbuttoned and rolled up to his elbows, which looked ridiculous, if you asked Teo. He figured that after spending most of their time in their spandex Academy uniforms, these jocks felt overwhelmingly restricted in suits.

The only ones who looked unbothered were Auristela (whose suit fit like a glove) and Dezi (but he'd look perfect in a paper bag). In front, Auristela waved enthusiastically, gaining a fresh wave of cheers as they walked out onto the dock. Halfway down the ramp, Niya kicked off her boots and proceeded barefoot.

People paused to cheer and wave to the competitors as they walked the main road through the city. Luna led them around a traffic jam that had been caused by a large steer standing in the middle of the street, contentedly chewing on a mouthful of hay. The commuters didn't seem particularly bothered. They waited patiently in their cars and followed the instructions of Fauna priests redirecting the vehicles so as not to disturb the beast.

Teo saw animal companions *everywhere*, which made him deeply homesick. His chest ached watching a girl cross the street with a cat riding in her backpack, and again when they passed a panadería where a man and a sloth shared a muffin.

The alebrije sanctuary was massive. Fauna priests led them around the campus on a tour. They showed the semidioses the veterinary clinic where injured and sick alebrijes were tended to with state-of-the-art technology.

A priest was explaining in a monotone the various diets they provided for the different alebrijes in the kitchens when Teo's attention wandered out the wide windows. Outside, there was a fenced-in area. Much like the spa in La Cumbre, the sanctuary thus far had been emptied of visitors for their private tour. But here, there were *actual* people.

Not priests in robes, but parents, teens, and loads of kids. Just normal people.

"What's that?" Teo asked, interrupting the priest midsentence.

"That's our petting zoo," he said, the annoyance clear in his voice. "One of the many ways we raise money for the sanctuary. People can pay to come feed alebrijes that wouldn't be able to survive alone in the wild. It's a very popular field trip destination."

Teo smiled. "Awesome, let's check it out!"

"W-wait!" the priest called after him. "You're not—"

But Teo didn't listen. He pushed through the doors and out into the sunlight, Xio and Niya following without question. This looked way more fun than listening to the boring old tour guide. "Can we feed the alebrijes?" Teo asked a priestess at the entrance to the small yard.

When she turned and saw Teo, her eyes went wide, quickly darting among the three of them. "Oh!" She blinked rapidly. "You—you want to?"

"If we can?" Teo asked, exchanging confused looks with Xio. He didn't understand the startled look on her face.

"They're so cute!" Niya lamented, her fingers hooked into the fencing.

This caught the attention of the people inside. When they saw the trio, kids and adults alike shared the same surprised look.

"Oh, I mean, I can try to clear everyone out," the priestess said hurriedly, motioning to a couple other priests standing by for their help.

"You don't have to make them leave," Teo told her with an uncertain laugh.

This seemed to fluster the woman even more. "Are—are you sure?"

"I mean, we're not contagious." He laughed. "And Niya might not be able to wait," he added, gesturing to Niya, whose fingers were shoved through the chain-link fence, reaching desperately for a maroon porcupine with an ostrich neck.

The priestess still looked worried. "All of you?" she asked, looking past his shoulder.

The other competitors had joined them outside, awkwardly lingering. Teo had never seen the Golds look so unsure of themselves.

"Looks like it."

The priestess flushed and she and her helpers tripped over themselves to hand each of them a paper cup packed with nutrient-rich pellets. Niya charged in first, followed by Teo and Xio. The adult chaperones and kids gawked at the sudden appearances of the semidioses. Niya didn't seem to notice as she ran around trying to get the colorful alebrijes to accept her love. A few kids giggled uncontrollably.

Teo fed pieces of food from his palm to a rainbow-colored llama with bat wings while Xio stood nearby.

"What are they waiting for?"

Teo looked to where he pointed. The rest of the Golds stood along the back fence, looking around. Teo shook his head. "I have no idea."

"Are they afraid of the alebrijes?" Xio wondered as the llama munched happily.

"No, that doesn't make sense . . ." They'd had no problem going after the alebrijes during the trial, so what was different now? That was when Teo realized their wary glances weren't directed at the alebrijes, but the adults and children standing nearby. A surprised laugh bucked in his chest.

"Have you guys *ever* interacted with mortals before?" Teo asked as he walked back over to the group.

They exchanged concerned looks. Marino's mouth opened.

"Who *weren't* priests," Teo specified.

His mouth closed.

"We literally save mortals every day," Auristela snapped, trying to maintain her haughty demeanor, but Teo could see through the cracks of her facade.

"Sure, but have you ever actually *talked* to one?" Teo pressed.

Auristela rolled her eyes and turned away.

Teo laughed and shook his head. "They're not gonna bite!" To prove his point, he walked over to a group of kids who were fawning over a small donkey with green fur and frog eyes.

Slowly, everyone seemed to loosen up. The alebrijes didn't care who they were. Dezi and Marino were the first to step away from the fence and the animals came swarming for their cups of food. A bright pink flying squirrel with the head of an axolotl took quickly to Dezi, and when an overly enthusiastic pig with yellow-and-green scales bowled over Marino, some of the parents rushed to help him up.

It wasn't long before the kids got brave enough to come up and start asking the semidioses hundreds of questions. A little boy and girl complimented Atzi's braids and the flowers in Xochi's hair. The latter got so flattered she immediately grew some orchids right there in the tanbark to give out.

Everyone got into it, talking with the kids and even pulling off full conversations with the parents. Only Auristela and Ocelo refused to participate, instead deciding to get frutas con chile from the small snack stand. Teo grabbed their pellet cups from where they'd abandoned them on the fence and told some of the kids to gather up. He walked down the line, placing some food on their heads and shoulders so a group of flying alebrijes immediately swarmed them. The kids dissolved into fits of laughter as the alebrijes' feathers tickled their cheeks.

When a little boy, startled by an aggressive monkey cat, dropped his pellets and began to cry, Aurelio hesitantly approached and offered him his cup. Teo couldn't help smiling, and his stomach—the betrayer it was—did a little flip.

"I love them so much!" Niya whined, practically melting into a gooey puddle as one of the priests showed the group some rainbow-colored baby rabbit doves that had just hatched. "How did you get a pet alebrije?"

"Oh, they're not pets!" the priest explained. "Lots of alebrijes wander into the southern cities from Los Restos. Usually we scoop them up and release them again, but a few get hurt and need to be rehabilitated, like these four."

"So you take care of them?" Teo asked.

He nodded. "Just until they're strong enough to go home."

"I want to take care of alebrijes when I grow up!" a little boy announced as he gently petted one of the tiny balls of fur.

"I want to be a Sunbearer!" a girl with curly hair said, beaming up at

Niya. A knot twisted in Teo's stomach. He thought of his conversation with Aurelio.

Auristela whispered something behind her hand to her brother and Ocelo, snickering cruelly at the silly little mortal girl.

But Niya returned her smile. "Me too!"

After thanking the workers at the sanctuary and saying bye to their new friends—alebrije and mortal alike—it was finally time to head to Fauna Temple, which Teo at first mistook for a tall hill in the middle of the city. Instead of stone or steel with sharp edges, the walls of Fauna's temple were covered in moss and grass. Massive trees grew around the structure, their thick, twisted branches providing support and homes for more wildlife. As they approached, Teo realized animals of all shapes and varieties were carved into every bit of wood.

Instead of the iconic stone steps that led to the observatories of most temples, Fauna's was a grassy, sloped ramp. At the top, the El Valle Sun Stone beamed into the orange-painted sunset sky.

They cut through the main courtyard, a series of wood-and-rope foot bridges suspended over water where manatees crunched on whole heads of lettuce fed to them by priests.

"Mind your step," Luna warned as they entered the ground floor, where they found animals roaming the halls freely. Birds nested in wooden houses along the walls, but Teo had to keep his eyes on the ground because tiny mice and dwarf porcupines scurried across the stone floors, a skunk waddling after them in an attempt to keep up.

They started up a set of stairs. Each floor they passed was devoted to a different ecosystem or climate. There was even an entire level containing a full-on aquarium.

"How do they not eat each other?" Niya asked as they walked through a jungle level where spider monkeys chased one another around a dozing ocelot.

"Fauna," Xio said, as if that explained everything.

When Niya and Teo gave him a blank look, he grinned.

"She's a calming presence for animals, so when they're in her temple, they're super chill and relaxed."

Niya turned to Teo. "Do you feel super chill and relaxed?"

Teo scowled. "I'm not an animal!"

"Well, technically—" Xio began, but Teo didn't let him finish.

"I'm not a *bird*," he specified. "I've got wings, yes, but the rest of me is one hundred percent human!"

"You're also half a god, though," Xio pointed out.

"So, you're, like, twenty-five percent human, twenty-five percent bird, and twenty-five percent bird god," Niya said, counting off on her fingers.

"That's only seventy-five percent," Xio told her.

"She's terrible at math," Teo whispered.

"*Teo!*" Niya stomped her foot. "You know that's what I'm sensitive about!"

Laughter shook Teo's voice when he tried to apologize. "I'm sorry!"

She sharply turned away from him, one of her braids flicking his cheek. "And twenty-five percent dumbass, how's that!"

Teo and Xio chased after Niya, singing her praises to get back on her good side. By the time they made it to their destination, she'd gotten over it.

The dining hall in the El Valle temple was smaller than La Cumbre's, but no less grand. The walls were lined with golden statues of animals, from a tiny mouse on a pedestal to a huge crocodile. The heavy wooden table in the center of the room was carved from a single tree, its many rings showing the centuries it had taken for a tree to grow to that size.

Fauna priests dressed in soft, wheat-colored robes stood in two lines, waiting to assist. Two women Teo didn't recognize stood by the head of the table, flanking the goddess herself.

"Welcome, competitors." Fauna greeted them in a soft voice. It was so soothing that Teo found the tension in his shoulders and wings melting away until he was standing there and smiling at her like a weirdo, but he couldn't help himself.

"Thank you for having us, Diosa," Luna said.

Fauna smiled back. "My daughters, Catalina and Alejandra, are equally pleased to meet you all as well." She gestured to the young women at her sides.

Catalina nodded in greeting. She wore a suit that was nearly identical to the ones they'd been outfitted with. Judging by the way she held herself, with her hands clasped behind her back, Teo got the vibe that she was pretty serious, which was in stark contrast to her sister.

Alejandra was shorter and far less severe. She wore a lumpy fur coat, which seemed weird considering the heat. There were bits of dried grass, twigs, and tufts of lint stuck in the fur and her tangled hair. Her smile was bright and beaming as she waved enthusiastically at them.

Niya was the only one to wave back.

"Please, have a seat," Fauna said. "I'm sure you're all tired and hungry."

"Do you know those semidiosas?" Teo whispered to Xio as they took their seats.

"Catalina is one of the most decorated active semidioses in Reino del Sol. She's the captain of the all-femme horse riders, Fauna jinetes, who escorted us to the trial," Xio explained. "They do search-and-rescue missions in places with difficult terrain like the mountains or desert, and they also respond to any emergency situations where animals are involved, like stampedes or if something dangerous wanders into a city."

"What about Alejandra?" Niya asked, nodding to where she sat across the table.

Xio shrugged and shook his head. "Never heard of her . . ."

"So is Fauna, like, your grandma?" Niya asked Teo.

He gave her a confused look. "What?"

"I mean, she's the diosa of animals, right?" Niya reasoned as Fauna priests brought out food on large platters. "And your mom is the diosa of birds—"

"You're thinking of it like a family structure," Xio interrupted. "It's more like a corporate ladder."

"My mom reports to Fauna," Teo agreed. "We're not related."

But he was still distracted by Alejandra. Maybe it was a trick of the light, but Teo could've sworn he saw something in her coat move. When a plate of rolls was set on the table, Alejandra picked one up and tore off pieces before placing them in her upturned palm.

That time, Teo *definitely* saw something under her coat move.

"What the—?"

Three small, fluorescent-colored creatures ran out of her sleeve.

Auristela, who was sitting next to Alejandra, gasped and jerked away, bumping into Aurelio and spilling the glass of water he'd been about to drink.

"*What are those?!*" Auristela shrieked. Aurelio made a disgruntled face and started carefully soaking up the water in his lap with a napkin.

"Oh, they're just my friends!" Alejandra said, smiling down at the tiny creatures like she didn't notice Auristela freaking out.

In Alejandra's hand, a neon purple axolotl with crab claws tore the roll into tinier pieces, while a bright blue ringtail cat pocket gopher nibbled on their share, and a chartreuse gecko millipede with several tiny suction-cup feet gummed a hunk of bread.

Teo grinned. "We met a bunch at the sanctuary," he said, leaning as far forward as he could to get a better look.

Auristela grabbed her brother's arm, forcing him to switch seats with her.

"*Ale*," Catalina chided while Fauna and Luna were deep in conversation at the end of the table, "do you have to let them on the table?"

"Don't worry, they're completely harmless," Alejandra said, ignoring her sister.

The gecko millipede waddled over to Aurelio with its many feet. It stared up at him and wiggled its tiny body, tail whipping while it made a strange croaking sound.

"Pepe likes you!" Alejandra told him.

Teo watched as Aurelio hesitantly reached out. Immediately, the alebrije—Pepe—flopped onto his back, exposing a lemon yellow belly. Aurelio tickled him with his pointer finger and Pepe squirmed and gurgled happily.

Aurelio chuckled, a warm sound from deep in his chest—a rare and fleeting phenomena that Teo hadn't witnessed in years.

"That's Gigi and that's Lala," Alejandra said as she pointed to the ringtail cat pocket gopher and then the crab axolotl. But then she frowned. "Where's Mauricio?"

Upon hearing his name, a tiny bright pink rabbit stuck its head out of Alejandra's sleeve, blinking sleepily.

"There he is!" Alejandra smiled.

Mauricio crawled out onto the table. A pink rabbit was shocking enough, but that did nothing to prepare Teo for the sets of long flamingo legs that followed.

A laugh jumped in Teo's throat. He clamped his hand over his mouth. "Oh my *gods*."

Standing on his thin little legs, Mauricio wobbled a bit. Xio held out a piece of bread and the alebrije's nose went wild, suddenly very awake as he took the offer and nibbled away.

"I help out at the sanctuary most days," Alejandra explained. "If there are smaller ones who need more one-on-one attention, I usually take them home and help socialize them before they're ready to join the other alebrijes who can't be returned to the wild."

"Did they teach you that at the Academy?" Teo asked, trying to picture it.

Alejandra laughed. "Oh no, I flunked out a couple of years in," she said. "Being a Hero wasn't for me, so I went to veterinarian school instead and took a liking to alebrijes."

Teo nodded and tried not to look annoyed. Apparently some Golds went to the Academy when they didn't even *want* to, but it still refused Jades.

Fauna priests brought out the main courses, careful not to disturb Mauricio, who had fallen asleep standing with one of his legs tucked under him.

"Whoa," Niya said as spiced, cooked meats appeared with hearty vegetables. "I figured everything would be vegan!" she added, loud enough that it gained Fauna's attention.

"We care for and respect animals here," Fauna said. "Including their sacrifices. We honor animals by making use of every part of them, in our clothes, our textiles, our food. Our winter coats are made of fur and insulated with feathers. We even use dried dung to fuel our fires."

"Doesn't that stink up the temple?" Atzi asked, too bewildered to censor herself.

Fauna smiled. "We specifically use herbivores, so it only smells like burning grass."

Atzi looked *very* impressed.

Meanwhile, Teo saw Auristela mouth the word, "*Ew.*"

"The outfits we gave you are made with the same principles," Fauna went on, gesturing to Dezi as Luna translated for him. "They're sewn together with needles made from bones and sinew used as thread. The buttons are made from antlers, the belts are rawhide, and your shoes are tanned leather. Even the sombreros are made from horse and rabbit hair."

"This has *got* to be the most sustainable city in Reino del Sol," Xochi said as she marveled at the stitching on her hat.

"Easily," Fauna said with a grin. It was obvious she took great pride in it. "We don't want any creature's sacrifice to go to waste, whether it is food, clothing, decorations, or tools." Her large eyes shifted to Teo. "Even your hollow bones, Teo, would make beautiful flutes."

Teo balked as everyone turned to look at him.

"Do you have hollow bones?" Marino asked in awe.

"Uh—I mean—yeah—" Teo stammered.

"Is that why you're so light and easy to throw around?!" Niya demanded.

"No, you're just freakishly strong," he told her.

"You're practically an alebrije yourself!" Alejandra pointed out.

Niya gripped the table, as if seeing Teo in a brand-new light. "Oh my *gods*."

"She's right!" Xio gasped.

Teo's mouth froze and his stomach churned as the whole table exploded with questions.

"Were you hatched from an egg?" Atzi asked excitedly.

"Do you perch?" Xochi wondered aloud.

"Yeah, like, if I put a stick against the bottom of your foot, would you just—" Marino made a gripping gesture with his hands.

"Do you eat *bugs*?" Ocelo asked with a snort.

Teo's face burned red. "*No!*"

Dezi signed something to Marino, who shook his head and signed something back, which somehow felt worse than knowing what they were actually saying.

Alejandra leaned across the table and tried to whisper, but everyone was listening and paying close attention. "Do you have a cloaca?"

"WHAT?!"

Catalina sighed and pinched the bridge of her nose. "Too far, *again*, Ale."

Teo leapt up from his seat, his wings knocking his chair over. "Excuse me," he murmured before bolting for the door. His heart rammed in his chest, humiliation coursing through his veins. Once in the hallway, Teo slumped onto a couch sitting against a wall and put his face in his hands. Why was it that just because his body was different from everyone else's, they thought they could ask whatever inappropriate questions they wanted?

"You guys went too far!" he heard Niya declare from the dining hall.

The doors flew open and Niya stomped into the corridor. When she spotted Teo, she plopped down next to him.

"You okay?" she asked, lightly nudging his shoulder.

"I guess," he grumbled before letting his hands drop to his lap.

"I didn't mean to embarrass you," she said, guiltily tugging on one of her braids.

"I know you didn't." Teo took a deep breath and exhaled through his nose. "I'm just tired of feeling like a freak of nature compared to everyone else."

"I'm sorry."

"I know." Teo leaned back and tried to give her a smile. "Thanks for apologizing."

Niya curled up and tucked her legs under her. "Hey, Teo?"

"Hm?"

She leaned her cheek against the back of the couch and stared up at him. "What's a cloaca?"

Teo shoved her off the couch.

Back on the boat, Teo had changed and was digging around in the bag of candy—which was mostly wrappers now—when there was a light knock on his door.

"Hey, Teo?" Xio poked his head in. "Can I ask you something?"

Teo angrily chucked a pillow onto the floor. "I don't have a cloaca!" he barked.

Xio blinked. "Uh, not that."

"Oh." Teo relaxed. "Sorry, I'm just—" He shook his head clear. "What's up?"

Xio stepped into his room and closed the door behind him. He was already in his pajamas—an oversize long-sleeve shirt and sleep shorts—and his tangled mess of curls made Teo wonder if he'd gotten out of bed to come talk to him.

"I was just wondering…" Xio twisted his sleeves around his fingers, not looking Teo in the eye as he inched closer.

Teo tipped his head curiously. Xio was acting even more cagey and uncomfortable than usual, which was saying something.

"SO YOU'RE, LIKE, TRANS AND STUFF," Xio suddenly blurted out, his cheeks bright red.

Oooh. This was going to be a Talk. An amused grin tugged his lips. Teo plopped himself down on his bed. "What questions you got for me?"

Xio's shoulders slumped; he looked relieved but still unsure. "What's that like—being on T?"

"Uh, mostly sweaty and a little smelly," he said, which earned him a laugh. It was a very broad question, but Teo tried to come up with something useful. The last thing he wanted to do was scare Xio off. "It's good, I guess? I didn't figure out my gender stuff until I was fifteen. My quinces and gender confirmation ceremony happened in the same week—"

"I remember," Xio said quickly. He cleared his throat. "That was kind of a big deal for me," he confessed, trying to sound casual. "Kinda helped me work up the nerve to have mine last year."

Teo had never been so flattered in his life. "I also remember," he bounced back.

When a semidiose discovered their gender didn't align with the one they were raised as, their gender confirmation ceremony was celebrated like any birthday. The ceremonies were even a bigger deal than quinces because it was such an important acknowledgement and celebration for the community.

"I don't know, it's like ..." When Xio spoke, the words were directed at his feet; he was unable to meet Teo's gaze. "It's like seeing you helped me understand something about myself, I guess. I've kind of always felt like I wasn't entirely myself, but couldn't figure out why, you know?" He cut Teo a nervous glance.

"I absolutely know." Teo had spent so many years feeling confused and lost, like he was wearing his shoes on the wrong feet, but constantly and with a lot more emotional breakdowns. "I started taking testosterone a few months after my ceremony," Teo guessed, trying to piece together the timeline. "I had to work up the nerve because I was so freaked out by needles," he confessed. "But now it's, like, nothing."

"And you got top surgery."

Teo nodded. "Last year."

"And that felt ... right?"

"Holy shit, it was like night and day." Teo laughed. He could still feel the relief of seeing himself flat-chested. "The clothes I wanted to wear finally looked right and *felt* right," he said. "The only downside was that my wings didn't transition along with the rest of me. So, while I didn't have to wear a chest binder anymore, I had to wear one to hide my wings because seeing them made me feel so ..." He searched for the right word.

"Dysphoric?" Xio guessed.

"Exactly. But now they're perfect and I can't stop staring at them," Teo said, fondly catching his reflection in the mirror across the room. "I don't know why they took so long, but transitioning is never one clean and clear shift, you know? It doesn't happen overnight." Teo shrugged. "It's just as much mental as it is physical, I guess. Puberty was a *bitch*," he added.

"*Seriously!*" Xio finally approached the bed and sat next to Teo. "It changed *everything*," he said, face pinched like he was in physical pain.

"You mean when you got your period?" Teo guessed.

"Yeah," Xio said, rubbing the back of his neck. He looked like he hadn't had a good night's rest in two years. "It showed me pretty much everything I hate most about myself. It was a really tough time for me."

"My period went away a few months after I started T," Teo said, trying to be helpful.

"I'm not on T," Xio said, toying with his bracelet again.

"Blockers?" Teo guessed.

He shook his head.

Maybe he was being shortsighted. "Do you want to be?"

Xio nodded vehemently, sending his curls bouncing.

"Then why aren't you?"

"My dad is ... weird with medical stuff."

Teo frowned. Something wasn't adding up. Transitioning genders was common and completely natural. Teo had never heard of someone being against, and especially not a god. "But you had your gender confirmation ceremony."

"He doesn't have anything against it!" Xio rushed to clarify. "It's really doctors he doesn't trust. I guess bringing bad luck into a hospital is kind of a bad idea."

"I guess ..." It still didn't sit right.

"I feel like there's still parts of me people can't see or understand," Xio explained. "I've never felt like I belong or fit in anywhere, and not just because I'm … a Jade. I'm still not sure who I am …"

Teo racked his brain, trying to figure out what that meant. "Oh! Do you mean maybe you're, like, agender or bigender or nonbinary or something?"

Xio lifted his shoulders in a weak shrug. "Something like that."

"Would you like it if I used they/them pronouns for you?" Teo suggested. Maybe that would help.

"I'm not sure yet."

"You know, not fitting into a gender binary is a totally normal thing," Teo went on. "I mean, Sol, literally our greatest and most powerful god, our damn *creator*, is nonbinary. That's pretty badass, if you ask me," Teo said, giving Xio a playful nudge.

Xio exhaled a small laugh, but Teo could tell he was still bothered.

"Well, it's okay if you haven't figured yourself out yet," he told the younger boy, trying to be reassuring. "You have literally all the time in the world."

Xio's expression fell and Teo's heart sank. Xio thought he was destined to die. Just like the other Jades. Just like Paloma. "Hey, don't—" Teo started, but Xio cut him off.

"Well, thanks for talking to me," Xio said, suddenly getting to his feet. "And letting me, like, be awkward at you." He forced a laugh. "I'm really tired now, though, and we've got a big day tomorrow."

Xio stretched and yawned. It was very obviously fake, but Teo didn't want to push him to talk about something when he wasn't ready. He'd have to just play the long game.

"Okay," he conceded.

"Thank you—and sorry," Xio quickly added. "Anyway, bye—or, good night, I guess." He gave Teo a jerky wave before disappearing out the door.

Teo crawled into bed. He curled onto his side and scoured TúTube for any videos he could find of Paloma. Did she have any friends during the trials? Was she like Xio, lonely and scared? The ache in Teo's chest was dull and all-consuming.

Xio probably thought these trials would cut short his time to figure out who he was. Well, Teo wasn't going to let that happen. The future wasn't decided yet. There were ten competitors in these trials for a reason. It couldn't be true for all of them, but Teo was going to make sure Xio got to go home and have the life he deserved.

CHAPTER 16

"The third trial will be held in the Opal Oasis and hosted by Diose Guerrero," Luna announced the next morning at breakfast.

Ocelo slammed their fists on the table, sending silverware clattering. "YES!"

"*That's not fair!*" Niya mocked in a whiny voice. Ocelo glared at her.

The Opal Oasis was located southeast of El Valle. As they made their way along the water, the terrain on the coast shifted from grassy plains to flat desert. It quickly became too hot to hang out on the deck, so they all moved inside and drank chilled juice in the air-conditioned common room until they entered the shade of a canyon.

The river wove back and forth between steep cliff faces. Here, the water was a bright turquoise blue, brilliant against the red-and-orange-striped rock formations. Slowly, plump cacti and green shrubs popped up along the river until they left the canyon behind and the view opened up, revealing the Opal Oasis.

Now *this* was what Teo expected a Gold city to look like.

It was a massive spot of sprawling green in the middle of the arid desert, built around a freshwater spring fed by aquifers. Bushy palm groves grew between huge buildings made mostly of glass and gold plating. In the setting sun, the city sparkled in shades of blue, green, pink, and orange. It reminded Teo of fire opals, which he supposed was how the war city got its name. The people of the Opal Oasis took great pride in their city. It was common to hear them brag about how only the strongest could survive and thrive in one of the most uninhabitable places on the planet.

The crown jewel of the city was Diose Guerrero's golden temple, sitting on a bank of the aquamarine spring. The sun glimmered against the gold so brilliantly that it hurt Teo's eyes to look at it directly.

The boat had to slow its pace upon approach. Since the city was so isolated, there was constant traffic of ships bringing in cargo through engineered canals that linked the river to a port. Smaller boats carried shipments of imports to the narrow channels that branched off into other parts of the city.

When it was time to walk to the arena, the citizens of Opal Oasis came out to support their semidiose in throngs. Seas of people lined the streets, chanting Ocelo's name as they walked in the procession. Whenever they waved, the cheers swelled to roars. People threw flowers and plush jaguars into the street, which Guerrero priests dressed in red robes gathered and loaded into a cart.

They adored Ocelo, which made absolutely no sense to Teo. He couldn't see how anyone would like the war semidiose, let alone a whole city.

It was hard to see the city through the crowd, but Teo got glimpses of gyms and sports bars. They even passed by a fancy shop that Teo thought was a jewelry store at first until he realized the glass displays held beautifully crafted weapons.

The third arena had been transformed into a tropical forest in the middle of the desert city. Mist hung in the dense tree canopies and even the air smelled thickly of damp soil. Their parents waited for them on a platform. The jumbotron showed Verdad and Chisme in conversation, obviously emceeing the trial but impossible to hear.

The cheers for Ocelo were louder here. A corner of the stands had even constructed a tifo of Ocelo's head, midsnarl. There must've been more than a hundred people acting in unison to hold the banner above their heads.

"Our lands have been peaceful for thousands of years," Luna said when everyone was gathered at the platform. The semidioses took their usual places in front of their godly parents. "But that doesn't mean our people wanted to live without the thrill of battle."

Standing next to her, Diose Guerrero grinned proudly, their fists resting on their hips. Fantasma kept throwing them nervous glances from the corner of her eye.

"In ancient times, cities would invade one another to capture prominent figures—not to kill them, not even for ransom, but simply to prove they could. These were nonviolent and honorable competitions. We re-create the tradition of the Bloodless Battle in today's trial. You'll be competing in pairs. If you're touched by someone on the other team, you're captured and unable to capture anyone else. You'll be marked as captured with the glyph of the semidioses who captured you," she said.

Auristela's face brightened with a sharp smile as she locked eyes with Aurelio, who responded with a small nod. Everyone's heads swiveled to silently search out a teammate and Teo suddenly felt like he was back in school, in need of a partner for biology class.

"The pairs will be decided by Sol," Luna finished, like she had been waiting for them to get their hopes up before swiftly crushing them.

Teo couldn't help smirking at the Golds' disgruntled expressions. Auristela looked especially murderous, but then he realized that this also applied to him.

Shit.

"Semidioses, please step forward and stand in a circle," Luna instructed, waving them on.

Teo's mom pecked a kiss on the top of his head before he moved to join the others. Teo sent a silent prayer to Sol, to take pity on him and pair him up with Xio or Niya. Or, at the very least, not Auristela or Ocelo.

All ten semidioses stood in a circle facing one another, shifting uncomfortably as they waited to see how the pairings would be chosen. Teo looked around, waiting for something to happen, when his eye snagged on Aurelio.

Aurelio gave him a nod—just a small dip of his chin—that sent Teo's stomach tumbling. Murmuring broke out in the crowd, pulling his attention away.

Above Marino's head, like it had been drawn midair, was the golden burning heart of Diosa Amor. Marino grinned across the circle at Dezi, whose dazzling smile gleamed as a matching glyph of Diosa Agua's wave hovered over his own head. The jumbotron displayed their portraits, side by side.

Teo would've been happy with either boy as his own partner, but he held out hope to be paired with one of his friends. Xochi and Atzi were next. Again, he would've preferred them over the alternatives, but it seemed like Sol was taking pity on them and pairing people who got along.

That was, until the next team was selected.

The light of a glyph appearing over Xio's head immediately to his left caught Teo's attention. Hope lifted in his chest. Teo's head jerked up, hoping to see his own glyph, but no such luck. It was the jaguar head of Guerrero.

"That's not fair!" Ocelo's voice boomed.

Across the circle, the jade eye of Mala Suerte illuminated above Ocelo's head.

And they were pissed.

"He's bad luck! He's gonna make me lose!" Ocelo complained.

Instantly, Teo's ears rang. He could see it ripple through the rest of the group as people winced and clamped their jaws shut. Teo pressed his tongue between his teeth as Mala Suerte's barely contained rage thrummed throughout the arena.

Diose Guerrero flicked the back of Ocelo's shaved head and growled a warning under their breath.

"Do you have so little faith in your own skill that you rely on your partner to carry the weight of your team?" Luna said in a cool, even voice.

Ocelo's mouth opened and closed uselessly like a fish's. Niya snorted and Teo used all of his willpower to not react.

"Or are you questioning the will of Sol—again?" Luna added.

Ocelo's mouth snapped shut.

Poor Xio shrank under the attention, shoulders hunching up to his ears, while his dad loomed behind him, looking ready to pull the teeth out of anyone else who dared to say something against his son.

Teo reached over and lightly knocked his knuckles against Xio's arm. "Don't worry—it'll be okay," he murmured, knowing full well that was a lie.

Xio kept his eyes trained on the ground, toying with his bracelet.

Now Teo was worried. Not only for Xio but for himself. Niya, Aurelio, and Auristela were the only options left. Any last hope he had was dashed as Auristela's and Niya's glyphs appeared above each other's heads. Auristela's full lips pressed into a hard line as she looked back and forth between Niya and her brother, high ponytail whipping.

Niya rolled her eyes as she adjusted one of her braids. "Get over yourself," she grumbled under her breath, sounding annoyed but mostly inconvenienced. With Niya and Auristela teamed up, that meant—

Teo's chest clenched.

He didn't need to look up to know what glyph was there, and across from him, the quetzal of Teo's mom glowed above Aurelio.

Sol really couldn't cut him a break, could they?

Aurelio still smiled for the crowd, but in a way that looked like it took effort.

Teo had to hand it to him—Aurelio was good at covering up his emotions. It was a skill Teo knew he severely lacked. He frowned, trying to get a read on Aurelio's reaction, but the boy's entire focus was on Luna, awaiting further instruction.

"Trade you," Niya said under her breath.

As much as he hated to admit it, Aurelio was an incredibly skilled competitor and Teo was definitely . . . not. Teo could feel the impending humiliation. Aurelio might have been willing to help him prepare in training, but that didn't mean he wanted to team up with a Jade.

"This trial is not timed and will end when the last team, or person, is left standing," Luna said, waving them toward the bridge that led to the arena. "It's time to get into position."

"Don't worry," Teo said discreetly to Xio as they fell into line behind Luna. "Niya and I will come find you as quickly as possible."

Niya nodded in agreement.

"Just try your best not to get tagged, okay?"

Xio nodded, but he didn't look reassured. His face was sickly pale and he kept shooting nervous glances at Ocelo, who moodily stomped after Luna like a toddler.

If they could find each other and regroup, they could play defense and outlast the others for as long as possible.

Until then, it was him and Aurelio. Partners.

Each team started at the outer edge of the island, equidistant from one another. There were only about ten feet between the water's edge and the tree line, making it impossible to see where anyone else was.

Standing next to Aurelio, Teo felt ridiculous. While Aurelio was tall and broad with that heroic stoicism, Teo was gangly and messy-haired and severely lacking in valor. He did his best to stand straight and keep his wings neatly folded against his back as Aurelio stood perfectly poised, ready to take off.

"You ready?" Aurelio asked, finally speaking to him for the first time since they were paired up.

"Of course I am," Teo shot back, keeping his eyes on the forest ahead and refusing to look over.

In the distance, Mariachi's cornet sounded and Teo's watch buzzed on his wrist.

Teo and Aurelio ran straight into the trees.

Immediately, Teo was hit with a wall of hot, damp air. It was still and heavy; no breeze managed to break through the dense foliage. It seeped into his skin, prickling sweat across his brow. Taking a breath felt suffocating. With the sun blocked out by the dense canopy overhead, they were plunged into gloomy darkness.

The rain forest was a sea of skinny rubber trees and bushy palms, towering well over a hundred feet tall. The thick, woody vines of lianas draped over everything, threatening to snag Teo if he stepped wrong. Luckily, the lack of light made it impossible for anything to grow on the forest floor other than short xate trees, their large leaves desperately reaching for any bit of sun.

"What's the plan?" Teo asked, his concentration split between keeping his wings folded so they didn't get caught on something and trying to breathe in the heavy, unrelenting heat.

"Divide and conquer?" Aurelio suggested, not even the slightest bit out of breath.

"Does that ever *actually* work?" Teo puffed. Aurelio was already trying to get rid of him.

"Sometimes."

"I mean, this is basically a fancy game of freeze tag."

Aurelio sighed. "I don't know what that means."

"C'mon, Golden Boy, you're the one with the fancy education, shouldn't you have some tips?"

"Don't get tagged."

"Oh, great, thank you, that was incredibly helpful!"

"And don't be so loud or the others will hear you," Aurelio said as they jumped over a fallen log, one much more gracefully than the other.

It was hard to be quiet when he was already panting like a dog. Teo was running as fast as he could, but it was obvious Aurelio was holding back in order to keep pace with him.

"You know, in horror movies, splitting up is what always gets people murdered," Teo pointed out.

"I don't watch movies," Aurelio said plainly.

"You *what*?!" Teo spluttered. His foot caught on a root and he pitched forward.

Luckily, Aurelio caught his upper arm and yanked him back upright, not even breaking his stride. As Teo scrambled to his feet, his gaze slipped toward the other boy, and found the vaguest hint of a smile on his lips.

"What kind torture are they putting you through in that place?" Teo demanded.

"Focus, Bird Brain," Aurelio told him.

Teo rammed his shoulder into him. "Shut up!"

Aurelio didn't even break his stride, but he did grin, which was nice. So nice, in fact, that it took Teo a moment to realize there were voices up ahead.

"I'll go left, you go right," Aurelio said sternly, an overly intense expression back on his face.

"I'll go left, *you* go right," Teo said, not one to take orders from a Gold. He cut across Aurelio's path before the other boy could stop him.

Teo was half convinced Aurelio was trying to ditch him, but it didn't matter. Teo was going to ditch him first to go find Xio. That was his top priority.

He heard heavy footfalls just in time for Ocelo to crash through the trees and launch themself into Teo's path.

With a strangled shout, Teo swept his wings down, propelling himself high enough that Ocelo tackled empty air. Teo landed again as Ocelo tumbled to the ground, crashing into the base of a tree. Undeterred, they got back on their feet.

"Get over here!" they snarled.

"Yikes, hard pass!" Teo said, quickly backing up.

Ocelo charged at him like a bull.

Beating his blue-and-green wings as best he could, Teo launched himself from the ground again. He was off-balance, tipping back and forth as he got higher. His desperately flapping wings crashed into foliage, startling a group of red-eyed tree frogs.

By some miracle of Sol, Teo was able to make it to the lower boughs of the canopy. Or, at least, he collided into a trunk and held on for dear life.

"*Come back down here!*" Ocelo shouted, their face red as they paced back and forth at the base of the tree like an angry jaguar.

"I'm good!" Teo called down, getting a firmer grip. The branches at least seemed strong enough to support his weight.

"*You can't stay up there forever!*"

A laugh bubbled in Teo's throat as he basked in how he'd managed to outsmart Ocelo. "Uh, yeah, I definitely can!"

Taking up the challenge, Ocelo stomped over to the tree. With a grunt, they transformed, muscles bulging.

"What are you gonna do, tear the tree down?" Teo asked, condescension dripping from his voice. Ocelo threw their hands out at their sides, unsheathing their claws. They sank them into the soft bark and very quickly began to scale the trunk.

Teo had forgotten jaguars could climb trees.

Abandoning ship, Teo scrambled down the branch and onto another tree. Luckily, the canopy was so dense with tangled branches that, with the help of his wings, it was relatively easy to leap from bough to bough.

Bark scraped against his palms and leaves snared in his hair as Teo raced from one tree to the next. The dense foliage kept him hidden and soon enough, he'd lost Ocelo, their angry shouts fading behind him.

Teo used the canopy to travel deeper into the rain forest. Going to the heart of the arena seemed like a good plan, since that was probably where the others were headed. He needed to find Xio and Niya before either of them got tagged. Teo felt a little bad leaving his teammate behind, but it wasn't like Aurelio was relying on him to win the trial.

The damp leaves provided ample cover, and being this high up meant he could sneak around without drawing attention to himself.

After a few minutes of running into nothing but an army of weaver ants and a chill little sloth, Teo got worried. But then he heard a commotion up ahead and followed the sound. He hopped into a strangler tree, his wings helping him keep balance as he crouched low on a branch.

In the middle of a clearing stood a huge kapok tree. The bottom section of the tree was a large mass of roots plunging into the soil, and sitting at the base was Xio.

A wide grin split Teo's face. Finally, something had gone right! He was about to drop down to Xio, but something about the way the boy was sitting made him pause.

He was sitting cross-legged, his hands in his lap, but slumped onto his side. The position of his body was strange, too stiff to be normal. That was when Teo spotted the glyphs hovering over his head. The wave of Diosa Agua and the burning heart of Diosa Amor.

Teo's stomach clenched. Xio was already tagged, and the culprit was still there. Dezi stood with his back to Xio just a few feet away, his attention caught on what had drawn Teo to the clearing in the first place.

Niya and Auristela were in an all-out fight. Auristela threw balls of fire at Niya, who deftly jumped out of the way before slinging a golden spear like a javelin. Auristela ducked just in time and the golden weapon sank into the tree with a *thunk*.

"You're always doing this!" Auristela shouted, her face violent red.

"Doing what?!" Niya demanded, teeth bared.

Their enraged gazes were locked, but there was something very wrong about them. Niya's eyes weren't their usual shade of hazel-brown, but black. Auristela's eyes had changed, too, and the skin around her eyes was dark, almost bruised looking.

Was it a trick of the light? The shadows of the canopies?

"Barreling through everything like an avalanche!" Auristela snarled.

"At least I'm a *natural* disaster, you grease fire!"

Auristela fumed. In one quick movement, she extended her arms and brought her hands together, palms facing toward Niya.

Whoosh.

Fire exploded from her hands like a flamethrower.

Teo lost his footing for a moment, a panicked cry lodging in his throat, but Niya was fast.

She threw her arm up and a large, silvery shield materialized. Niya ducked behind it, saving herself from the licking flames. The metal grew hot, glowing a deep, angry orange but thankfully not melting.

Teo ground his teeth. He wanted to shout at them, tell them they were acting like complete fools—they were on the same damn team! Why were they fighting each other?

But he didn't because Dezi was completely distracted by their temper tantrums.

If Xio was already out of the game, Teo could at least avenge him by taking out Dezi. Anger swelled in Teo's chest and clouded any thought other than *make Dezi pay*.

He dropped from the tree, angling his wings to swoop down on Dezi. He stretched his wings out like Aurelio had shown him, but the sinewy new muscles weren't strong enough to stop the momentum of his body as he flung himself forward.

Teo cried out. Searing pain tore through his shoulders.

Dezi must've felt the air shift and jerked to look over his shoulder. His eyes locked onto Teo's, wide with surprise.

Teo flung himself forward, reaching for the other boy. He smirked, knowing it was too late for Dezi to evade him. But then something strange happened.

Dezi didn't jerk back or even have the common decency to acknowledge defeat. Instead, Dezi *smiled*.

And in that moment, Teo knew he'd fucked up.

He tagged Dezi's arm. Something like a static shock stung Teo's fingertips and raced up his arm. Immediately, Dezi's body went rigid, and he fell to the side, Teo's and Aurelio's glyphs appearing above him.

At the same time, a wave of drowsiness washed over Teo. He stumbled forward, swaying on his feet. The anger he'd felt moments before had completely dissolved. Teo frowned, trying to remember *why* he was upset to begin with.

Suddenly, Teo didn't even care about why he'd been angry. Instead, something warm and sweet like honey spread through his body, from the top of his head to the tips of his toes. A deep, satisfying breath filled his lungs, and when he exhaled, his arms and wings went limp as all his muscles relaxed.

He felt good—*really* good and completely at ease. It reminded him of summer afternoons, lying out in the sun on the docks of the canals after a long day of swimming. He wanted to curl up and take a nap.

Teo knew there were other people around, but through the fog in his head, he didn't care about them. They were nothing but shadowy figures, completely inconsequential, until he turned and Dezi came into sharp focus.

Dezi smiled up at him and every nerve in Teo's body tingled.

Dezi. Dezi was so perfect. Why weren't he and Dezi better friends? Teo bet they had loads in common. Like, they both thought Dezi was the prettiest boy to ever live. And he *was*! How had Teo never noticed it before?

With a sigh of relief, Teo dropped to his knees and scooted up to Dezi's side. Lying his head on Dezi's shoulder, Teo took another deep breath and closed his eyes. He felt like he was on the receiving end of the world's warmest hug. Through the haze, someone called his name, but Teo ignored it. As long as he was with Dezi, he would be happy. As long as he was with Dezi, he was safe and nothing could go wrong. He curled closer, squeezing Dezi's arm as his wing draped over them. He could fall asleep right there on the jungle floor, knowing nothing bad would ever happen.

Someone shook his shoulder, rough.

"Go away," Teo grumbled, knocking them back before pressing his face into Dezi's neck.

Unceremoniously, Teo was dragged to his feet.

"Snap out of it," the person said, stern and loud.

Teo cringed. Being taken from Dezi's side sent a deep ache tearing through Teo's chest. His skin crawled and itched. He *needed* Dezi—needed the sense of safety and comfort. Without Dezi, something terrible would happen to him.

Panic squeezed Teo's throat with an iron grip. "Leave me alone!" He thrashed and fought, struggling to break free of his captor.

But they refused to let him go. "*Stop*," they ordered, squeezing his upper arms and shaking him.

Teo's heart raced, and his vision started to clear. Before him, Aurelio's face came into focus. His expression was taut, fiery eyes blazing.

Aurelio gave off his own heat. Not Dezi's gentle warmth, but an intense burn that made Teo's skin prickle beneath Aurelio's touch. "You need to get away from Dezi."

Teo seethed. Aurelio, who only caused him hurt and heartache, wanted to take him away from the only person who made him happy.

"No!" Teo wrenched himself free and dove back to Dezi's side. Instantly, the sleepy contentment quelled the rising pain and panic.

"What you're feeling isn't real."

Teo glared up at Aurelio, eyes stinging and throat burning. What a terrible, *cruel* thing to say.

"Go away!" Teo shouted, desperate to chase down the euphoria that Dezi made him feel. Aurelio was *ruining it*. Aurelio ruined *everything*.

Aurelio's eyes flicked past Teo's shoulder. He leapt to his feet and hurled a ball of fire.

Teo ducked and threw himself across Dezi. When he looked up, Marino had entered the clearing. Fire burned at the base of the tree next to him. When Aurelio closed his fist, it immediately went out.

Marino stood, arms twisting and pulling rhythmically as a stream of water curled around him, like a silvery blue snake circling him mid-air. Teo had tagged his partner, and now he was looking for retribution.

Aurelio edged away from Teo and Dezi, igniting twin flames in his palms.

For a moment, they stared each other down and then in a blink, they charged at each other, a flurry of fire, water, and hissing steam.

"Teo, watch out!" Niya's voice rang out.

Auristela, soot smeared across her cheek, was sprinting for Teo, a fierce look of determination on her face.

Teo didn't even care. If she wanted to tag him, he'd let her as long as he could stay with Dezi.

But before she could get close, a golden net flew through the air and wrapped itself around Auristela, knocking her to the ground. Auristela let out a furious noise as she thrashed, trying to get herself free as Niya caught up to her.

"Traitor!" Auristela screeched, sneering up at Niya from the floor.

Catching her breath, Niya propped her fist on her hip and rolled her eyes. "Bite me, princess."

Auristela slammed her fists into the ground. Fire ignited, covering her entire body. Through the flames, Teo watched as the golden netting melted and Auristela was back on her feet.

"Dammit," Niya groaned before Auristela chucked a ball of fire at her head.

The two teammates went back to battling each other in a flurry of flames and slashing metal, disappearing through the trees.

Teo crouched next to Dezi, ready to fight Aurelio off again, but Aurelio's focus was on Marino. As the other boy slung streams of water at him, Aurelio ducked and dodged out of the way, slowly edging closer until he was standing right in front of Teo. Before Teo could figure out what the hell he was doing, Aurelio rolled to his left—

And a heavy stream of water sprayed Teo directly in the face.

It shot up his nostrils and completely doused him. Teo's lungs tightened as the icy water sent a shock through his system. He coughed and spluttered, shaking the water from his face. "What the hell!"

A hand grabbed his arm and hauled him to his feet.

"Have you snapped out of it now?" Aurelio demanded, irritation edging his voice as he scowled at Teo.

Snapped out of it?

"The hell happened?" Teo asked, wiping water from his eyes.

"Dezi happened."

Before Aurelio could elaborate, he shoved Teo back and darted out of the way as another stream of water struck the kapok tree. Marino stood opposite them, looking aggravated and worse for wear. Aurelio also looked rough. Teo couldn't remember ever seeing him so sweaty and out of breath.

"Dezi?" Teo looked back to where Dezi was on the ground, still frozen but now with a bemused expression on his face. Teo's heart sank. Had he been...cuddling Dezi? In the middle of the trial? In front of everyone? *On television?!* "Oh my *gods.*"

"Addictive contentment," Aurelio said. With effort, he threw another fireball at Marino, who dodged out of its way.

Idiot. Huemac had warned him, and he'd even seen it himself during the second trial when Dezi had touched the bull-horned rooster!

Teo quickly moved away from Dezi, afraid to get sucked into his powers once again. "Shit, did I make a complete ass out of myself?" he hissed.

"A bit," Aurelio agreed, out of breath.

Teo looked over to Xio, who was still frozen in place but otherwise looked okay. Getting tagged out so fast would not be good for the younger boy's rankings, but that was something they could worry about later.

Time was not on their side.

Marino made another attack and this time Teo threw his wing out, doing his best to shield himself and Xio. The stream of water had the strength of a fire hose. It hit Teo with brute force, tearing off a few feathers. He cursed loudly.

"I'll handle Marino," Aurelio said, moving away from Teo and the others.

Teo frowned at him, confused. "Are you sure?"

Aurelio nodded, attention going back to Marino as he ignited flames in his hands. "Go find someone to tag," he said, expression pinching.

"But—"

"And *don't* get caught."

Heat warmed Teo's cheeks as Aurelio sparked his flint gloves and threw up a wall of fire. He didn't need to be told twice. Pushing off with his legs as hard as he could, Teo took off, back into the cover of the canopy, leaving Aurelio behind to hopefully overtake Marino.

Things weren't going smoothly, but they weren't going badly, either. At least he and Aurelio weren't at each other's throats like Niya and Auristela. Teo had even managed to tag Dezi.

Now he just needed to find someone else to tag, but that was easy for Aurelio to say. Teo was still a Jade in an arena full of Golds. The only upper hand he had was his wings. If he was going to take someone else down, he'd have to be sneaky about it.

Teo moved through the canopy, going as quickly as he could without making too much noise. The wind against his cheeks and rippling through his feathers felt euphoric. Teo made a wide circle around where he'd left Aurelio so he'd be able to find him again if he got into trouble. The concept that he was actually relying on Aurelio for anything was still absolutely wild, but he had to play the game.

When he heard a commotion, Teo followed the sound through the trees.

Apparently Auristela and Niya had come to their senses, or maybe the former had finally killed the latter, because he found Atzi and Auristela battling it out. It was a strange game of cat and mouse, both dancing around each other but with Atzi clearly on the defense as Auristela relentlessly lunged forward. Atzi threw lighting, keeping Auristela back, but just barely.

Teo felt kind of bad for Atzi, but not enough to get between the two powerful Golds, so he went on his way. Atzi would keep Auristela busy until Auristela inevitably tagged her.

"Oh my *gods*, will you chill?!" Niya's voice cut through the trees.

Relief sent Teo racing through the boughs.

When he found her, Niya was standing over Ocelo, who was lying facedown on the ground. Niya's and Auristela's glyphs hung over their head.

"There you are!" Teo said, dropping down to her side.

"Here I am!" Niya smiled brightly.

"Are you okay?" He searched her eyes. The black was gone, leaving them their usual shade of hazel brown.

Niya exhaled between pursed lips. "'Course I am! I took down Meat Head!" she said, proudly pointing to where Ocelo glared up at them from the ground, their cheek pressed into the dirt, absolutely seething.

"Not that it was that difficult," Niya continued. She crossed her arms and gave Ocelo a disapproving look. "Y'know, if you didn't lose your temper so quick it wouldn't be so easy to trick you."

Ocelo's body jerked.

Teo took a large step back. If anyone could somehow manage to break the magical bindings of the trial, it'd be Ocelo. And Teo would *not* want to be in their way.

Niya nudged them with her foot. "Calm down!"

"Speaking of temper—I thought you and Auristela were going to murder each other," Teo said, looking around in case she decided to jump out.

Niya frowned and shook her head. "I swear I'm usually better at ignoring her, but it's like ever since the trials started I just *can't help myself*, you know?" she said, rubbing her eyes.

"Yeah, I get it," Teo agreed. Maybe the stress of the trials was getting to all of them.

"So, what's the plan?" Niya asked, turning to Teo.

"Why do I have to come up with the plan? You're the Gold!" he shot back.

"Yeah, but you're, like, the plan guy!"

"The *plan* was to keep Xio from getting tagged," he grumbled.

"Well, that didn't work out, so what's plan B?"

"I need to come up with plan A *and* plan B?!"

"*You're the plan guy!*"

"I—"

Two people came crashing through the trees.

Both Teo and Niya screamed. She reached to grab Teo, but Teo quickly twisted out of her reach.

"YOU ALMOST TAGGED ME!"

"I'M SORRY, I GOT SCARED!"

Marino had chased Aurelio into the clearing, relentlessly blasting him with water. Aurelio threw his arms up in an attempt to shield himself, but it was useless against the deluge.

Teo waited for Aurelio to get up and flamethrower Marino's ass, but he didn't.

With another hit of water, Aurelio was knocked off-balance, dropping down on his knee.

"Your partner's not looking so good," Niya said warily.

Teo never thought he'd see the day when Aurelio was bested. It didn't make any sense, but then he realized—Marino was the semidiós of water, and Aurelio was the semidiós of fire. They were opposing elements. He remembered poring over Xio's trading cards and the weaknesses listed at the bottom. Marino's was fire and heat, and Aurelio's was water and cold.

And if he was drenched, that meant his flint gloves didn't work.

He needed help.

Thinking fast, Teo took off into the air and dropped down in front of Aurelio just in time to get hit with a face full of water. He threw up his wings to shield himself. This time, Marino's hit wasn't as hard. Maybe he was running out of steam, too.

As water sprayed uselessly against his wings, Teo looked down to where Aurelio was crouched behind him.

"You good?" he asked.

Aurelio looked up at him, more than a little dazed. His cheeks were red and his soaked clothes clung to his heaving chest as he tried to catch his breath. Aurelio wiped the water from his face before nodding, a determined look in his eyes.

Marino was closing in. One step closer and he'd be able to reach out and tag Teo's wings.

"Take off," Aurelio told him, his attention focused ahead.

His stubborn ass was going to get himself tagged. "But you—"

"Now!"

Teo flew up into the air, well over Marino's head. Marino lunged forward, only to swipe at empty air, as Aurelio dove at Marino's feet, tagging his right leg.

Instantly, Marino's body locked up and he toppled to the muddy ground.

Teo whooped, punching his arm into the air—which nearly made him fall, but he quickly recovered. Aurelio pushed himself up from the ground, unsteady but upright.

Now he and Aurelio had both tagged someone. By some miracle of Sol, they actually stood a chance of winning this trial. The victory, however, was short-lived.

"Sonofa—!"

Down below, Niya was flat on her back, her wrists and ankles bound by vines. Xochi stood a few feet away, a triumphant grin on her face as she used the vines like rope to drag Niya toward her.

Teo swooped down, landing so hard he nearly fell over. He raced to Niya, grabbed the vines, and pulled, trying to wrench them free of Xochi's grip, but the springtime semidiosa was stronger than him.

"Do you remember what Xochi's weakness is?" Teo demanded, holding on for dear life.

"No, I thought you knew!" Niya answered as she wrangled with the vines.

"Cut the vines!"

"I can't, my hands are stuck!" Niya struggled against the restraints, but it was no use.

With a hard yank, Xochi knocked Teo off-balance. He scrambled to hold on, digging his heels into the dirt, but it did little to slow Xochi down. This was a tug-of-war that Teo was not going to win.

In a flash of orange light, flames cut through Teo's vision, severing the vines. Teo stomped out the charred ends as Xochi let out an incoherent shout of anger.

Aurelio was back on his feet, small flames dancing across his fingers.

With the vines loose, Niya wrenched her arms apart, snapping her bindings.

Xochi sprinted toward them, but before she could tag Teo, Niya slammed her open hand against the ground and made a fist. The mud swallowed Xochi's feet up to her ankles, knocking her forward. While she was still disoriented, Niya quickly tagged Xochi's arm.

"I didn't know you could do that!" Teo gaped.

Niya got to her feet and tossed her braid over her shoulder. "I've got loads of tricks you don't know about," she told him, grinning ear to ear. "Come on." Niya offered her hand to help him up.

Teo started to reach for it.

"Don't!" Aurelio shouted.

Teo jerked his hand back. "Were you gonna tag me?!"

Niya laughed and shrugged her shoulders. "It was worth a shot!"

Teo glared up at her. "We're supposed to be working together!"

"We're the only four left!" Niya pointed out with a huff. "It's either me or—"

Blazing white light exploded before Teo's eyes, followed by a thunderous boom.

When his vision cleared, Niya was sprawled out on her side, unmoving. A fresh cut across her cheek dripped golden blood. Atzi stood behind her, fists raised and poised as she looked between Teo and Aurelio.

Teo's heart clenched painfully in his chest. "Niya!" He moved to race to her side, but Aurelio's voice stopped him.

"She's fine—if you touch her now, you'll get electrocuted, too," he warned, keeping his eyes on Atzi.

Small flickers of lightning danced across Niya's body.

"She's not fine, she's unconscious!" Teo barked.

"She's gotten zapped by Atzi dozens of times," Aurelio said calmly. Teo glared, but Aurelio grinned. "You ready to finish this, or what?"

"I don't want to get struck by lightning again." He hadn't exactly had a good reaction the first time.

"She's been throwing a lot of bolts, which means she's low on power," Aurelio said, nodding in Atzi's direction.

Looking at her now, Teo could see the quick rise and fall of her chest. The silvery ribbons she always wore braided into her hair were falling out, crooked and unraveling.

Atzi was tired but determined.

If she was still standing, that meant she must've won the fight between her and Auristela. Teo would've paid good money to see the look on Auristela's face when Atzi tagged her.

"How many people did you tag?" Teo asked, moving to Aurelio's side.

"One."

"Me too."

A grin curled Teo's lips.

Aurelio glanced at him from the corner of his eye, arching an eyebrow.

"Race you," Teo said.

Aurelio exhaled sharply through his nose.

"Unless you're scared—"

Aurelio smiled and warmth flooded Teo's chest. "On the count of three."

A laugh jumped in Teo's throat.

"One, two—"

Teo ran as fast as he could.

Atzi turned and took off through the trees. It took less than five steps for Aurelio to catch up and fall into stride next to Teo.

Atzi wove through the trees in an attempt to lose them. She spun around and threw up a wall of rain, but it was little more than a drizzle and did nothing to slow them down.

Try as she might, Atzi started to falter. As they closed in, Aurelio lengthened his stride, gradually pulling ahead. Adrenaline and stubborn determination coursed through Teo's veins. He urged himself to run faster, go harder, *push, push, push*.

A slick, mossy log lay across the path and Atzi jumped over it. Teo and Aurelio got to it at the same time, but instead of jumping over it, Teo jumped onto the log and launched himself into the air.

Teo thrust his wings down and shot forward, tagging Atzi between her shoulder blades. Her body locked up and fell to the ground. Overhead, Dios Mariachi's cornet sang the end of the trial as Teo's watch vibrated.

Teo tumbled through the air and hit the ground hard, somersaulting a couple times before skidding to a stop at the base of the tree. His lungs burned and several parts of his body were definitely bruised, but it was totally worth it.

Teo raised his hands over his head. "We won!" he announced, breathless and half drunk on victory. He couldn't believe it—he'd actually gotten through a trial without complete disaster. And, more than that, he'd tagged *two* Golds!

Aurelio walked over to Teo.

"I did it!" Teo beamed up at him, still barely able to believe it himself.

"You did," Aurelio agreed, holding out his hand for Teo to take.

Delirious laughter bubbled in Teo's chest as he was pulled to his feet. Aurelio's tight grip was only on his hand for a moment, but the sensation lingered like a burn.

"I can't believe it!" Teo said, bending over and bracing his hands on his knees as he tried to catch his breath. "That was awesome!"

Aurelio looked at him, an amused look on his handsome face. It wasn't exactly a smile, but it was definitely adjacent. He seemed to have recovered from Marino's attack. Even as he stood there, Aurelio's abnormally high body heat was drying his clothes, wisps of steam billowing off his shoulders.

He looked great, actually. They'd chased Atzi through the rain forest and he wasn't even winded.

Teo frowned. "Wait," he said, forcing himself to stand upright. Something didn't add up right. If Aurelio was still weak from Marino's attack, then he should look haggard right now. But he didn't. And if he'd recovered already, then Aurelio *easily* should've outrun him in a matter of seconds.

"Did you let me win?" Teo demanded.

"I don't know what you're talking about," Aurelio said, cleaning his soot-covered hands and gold armbands off on the hem of his shirt.

"Yes you do!"

Without looking up, he turned around and started walking. "Come on, it's time for the rankings."

Teo fumed and stomped after him. *"Get back here, you bastard!"*

CHAPTER 17

The semidioses gathered back at the platform with Diosa Luna. Looking around at the group, Teo noticed how different the mood was compared to the first trial. When the trials had first started, there was a charged energy of competition. Now, everyone's cracks were starting to show. Excitement and eagerness were replaced by exhaustion and wariness as they all awaited the rankings.

Dressed in her crisp white suit, Diosa Médica was summoned to assess Niya, who'd been forced to sit in a chair. She checked Niya's heart and lungs with her golden stethoscope, a serious expression on her face. Poor Dios Tierra was a wreck, hovering behind Niya as he switched between nervously fidgeting with his tie and wringing his gloved hands. He looked distraught—or as distraught as someone in a mask could look, anyway.

Hard-as-rocks Niya, who always seemed so indestructible, was sluggish, wincing every time she moved. Little red lightning burns streaked her arms and neck in feathery patterns. Diosa Médica finally cleared her, and when Niya stood up, encouraging cheers rippled through the crowd.

"You okay?" Teo asked under his breath as Niya and Tierra took their places next to him and Diosa Quetzal.

"Pft, it's gonna take more than that to take me out," she said with a tired grin and a wink.

Relieved, Teo smiled back, but it didn't last long.

Diosa Luna looked very displeased as she approached the stone slate. With no preamble, she said, "Sol has determined the rankings."

This time, when the glyphs rearranged themselves, most of the movement was at the top, but Teo was focused on the bottom. He held his breath, waiting to see where Xio got placed.

Teo exhaled a heavy breath. Xio was still in eighth, and while he certainly hadn't moved up in the rankings, at least he hadn't moved down. While it was a relief, it was also confusing. Hadn't Xio been tagged first? And somehow Ocelo was beneath him again.

When he looked over, he assumed they would be fuming mad again, but to his surprise, Ocelo was uncharacteristically still. Instead of anger, fear hid in the lines of their face.

Diosa Amor raised her hands and shook them over her head as she shouted triumphantly. She practically danced in place over her son's success, vehemently signing to him as Dezi stood there beaming. Dios Tormentoso had to practically double over to speak soft, reassuring words to Atzi, who was on the verge of tears. Her eyes glistened and her chin dimpled, but she stayed strong, nodding at whatever her dad said. When he stood upright again, Tormentoso's expression was stormy, the thunder in his beard rumbling moodily.

Even though Auristela had drastically moved down to fifth place, a bright smile lit up her face. She grabbed Aurelio's arm, shaking it fiercely. Teo realized she wasn't reacting to her own rank, but celebrating that Aurelio was now first. Auristela had a new orange light behind her eyes and Aurelio wobbled under her enthusiasm.

As Verdad tugged at Aurelio's arm, pulling him away for an interview, Aurelio looked over his shoulder and caught Teo's eye. Aurelio smiled at him. It wasn't the forced smile that seemed to be part of Aurelio's uniform, but a *genuine* smile. The kind that bunched up his cheeks and crinkled his eyes. It stole the breath from Teo's lungs.

"Teo!"

His mother's gasp startled him.

Dread dropped into his stomach. "What?" Frantically, he searched for his glyph, scouring the bottom of the list.

"Look!" Quetzal pointed at the slate.

Not toward the bottom, but the top.

"Fourth?" Teo practically shouted, absolutely stunned. That couldn't be right, could it? "Wait—how?"

"You and Niya were the only ones to tag two people, mijo," his mother said, beaming.

"I believe that's the highest rank a Jade has ever achieved," Mala Suerte said, his voice smooth as silk, eyeing him curiously.

"Holy shit," Teo breathed, unable to believe his eyes. It couldn't be real. "*Me?*"

At his side, Xio stared up at the rankings, looking just as confused as Teo felt.

Mala Suerte wasn't the only one whose attention had turned to Teo. Other Gold gods regarded him curiously. Diosa Amor smiled at him, her attention flicking between Teo and Dezi, who signed quickly to his mom with emphatic facial expressions. Diose Guerrero narrowed their eyes at him suspiciously, but Dios Tierra, the kindhearted man that he was, flashed Teo a discreet thumbs-up.

And then there was Diosa Lumbre. Her scorching ember eyes stared him down so intensely, so calculatingly, that Teo was convinced his skin would blister. At her side, Auristela gave him an equally searing look. Maybe she was pissed about him overtaking her in the ranks.

"How in the heck am *I* in second?" Niya blurted out, genuinely perplexed. "I was unconscious for, like, the last five minutes!"

"Why am I still so low?" Atzi asked quietly. Dios Tormentoso stood dutifully next to his daughter with a hand on her shoulder.

"While you were indeed rendered unconscious for the end of the trial, Niya," Diosa Luna said before anyone else could voice their objections, "*You* were never tagged out and you did tag two of your competitors."

Niya tipped her head back and forth, squinting one eye like she was trying to do the calculations in her head.

"Atzi," Luna said, turning her attention to the rain semidiosa. "The name of this trial was the *Bloodless* Battle. You were told to cause no physical harm to your competitors. You did not follow those instructions."

Atzi shrank against her dad, who wrapped his burly arm around her shoulders. She nodded her understanding, but her lips quivered.

"This challenge was designed to test your ability to work as a team. Teo and Aurelio were the only team to work together," Diosa Luna explained. "Meanwhile, Ocelo abandoned their teammate as soon as the cornet sounded."

Teo looked to Xio for confirmation. The younger boy had a smug look on his face, like he was glad to see Ocelo called out. It made Teo smile, too.

"This isn't a scored test like you'd take at school," Diosa Luna told them all in a cool tone. "There isn't a grading rubric or numerical value assigned that determines your rank."

Niya made a disgruntled sound. Teo knew her brain worked by finding literal solutions. She saw things in black and white and had a hard time understanding gray areas.

"Sol is looking for the heart of their champion as well as their sacrifice," Diosa Luna continued. "*That's* how the Sunbearer is chosen. You would all do well to remember that."

※

"This is so annoying!" Xio grumbled, stuffing his hands into his pockets with a petulant scowl. As always, the three drifted to the back of the group as Luna led them to the temple. "It's, like, impossible to figure out how the rankings work!"

"Yeah, none of this is going the way I thought it would," Teo agreed with a shake of his head. "I mean, I guess that's the point, right? Sol seeing through the surface stuff to decide who's worthy . . ."

"Aye, at least you're not in last place!" Niya pointed out, ruffling Xio's curly hair. "Meanwhile, *this guy* might actually have a shot at being Sunbearer!" she added, giving Teo a playful shove that sent him stumbling.

Teo rolled his eyes dramatically, but it didn't feel as impossible anymore. It was Niya who was supposed to overtake the other Golds. He had no *real* belief that it could be *him*. There was no way Sol would see him as a viable contender, but now he was sitting in *fourth place*. It was absolutely wild and while he knew there was no way Sol would deem him worthy of being Sunbearer . . . Well, what if they *did*?

A Jade had never won the Sunbearer Trials before. If he did win, it'd be a huge upset. He thought of Paloma and how she'd bravely faced her end.

If he did win, maybe people would finally have to start taking Jades seriously.

"You know what? You're right," Xio said, his mood suddenly shifting as he grinned up at Teo and Niya. "I mean, I *really* thought I'd be dead last right now, but I'm actually doing okay."

A relieved laugh bucked in Teo's chest. "They said one of us was going to end up being the sacrifice, but look at us now!"

"That's the spirit!" Niya sang.

The three dissolved into laughter. It was the best he had felt since arriving at Sol Temple. Teo's hope was small and featherlight at first, but it smoldered as he dreamed. Winning would mean getting back at everyone who thought Golds were better than Jades. He'd show the dioses how wrong they were for barring Jades from the Academy.

Determination caught fire in his veins. The thought latched on to his brain and took hold.

He could do it, not just for himself, but for every Jade who'd ever been made to feel less than.

It was more than making sure the bullies lost.

Before, Teo had wanted to protect and survive. Now, he wanted to *win*.

During dinner back on the boat, the Golds were somber and in various stages of exhaustion. Ocelo frowned at their plate the whole time, their knees bouncing anxiously. Atzi never showed up, but Xochi volunteered to take her some food. Poor Niya had gone to bed early, the bolt of lightning she'd received from Atzi having done a number on her already exhausted body. She kept saying she needed extra rest in order to regain some brain cells. Teo didn't bother explaining that that wasn't how brain cells worked.

Everyone was worn out, feeling sorry for themselves, or both.

Everyone except for Teo and Xio. Xio was in the best mood Teo had seen him in since the trials began. His smiles came easily and he even laughed at Teo's terrible jokes, and Teo was happy to ride the good vibes.

Five days of physically demanding trials, restless sleep, and learning how to use a whole new set of limbs was wearing Teo down. He had a constant, dull ache in his muscles and a low-level headache, but he was still in a great mood from today's success.

He kept trying to catch Aurelio's eye, but his back was to Teo as Auristela spoke to him in hushed tones. Every time she caught him looking over, Auristela threw Teo a dirty look. It didn't seem like Teo would get the chance to congratulate him.

Most people went to bed right after dinner. After taking a shower, Teo changed into a pair of sweatpants and a T-shirt the Sol priests had cut slits into for his wings. Teo paced back and forth in his cabin for several minutes. His skin crawled with pent-up energy—the punch-drunk kind from too little sleep and too much excitement. He was still riding high from the trial and just felt so *good*. It would be a waste to stay cooped up in his room all night. It'd been a while since he'd gotten into any mischief and he was starting to feel itchy.

So, he came up with a plan.

The wood floor was cold against Teo's bare feet as he crept down the hall, making sure to be especially quiet as he passed Xio's and Niya's rooms. He felt a little guilty, but he didn't want to have to explain himself if he got caught.

Lightly, he rapped his knuckles against the fire glyph painted on the door. His heartbeat fluttered in his pulse.

Teo half expected Aurelio to be asleep already, but after a pause, he heard the padding of footsteps.

The door opened to reveal Aurelio standing in a pair of tiny shorts and one of those gray oversize douchebag tanks with the huge arm holes that dropped down to his waist. This was the first time he'd ever seen Aurelio with his hair down. It cascaded to his shoulders, hiding the shaved sides in thick, shiny waves.

Dressed down, soft and sleepy, this was a version of Aurelio that Teo knew he had never been meant to see. It sent a trill down his spine, plunging into the pit of his stomach.

For a second, Aurelio blinked at him, his bleary eyes widening with surprise while Teo gaped at him.

"Damn, dude, I can see your nipples," Teo blurted out, taken aback by the sheer expanse of brown skin and muscle.

Aurelio crossed his arms over his chest. Red bloomed in his cheeks.

Teo grinned. "Seriously, why even bother wearing a shirt if it doesn't cover anything?"

Aurelio scowled. "I run hot," he said, voice gravelly with exhaustion.

"Do you sleep in those, too?" Teo asked, pointing at his golden arm-bands. "Is it, like, a security blanket thing?"

"Do you need something?" Aurelio interrupted. He shook his head a little, the force making his dark hair glint and sending the delicate ends brushing against his shoulder.

Teo shook his head, escorting his eyes back to Aurelio's face. "What are you doing right now?"

"Watching baking videos," Aurelio said, holding up his phone. Sure enough, a video of someone piping a cupcake while faint piano music played.

"Seriously?" Teo chuckled. "I thought you were messing with me the other day."

"They're relaxing," Aurelio said a bit defensively.

"Well, I've got other plans!" Teo held up his backpack and wiggled his eyebrows. "Wanna come with me?"

Aurelio tipped his head to the side and cut Teo a suspicious look. "What are you doing?"

Teo scoffed. "Come on, what's the worst that could happen?"

Aurelio's gaze flicked toward his sister's room. "That's not an answer."

"Oh my gods," Teo grumbled. "Look, come or don't come, I don't care!" He turned to leave but Aurelio stopped him.

"Wait—I'm coming."

Teo beamed triumphantly. "Great! But make yourself decent first, for Sol's sake. I don't want your nipples staring at me all night."

Aurelio ducked back into his room and tugged on a black hoodie.

"Where are you taking me?" Aurelio asked as Teo led him out onto the deck.

"Keep your voice down," Teo told him in a sharp whisper, checking to make sure the coast was clear. "We're on a mission."

"What mission?" the other boy asked, quieter this time as he followed.

"To get Niya some candy as a get-well-soon present," Teo said as he waited for one of the deckhands to finish making her rounds. "I ran out of stock and it's always a surefire way to cheer her up."

"Wait, you mean sneak off the boat?"

"Yes!" The deckhand went inside and Teo sprinted for the dock. He got halfway across before he realized Aurelio hadn't followed him. He turned back to find the fire semidiós still standing on the boat.

"What are you waiting for?" Teo whispered harshly.

Aurelio glanced around. "We're not supposed to leave the boat."

Teo huffed. "Do you always do what people tell you?"

"I mean, yeah."

"Listen, I was *supposed* to be spending my time checking out all these cities on my own, but instead I got chosen to compete in the trials, so I'm taking back time that's owed to me!" Teo insisted.

Aurelio rolled his eyes but finally relented.

It seemed impossible that even winning the Sunbearer Trials could rival the triumphant brightness that exploded in Teo's chest. Equally surprised and delighted, he tugged on Aurelio's sleeve. "Come on!"

Together, they slipped off the dock and raced for freedom.

Opal Oasis was surprisingly lively late at night. People spilled out of sports bars and loud conversations filled the streets. With all the bustle, it would be easy for someone to spot Aurelio, the currently top-ranked competitor in the Sunbearer Trials, and Teo, a boy with *wings*. Teo at least had had the foresight to tuck his wings inside his hoodie, and when they got off the boat, he immediately pulled Aurelio's hood up over his head in an attempt to hide his face.

Teo had no idea where they were going, but it was easy enough to follow the main road until they found a little bodega on the corner. The inside of the shop was full of metal shelves packed with items. There were towers of every flavor of chip imaginable and a section of toiletries, and the far wall was lined with coolers full of soda, energy drinks, and beer. There was a whole section dedicated to cleaning products, and colorful pinatas—some bleached pale from the sun—hung from the ceiling.

Teo made quick work of finding Niya's favorites and dumping them on the counter while Aurelio wandered the aisles, his fingers sliding over the stacks of colorful candy. After paying the gray-haired woman at the counter, Teo grabbed the bulging paper bag and led Aurelio to a bench in a well-lit park.

"What are they?" Aurelio asked as he sifted through the pieces of candy Teo dumped out between them.

"What do you mean, 'what are they'?" Teo said with an uncertain laugh. "It's candy!"

Aurelio hummed. He gave the array of candy an intense look of concentration that seemed better suited for a chess board.

"Lucas, Paleta Payaso, Pulparindo, Vero Mango—" Teo listed off. "Do you seriously not know what candy is?" Teo demanded.

Aurelio gave a small, self-conscious shrug. "I know what candy *is*, I just don't eat it," he said, pushing his hood back down.

Teo balked. "What—why?"

"We don't have it at the Academy."

"At all?"

"We're not supposed to, but people sneak it in." Aurelio specified, "Like Niya."

"That's *horrible*."

"Pan Dulce makes us sweets sometimes, and hot chocolate," he said, hesitantly picking up a packet of Limon 7.

Aurelio poured it into his mouth. Immediately, he coughed and spluttered, sending bits of powder flying from his mouth. "That's *horrible*," he said, eyes watering. "It's like *sea water*."

Teo threw himself back, wrapping his arms around his stomach as he laughed. "It tastes better on pickles!"

Aurelio's eyes were wide and his lip still curled in disgust, and the ridiculous alarmed expression threw Teo into another fit of laughter.

"Here, try this," Teo said, wiping the tears from his eyes as he handed Aurelio a blue cachetada. "It's tamarind."

"Uh, how does this work?" Aurelio asked as he carefully inspected the long oval shape. He held it up with both hands, closing one eye and peering at Teo through the candy like it was a magnifying glass. There was an uneasy smile on Aurelio's face, so wide that it bordered on goofy. It was, Teo realized with a treacherous flutter, the kind of thing he would've done when they were kids.

Teo huffed out a dramatic sigh and held out his open palm. "You really are helpless."

Aurelio hesitated for a second before handing it over. Teo laid the candy on his leg and peeled back the top layer of cellophane.

"It's easier if you have a table," he said, folding the other plastic layer onto itself. Teo pressed his palm against his thigh to flatten the pliable candy and tried not to swelter under Aurelio's gaze. Teo made slow, deliberate movements, twisting the stick between his fingers, folding the sweet again and again until the candy had become a narrow rectangle. Light no longer shone through it. "The perfect fuel for becoming Sunbearer," Teo said as he handed it over.

"If candy is the deciding factor, Niya's probably got us beat," Aurelio said, jaw working as he chewed the sticky candy.

Teo shook his head disapprovingly. "Damn, I was just starting to think I might like attending the Academy, but now I've changed my mind," he joked. "Don't they have candy in your home city?"

"I'm sure they do, but I don't leave campus much except when I get summoned on missions," Aurelio confessed.

"Don't you go home to visit your dad?" Teo asked.

"My mom lets me and Auristela go home for our birthday," he said. "But that's about it. She thinks our time is better spent training instead of wasted at home."

Wow. And Teo thought *he* spent too much time at school. He couldn't imagine what it'd be like living there 24/7 and only getting to leave once a year. It sounded like torture.

"What about your mom?" Aurelio asked.

Normally, Teo wouldn't take a diversion as an answer, but Aurelio looked so tired, he decided to let him get away with it.

"I get to see her a lot," Teo said. "She gives out blessings in the temple during the week and spends longer visits with me on the weekends. She still leads all the holiday celebrations and even makes special trips for quinces and stuff," he explained. "I guess that's a perk of being a Jade—less responsibilities and more time to do what you want."

"Sounds nice," Aurelio said with a wry smile.

"But I've got Huemac, who's my guardian when my mom's not around. He basically raised me, the poor guy," Teo said with a grin.

"I know. I remember," said Aurelio, voice low. "I always liked him."

Teo swallowed hard. He didn't know which part was harder to digest: the fact that Aurelio had memories of them, or that they were fond.

"You're lucky," Aurelio went on. "Stela and I just had a rotating cast of pissed-off priests. Being our nanny was the least popular temple duty."

Teo's grin slipped away. The more he talked about it, the more it seemed like Aurelio's life as a Gold maybe wasn't as great as Teo thought it was.

Was it the same for every Gold semidiós? He knew Niya loved going home. Teo couldn't fathom a situation where Dios Tierra wouldn't be thrilled to see his daughter. In fact, Teo was pretty sure the golden-masked god looked forward to being with his daughter more than even Niya looked forward to being with her dad, which was saying a lot.

Aurelio's upbringing sounded painfully lonely. Teo had grown up with Huemac always by his side, looking after him, and the other Quetzlan priests were like his family. Even the people of Quetzlan itself had helped raise Teo.

What was it like for Aurelio and Auristela to only have each other?

Aurelio reached for one of the small disks of mazapan and tore open the wrapper. Immediately, the delicate candy crumbled to bits in his large hands.

Teo lurched forward. "Whoa, whoa, whoa!"

Aurelio froze, powdered mazapan sprinkling his lap. "What?"

"You're doing it all wrong! You gotta open it *gently*, without breaking it." Teo picked one up and carefully undid the wrapper. Most of the mazapan remained intact except for an edge that crumbled away. "See?" he said, holding it up. "You gotta do it like that."

Aurelio furrowed his brow. "Why?"

"I don't know." Teo shrugged. "You're just supposed to! No one questions it. Just like biting into your cake on your birthday."

Now Aurelio looked *really* confused. "Why do you have to bite your cake?"

"You just do!" Teo said, laughter shaking his words. Aurelio was so out of touch with anything fun. "I really have a lot to teach you," he added with a disapproving shake of his head. "Here, try another one."

Aurelio took another mazapan and slowly started to undo the rose wrapper, but it immediately turned into a crumbly mess.

Teo snorted.

"If you become Sunbearer, you'll see all the other cities," Aurelio pointed out as he started on another mazapan. "Each one throws a huge party."

Teo knew the broad strokes of what being the Sunbearer entailed. At school they mostly stressed the whole sacrificial ceremony part and didn't go too in depth on what happened after, other than the Sunbearer being the one who delivered to each temple the elixir that was made from the sacrifice and fueled the Sun Stones.

The pride of being fourth in the rankings still burned fiercely in his chest. Despite himself, Teo grinned. "That'd be really cool," he said. "Though I'm surprised you're even entertaining the idea of me winning."

"Everyone's got a chance," said Aurelio pointedly.

"I guess, but everyone *expects* it of you. Us Jades don't have very exciting prospects back home," Teo said as he chewed on the stick of his lollipop.

Aurelio tipped his head curiously. "What do Jade semidioses usually do?"

"Kind of depends on their parent, honestly. Mariachi's and Baile's kids usually become performers. Médica's oldest daughter just became the head athletic trainer for the city's soccer team," Teo explained. "After I graduate I'll probably just keep living in Quetzlan Temple, helping Huemac out with running the city and taking care of the birds," he confessed.

"That all sounds really nice," Aurelio said in a strange voice that Teo couldn't quite place.

"It's nothing compared to being a Hero," Teo pointed out. "You guys get to travel all over Reino del Sol, rescuing people and saving lives. Everyone knows who you are."

"They know *about* me but they don't really *know* me," Aurelio said, his intense focus aimed at the mazapan in his hands. "Being a Hero means always being busy, always traveling to where I'm needed," he explained. "I don't really get to settle down anywhere or get to know anyone who isn't on my team. At least you have options."

Teo hadn't thought of it that way before. He figured the Gold semi-dioses got to live lives of fame and luxury. He hadn't considered what it actually entailed. Aurelio already didn't have much of a family other than his sister.

Was being a Hero all it was cracked up to be? Was it worth being lonely and not having a life of his own? To be famous and beloved, but at a distance?

There was only a year left until they graduated. Teo thought maybe this was his chance to be friends with Aurelio again, but the truth was, this was probably the last time they'd cross paths. After this, their lives would take them even further apart from each other.

Suddenly, Teo's stomach wasn't in the mood for candy.

He leaned over to toss the lollipop stick into a nearby trash bin and his wings shot out abruptly, deciding they needed to stretch.

Aurelio's eyes immediately snapped to them.

Heat flooded Teo's face. "Sorry." He leaned away from Aurelio and attempted to wrangle them against his back again, pulling his sweatshirt down. Feeling uncomfortable and defensive, he asked, "Do they weird you out or something?"

Aurelio glanced around like he was trying to find what Teo was talking about. "What?"

Teo crossed his arms tight over his chest. "My wings."

Aurelio's face screwed up in confusion. "Of course not."

Teo blinked. "Oh."

"Why would you think that?" Aurelio asked, toying with another mazapan.

Teo shrugged as embarrassment crawled up his neck. "I don't know, you always look at them funny," he said, shifting awkwardly in his seat. "Even when we were kids."

When they were little, Teo used to always catch Aurelio staring at his wings from the corner of his eye. When Aurelio stopped talking to him,

Teo had assumed his wings were another reason Aurelio hadn't wanted to be his friend anymore.

But now, Aurelio gave him a small shake of his head, like he didn't understand what Teo was saying.

"I know they're kinda—"

Aurelio cut him off. "I like your wings," he said, simple but earnest.

Teo's heart gave a heavy thud. "I just thought—" He was suddenly flustered and struggling to string words into a complete sentence. "You always avoid touching them—"

Aurelio shook his head, a small crease between his brows. "No I don't."

"Then why haven't you?" Teo asked, frustration edging his voice. Everyone else constantly touched his wings without batting an eye. If Aurelio wasn't repulsed by them, why did he seem to go out of his way to avoid them?

Aurelio lifted his shoulders in a small shrug. "You never said I could."

Teo stared at him, the tension quickly melting from his muscles as he sank back onto the bench. Completely caught off guard, Teo let out a small "Oh."

He was so used to people grabbing and touching his wings without consent, he hadn't even considered that Aurelio didn't touch them because Teo hadn't given him permission to.

Teo cleared his throat, doing his best to put on a facade of nonchalance and composure. "Well, you can touch them if you want," he offered as casually as possible.

Soft pink tinged Aurelio's cheeks. "Are you sure?"

The way he asked it, so uncertain, made Teo laugh. "Yeah, dude, don't make it weird."

He scooted forward on the bench so he could turn around.

"Just be careful, they've got a mind of their own sometimes," he warned. Apparently, this time his wings wanted to behave, because they lay neatly against his back, waiting.

❋

The nervous energy of anticipation would've made Teo laugh if he wasn't having such a hard time dealing with how fast his heartbeat was thrumming in his veins.

After a long pause, Aurelio's fingers brushed lightly against the small covert feathers on the top of his wings. They shuddered in response and Teo let out an awkward laugh. "Sorry, that tickles," he said, goose bumps running down his arms. Aurelio's touch was surprisingly gentle and always, always so warm.

Aurelio's fingers followed the path of his feathers, down to the long primaries that ended at the tips of his wings. "I didn't think they'd be so soft," Aurelio said quietly.

Teo tried to cover his shiver with a laugh. "Were you expecting scales?" he asked, turning to look at Aurelio over his shoulder.

Aurelio gave him a withering look, but the corners of his lips pulled into a smile. The kind that warmed his eyes and softened his always-so-serious expression. It was so distracting that Teo caught himself staring. Every nerve in his body danced and tingled.

Aurelio's smile shifted to an expression so soft, it made Teo hold his breath.

"I could've sworn I made it clear you were supposed to stay on the boat."

Teo and Aurelio jumped, immediately springing apart.

Luna stood before them, a severe expression on her face. Auristela stood at Luna's side with her arms crossed tightly over her chest. She glared at Teo, which was nothing new to him, but Aurelio's shoulders hunched guiltily.

"Luna!" Teo said, holding his arms out in greeting. "We were just—" He glanced in Aurelio's direction but the other boy was entirely useless, the color having drained from his face as he stared, terrified, at the diosa. Teo's mind raced to come up with some kind of excuse but he had nothing. This was possibly the first time he couldn't talk himself out of trouble.

"Do you want some candy?" he asked with a guilty smile.

Teo, Aurelio, and Auristela followed behind Luna as they made their walk of shame back to the dock.

"What are you doing here?" Aurelio asked his sister, trying to be quiet.

"Luna caught me sneaking out to look for *you*," she hissed back.

Teo rolled his eyes. Typical.

"Back to your rooms," Luna said sternly when they were back on the boat. "All three of you. If I catch you breaking the rules again, there will be dire consequences."

Side by side, Teo and Aurelio boarded the boat. Auristela jerked her head in the direction of the bedrooms. "Come on, Relio."

For a moment, Aurelio didn't move and Teo thought he might stay, but it was short-lived.

"Okay, I'm coming."

When Auristela didn't move, Aurelio exhaled a breath. He turned to Teo. "Here." Aurelio held out his closed fist and Teo offered his upturned hand.

Very carefully, Aurelio placed a perfectly unwrapped mazapan in his palm. A small laugh bucked in Teo's chest.

"See you tomorrow," Aurelio murmured.

"See you."

With that, Aurelio followed his sister inside, leaving Teo alone with the mazapan and an ache in his chest. He hadn't noticed how Aurelio's body heat had been keeping him warm until it was gone.

CHAPTER 18

As punishment for his escapades the previous night, Teo wasn't allowed to go to the soccer match that Diose Guerrero had arranged for them to attend. Aurelio, as noble and principled as he was, said he should get the same punishment, but Teo argued it had been his idea, that he'd quite literally dragged Aurelio along with him. Luna readily accepted that as the truth, which probably should've offended him. Either way, it didn't make sense for both of them to miss out.

When the group left, Teo went into the common area and talked some of the priests into playing dominoes with him as the soccer match played on the television. As if to rub it in, the cameras kept panning to where the other nine competitors had their own box seats, surrounded by a lavish spread of food and drinks. After he lost two rounds of dominoes in a row, the priests took pity on him and brought up a tray of pan dulce handmade by the diosa herself.

Eventually everyone came back, loaded down with souvenirs. Niya gave him her stuffed jaguar—the mascot of the Opal Oasis team—and Xio gave him his yellow-and-red-spotted scarf. While Niya raved about how fun it had been, Xio at least looked guilty for having a good time without him.

For their trip to Guerrero Temple, they were given sleeveless black tunics with matching pants adorned with gold fasteners down the outer stitching. There was also a red cape that they wore knotted on the left shoulder and draped across the right with their parents' glyphs embroidered onto it. Niya had to help Teo get into his because his wings kept getting in the way.

Finally they disembarked, with Ocelo leading the way.

After being cooped up all day, Teo was happy to get off the boat, but Guerrero Temple felt less than welcoming. It might've had something to do with the two ginormous gold jaguar statues sitting atop each wing of the massive building. Their empty, staring eyes made Teo shiver. He didn't like cats, especially big ones, and the ominous statues gave him the heebie-jeebies like any second they'd hop down and swallow him in one gulp.

The courtyard of the temple housed a small grove of jungle trees, complete with heavy branches and hanging vines surrounding a pond. A larger-than-life golden statue of Diose Guerrero stood at the edge of the water with a black statue of a jaguar lying across their feet.

That is, Teo thought it was another statue until they approached. It lifted its large square head, amber eyes practically glowing against its melanated fur. It stood up and stalked toward the group. Before Teo could do little more than yelp and latch on to Niya's arm, the jaguar launched itself onto Ocelo, knocking them off their feet.

A terrified shout ripped through Teo's throat as the jaguar—

Licked Ocelo's face.

Teo looked on, absolutely baffled as three other jaguars with normal coloring emerged from the trees and piled onto the war semidiose. Ocelo laughed and greeted their massive friends, wrestling and pushing them affectionately as they rubbed their large heads against Ocelo in welcome.

"You good?" Niya asked with an amused grin.

Teo realized he was still clinging to Niya's arm for dear life.

He quickly let her go and wiped his sweaty palms on his thighs. "*Yes.*" He scowled. "I just—"

Xio at least had the decency to hide his chuckles behind his hand.

Something tugged Teo's wing.

He looked back to find a jaguar cub pawing at him, snuffling curiously at his feathers.

Teo jumped onto Niya, practically climbing onto her back. "HELP!"

But Niya was too busy laughing to do anything while the cub sat back on its haunches, swatting playfully.

Ocelo walked over and scooped the cub up into their arms. "That's my good girl," they said, grinning as they walked back to the front of the group. The cub placed her massive paws on either side of their head, long tongue grooming their buzzed hair. Ocelo's dyed jaguar rosette patterns matched the fur of the cub's almost perfectly.

Teo turned on his friends, his face red. "Thanks a lot, you two!" he snapped while Niya continued to cackle.

Xio was doubled over, cracking up, his arms wrapped around his stomach. "I'm gonna pee!"

To worsen the humiliation, he caught Aurelio watching him with amusement. Teo quickly turned away to hide his ever-reddening cheeks.

The black jaguar walked next to Ocelo and Luna as the group made their way through the courtyard. The rest of the cats stayed behind, but Teo swore they were staring at him. Instead of greeting them at the dining hall like the others, Diose Guerrero's massive form stood waiting for them at the entrance of the temple.

"WELCOME HEROES!" they called, sharp teeth flashing as they grinned ear to ear. They waved everyone inside, giving friendly hellos before falling into step next to Ocelo, their large arm draped across their child's shoulders.

The dining hall was small but cozy. The table was already piled high with nearly every kind of meat imaginable, but heavy on juicy, rare steaks. The priests in red were talkative and not once did Teo's glass go empty.

Diose Guerrero shared the head of the table with Ocelo. The black jaguar made itself comfortable on an overstuffed pillow, chewing on hunks of meat and bones that Guerrero shared from their own plate. The jaguar cub remained in Ocelo's lap, being hand-fed and sucking on Ocelo's fingers in between.

Diose Guerrero was a lot different than how Teo pictured. He'd figured the god would be surly and intimidating, like Ocelo, but Guerrero was the complete opposite. They were loud and friendly with an easy, albeit sharp-toothed, smile. Guerrero liked to make jokes and then promptly crack themself up, sending their booming laughter echoing across the room. Stranger still was to see Ocelo in their natural habitat, smiling and laughing right along.

By the time they returned to the boat, everyone was stuffed. The other Golds piled onto the couches in the common room, nursing their food comas and flipping endlessly through channels on the TV.

Teo, Xio, and Niya sequestered themselves in some armchairs in the corner, watching clips of previous trials Diose Guerrero had hosted. When it came down to it, they all involved some sort of head-to-head competition. One year, competitors were paired off in a ring and forced to battle one another until someone got pushed out of bounds, while another involved a variation of capture the flag.

As the night went on, Xio got quieter and quieter. Niya didn't seem to notice, but Teo could literally watch the tension creeping into his shoulders. They were the last ones left in the common room and when Niya nodded off and started to snore, Teo decided it was time for bed.

"Do we have to?" Xio asked in a small voice. He kept anxiously twisting his bracelet around his wrist.

"It's pretty late. You should get some sleep so you're well-rested for tomorrow."

"I guess . . ." Xio trailed off, staring at the door that led outside.

"You okay?" Teo asked. Suddenly, he was worried that Xio might be a flight risk. He didn't know what happened to competitors who tried to run away during the trials, and he was too scared to look it up.

Xio was silent for a moment, but then he turned back to Teo and forced a smile. "Yeah, I'm fine." Teo knew he was lying, and maybe that was obvious, because Xio hastened to add, "It's just nice to have company, I guess. Back home I share my room with three of my siblings. It's kinda weird and quiet by myself."

"You can stay with me," Teo offered, feeling bad for the kid. He had no idea what it was like sharing a room since he was the only child of Quetzal—well, the only living one—but he could imagine the change would be jarring. "I'm sure one of the Sol priests could bring in a spare bed—"

But Xio quickly shook his head. "No, that's all right," he said, using that same forced smile on him again. "I've got some stuff I need to do before bed, anyway." When Teo gave him a questioning look, he added, "Just want to go over my notes one more time."

"I can keep you company if you want—"

"No, no, it's okay, really," Xio said hurriedly.

Teo sucked his lips between his teeth. He didn't like the idea of Xio being lonely, but he also didn't want to treat him like he was a child. "All right, well, I'm across the hall if you change your mind. Okay?"

Xio nodded.

Teo reached over and gave Niya a shove. She was a heavy sleeper and if you weren't a little rough with her, she stayed dead to the world.

A short snort rattled Niya's nose and she sat bolt upright. "Wha' happened?" she asked groggily, looking around.

"Time to go to bed, Sleeping Beauty," Teo teased as Xio picked up his binder of cards.

Niya yawned and stretched. "Oh good, I was starting to get a little tired."

＊

Teo tossed and turned the entire night. His body was full of restless energy. Unlike the night before the other trials, this time he felt a buzz of excitement instead of the usual dread. He still couldn't believe that he'd come in *fourth*. Everyone had a chance, Aurelio had said so himself, but did he really believe it?

At breakfast the next morning, Teo's knees bounced uncontrollably under the table and his gaze kept slipping to Aurelio. When Aurelio glanced back, it set a fire low in Teo's stomach that continued to smolder as Luna arrived to tell them where they were headed next.

"For the fourth trial, we will be traveling to Laberinto," she announced.

Teo sat there in shock while confusion passed around the table.

"Laberinto?" Xochi repeated, like she hadn't heard of it before. Atzi shrugged, just as lost.

"Laberinto is a Jade city," Teo said, louder than he meant to. He looked at Luna, waiting for some kind of explanation, but she only nodded.

"That is correct."

Teo didn't know whether to laugh or cheer or do something else entirely.

"Holy crap," came Xio's small, awed voice.

"Why are we going to a *Jade* city?" Auristela demanded, spitting the word like it left a bad taste on her tongue.

"Because Diosa Opción is hosting the fourth trial," Luna said, choosing to ignore Auristela's attitude.

"There's never been a trial held in a Jade city before," Aurelio said slowly, though not unkindly.

"Yes, and we've never had two Jade competitors, either," Luna pointed out, casting a quick glance at Teo and Xio. Teo could've sworn she was holding back a smile. "I think this is a trials full of the unprecedented and unexpected."

"I can't believe it!" Teo said, half delirious as he, Xio, and Niya went to the aftdeck to talk over what they'd just learned. "A *Jade city*!" he repeated, pushing his hands through his hair.

"I don't know what to make of it," Niya confessed as she sank onto the couch.

"Me, neither! It means *something*," he insisted. "I just don't know what!"

Were the other gods finally seeing that Jades weren't entirely useless? If they were being chosen by Sol to compete, and a Jade god was even *hosting* one of the trials, did that mean maybe, finally, Jades were going to get a chance?

It was an opportunity, one that Teo didn't want to waste. If he could pull this off, he would have the chance to change things for Jades on a monumental level.

While Teo juggled his internal crisis, Niya started asking more practical questions.

"What's Opción the diosa of, anyway? There are so many Jade dioses, it's hard to keep track," she said before hastily adding, "No offense!"

"Problem-solving, ingenuity, and choices," Xio supplied with his encyclopedic knowledge. His trading card binder had been searched and cast aside. There was no historical information that would help them this time around.

"Sounds hard," Niya said with a look of concern.

"I just can't believe it's a Jade city!" Teo repeated for about the tenth time as he paced.

"Maybe it'll be like a puzzle?" Xio guessed.

Niya scoffed. "If the fourth trial is a damn board game, I want my money back."

They bounced around ideas as Marea steered them east.

Laberinto was a coastal city, nearly on the opposite end of the equator from Quetzlan. As they made their final approach, the river grew wide until they entered a channel where the freshwater met the ocean and Laberinto came into view.

Teo, Xio, and Niya went onto the deck for a better look.

It was a small cliffside city perched on a peninsula and overlooking the eastern ocean. The sound of crashing waves and singing gulls traveled in the wind. The air smelled briny, like sea salt. While the western ocean, which Quetzal bordered, was calm and bright blue with sandy beaches, the shores at the base of Laberinto were the complete opposite. Whitecaps slapped against the sides of the boat while dark, frothy waves crashed against the rocky shore, sending streamers of seaweed rolling in the surf.

Far above, at the top of the cliffs, rested Laberinto. It was too congested to have an arena within city limits, so one had been constructed on a bit of land near the sea. The wind whipped through the air, carrying with it the cheers of the waiting crowd. It seemed oddly louder than usual, but Teo thought little of it—he was too busy getting stuck in his own head.

It was down to the wire now. He had two more trials left to succeed. He had to be focused and not let himself get distracted, which was why when they walked into the arena and thunderous cheers erupted, he barely noticed.

"Holy shit." Niya stopped abruptly, causing Teo to collide into her very solid back.

"Give a guy some warning, Niya—"

"Look!"

"Nearly broke my nose on your—"

"TEO!" Niya grabbed him by the shoulders and spun him toward the stands. "LOOK!"

At first, Teo didn't understand what he was supposed to be looking at. The tiered seating was packed full of people sitting shoulder to shoulder. They waved pennants and flags in the air, just like every other trial, but then he realized—

They weren't the white flags of the Golds, or even Sol. They were bright blue-green.

Jade.

Teo's breath caught in his throat.

And not just any Jade flags. They all bore the spread-winged quetzal, his mother's glyph. Fans held handmade signs with his name and posters with his terrible picture from that very first day. There were even hand-painted posters of quetzals.

HERO OF THE JADES, one sign read.

Clips of Teo from the previous trials flashed across the giant jumbotron. Teo kneeling before the mother alebrije as she loomed over him. Teo dodging attacks in the trees. Teo flying above Tierra's mountain with his new wings. They didn't even show the part where he was struck by lightning out of the sky.

The jumbotron switched to a live feed, focused on his stunned, open-mouthed face.

The crowd erupted in screams, shouts, and whistles. They thundered so loudly, Teo could feel it reverberate deep in his chest. Garbled words slowly filled the air until it became one resounding chant.

"Pa-ja-ri-to! Pa-ja-ri-to!"

He couldn't believe it.

"They're here for *you*!" Niya practically screamed in his ear.

Xio turned to look up at Teo, eyebrows lifted and lips parted like he couldn't believe it, either. A spontaneous laugh jumped in Teo's throat. His eyes stung and his chest was so tight, he could barely breathe. He pressed his palms into his cheeks and shook his head. How was this possible? His stomach tumbled as he went to his mom.

"This is amazing, Teo!" she said, squeezing him tight. "You're their Hero!"

Hero.

Teo turned, seeking out Aurelio.

When he found him, Aurelio was already watching, an open, unabashed smile gracing his features. Teo smiled back so big, it made his face ache. He didn't even care that Auristela was seething next to him. She didn't matter.

Teo, a lowly Jade from a tiny, forgotten city, was standing in the ranks of the best young Heroes in all of Reino del Sol. The people were calling to him. They wanted him to win.

And Teo was not going to let them down.

For the fourth trial, a temple loomed in the center of the arena. Only it was less a temple and more the ruins of one. It was covered in glistening ferns and slick moss. Caved-in sections of roof yawned open, pitch-black and draped with vines. The stone steps going up the center of the temple were split and broken by thick roots.

It was a strange sight. Something about it was unsettling and made him move closer to Niya's side. Teo had never heard of a temple in such a state of decay. Even the poorest of Jade temples was still lovingly tended to by their people.

It was like getting a glimpse of a desolate future, or a long-ago past.

"For the fourth trial, competitors must collect stones from caches hidden within this temple," Diosa Luna instructed and signed. "There are four different kinds of stones, each of which are worth a different number of points. Obsidian stones are worth ten points, jade stones are worth twenty-five points, and gold stones are worth one hundred points. Lastly, there is one replica of the Sol Stone hidden within the temple. It is worth five hundred points."

Marino let out a low whistle.

It sounded simple enough, but even Teo could spot that this would be a lot more complicated than the past trials. Trying to find stones hidden in an unfamiliar temple would be like searching for a needle in a haystack.

"Lower-value stones are easier to find and can be found in higher quantities, while gold stones will be fewer and more difficult to locate," Luna continued. "Competitors have one hour to collect as many points as possible."

Sol priests stepped forward to hand out black drawstring backpacks and what looked like fancy sportswear watches. Teo murmured his thanks as he took his. When he fit the watch around his wrist, the face lit up with acid green numbers.

60:00

"You must deposit your stones at the altar at the top of the temple before the hour is up," Luna said, gesturing toward the temple.

Teo craned his neck to squint up at it. He couldn't quite see the top, but something shiny caught the sunlight.

"You can deposit your stones at any time, but you may only do so once. Once you've deposited your stones, your score is locked in for the trial." Luna's midnight black eyes swept down the line of semidioses. "You can use whatever means are at your disposal to collect stones or interfere with other players," she said.

Luna smiled like she knew something they didn't.

They were ushered to the edge of the bridge to all start at once.

Since his wings were too cumbersome to allow him to carry his backpack on his back, Teo wore it on his chest to avoid the hassle. Some of the Golds had a similar idea. If nothing else, it'd be easier to put stones into and keep them safe.

"I've got a bad feeling about this one," Xio said, his eyes locked on the temple.

"Hey, no negative thoughts!" Niya ordered as she helped him put on his drawstring backpack, securing it in place. "Only positive vibes here—right, Teo?"

"Right," Teo agreed blindly. He was distracted by Aurelio and

Auristela, who stood nearby, stretching and probably talking about their strategies as they awaited the start of the trial.

"We'll be able to stick together this time," Niya reassured him. "We'll gather as many stones as possible, and then split them up. We'll give extra to Xio since he's so low in the rankings. I bet anything those fools are gonna be battling it out for the higher-point stones, so just stick to the jade and obsidian ones—"

Niya's voice faded into a low thrum as Teo edged closer to Aurelio and nudged the back of his knee with the toe of his shoe.

Aurelio's knee buckled.

When he whipped around, Teo smirked.

"Ready to get knocked out of first place, Golden Boy?"

Auristela's attention snapped to Teo, her face pinching with restrained anger.

But Aurelio's expression softened to an amused grin. "You think you can get more points than me, Bird Brain?"

"Oh, I *know* I can."

A spark ignited behind Aurelio's eyes. "Prove it."

Something burned deep in Teo's chest, and he didn't even care when Auristela grabbed her brother's arm and turned him away.

When Teo turned back to his friends, Niya immediately smacked his arm, which felt more like a punch coming from the burly semidiosa.

"Ouch!"

"*Ew*, Teo!" Niya snapped accusingly.

"What?!" he said through guilty chuckles. "A little friendly competition never hurt anyone!"

While Niya gagged, Xio's eyes shifted curiously between Aurelio's back and Teo.

"Semidioses, on my mark," Luna's amplified voice boomed.

Mariachi's cornet sounded at the same time Teo's watch buzzed on his wrist.

Everyone ran across the bridge, Aurelio and Auristela leading the pack. Teo and Niya slowed to keep pace with Xio. The closer they got to the temple, the less confident Teo felt. The cheers from the stands were crushing this time, ringing in his ears.

The first cache they came upon was in the courtyard. The ground was covered in dense undergrowth, threatening to snag Teo's feet if he stepped wrong. Sections of the outer temple walls had streaks of ash peeking out between blankets of greenery.

In the center of the courtyard stood a humanoid statue made of cracked and weathered stone. Time had worn away any facial features there once had been, leaving only a jagged gash.

Everyone sprinted toward the statue. Teo could see the gold stone, about the size of his fist, resting atop its head. Immediately, the Golds up ahead raced for it.

"That's creepy," Teo said as they slowed to a stop.

"Blech," Niya agreed, crinkling her nose.

"We should—" Teo looked to Xio, but he was no longer standing between them.

He'd come to a stop a few yards back. Frozen in place, he stared up at the statue with wide eyes, the color draining from his face.

Teo quickly retreated back to his side. "Hey, it's all right," he said, gently bumping his shoulder into Xio's. "We'll look out for each other." The kid was clearly terrified and Teo couldn't blame him.

"We're sticking together this time!" Niya reminded him. "Let's get some rocks and get this over with!"

"The sooner the better," Teo agreed.

Xio nodded, a short jerky movement, his eyes still stuck on the statue.

By the time they reached the statue, Aurelio had swiped the gold stone and Auristela had grabbed one of the three, slightly smaller jade stones in the statue's upturned hands. Ocelo got the second and Xochi the third.

The others had completely bypassed the statue and run into the temple.

"No one even touched the obsidians," Teo said as they approached the deserted statue. A small pile of polished obsidian stones about the size of chicken eggs sat at the statue's feet. "Did they not see them?"

"They probably think they're too *good* for them," Niya growled.

"Seriously?"

"Seriously."

"That seems like a bad strategy," Teo mused as he picked up two. The stones were cool against his fingers as he slipped them into his bag.

"Most of them are going to want the gold stones," Niya said as she dumped the remaining eight into Xio's backpack.

"Don't you need some?" Xio asked, giving Niya a surprised look.

Niya waved him off. "We'll find more. 'Sides, I'm doing fine in the rankings. Not to brag or anything," she added with a wink.

But something wasn't sitting right with Teo. "This seems too easy, doesn't it?" he said, looking around the now-abandoned courtyard. "Just stones waiting out in the open?"

"Teo!" Niya snapped, cutting her hand across her body in the slashed-throat motion. "Just accept the nice gifts from the dioses and let's move on—don't jinx it! No offense," she added to Xio.

He shrugged his small shoulders. "None taken."

Teo tried to push the nagging feeling to the back of his mind. Right now, he needed to focus on getting through this trial, especially if he was going to beat Aurelio.

"Let's go before all the good stones get taken," Teo said.

He led the way through the courtyard where the crooked stone steps led up to the top of the temple. Two large, dark archways stood on either side every couple flights.

"Left, right, or up?" Teo asked.

"Aurelio, Auristela, and Ocelo went to the left," Niya said.

"I saw Xochi, Marino, Dezi, and Atzi go right," Xio added, clutching the straps of his backpack.

"Then let's go up," Teo said, not waiting for confirmation as he took the uneven steps two at a time. "Better we find an untouched cache first and not just their leftovers."

When the path split in two, Teo immediately went for the left. "Let's go!"

With one last glimpse of daylight, they crossed through the arch and were plunged into darkness. Immediately, the noise of the cheering crowd cut off. The sudden silence sent Teo's heart lurching in his chest.

All three skidded to a stop on the slick floors.

"Did you guys hear that, too?" Xio asked, experimentally rubbing his ear.

"Yeah," Teo said, taking in their surroundings.

Unlike the open-air floors of Quetzlan Temple, these dimly lit halls were cramped and split off in several different directions. Pitted stone floors were flanked by walls covered in faded carvings and dark mold. The echoes of water dripping and wind slipping through empty halls were the only sounds.

"How the hell are we supposed to navigate this place?" Teo said. Without windows or a guide, it'd be impossible to orient themselves. Torches lining the walls were the only source of light.

"Well, we know going up will get us to the finish point," Niya offered as she sniffed a green, spongy growth on the wall.

Teo rolled his eyes. "Yeah, no shit. And don't lick that."

She shot him a scowl. "I wasn't going to!"

"I guess we should pick a direction and hope for the best?" Xio cut in with a doubtful look.

Niya threw her hands up in an exaggerated shrug. "I guess so!"

"We haven't had a real plan for any of the other trials, so why start now?" Teo grumbled.

"Let's try this way," Xio said, pointing to a hallway lined with arched doorways. As they ran past, it was so dark that Teo couldn't even see what was on the other side.

"Dios, how big is this place?" Teo wondered as they jogged down the corridor. It seemed to stretch on forever ahead of them; it was impossible to see where, or if, it ended.

"Can't be any bigger than the arena, right?" Niya said, but even she looked doubtful.

"Let's try this one," Xio said, veering off to jog through one of the shadowed arches.

Once they passed through, they found themselves in another identical hallway. Uneasiness churned in Teo's stomach. A slow, creeping feeling worked up the back of his neck as he and Niya followed Xio through another doorway—

And into another identical hall.

"Is this the same hallway?" Niya asked, stopping to spin in a circle.

"I don't think so," Xio said, not sounding too concerned.

"I have no idea," Teo admitted, squinting into the dark. "I can barely see anything."

"Hang on."

Teo turned to see Niya, with a tinkling of metal, transform her bangles into a shiny ax. She lifted it above her head before swinging it down at the floor. The blade struck the stone, leaving a splintered crack.

"There!" Niya said, leaning the ax against her shoulder like a bat. She proudly gestured to the circle of crumbled stone. "Now we can tell if it's the same hall!"

Ready to go, Xio led the way through a different doorway. "This way!"

Teo followed and, once again, they were spit into a hallway.

And there was the large gash in the stone Niya had left.

Teo groaned. "This is definitely the same hallway." He barely got the words out before Niya shoved his arm, sending him stumbling forward.

"You jinxed us!" she barked.

Teo caught himself before he could run into the slimy wall. "No I didn't!"

"You said, 'This seems too easy!'" Niya mimicked him in a ridiculously deep voice. "Tell him, Xio!"

"I don't sound like that!" Teo said, shoving her back, which of course did nothing. Annoyance itched under his skin. "And it's not my fault we wound up in this stupid hallway!"

Xio stood between them, eyes bouncing back and forth as they bickered.

"Well it's certainly not *my* fault!" Niya shot back.

Teo let out a groan so frustrated that it almost became a squawk. "We need to focus! We've only hit one cache and we have no idea how many there are in total! Which way should we try next?"

"This way!" Xio said.

Teo and Niya chased after him as he took off through another doorway.

Over and over again, they found themselves in the same hall.

"Wait!" Teo said before Xio could run through another doorway. Xio and Niya both skidded to a stop. "This isn't working," he said, wiping sweat from his brow. The damp, trapped air felt thick in his lungs.

"This doesn't make any sense!" Niya shouted, her voice echoing as she stomped her foot. "These stupid doorways aren't working!" The bangles against her wrists melted and grew into a large metal club in her hands.

"Niya," Teo warned, but it was too late.

Holding it like a bat and with a fierce look of determination, she swung the ax into the wall.

The hit cracked through the stone, echoing against the walls. The ground beneath Teo's feet shook violently. Teo grabbed Xio's hood and dragged him back.

Luckily, the only damage Niya caused was a jagged hole in the wall.

"There!" Niya smiled happily. "If those doorways don't work then we'll use a new one!" As the club turned back into bangles, Niya pushed some of the loose rocks to widen the gap. The ancient stone didn't put up much of a fight.

"Niya!" Teo snapped. "You could've caused the floor to collapse!"

She scoffed. "Don't be so dramatic, I barely put any force behind it!"

"That was *barely*?" Xio asked, staring up at Niya with wide eyes.

Niya preened in response.

"Let's *try* not to cause any cave-ins while we're in here," Teo said, rubbing his temples. He checked his watch to see that more than five minutes had already passed. "Let's go!"

Niya squeezed her way through the hole first and Teo waited for Xio to go next before following.

As he stumbled through, he heard Niya say, "Uh-oh."

"*Now* what?"

There wasn't another hallway on the other side of the wall. Instead, it opened up into a small room. Other than some moss and the questionable smell of mildew, it was empty. On the far wall stood a single door made of dark, water-stained wood.

"Well, it's not *worse*," Teo said as he hesitantly stepped closer to the door.

"It smells bad in here," Xio said, covering his nose with his sleeve.

"I'm getting bad vibes from that door, Teo," Niya added, her voice tight.

"Oh, come on, Niya, since when are you afraid of—"

Teo turned around to face his friend. Niya's brow was bunched as she stared at the door and Xio's face was scrunched in distaste.

But what made him pause was the hole in the wall. Or rather, lack thereof.

Teo's shoulders slumped and his stomach dropped through the stone floor. "Okay, maybe it *is* worse." He pointed to the blank wall behind them, which showed no sign of Niya's earlier destruction and, more important, no exit.

"What the *shit*?" Niya gasped, running her hands over the slick stone. "Should I make another hole?"

"No! I've got the feeling trying to take shortcuts is what got us in here," Teo said, trying to keep his voice even.

He didn't want to admit it, but panic was starting to claw its way up his throat. He wasn't used to being stuck in small places and didn't like the feeling of being encased in stone one bit. Teo's wings kept readjusting themselves and it took all his concentration to keep them under control.

"Maybe someone should try the door?" Xio offered.

He was right, of course, and the quicker they got out of there, the better. Teo needed fresh air and sky.

Niya rolled her shoulders back and lifted her chin. "Welp, let's give it a try!" She marched up to the door and grabbed the handle. By some miracle, it groaned open.

Relief was like a splash of cool water on Teo's face.

Niya turned back to them with a smile. "It worked!"

No sooner had the words left her lips than Teo saw something move on the other side.

Before Teo could do anything more than let out a strangled shout, a massive stone hand shoved Niya. Knocked onto her back, Niya skidded across the floor to Teo's and Xio's feet before the door slammed shut.

"Son of a—!"

"Niya!" Teo dropped down next to her as she gasped for breath. "Are you all right?!"

"The fuck was that?!" she croaked, rubbing her chest and coughing.

"Looked like a hand," Xio said with keen curiosity as he squinted at the now closed door.

Teo helped her onto her feet. "I think we need to stop and think—"

But Niya was already stomping back to the door. "I've got this, don't worry," she said as the metal club materialized in her hand again.

"I don't think—!"

Too late.

Niya threw open the door again, ready to swing, but the stone hand appeared once more. This time, it flicked the club right out of Niya's grip. Teo grabbed Xio and used his wings to jump high enough to avoid it as it skittered across the floor right under them.

Before Niya could react, the hand shoved her again and she went flying. Her back slammed into the wall before she ended up in a heap on the floor along with her bat. Anyone less than a demigod would've had their skull cracked open by now.

"I don't think that's working," Xio observed calmly as Teo helped her stagger to her feet yet again.

But Niya wasn't listening. She held her hand out and the club flew back into her grip like a magnet. This time, the bangles from her ankles joined to morph into a large hammer. "We're getting through that door!" she shouted, stalking forward with grime streaked across her bare thighs and muscular arms.

This time, Niya was faster. When the door opened, she was ready and struck the stone hand with her hammer, but it simply caught the weapon in its palm and squeezed. The mangled hunk of metal dropped uselessly to the floor.

"YOU—!"

Before Niya could get out her insult, the hand picked her up and chucked her at Teo and Xio. They dove out of the way as she collided into the wall with a *crack*. This time, when she slid to the floor, her body left a spiderweb of cracks in the stone wall.

"For Sol's *sake*, Niya!" Teo said, racing back to her side as the door slammed shut again. "Would you stop? It's not working!"

When he got her into a sitting position, chunks of her hair had escaped her braids, sticking out at all angles. Niya spat, her golden blood splattering on the ground and shining on her lip. When she looked up, anger glinted in her bronze eyes.

"RUDE, ASSHOLE!" she roared.

"I don't think it cares," Xio mused. But something in Teo's mind clicked.

"I've got an idea," he said, turning back to the door. "If the temple threw us in this room because it didn't like that we crashed through the wall—"

"*We?*" Niya pressed.

"Because *you* crashed through the wall," Teo corrected, doing his best not to sound annoyed. "Then maybe *we* were the rude ones."

"I don't get it," Xio said.

"Maybe we're playing the game wrong," Teo said as he slowly approached the door. Every fiber in his being was screaming at him to stay away. Even his wings flung themselves out, knocking him off-balance, like they were going to take flight, but there was nowhere to run away to.

Teo stopped in front of the door. His heart hammered in his veins as he clenched his hands into fists, trying to steady himself. He sucked in a breath and said a silent prayer to Sol before knocking on the door.

The echoes faded without anything happening.

Swallowing hard, Teo cleared his dry throat. "May we go through?" he asked.

The door groaned open and Teo immediately dropped to the floor, flinging up his wings to cover his head.

But no stone hand threw him across the room.

"Well, *shit*," Niya said through a laugh.

Teo peeked between the feathers of his wings. The door stood wide open and the hand was nowhere in sight.

"Did—did it work?" Teo asked, hardly believing it himself.

"Looks like it!" Niya jerked him to his feet. "Who knew you'd be the brains to my brawn?" she said, thumping him so hard on the back it knocked the wind from his lungs.

"*Thanks.*" Teo coughed.

"How'd you know to do that?" Xio asked, frowning up at Teo.

"I didn't," he admitted with a shrug.

Xio didn't seem satisfied with that answer, but there wasn't time to discuss it further.

"Onward and upward!" Niya announced, as if she hadn't nearly been made into human pulp mere moments ago.

Teo led the way through the door. On the other side was another, much bigger room. It was narrow but quite long, with flickering torches lining the walls and illuminating the next cache.

"*Finally,*" Teo sighed in relief.

Three stone pedestals sat equidistant from each other. The closest held ten obsidian stones, past that were the four jades, and at the very back of the room a gold stone glimmered on its own. All the stones present meant no one else had found the cache yet.

"We should take all of them, right?" Teo asked, looking to Niya and Xio for a morality check.

"Hell yeah, screw those other guys!" Niya agreed with a snort.

Xio stepped forward but Teo grabbed him by the back of his jacket. "Wait!"

"What?" Xio asked, giving him a confused look.

"There must be a catch, right?" Teo reasoned. "I mean, we just got stuck in a neverending hallway and Niya nearly got creamed—"

"*But did I die?*" she interjected.

Teo decided to ignore her. "We need to be careful and not go charging in."

"The floor *does* look kind of weird," Niya said, pointing down.

The floor was made up of stone tiles. "They're glyphs," Teo realized.

Lumbre's sun, Amor's sacred heart, and his mother's quetzal were easy to spot. "It's not all the dioses' glyphs, but definitely all the competitors.'"

"There's my dad's!" Niya chirped, pointing excitedly to the glyph with three mountains.

"I don't recognize this one," Teo said.

Among the familiar glyphs, there were a series of tiles with a goat head. It was grinning, its open mouth lined with sharp teeth.

"Damn, that's Venganza," Niya said, backing away from the tile.

"The god of vengeance," Xio explained, the color draining from his face.

"Oh." Teo had only learned about the Obsidian gods in school. He clearly wasn't as well versed in the history of the betrayer gods as the Golds were.

"Yeah, let's not step on those ones," Niya said. "Nothing good will happen."

"Maybe we're only supposed to step on the tiles with our parent's glyph?" Teo guessed, pointing out the path of Quetzal glyphs that led to the pedestal of obsidian stones. "The tiles get smaller the deeper you go into the room," he pointed out.

"Probably to make it harder to get the jade and gold stones," Niya guessed.

"Could you just use your wings to get the stones?" Xio said, turning to Teo.

Teo shook his head, embarrassment warming his cheeks. "The ceiling isn't high enough. I don't think I could get the stones without accidentally bumping into it and dropping onto the tiles," he admitted. Guilt squeezed his stomach as Xio stared at the tiles, his hands white-knuckled as they gripped the straps of his bag. He looked especially small and younger than his thirteen years.

Once again, Teo was hit with the realization of how truly unfair it was that Xio was even in the trials to begin with.

"Aye, Teo and I can get the stones," Niya said, lightly bumping her shoulder into Xio's.

"You don't have to—" Xio started, but Teo cut him off.

"Yeah, you stay here and stand guard!" he agreed.

"I can go for the jades and gold if you can get the obsidians," Niya said, looking to Teo for confirmation.

"I don't know, you've got really big feet," Teo teased with a grin. "You sure you can handle the little tiles?"

"I might have big feet, but I've got way better balance than you and your wings flapping around like a baby bird's!" Niya shot back.

A laugh bucked in Teo's chest. "You've got me there."

Xio managed a small smile. "Thanks, you guys."

Teo insisted on testing out their theory, catching Niya before she jumped into action. She acted as an anchor, gripping Teo's arm in her rock-solid grip as he inched to the tiles and experimentally stepped on a Quetzal glyph. The stone remained steady. They swapped spots so Niya could try hers, and when it held true, that was good enough for Teo.

Niya headed out first, quickly moving from tile to tile with ease. She went for the gold at the far back of the room first. The way she leapt from one tile to the next without even pausing made Teo's heart clench so tightly he had to stop watching and focus on his own path. Carefully, he stepped from tile to tile, looking three steps ahead for his mother's glyph so he didn't get stuck and have to double back.

"Got it!" Niya announced, beaming as she held the gold stone for them to see before tucking it into her backpack.

When she headed back for the jade stones, Teo had only just reached the Quetzal tile closest to the pedestal. He loosened the drawstrings of his pack and carefully dropped in all ten obsidian stones. The downside to collecting all the obsidians was his bag was quickly filling up and getting heavy to carry.

"I've got the obsidians!" Teo called out, tugging the bag tightly closed. "Get the jades and let's get out of here," he said to Niya.

"On it!" Niya replied, already nearing the last pile of stones.

Teo exhaled a huge sigh of relief. The beginning of the trial may have been a disaster, but at least they had it together now. "Be sure you don't—"

The cracking of stone cut through the air.

Teo's head whipped to Niya. She stood perched on a tile, eyes wide. "It wasn't me!" she said with a jerky shake of her head.

Panic squeezed Teo's throat. He turned to find Xio. His foot was on a tile, the stone completely shattered.

"I slipped!" Xio cried out, eyes bulging.

Before Teo could react, the ground beneath his feet shuddered.

The thunderous sound of stone grinding against stone filled the air. The floor dropped out from under Teo, tilting suddenly like it was on a hinge. His wings shot out, trying to catch him, but it was too late.

He fell back, sliding across the stone toward the chasm that had opened up in the floor.

Xio scrambled, trying to catch hold of anything, but his small hands slid uselessly against the slick stone.

"TEO!" Niya shouted. He could see the terror in her eyes before she fell into the pit.

"NO!" The word tore through his throat, but there was nothing he could do.

Teo plunged into darkness.

CHAPTER 19

Teo's wings scraped against rock as he shot through what felt like a cramped tunnel. Unable to see in the pitch black, he bumped over fists of stone that tore at his skin and feathers. He tried to slow himself down but his hands and feet slipped uselessly against the slimy sides.

It was officially the worst slide he'd ever been on.

There was a flash of light at the end of the tunnel before Teo was unceremoniously spit out onto a metal grate. He groaned, cold metal biting into his cheek and the taste of blood on his tongue. The heavy stones in his bag dug into his chest.

With a great deal of effort, Teo pushed himself up onto his feet and looked around.

Water droplets rained down on him from twisted roots dangling from the ceiling. The tang of mildew and algae hung in the air. There were multiple tunnel offshoots on the knobby rock walls behind him, spilling streams through the grated floor and into the murky water below.

The gaps in the iron were about the size of his fist. Not big enough for his foot to fall through, but definitely big enough to trip on if he wasn't careful.

"*Dammit,*" Teo cursed. Getting separated from his friends was the last thing he needed. And where the hell *was* he?

Small shafts of light cut through cracks in the stone, which was a relief. Sunlight meant he wasn't belowground. Hopefully, he could still get to the top of the temple to deposit his stones, but time was ticking away. He needed a way out.

Teo turned and found himself face-to-face with another cache.

Three stone chests sat in the middle of the room in a line, their lids open and revealing the stones inside. The obsidian stones sat on his left, the jades in the center, and the single gold stone was laid in the chest to his right.

And, most importantly, a set of stairs waited on the other side.

Teo's heart leapt. He wasn't *totally* screwed! He could grab some stones and use the stairs to escape.

But, of course, he'd have to get through whatever obstacle was awaiting him.

The smart move was to try to get the obsidian stones first, since they were easier. Teo slowly crept across the grates, eyes sweeping back and forth for any sign of danger. Ripples dragged through the water below, but when Teo stopped, so did they.

It was agonizing work, moving closer to the chest when he *knew* there was something lurking down below but he didn't know *what*. By the time he reached the chest, his stomach was so queasy with nerves, he was ready to barf. The anticipation was worse than anything that could be waiting for him in the murky depths.

Gathering any last ounces of bravery he had, Teo reached out and touched one of the black stones. Still, nothing happened.

Slowly and ever so carefully, he started to pick up the stones and place them into his bag, trying to make as little noise as possible. But as he did, the water beneath him started to churn.

Teo stuffed them into his bag faster.

The seventh stone was in his hand when Teo's feet got stuck on something. He looked down. Through the iron grates, two pale green tentacles had hooked themselves around his ankles.

Teo let out a strangled shout. He tried to back away, but they only tightened their grip, sending him crashing back onto his wings. Frantically, he tried to pry his ankle free, but then another tentacle grabbed his wrist and tugged hard, pulling him down onto his back once again.

He tried to rip the tentacle off with his free hand, but it wouldn't budge. They tightened, making his hand and feet tingle as they cut off his circulation. In an act of desperation, Teo leaned over and bit down on the tentacle as hard as he could.

They released him and retreated back into the water as something let out blood curdling screech. Teo had no intention of finding out what exactly that 'something' was.

Ignoring the rank taste in his mouth, he scrambled to his feet and lunged for the chest. Wrenching open his bag, he dumped the last three obsidian stones inside before a tentacle shot out for his ankle again. This time, he stomped down at it as hard as he could.

The creature cried out again. The arm flashed from pale green to angry red, which was probably a bad sign.

Teo jumped into the air, his wings lifting him up in an attempt to make a break for the stairs, but another tentacle shot out through the grates. It snatched his ankle and slammed him back down on the grate with a loud *clang*.

Teo cried out as pain exploded in his wings.

Quickly, he rolled onto his stomach and tried crawling for the stairs. Before he could make it to safety, another tentacle arm snaked around his thigh. It constricted and pulled, trying to drag him back. Teo shoved his fingers between the grates and held on tight. The iron bit painfully into his skin.

He was losing his grip. If he didn't think fast—well, Teo didn't want to think about what fate awaited him.

Hanging on for dear life, Teo was out of options. There were no tools for him to fight back with.

Except for the empty chest.

Frantically, his brain tried to piece together a plan. What it came up with was objectively terrible. A truly shitty plan that could go wrong at least half a dozen ways, but it was all he had. His fingers were slipping. He was out of time.

After saying a silent prayer to his mom, Teo let go.

He rolled onto his back as the tentacle pulled him, dragging his wings painfully against the grates. Teo threw himself to the side as he passed the now empty stone chest, grabbing it in his hands. With all the strength he had left, he heaved the chest over his head and slammed it down on the tentacle, just below its grip on his thigh.

The creature screamed, its rubbery skin flashing white. There was a flash of moldy blue blood before the tentacle retreated back into the water.

Finally freed, Teo ran for it. He threw himself onto the steps and turned around, ready to fight off more tentacle arms. Instead, the arms retreated, slipping back through the grates and disappearing into the water below.

"Holy shit, holy *fuck*," Teo panted, his pulse roaring in his ears.

He made sure his bag was still strapped to front with the obsidian stones safely inside before checking he still had all six limbs. Other than some scrapes and suction cup–looking welts on his wrist, he was fully intact.

Teo collapsed onto the steps and tried to catch his breath.

If it was this difficult to just get the lower-point obsidian stones, he couldn't imagine what terrors awaited anyone who tried for the jade or gold stones.

As if on cue, a shout echoed from across the room.

Someone flew out from one of the tunnel offshoots, landing in a heap. Teo immediately recognized them as Ocelo.

Dazed, Ocelo pushed themself up into a seated position. They shook their buzzed head roughly, like they were trying to rattle their brain back in place. Ocelo looked around the room. When their jaguarlike eyes landed on the undisturbed gold stone waiting in its chest, their smile was all teeth.

But then they spotted Teo, and their smile immediately twisted into a sneer.

Ocelo got up and stomped off toward the gold stone, the grates rattling loudly under their feet.

"Watch out!" Teo attempted to warn. "There's—"

"Shut up!" Ocelo snarled without even looking in his direction.

A second later, a fiery red tentacle as thick as Teo's chest burst out of the water, sending a section of grate flying through the air.

"I tried to warn you!" Teo called out as the arm snatched Ocelo up and threw them to the ground.

The tentacle dove for Ocelo. Teo winced, expecting to see the semidiose get ripped apart.

Instead—in absolutely the wildest shit Teo had ever seen—Ocelo caught the slimy tentacle. They squeezed their thick arms around it like they were putting it in a choke hold. It thrashed wildly, slamming Ocelo against the grates, but Ocelo held tight, biceps bulging. The tentacle flashed between scarlet red and frightened white.

"For Sol's sake," Teo murmured to himself as Ocelo straight up wrestled the monstrous creature.

They managed to shift their grip, strangling the tentacle with one arm while they punched it mercilessly with the other.

Ocelo was an asshole, but damn were they strong.

"Well, I can see you have your hands full!" Teo said, getting to his feet. "Good luck!"

Teo ran up the steps as quickly as his battered body could manage. As he ascended several flights, Teo checked his watch. They were nearly halfway through the trial already. If he had any chance of getting ranked first, he would need to speed-run any other caches he came upon.

Once he thought he'd gone high enough to be near the top of the temple, Teo veered off down a hallway in search of another cache. A strange, rhythmic *swish*ing sound caught his attention. When he followed it, he found a huge, cavernous room.

From where he stood at the entrance of the room, three paths branched out in different directions. Thick logs swung back and forth across the paths from the ceiling like pendulums. Huge curved blades made of polished obsidian tipped the ends of the logs.

Instead of being grouped all together in one place, Teo saw the ten obsidian stones were placed at different intervals between the swinging blades.

This time, Teo wasn't the first one to find the cache. The gold stone must have already been taken because he didn't see it at the end of the path—but to be fair, the dozens of quickly slicing blades made it difficult to see.

In the middle path, two competitors were battling it out for the jade stones. Marino and Xochi danced between the blades, trying to snatch the last one at the very back of the room. It was dizzying to watch as they tried to knock each other off-balance, Xochi slinging her vines like whips and Marino sending jets of water back into her face.

Wasting no time, Teo rushed to grab the obsidians before they noticed he was there. He bounced on the balls of his feet, trying to get the rhythm, like he was back in grade school playing jump rope at recess. It took some time to figure out the timing of the blades, but once he got it, it was almost easy to leap between them, scooping up the small stones on his way.

He reached the last one at the same time Marino and Xochi made it to the final jade.

Just a hair faster than Xochi, Marino swiped the stone right out from under her.

Xochi let out an angry noise as Marino bolted back to the exit. In a show of extreme skill, Xochi threw out her vines. Like grasping fingers, they snatched Marino's backpack right off his shoulders and into her awaiting hands.

"Hah!" she said sharply before ripping the bag open and plunging her hand inside.

The smirk didn't fall from Marino's face as he kept running, making Teo pause at a safe space between blades.

From the depths of Marino's bag, Xochi pulled out—

Plain, dusty rocks.

She sucked in a breath, her eyes flying wide open as she looked at Marino.

As he hopped between the blades, Marino pulled open a zipper of the pouch on the front of his jacket. He reached in and pulled out two jade stones, flashing a wide smile. By the shape of the pocket, Teo could tell more were inside.

Marino, the clever bastard, must've filled up his bag with decoy rocks from the ruins and hidden the real ones in his pockets.

Xochi fumed. No, more than fumed. Her eyes grew dark, an angry snarl contorting her features.

Marino stopped smiling.

A shout leapt in Teo's throat, to tell him to run, but Xochi was too quick.

She thrust out her hands and vines shot forward, but they weren't the slick, bright green ones she usually conjured. These were a deep blueish green, thick and twisted. Marino tried to dodge them but it was no use—they snatched him up and threw him to the floor.

The slap of his body against wet stone made Teo wince.

Xochi curled her fingers and the vines thickened and twisted around Marino's torso, pinning his arms to his sides

"Xochi, knock it off!" Marino shouted, the whites of his eyes circling his pupils.

Xochi didn't listen. She closed her hands into fists and the vines tightened and squeezed around his chest.

Frantic now, Marino thrashed, his legs kicking wildly. "*Stop!*" his strangled shout echoed.

Teo was rooted to the spot in shock. Xochi, while competitive, had never shown a violent streak during the trials. He could hardly believe what he was seeing.

Dark shadows hollowed Xochi's eyes. Violent red thorns sprouted from the vines, cutting into Marino and drawing golden blood against his dark skin. Marino screamed, a sound so terrible and frightened that it snapped Teo into action.

Without thinking, he raced forward and launched himself into the air, straight for Xochi. Her entire focus was on Marino, allowing Teo to slam into her and knock her off her feet. They both went sprawling.

Pain dragged across Teo's palms as he hit the ground, but the important part was that he'd broken Xochi's concentration.

The vines released Marino, who scrambled back as they withered and fell uselessly to the floor. Teo got on his feet and backed up, trying to put as much distance between himself and Xochi as he could. He expected to be the new focus of her anger, but when she sat up, instead of seething with rage, Xochi looked horrified.

She looked at Teo, brown eyes wide with shock, before turning to where Marino gasped for breath. She saw the vines. The pinpricks of golden blood on Marino's skin. Xochi looked down at her hands, jerking back like she was afraid of them.

"Marino! I'm so sorry! I didn't—!"

But Marino wasn't waiting for an explanation, and neither was Teo. Both boys ran for it.

"Are you okay?" Teo panted as he struggled to keep up with Marino.

"I think so," Marino said, though he still looked in shock. He cut Teo a glance. "You saved my ass back there. I owe you one."

"Yeah, well, just returning the favor," Teo said. "But if you want to repay me with stones—"

Marino grinned. "I don't owe you *that* much."

Teo let out a breathless laugh. "Worth a shot!"

Marino thumped him on the back. "See you at the finish!"

With that, the corridor branched off in two separate directions, and they split ways. Teo was more careful to check corners this time. Shit was getting dangerous. He didn't know why—maybe it was all the pressure and stress of the competition—but people were getting more and more brutal as the trials went on. He didn't want to think about what might have happened to Marino if he hadn't interfered.

He needed to finish the trial and meet up with Niya and Xio.

Teo looped around and ran up the stairs once again. He'd gone up a few flights when he rounded a corner and caught a glimpse of someone dashing through a doorway. In a split-second decision, Teo veered off to follow them.

In the dark halls, Teo barely saw them duck through a doorway up ahead. He threw himself forward, running as fast as he could.

If they found a cache, Teo wanted in on it.

Following them through another doorway, Teo skidded to a stop. This room was tall and narrow, almost like he was standing on the bottom of a square well. It was a tight fit, with maybe three feet of space from one side to the other. Ropey roots lined the curved walls, dangling through the hole at the top where daylight streamed in. Through it, he could see a blue sky dotted with fluffy clouds.

A few feet in front of him stood Dezi. With his back to Teo, Dezi didn't notice him enter. His head was craned back as he inspected the walls.

Teo followed his gaze and saw that there were three small ledges. The ten obsidian stones sat at eye level, the four jades were halfway up, and the single gold stone was a few feet from the opening in the ceiling.

Dezi turned slowly in a full circle, his bag hanging from his wrist. Teo saw the intense look of concentration on the other boy's face a split second before Dezi's eyes landed on him.

Startled, Dezi jumped, which made Teo jump, which in turn made Dezi clutch his bag protectively to his chest.

Without a moment's hesitation, Dezi sprang into action.

As if he were a character in a video game, Dezi scaled the wall, pulling himself up by the hanging roots before springing back and forth from side to side.

Teo gaped.

What the *hell* were they feeding Golds at the Academy?! To be honest, Teo wasn't even mad about it. Just impressed.

With the ease of a cat, Dezi made it to the second ledge where the jade stones waited. Anchoring himself on footholds Teo couldn't even *see*, Dezi smiled triumphantly as he reached for a stone. But his triumph was short-lived.

As soon as Dezi picked up the jade stone, the walls shook violently. Behind him, a slab of stone dropped, cutting off the exit.

Teo stumbled while Dezi latched on to the roots, swinging side to side.

At first, Teo thought his eyes were playing tricks on him, but no. The walls had slowly started to close in.

"Watch out!" Teo shouted uselessly to Dezi.

Regardless, Dezi swiped the rest of the stones into his bag before bounding up the walls again.

Teo suddenly realized *he* was the one who needed to watch out. The walls were slowly closing in, and if he didn't move fast, he'd be crushed, too. As the first trial had proven, he was a shitty climber and definitely had none of the skills to scale vertical walls. Cold, desperate panic cracked through Teo's head. As if on instinct, his wings shot out.

Maybe he couldn't climb, but he could fly.

Teo dashed forward and dumped the obsidian stones into his bag with fumbling hands. He looked up. Dezi stared down at him from the opening of the shaft. With the gold stone in one hand, he frantically waved at Teo to hurry with the other.

Hoping against hope that this would work, he used all the strength in his legs to launch himself into the air and flapped his wings twice in quick succession.

Teo shot upward. Hopped up on adrenaline and perilously clumsy, Teo bumped into the walls as he ascended as quickly as he could. The walls continued to close in. Stone scraped against his wings.

He was so close to the top. He was *nearly* there.

Teo stretched his hand up as far as he could. There were only a few more feet left before he'd make it clear. He just needed *one more* flap of his wings—

But there wasn't enough room.

His wings jammed against the rough walls.

Teo lost his momentum. For a moment, he hovered in midair, just a split second before he'd plummet down and inevitably be crushed to death.

His stomach dropped out from under him. Teo squeezed his eyes shut, anticipating his hopefully quick death.

But a hand caught his forearm. With a tug so strong it nearly pulled his shoulder from its socket, Teo was yanked through the opening.

He tumbled head over feet before landing in a heap of tangled limbs with someone else.

A few feet away, the shaft closed with a dull *thud*.

Teo rolled over, gulping down air. *"Holy shit, holy fuck."* Cheers roared to life. Miraculously, they had made it to the top of the temple.

Dezi was sprawled out at his side in a similar state. His handsome face was ashen as he stared back at Teo, looking just as terrified as he felt.

"DEZI!"

Marino was at his side immediately, pulling his friend up to his feet. "Are you okay?" he demanded, frantically signing with one hand. Dezi nodded, albeit a little dazedly. He turned to Teo, jerking his chin up with his eyebrows pinched in question.

Teo nodded and flashed an exhausted thumbs-up from the floor. "I'm okay," he said. When he got to his feet, the crowd roared to life again. Teo turned to the sea of jade. The jumbotron zoomed in on him as he smiled and waved.

"Pa-ja-ri-to! Pa-ja-ri-to!"

It was like a shot of pure adrenaline to his heart.

Marino must've reached the top about the same time as Teo and Dezi. Atzi had already made it to the finish and stood behind the undulating barrier. Next to her, a large gold bowl sat in the center of a raised dais. Dezi approached and dumped out the contents of his bag inside. A few jade stones and one gold spiraled down along the rim before disappearing through a hole at the bottom, locking in his points. Marino followed him through the barrier and did the same.

By some miracle, Teo had made it to the top of the temple without getting killed and even with time to spare.

Ready to hand over the obsidian stones he'd collected, Teo removed his bag. But as he approached the barrier to cross the finish, he overheard Marino say, "Did either of you find the Sol Stone?"

Dezi shook his head no, but Atzi nodded.

"It's on the floor below us," she said and signed, nodding toward the main outer steps. "But it's impossible to get," Atzi added. "It's hanging over this huge pit. I gave up, like, immediately, but the twins were still trying to figure it out when I left."

Aurelio and Auristela.

Teo checked his watch. There were fifteen minutes left before the trial was over.

"Pa-ja-ri-to! Pa-ja-ri-to!"

There was no way he was going to come in first with only the obsidian stones he'd gathered. There was still time left. Niya and Xio hadn't even made it to the top yet.

"Pa-ja-ri-to! Pa-ja-ri-to!"

He could get the Sol Stone. He could get it and *win*.

"Pa-ja-ri-to! Pa-ja-ri-to!"

Teo turned and sprinted down the steps.

CHAPTER 20

There was only one entrance into the temple on the level below. Through it, a single corridor led to the chamber where the replica Sol Stone was held. At first, Teo was suspicious of how easy it was to find, but then he saw why.

It was a large, dome-shaped room with a huge pit in the middle of the floor. From the ledge he stood on, Teo couldn't see how deep it went, but the groaning wind that tickled his face suggested it dropped to the very bottom of the temple. It must've been a hundred feet wide, impossible to jump even for a Gold semidiós.

Overhead, a large hand carved out of obsidian reached down from the darkness of the ceiling, its palm upturned. It had knobby fingers and sharp nails. The ceiling undulated in deep shades of celestial indigo and midnight blue. Pinpricks of stars blinked in familiar constellations.

Shining with golden, glimmering light, the replica Sol Stone waited in the palm of the cupped hand. It was seemingly impossible to get to. Teo understood why the others had given up.

That was, except for Aurelio and Auristela.

Across the pit was the only other exit and a ledge identical to Teo's. On it stood Aurelio and Auristela. Their heavy-looking bags sagged on their backs as they stared up at the Sol Stone. Auristela pointed up, explaining something to her brother while Aurelio nodded along, dark eyebrows bunched. When Auristela spotted Teo, anger flashed behind her flinty eyes.

Following his sister's gaze, Aurelio's eyes landed on Teo from across the room. His lips popped open with surprise.

Teo smirked, warm satisfaction flooding his stomach.

Finally, an obstacle where he had the advantage. Now he just needed to not fuck it up.

Head held high, he inched closer to the edge, doing his best not to look down and psych himself out. He had this. He needed to fly up there and grab the Sol Stone, and then he'd have more points than any of the other semidioses.

Teo took a deep, steadying breath before launching himself into the air.

Taking off was easy. Landing was a bit more difficult. Because of how the hand was curved, there wasn't a flat surface for Teo to perch on. Without an ounce of grace, Teo wrapped his arms around the wrist, but it was too wide to completely reach around.

Skin damp with sweat, he lost his grip and slid down the polished obsidian into the palm.

Teo's foot nudged the Sol Stone.

And it rolled, teetering precariously at the edge, the pit yawning open far below.

Teo's heart dropped. "NO!"

As the Sol Stone rolled over the edge, he threw himself forward, slamming his chin into the palm. Teo latched on to the Sol Stone, his fingers slipping across the smooth surface. Quickly, he hauled it back over the edge and hugged it against himself as he caught his breath. He was surprised how cool it was to the touch as he tucked it under his chin. Then again, it was only a replica.

Up close, it was dizzying to stare at. Swirling solar flares twisted between Teo's fingers. What looked like liquid sunshine danced under the surface of the stone. If he squinted, Teo could've sworn there was something hidden inside. Two shadows almost made it look like someone was staring back at him, but it must've been his reflection. Just a trick of the light.

I did it! he sang in his head as a delirious laugh bubbled in his chest.

Without any room left in his bag for such a large stone, Teo wrapped his arms securely around the Sol Stone before unfolding his wings. Careful not to look down, he glided down to the opposite ledge. He stumbled a bit but otherwise made a smooth landing.

With a huge grin on his face, Teo turned to show Aurelio.

"*Stela!*"

A violent force knocked into Teo, throwing him down. Bewildered, Teo looked up to find Auristela on top of him.

She pinned his wings down with her knees, rendering them useless as Auristela wrenched the Sol Stone out of his grip. Her eyes were dark as night, the skin around them angry blue and purple.

"No!" Teo shouted, trying to grab it back, but she leaned her weight harder onto her knees.

Hot pain tore through Teo's shoulders.

Instead of taking the stone and running for it, she held the Sol Stone out. "Here!" Auristela said, trying to hand it to her brother.

Aurelio stood rooted to the spot, shock and alarm written across his features. His eyes flickered Teo, then back to Auristela. "What are you *doing?*"

Teo tried to get up. "Get off me!"

"Shut up!" Auristela snarled, her teeth bared. "*Take it*, Relio!"

The color drained from Aurelio's face. He took a step back. "I won't."

Teo slumped with relief, but it was short-lived.

Auristela jerked back as if he'd slapped her. For a moment, hurt flashed across her face before it was quickly consumed by rage. "I *told you* he was manipulating you!" she seethed. Black veins splintered out around her eyes.

Teo balked. "What are you *talking* about?!"

"Stela, *stop this*!" Aurelio insisted, but she wouldn't listen.

Auristela raised the Sol Stone over her head.

Aurelio lunged.

Terror squeezed Teo's chest. He threw his arms over his head and squeezed his eyes shut.

Crash!

Debris hit Teo's cheek. When he opened his eyes, he saw Aurelio had thrown out his arm in an attempt to shield Teo.

Auristela had smashed the Sol Stone on the ground. Pieces of glass and shards of white that looked eerily like bone skittered across the floor.

For a moment, no one moved.

Teo stared up at Auristela, fear and anger freezing him in place. Her chest heaved as she sucked in sharp, loud breaths between clenched teeth, staring at what was left of the fake Sol Stone.

It was more than shock on Aurelio's face. It was fear. "Stela," he said quietly. He reached out and touched her shoulder.

She flinched like she had forgotten he was there. Auristela blinked and shook her head, almost like she was clearing her vision and everything suddenly came back into focus. The bruises faded and her eyes went back to smoldering brown. She looked at her brother, at the shattered pieces, and then down at Teo, still pinned beneath her.

Auristela reeled, quickly crawling off him.

Teo took the opening and jumped to his feet.

Suddenly, all three of their watches chimed at the same time. Teo's watch buzzed on his wrist. When he checked it, he saw the timer was counting down the last five minutes in angry red numbers.

Time was almost up.

Auristela leapt to her feet. Aurelio called after her, but she ran through the exit.

Teo couldn't make heads or tails of what the hell had just happened.

All he knew was his hands were shaking and his heart was pounding painfully in his chest.

Aurelio's head swiveled back and forth between Teo and the door his sister had disappeared through. He checked his watch again and growled at the back of his throat. "Come on," Aurelio said to Teo, waving him forward as he started to jog for the doorway. "I know the way up—*hurry*."

There was no time to second-guess. Teo ran for it.

Aurelio let him get ahead, giving directions and shoving him in the right direction when he almost made a wrong turn. He guided them back out into the sunshine and both of them tore up the steps.

When they reached the top, Teo was only vaguely aware that the dioses and Diosa Luna were already waiting.

Niya stood next to the golden bowl, her stones piled in her arms. "Where's Xio?!" she shouted, frantically looking for him behind Teo, but he wasn't there.

"I—I don't know!"

His watch shuddered, counting down the final seconds.

Panic gripped Niya's voice. "What do we do?!"

"*Dump your stones!*" Aurelio shouted, like he couldn't believe they were stalling.

Niya jerked, a bewildered look on her face as she stared at Aurelio before looking at Teo.

There was no time to question it. They had to act now, or else it wouldn't be just Xio who got disqualified.

"Dump them!" Teo told her.

She hesitated for only a second, glancing once more back to the steps, before she turned and dumped her stones into the bowl.

As Teo ran forward, he pulled his bag off his chest, wrenching open the drawstrings.

Aurelio shoved Teo's back, throwing him forward. His stomach rammed into the edge and he upturned his obsidian stones into the bowl. Aurelio was right behind him. They tossed in their stones at the same time, gold and jade tumbling together. The last one slipped through the hole at the bottom.

Just then, Xio appeared at the top of the steps, obsidian stones cradled against his chest.

"RUN!" Teo shouted.

"HURRY!" came Niya's frantic voice.

Xio flung himself forward, but his foot caught on the last step. He crashed to his knees.

A gasp caught in Teo's throat, dread spilling over him like icy water.

Three obsidian stones fell from his hands and clattered across the floor just as Mariachi's cornet sounded.

Teo retreated back to his mother's side as thunderous applause shook the arena.

"Are you okay?" she asked. Quetzal swiped her thumb against his chin and when she pulled back, his jade blood was on her skin.

He nodded numbly, distracted as he watched Xio get swept into Mala Suerte's embrace. Niya paced back and forth in front of Tierra like a caged animal.

As the rankings board was brought forward, Teo stole a look at Aurelio.

There was a slight sheen of sweat on his brow. He was trying to smile for the cameras, but he kept glancing over at Auristela, who stood stick-straight and rigid, staring ahead and barely moving.

The events of what had happened just minutes before pinged around in Teo's head. What the hell was that? Was Auristela really that ruthless? His legs quaked as he watched her, paranoid she might go off on him again.

"Sol has determined the rankings," Diosa Luna announced. The glyphs slid on the stone slate.

Teo tore his eyes away from the twins to the rankings.

The crowd exploded with thunderous applause as people screamed for Teo. Jade banners waved and their chanting rose. "*Pa-ja-ri-to! Pa-ja-ri-to!*"

Teo's mother squeezed his arm. "You're *third*!" Quetzal sang, her voice trilling.

He couldn't believe it. "Third?" Teo repeated.

The jade quetzal sat in third among the gold glyphs bunched at the top.

"I'm *third*!" Teo let out a booming laugh and buried his fingers in his hair. He couldn't believe it! Teo pulled in a deep, satisfied breath. He was *almost* there. He actually stood a chance at becoming Sunbearer.

"Auristela," Teo heard Atzi gasp.

He searched for Lumbre's glyph with the "a" in the middle. He'd expected it to be somewhere near the top and was confused when he couldn't find it. His eyes trailed down, down, down until finally he spotted it.

Eighth. In one trial, Auristela had dropped from fifth place to *eighth*.

She stood next to her mother with her hands tightened into white-knuckled fists at her sides. Auristela remained still, but Teo could've sworn he could see her lips and chin trembling. Aurelio wasn't smiling anymore.

And then there was Xochi, who had dropped all the way to

ninth. She stood huddled against her mother, her hands pressed over her mouth as tears sparked in her eyes.

Every semidiose looked upset, including Dezi as he was led away for his interview. It made the roaring cheers of the crowd feel ominous and out of place.

Teo searched for his friends. Niya's glyph hovered safely in fourth, but Xio—

Teo's blood ran cold. The jade eye of Dios Mala Suerte had plummeted to last.

"Xio," he breathed, searching for him in the crowd.

Xio stood next to Mala Suerte, leaning against his father's side. His nose was red, his eyes glassy as his father wrapped his arm around his small shoulders in a viselike grip.

"Wh-what happened?" Teo stammered.

"I tried to do what you guys told me to," Xio said, his voice tight. "But I barely found any stones. I couldn't find you guys and I didn't know where the finish was."

A wave of nausea rolled in Teo's stomach. They'd failed.

There was no celebration among the semidioses this time. Reality hit them all in the stomach, swift and cold as iron.

In the pursuit of becoming Sunbearer, Teo had forgotten his main goal—to keep his friends safe. Now Xio was in danger of being sacrificed.

Back on the boat, Xio went right to his room and didn't come back out.

"Should we try talking to him?" Teo asked.

"I don't know, when I'm upset, I usually need my own space," Niya reasoned, but she wasn't happy with her own answer, either.

Teo's guilt was eating him alive from the inside out. Niya's worry manifested as anger, and without somewhere to focus it, she ended up pacing back and forth in the common room. Even Auristela and Ocelo were silent, the former looking pale but still desperately trying to maintain an air of superiority.

Teo took a long, hot shower and stayed in his room through dinner. He wasn't hungry and he couldn't face the other competitors. Instead, he lay in bed and obsessed over how they could've done things differently, rethinking every move the three of them had made during the trials that had led them to this point.

If he hadn't gone back for the Sol Stone, maybe he and Niya would've been able to look for Xio. When he found the finish, maybe he could've gone back for Xio and gotten him there on time. They could've shared their stones. If he hadn't been so concerned with winning, who knew what else he and Niya could've done to help him.

Teo's stomach gave a sickened lurch. He remembered their first night in the temple, how he and Niya had talked Xio into begging Diosa Pan Dulce for hot chocolate. How it felt seeing Xio—this small, resigned little kid—smile for the first time since arriving. Teo had thought he could help Xio and keep him safe, but clearly he was wrong.

That wasn't how the trials worked.

Teo curled up in bed and his wings hugged tightly around him. Aurelio had been right from the start. He didn't belong here. He didn't deserve this. Sol had seen something inside of him that simply didn't exist.

The next morning after breakfast, the Sol priests brought in new clothes for Teo to change into. This was the first time he was given a choice of what he wanted to wear.

There were too many choices, if you asked Teo. Instead of a carefully laid-out ensemble, a whole rack was waiting for him. All the pieces varied in style and color. It took Teo a while to pick out something he liked that went well together, but he finally decided on royal blue slacks, a pastel green short-sleeve button-down, and a black sweater.

When he met up with the others, Teo wasn't at all surprised to see that Aurelio and Auristela had coordinated in matching black-and-red outfits, somehow still looking like supermodels. Teo eyed Auristela, hating that he was actually, genuinely afraid of her now. Dezi had seemed to pull on every piece of blush pink clothing he could find, and Ocelo wore such a heinous mix of colors that Teo suspected they might be colorblind.

"You look cozy," Teo said to Xio with a grin.

He was bundled up in jeans and a deep purple hoodie. "I'm freezing," he grumbled, shivering on the deck.

"Here!" Niya took off the long white cashmere scarf she'd been wearing and wrapped it snuggly around Xio's neck several times until all that could be seen of him was his nose and eyes.

"Thanks," came Xio's muffled voice.

"How are you?" Teo asked, trying hard to sound nonchalant. The last thing he wanted was to scare Xio off or make him feel even worse about being in last place.

Xio shrugged, causing Niya's scarf to conceal even more of his face. "Fine. Why?"

Teo looked to Niya for help. He pressed his brows together and gestured slightly to the younger boy. She shrugged in response, as if to say, *What can you do?*

This time, there was no fancy tram to take them up to the city. Instead, they had to climb a very steep, very rickety set of wooden steps to a platform where three vans waited for them.

"*Gross*," Auristela sneered under her breath as they split up and got in.

Opción priests dressed in white-and-black-checkered robes drove them through the city. It was a bumpy ride that reeked of exhaust, taking a gravel road from the dock to where the main streets were. When they curved around a bend, Laberinto finally came into view. The peninsula sloped up toward the cliff face, putting the entire city on display.

It was inarguably the strangest city Teo had ever seen. No two buildings were the same. Many were half finished, while others started off in one style but continued in a completely different one. The residential areas were also eclectic, with no common theme between houses. They were brightly colored and stacked tightly together in what seemed like random streets until Teo realized—

"It's a maze!"

Indeed, the tightly packed streets crisscrossed and twisted around each other, several ending in dead ends.

Niya let out a low whistle. "I feel sorry for whoever has to deliver the mail."

The Opción priests delivered them to Laberinto's famous outdoor market, *where the options never run out!* They were given an hour and half before dinner to shop to their heart's content, in whatever shops or restaurants they liked.

The outdoor market was arranged in a long, rectangular block of small buildings and stalls with finely paved walkways blocked off from the traffic of the city. The smell of sizzling meats from one of the many cart vendors spread throughout the market. Auristela immediately grabbed Ocelo's and Aurelio's hands and ran off in the direction of a high-end clothing store.

"Aw, yeah!" Niya exclaimed. "Shopping day! I wonder if they have an athleisure store. *Ooh*, or a jeweler—I could get some new bracelets to make into weapons! Where do you wanna go, Teo?"

Teo had his eyes set on a long fountain at the center of the strip. The ledge was flat and roughly bench height. "I think I'm just gonna hang out over there, actually. I'm not in much of a shopping mood."

"Me either," Xio agreed.

Niya groaned. "C'mon, you should at least *try* to have some fun!"

But Teo shook his head. "Seriously, Niya, you go ahead. We're beat from the trials and it's not like there's anything here we *need*. Xio and I will chill by the fountain; you can come find us when you're done."

"Ugh, *fine*," Niya agreed. "But I'm totally looking for some new basketball shorts for you. Those ratty ones you wear to bed are embarrassing."

"What's embarrassing about my shorts?" Teo demanded, but Niya was already walking away, waving him off dismissively. Teo sighed and started toward the fountain with Xio tagging along.

Once they were seated, Teo decided to try to broach the subject of Xio's standing in the trials one more time. He could understand Xio wanting to seem tough and unbothered, but the poor kid had to be scared.

"Sooo," Teo began, but before he could say any more, Xio shook his head.

"I'm *fine*, Teo," the other boy insisted. "Seriously. It's a miracle I lasted this long out of last place. We have one trial left, and all I can do is try my best."

"That's ... very healthy," Teo admitted. So why did *he* still feel so bad?

"Can I join you guys?" a voice asked from above. It was Marino, looking longingly toward the water behind them.

"Of course," Teo said, gesturing to the empty space beside him.

Marino took a seat, a look of relief spread across his face. "Thanks. Don't get me wrong, the market is cool and everything, but I'm just ..."

"Not in the mood?" Xio offered.

Marino nodded enthusiastically. "How are we supposed to unwind with the pressure up this high?"

"*Seriously*," Teo agreed. Across the walkway, he could see Ocelo and Auristela piling dresses and suits into the hands of a poor mortal shopkeeper. While they were busy, Teo saw Aurelio wander farther down the street on his own, his head swiveling back and forth like he was looking for something specific.

"Are y'all talking about the trials?" Xochi asked, approaching and taking a seat beside Marino. She leaned back so her head was tilted over the water, stretched her long legs, and crossed them at the ankle. "I'm *so* over it all, you know?"

"I just want to go home," Atzi agreed, materializing beside her. But rather than sitting beside the other Golds, Atzi shuffled down the line to take the space next to Xio. Teo thought he noticed a flush of pink beneath Xio's massive scarf.

Xochi snorted. "I doubt the Academy will even give us leave to go home between the end of the trials and returning to school."

"For real?" Teo asked. "Even though you were all competing?"

Marino and Xochi shook their heads, frowning. "We'd lose precious training time," Marino explained.

"I would *kill* for a week off." Xochi winced. "Sorry, poor turn of phrase. I just meant I would do anything to spend some time with my mom in the gardens."

"To just float out on the open sea," Marino agreed. "Not fighting a monster or rescuing civilians, just for a little bit."

An uneasy silence fell between them. Teo felt a strange surge of sympathy for all the Gold students of the Academy. Sure, they were spoiled, selfish attention hogs, but they were still people, no matter how much they wanted everyone else to think otherwise. Teo couldn't imagine not being allowed to go home when all this was over.

A few minutes later, Niya emerged, dejected, from the athleisure store she'd found with Dezi in tow. She plopped down right on the ground at Teo's feet, leaning her head back to rest in his lap.

"I shopped till I dropped," she declared and signed.

Dezi gave her a sympathetic pat on the head.

"You didn't even buy anything!" Teo laughed.

"I know!" she cried. "Isn't it pathetic? I can't bring myself to get into it. These stupid trials are really harshing my vibe."

The other kids murmured in agreement.

And so for the rest of their allotted shopping time, they sat and thought about the impending final trial. Every few minutes, one of them would make a half-hearted attempt to distract the others from their thoughts, but any conversation they tried quickly sputtered out. Niya was right. The vibes were *way* off.

The remaining three competitors materialized back from their shopping sprees. Auristela held a bag in each hand, full of clothes and accessories. Ocelo had somehow managed to purchase an entire punching bag full of sand and was trying to fit it into the back of the car, much to the priests' annoyance.

Meanwhile, Aurelio held only a small paper bag in the crook of his arm.

"Relio," Auristela said, equal notes of concern and annoyance in her voice. "You didn't even buy anything."

"I did," Aurelio said, digging his hand into the paper bag. "I didn't really know what anything was, so the shop owner picked everything out for me." He pulled out a handful of colorfully wrapped pieces of candy.

"Candy?" Auristela said, giving her brother a confused look.

A surprise laugh jumped in Teo's chest.

Aurelio gave him a piece of mazapan along with a small, embarrassed smile.

"Pulparindo chamoy?!" Marino gasped, eyes going wide.

"Borrachitos!" Atzi sang.

"I haven't had Coconugs in *years*," Xochi added.

"Can we have some?" Niya pleaded, clutching her hands to her chest.

"I've got more than I need," Aurelio said, holding the bag out. The others swarmed him immediately.

"This is awesome!"

"You're the best!"

"Thanks, Aurelio!"

Aurelio just nodded awkwardly, blushing. When Teo smiled at him, he was pleased to see his cheeks burn an even darker shade of crimson. When the priests returned to escort them all to dinner, Aurelio continued to be the center of everyone's attention as they ate candy and cracked jokes. Teo enjoyed his piece of mazapan on the drive back, choosing to ignore Auristela, who kept shooting him a venomous glare.

The drive to Opción's Temple took them through the city's winding streets. They passed the restaurant district, where eateries bordered a courtyard with picnic benches. There were several tables and chairs with board games set outside office buildings for public use.

When they pulled up to the temple, Teo wasn't surprised to find it matched the chaotic nature of the rest of the city. The architecture was a hodgepodge of different styles; some sections were plain stone while other levels were brightly painted. Every window was a different shape, some with intricate moldings and others just boring squares.

It looked like almost every resident of Laberinto got to contribute to the design of the temple and, judging by the scaffolding on the west wing, it changed regularly.

Opción priests guided them through the seemingly endless rows of hallways until they were brought into the dining room.

Diosa Opción stood in the middle of the room. Her hair was cropped so short it was barely a shadow and she wore a simple white dress. Her face was round, and while she looked very friendly, there was something about her expression that made it seem like she knew something you didn't and found it amusing.

"Welcome, competitors!" She gave them a warm and friendly smile as they filed in. "Please, help yourselves and sit where you'd like," the diosa said, gesturing. Unlike the other cities where the tables had been long rectangles, this one was round.

The smell of food immediately made Teo's mouth water. Instead of being served by priests, the food was laid out on long tables along the far wall. There was every food imaginable, but an especially large assortment of fish, which Teo figured had to do with them being so close to the ocean.

When they had their food, Teo, Niya, and Xio picked a spot to sit.

Diosa Opción waited for everyone to settle before taking the empty chair next to Teo. When he turned to thank her for her hospitality, the diosa looked almost completely different. If it weren't for the fact that she was the only one well over seven feet tall, he would've thought she was an entirely different person.

In a blink, her hair had grown, now presenting as deep brown curls that hung below her suddenly cleft chin. Teo realized that when she moved, the color of her dress shifted, like it couldn't decide what color it wanted to be.

She gave Teo that same secretive look again as he gaped at her.

"Whoa," Xio breathed, openly staring at her.

"Thank you," Diosa Opción replied with an amused grin. When she tucked a lock of hair behind her ear, it changed again, now long and straight and the color of sun-dried wheat.

They ate as they quietly conversed, watching the diosa change as often as she chewed.

"I'm surprised you're considered a Jade," Xio said to her.

"Why's that?"

"You're just—" He blushed. "*Very* powerful."

Ocelo snorted.

"You disagree?" Diosa Opción said, studying them thoughtfully.

Before their eyes, Ocelo's hair shifted until its jaguar rosettes were pale pink and dark fuchsia. Dezi gasped in delight and Xochi laughed.

"What?!" Ocelo demanded.

Xochi dug into her pocket and pulled out a compact mirror. "I think pink suits you," she said as she handed it to them.

"You did this?" Ocelo said, somewhere between surprised and impressed, darting their eyes at the diosa—but they couldn't seem to look away from their own reflection.

"Just a choice," Diosa Opción said. "A simple choice for a single creature."

As quick as it had changed, Ocelo's hair shifted back to normal. They snapped the mirror closed and tossed it back to Xochi, glaring at their plate.

"Choice is the most powerful force in existence. Much more powerful than me," the diosa said casually, gaining some shocked looks. "Jades, Golds—these descriptions mean nothing, really," Opción said, dismissively waving her hand. "We gave them to ourselves. It's humanity that has all the power."

"How can you say that?" Auristela snapped, as if the diosa had insulted her personally.

"So much like your mother," Diosa Opción said, and Auristela sat up straight like someone had smacked her between the shoulder blades. "You think humans serve us, don't you?"

No one said or did anything. It sounded like a trick question, but Teo didn't understand how. That was the way the world worked, everyone knew that.

"*We* serve *them*," Opción clarified. "That's our power. It is a privilege they've granted us. Our people have free will and our power would mean nothing without them believing in it."

"Without the gods, the world would end," Niya said, talking slowly like she thought the diosa was confused.

"They keep us safe, just like Sol and their sacrifice," Marino added.

"Yeah, that's the whole reason we have the Sunbearer Trials, isn't it?" Atzi said, unsure.

"To keep the Sol Stone fueled."

Everyone turned to Aurelio. He was usually so quiet whenever they ate together, it was a bit startling to witness him speaking up. But he ignored the stares and kept his focus on Diosa Opción, his expression stony and serious. "Without them, the world would end."

"Yes, a single choice could end the world," Opción agreed. "And only one of you gets to make that choice. What does that say about the rest of your power?" She smiled. "But I suppose that's why you're all here, isn't it?"

Teo wasn't sure what to make of her knowing look.

"That was weird," Xio said as they walked back down the rickety steps to the dock.

"Yeah, it was like she was talking in riddles or something!" Niya agreed, rubbing her temples. "It gave me a headache! What the heck did she mean by any of that?"

"I don't know," Teo said, but he was deep in thought.

A single choice could end the world. Opción had said it like some offhand comment, but it was fucking with his head. Something about it made him think of all the arguments he and Aurelio had gotten into. About what it meant to be the Sunbearer or the sacrifice. It was like the answer was right there, he just couldn't see it.

Back on the boat, Teo, Xio, and Niya tried to be productive and do some last-minute brainstorming in the common room. Tomorrow they would return to Sol Temple and have one final day before the fifth trial, but they were entirely wiped out. Niya fell asleep first, her quiet snores becoming background noise while Teo listed off previous trials from Xio's notes, searching for a hint of what was to come.

After asking a question and getting no response, Teo looked up to find Xio slumped against Niya's side, fast asleep.

"We should go to bed," Teo whispered, plucking at Xio's sleeve.

His eyes flew open and he sat upright. "Now?" Xio asked groggily, blinking his eyes to get them to focus. "Already?"

"It's almost morning," Teo told him.

"Can we stay up a little longer?"

The way he cast a furtive glance toward the cabins and the strain in Xio's voice gave Teo pause. Maybe he was just dreading the final trial, or simply didn't want to be alone. Either way, Teo didn't have the heart to tell him no.

He sighed. "Fine, a little while longer, but then we have to sleep."

Xio nodded.

Teo sat down next to Xio and flicked the TV on before turning the volume low. As Xio settled back against the cushions, Teo idly flipped through the channels. When Chisme's annoying face came on-screen, he changed it immediately to some nature documentary. Xio's deep, quiet breaths mixed with the droning voice of the narrator, letting Teo turn off his brain, if only for a little while.

CHAPTER 21

The trials were almost over. When the boat docked, they were back at Sol Temple, where this all had started and where, tomorrow night, it would all end.

They had one more day. As a final celebration before the fifth trial, they would be having one last feast. All of the competitors, their parents, and their priests were invited to eat, drink, and celebrate. It was supposed to be a huge deal, something the Golds kept talking about and were looking forward to, even under all the tension that hung in the air. But to Teo, it sounded awful. He didn't want to pretend that he was happy, or that this was an honor. He was tired and he was scared, and he felt entirely powerless to do anything about it.

They disembarked and were led back to Sol Temple and once again given the warning to stick to their quarters and not go wandering around. It felt like a year had passed since they'd left, not nine days. The competitors went back to their old rooms and were told to make themselves presentable. Dinner would start at six o'clock sharp and they needed to wear their regalia again, which was the last thing Teo wanted to do. When he walked into his room, his outfit was already waiting for him, hung on a clothing rack.

Teo wanted to chuck the whole thing out the window.

He was about to take a shower when someone knocked on his door. Teo raced to open it, hoping it would be Aurelio on the other side, but it wasn't. It was much worse.

"Hello, Teo," Verdad greeted in her perpetually professional tone. Chisme winked from behind his sister's shoulder, wiggling his fingers in a small wave.

"Uh, hi," Teo replied. He glanced down the hall, dread dropping into his stomach. Why the hell had these two showed up to his room? "Is something wrong? Am I in trouble?"

"Not at all," Verdad assured him.

Chisme arched his eyebrows. "Is there a reason you'd be in trouble?"

"No," Teo said quickly.

"We were wondering if you'd be willing to sit with us for an interview," Verdad explained. "I'd love to hear from the Jade semidiós who climbed up the ranks to third place. You're a great inspiration to your people."

"Or you would be, if you'd talk to them," Chisme added. "We have the audience to facilitate that!"

"I guess," Teo said, though he still wasn't certain. He had such a grudge against Chisme, and he wasn't sure whether Verdad was just as untrustworthy. "I have to go to that fancy dinner thing soon—"

"We won't keep you long," Verdad rushed to add.

Teo sighed. "Yeah okay," he finally agreed.

They led him to one of the lower levels in the temple and into a large room that Verdad and her team had transformed into a control center. It was filled with desks and chairs, the room dark but illuminated by the blue lights of the huge wall of televisions. Reporters and editors sat at computers, splicing together clips of scenes from the trials while the news played in real time on other screens.

"Take a seat," Verdad said, leading him to what he assumed was her work space. The desk had three monitors and huge stacks of paper meticulously organized next to an even row of pens. There was a second chair at the desk before a messy stack of tabloids and notebooks where Chisme sat.

Teo pulled up a chair and sat down, tense and expecting cameras to be shoved in his face, but all Verdad did was pull out a yellow notepad.

"I'll start," she explained. "And then my brother will have some questions for you, too. For my piece, I'd like to give the people a more holistic view of the Jade demigod who has been dominating in the trials—to *humanize* you a bit, if you'll pardon the pun."

Verdad started the interview with some softballs—what it was like living in Quetzlan, if he'd ever traveled through Reino del Sol before this, what his relationship with his mom was like—before diving into more probing questions.

With a few taps of her keyboard, a still frame popped up on one of the monitors. It was from the very first trial. Ocelo stood at the top of the mountain, eyes cast in shadows as they glared, the boulder raised above their head as Teo stared up at them, wide-eyed.

"You've been in quite a few precarious situations during the trials," Verdad said, studying him through her glasses. "And without any of the training most of the other competitors have received. What's that like?"

Teo wasn't sure how she wanted him to answer. "Well, it *is* the Sunbearer Trials," he said, casting an uneasy glance at the still frame. "Not exactly a walk in the park." He didn't know where she was going with this, but already he regretted agreeing to it.

"True," Verdad agreed. "But this year, the competitors seem especially ... driven, let's say."

"Do they?" Teo asked.

"Kid," Chisme cut in, "these have been the juiciest Trials since Pan Dulce's son confessed his love for Guerrero's daughter in the middle of the fifth trial."

Verdad adjusted her glasses and cut her brother a look. Chisme raised his hands in surrender. "Sorry, sorry. Go ahead, I can wait my turn."

Verdad pulled up a video of the fourth trial, distinctive for its verdant green plants and stone walls. She pressed play and Teo watched himself being knocked down, Auristela slamming on top of him and wrenching his wings back with her knees. Teo had been scared in the moment, but even now, in this quiet room with a solid chair beneath his legs, terror still crept up his spine.

"What happened here?" Verdad asked.

"Auristela took me down," Teo said, shifting uneasily.

"Some people think if Auristela hadn't interfered, you would have been locked in for Sunbearer," Chisme said.

Teo gave him an uncertain look. "I doubt it." He might have ended up with the most points, but there was no way he was that close to being the Sunbearer.

Verdad paused the video on Auristela, the Sol Stone raised up above her head. She was so angry her face was grotesque. The footage, clearly from a hidden camera, was a little blurry, but Teo could still make out the darkness of her eyes, could remember how they looked as she snarled down at him.

When Verdad spoke, her voice was quiet as she studied his face, watching for his reaction. "What was going through your head in this moment?"

Teo's palms were sweating. He wiped them on his thighs. "I don't know…"

"Did you think she was going to kill you?" Chisme asked.

"*Chisme,*" Verdad scolded. "Please stop leading the responses."

But Teo looked at himself at the bottom of the frame, his eyes squeezed shut and arms thrown over his head.

"Yes," he admitted, because it was true. "I thought—for a second, I thought she might kill me."

Chisme's mouth twisted into a terrifying grin, like a predator that had cornered its prey. "Do you have a longstanding rivalry with Auristela?"

Teo snorted a laugh. "Most of the Golds and I aren't friends—"

"Killing you would be quite a leap, though, wouldn't it?"

He hesitated. Something prickled at the back of his mind, a nagging feeling he hadn't been able to shake ever since the first trial.

Yes. It would.

"But I'm sure it must be easy to get caught in the heat of the moment during the trials," Chisme reasoned, inspecting his nails.

"I can only speak for myself, I guess," Teo said, trying to focus. "But yeah, I'm very, uh—goal-oriented."

But Teo's goal had always been straightforward, just to do as well as possible and look out for his friends. He stared at Auristela. In that moment, her goal hadn't been to win, but to hurt Teo, to keep him from winning.

"That's worked very well for you," Verdad said, clearly trying to steer the interview back in her preferred direction. "You've defied the odds over and over again during these trials."

Teo frowned. "I guess so . . ." Truth be told, he had been so young during the last trials, he didn't really know what the standard behavior was for the competitors. He'd just assumed that, as Golds, they all were cutthroat and would do anything to become Sunbearer—until he'd met Niya, anyway.

Verdad tapped around her keyboard and turned a monitor back to Teo, this time with the warm brown La Cumbre mountainside on the screen. He saw his own form gripping the rocks for dear life during the first trial, and Ocelo looming above him, poised to throw a boulder down at the other competitors. The camera panned out to capture Teo hovering in the air with his freed wings shimmering in the sun, but he was distracted by Ocelo at the top of the cliff, bringing the boulder down and staring at it like they didn't recognize it, didn't recognize themself.

Teo's mind flashed back to the jaguar jumping on Ocelo, the open, easy joy on the other semidiose's face. That wasn't the same person at the top of the cliffs.

Verdad asked another question but he wasn't paying attention to her anymore. His mind raced as he searched the clips and still frames. The burning nest from the second trial. Niya and Auristela battling it out during the third. Xochi's thorny vines squeezing the air out of Marino.

Teo had thought he'd just imagined it—it was so easy to overlook—but now he could see it, even in the shaking videos and blurred images. Each time someone had acted with particular violence, their eyes had gone the same glassy black. Some instances were fleeting, like Niya during the third trial, but others were more prominent, like the black veins he'd seen webbed around Auristela's eyes when she held the fake Sol Stone over his head.

Something, or someone, was messing with the competitors.

"Oh, I'm afraid we've kept you too long," he heard Verdad say. "The banquet has already started—"

Teo stood up abruptly, nearly knocking over his chair. "I have to go."

"What about my turn?" Chisme asked.

"I think you got quite enough," his sister replied dryly.

As Teo stood to walk back toward the door, Verdad grabbed his forearm and squeezed. "Teo," she said, eyes steady as she stared up at him. "Good luck."

Teo raced toward the banquet hall, furiously tapping around videos of the trials from TúTube, looking for better angles and moments that teased at his memory. Niya and Auristela fighting in the jungle at Opal Oasis, the viciousness between them. It wasn't normal. Something was *wrong*. Teo threw open the doors to the dining hall, skidding to a stop. The room was full, all the dioses, competitors, and priests sitting at a large table with Luna at the head. Everyone turned to stare at him, including Aurelio.

"Teo, where's your regalia?" his mother asked, confused as she looked him up and down. At her side, Huemac frowned, caught somewhere between confusion and the instinct to scold, but Teo couldn't care less about what he was wearing right now.

"Is everything all right?" Luna asked, standing from her chair.

All right? Was *everything all right*?

"Something's wrong with the trials!" Teo shouted.

Gasps and alarmed looks bounced around the table.

Luna stared at him, bewildered. "What are you talking about?"

Teo ran down the table, ignoring his mother's startled look and the others' murmuring. "Look!" He held up his phone, quickly scrolling through videos and images from the trials. "Do you see their eyes? Something's been messing with people's minds during the trials, making them angry and violent, and, I—I don't know," he stammered, trying to make sense of his jumbled thoughts. "Just *look*!"

Teo thrust his phone toward Luna, but before she could move, Lumbre lurched to her feet.

"Silence!" she demanded.

Teo saw his mother's face oscillate between confusion and offense as she looked back and forth between the Golds and her son.

"Him *being here* is already making a mockery of this sacred tradition. This is yet another desperate play for attention!"

"*Excuse me?*" Teo snapped, in what was perhaps not the wisest tone. Lumbre seethed. "I am *not* the first Jade to compete in the trials, but this *could* be the first time the competition has been sabotaged."

The final word elicited a gasp from somewhere down the table.

"If we're supposed to be judged on our heroism, on how we act, but something else has power over us, doesn't that make the whole competition unfair?"

"I have had enough of you and your dramatics!" Lumbre knocked Teo's phone from his hand. It clattered to the floor, screen smashing as it skittered across the stone.

Teo's heart thrashed. "*No!*"

Aurelio leapt to his feet.

"*Sit down!*" Lumbre ordered her son, but he didn't move. His eyes darted between his mom and Teo, unsure of what to do. Auristela grabbed his arm from where she sat next to him.

Teo took a deep breath, trying to calm the storm of emotions rising up in his belly. "Luna, *please*. Listen to me. You of all people must have noticed that something isn't right!"

Luna swallowed, her hands restless before her. "It is not my place to question the will of Sol."

"So you *have* seen it!" Teo exclaimed. He looked around to his friends, waiting for their outrage to join his own—Niya, Xio, hell, even one of the Golds—but instead, they all looked just as confused and unsure as Luna.

"Teo ..." Quetzal said gently, resting a hand on his shoulder.

No one was *listening*. "Mom, this is serious! I can show you—"

"The show is over, Son of Quetzal," Lumbre snapped. "Take your seat, and be grateful. To show up late for a banquet held in your honor as a competitor is enough of a disgrace. Do not embarrass your mother further!"

"Someone's going to get killed tomorrow!" Teo shouted back, his voice echoing off the walls. "And all you care about is that I'm late to this stupid dinner?"

The room was silent. No one had said it plainly like that, the whole length of the trials. Everyone had quietly agreed to ignore half of what this was all leading to.

"How do the rankings work, Luna? How is the great Sol deciding who will be killed tomorrow? Are any of us safe?"

Luna only gazed at him, apparently aware that he didn't expect an answer from her.

"All this time, the rankings have been weird! We all know it." Teo's heart was racing. He couldn't keep track of the words tumbling from his own mouth—it wasn't just about what Verdad had shown him anymore. It was like all the anger and frustration he'd felt during the trials was finally coming to a breaking point.

"Your daughter could be killed tomorrow, Diosa Lumbre, don't you care about that?" he shot back.

Fire blazed in her molten eyes. "How *dare you*—"

"*Stop it, Teo,*" a voice suddenly said at his side.

Xio sat at the table next to his father, his face pale.

"Xio," Teo said, shocked. Didn't he care? He was ranked last!

Tears shone in his dark eyes. "You're making things *worse*," he said in a strangled voice. Mala Suerte protectively wrapped his arm around his son's small shoulders.

"You knew what this was when you came here," Luna said, slowly and deliberately.

"I didn't choose to be a competitor!" Teo argued, but he could hear the defeat in his own voice.

"This runs our world, Teo," she said calmly. "You knew that. You just didn't care when it didn't affect you."

Teo took a step back, the words like a punch to his gut. He looked around. Niya, for once at a loss for words, stared at him, confusion puckering her brow. The other competitors exchanged wary glances while priests whispered to one another behind their hands.

Aurelio was still on his feet, ready to do *something*, but even he looked at a loss.

"But, the eyes . . ." He looked to where his phone laid broken and useless on the floor.

"Teo . . ." His mom stood up and gingerly took a few steps closer to him. "I think you're very tired," she said, softly and slowly like she was talking to a frightened bird. "You've been through a lot. Maybe you need some rest."

Teo's heart sank. Even his mom didn't believe him.

"This is a disgrace!" Lumbre roared. "I want him punished!"

"It's the night before the final trial, Diosa Lumbre," Luna said calmly.

That hung heavy in the air. What could be worse than what they'd have to go through tomorrow?

"Then I want him confined to his room!" Lumbre slammed her fist on the table.

Luna sighed but didn't argue. "Teo, please go to your room and cool off," she said, waving him off before rubbing her brow. "Tomorrow is the fifth and final trial. I'd like it to go better than tonight."

Humiliated and angry, Teo stormed back to his room before anyone could try talking to him. Once inside, he slammed the door behind him. Why did no one believe him? He knew it was far-fetched, but the evidence was there! Wasn't it?

Doubt was sour in Teo's stomach. He could've sworn he could see it, whatever *it* was, in people's eyes from the footage. His mom was right, he was exhausted, but that didn't mean he'd made it all up. Or had it just been a trick of the light? Teo squeezed his eyes shut and rubbed them with his fists.

What was happening to him?

Someone knocked on the door and Teo jumped.

Dread sank into his stomach. Was it Lumbre, back to chew him out? Or maybe Luna, coming to give him another punishment? He was tempted to just ignore it, but when they knocked again, this time more persistent, Teo dragged himself to the door and opened it.

It was Huemac. He looked like he hadn't slept in days. Teo braced himself, waiting for the priest to scold him or chew him out for his behavior at the banquet.

Instead, Huemac sighed. "Troublemaker," he said softly.

Tears immediately filled Teo's eyes and when he tried to blink them away, it only got worse.

Huemac stepped into the room and closed the door behind him. "What a mess you've gotten yourself in, troublemaker," he said with a tired smile.

Teo all but collapsed into the old man's arms, his tears spreading dark across Huemac's emerald green robes in a way they hadn't since he was a little kid. Huemac held him tight and rubbed the soft ridges between his wings. Teo hadn't felt that comforting touch in years.

"Your wings are so handsome," Huemac said, voice gruff even after clearing his throat. "I've been wanting to tell you. I'm so proud of you."

Teo let out a bitter laugh. "Why? I haven't done a single thing for you to be proud of."

"Why?" Huemac pushed him back with warm hands on his shoulders and made him stand up straight. "Teo, you have become so completely yourself. I am in awe of the young man before me."

Teo shook his head. "I shouldn't even be here."

"You didn't exactly have a choice."

Teo thought back to what Diosa Opción had said. *We all have a choice.*

"I'm just a fuckup," Teo said, rubbing at his eyes. "I fuck *everything* up."

"Oh, Teo," Huemac sighed. He sat on the edge of the bed and motioned for Teo to join him. "I have called you Troublemaker since you were two months old," he said. "I've never told you this story, but I was holding you while your mother gave a speech. You had just gotten fed and you wouldn't burp." He shook his head disapprovingly, but an amused grin curled his mouth. "Finally, I had to give you back to the diosa before she went back to the podium and as she took you, you puked right down the front of her dress. And you laughed at me. I swear you did." Huemac chuckled. "That was the first time I called you that."

"Not sure what baby barf has to do with this," Teo said weakly.

"And it didn't matter, Teo," Huemac continued, ignoring him. "Your mother laughed, too. She had many, many photos taken with spit-up on her after that. You taught me it didn't matter. You've never respected authority or formality, from the very beginning."

Huemac fixed Teo with a serious look. "But you don't cause trouble for the sake of hurting others. When you see things that are unjust, when you see people who are acting unjustly, you cause trouble by interrupting them."

"That's not why I—"

"You are a loud, impulsive, persistent seeker of justice," Huemac cut in, not letting him finish. "And that makes people uncomfortable, but it doesn't make you bad. It makes you very good, in fact. Far better than the rest of us who stay quiet because they're afraid to speak up."

"I think that's the nicest thing you've ever said to me," Teo teased through sniffles.

"You'd do well to remember it."

A surprise laugh bucked in Teo's chest, releasing some of the tension knotted in his body.

"I think I made a fool of myself," Teo confessed.

But Huemac shook his head. "No, Teo, you spoke up because you had to. It's not your fault the Golds don't listen."

"It wasn't just the Golds." Teo recalled the sinking feeling in his gut when he realized Quetzal didn't believe him, either.

Huemac sighed. "I'm only mortal, Teo. I understand what it's like to feel that my actions are inconsequential. But we must try to do what is right, regardless of who is willing to listen."

They sat in silence for a moment before Teo said quietly, "I'm scared."

Huemac smiled and patted his knee. "You'd have to be an idiot not to be. Troublemakers make change, Teo. You are your mother's son. You are the Hero of Quetzlan—whether you want it or not," he added when Teo made a face. "That's a lot of responsibility."

A responsibility Teo still didn't think he'd earned, but he could start to.

"I ruined that stupid fancy dinner and people think I'm making up stories about the trials," he said, rubbing his nose. "Everyone hates me now."

"If your friends know you, they know you're a very good person with good intentions."

"And if they still hate me?"

"Niya knows you, Teo, don't sell her short," Huemac said. "It would have been much easier for her not to be your friend all these years, you know. She won't give you up so easily." When Teo still didn't look convinced, he added, "If all else fails, buy her forgiveness with all the candy you've got stuffed in your bag."

Teo gave him a wry smile. "You knew about that, huh?"

Huemac chuckled and clapped Teo on the back. "Sol isn't the only all-seeing one."

CHAPTER 22

After Huemac left, Teo couldn't stand being cooped up in this room that wasn't his in a bed that was still too soft to ever be comfortable. Even the clothes he wore were branded with the Academy's logo, reminding him he was only playing dress-up for a fucked-up show of pageantry. He tore off the sleek Academy-approved pajamas and dug out his black basketball shorts and stiff jade blue gym shirt from Quetzlan High from his duffle bag.

Once again, Teo broke the rules and left the competitors' wing. He didn't care if he'd been banished to his room. There wasn't any other punishment Lumbre or Luna could hand out that was worse than being forced to compete in the trials.

He climbed the steps to the top of Sol Temple. The observatory was empty except for the Sol Stone and the waiting altar.

Without anyone else around, Teo realized the stone was giving off a soft humming sound as it rotated, small solar flares licking its sides.

Up here, he could see all of Reino del Sol stretching out into the darkness around him. Lights blinked from far-off cities, the beams of the Sun Stones shining from their temple homes. Back home, there was too much light pollution to see the stars, but here they sparked brightly overhead.

Teo plopped down on the edge of the observatory, his legs dangling over the side as the Sol Stone warmed his back. He faced the small beam of light farthest to the west that he knew was Quetzlan Temple. Teo missed home. It felt like months since he'd left instead of days.

Teo propped his elbows on his knees and scrubbed his hands over his face.

"There you are," came a familiar voice.

Teo jumped and turned to find Aurelio standing behind him. He wore the Academy shorts and a crop top that matched his uniform, his hair pulled back into a knot as always. The corner of his lip was tugged into a tired grin.

"How'd you find me?" Teo asked, his wings tucked in tightly against his back.

Aurelio lifted his shoulders in a small shrug. "There's only so many places to hide around here."

Teo squinted up at him suspiciously.

"Actually, the temple's pretty big." Aurelio sat down next to him with a heavy sigh. Teo liked how the soft parts of his stomach rolled when he was sitting. "I've been looking for a while," he admitted.

"We were supposed to stay in our rooms for the rest of the night," Teo said. "Won't your mom be pissed at you if she finds out?"

Aurelio shrugged. "She's usually mad at me, so I'm not sure it'd make much of a difference."

Not sure what to say to that, Teo kept quiet. Sleepy soft warmth radiated from Aurelio, warming Teo in the cold night air. Next to Aurelio's bare, muscular thigh and deep brown skin, Teo looked comically pale and thin.

"Which one's yours?" Aurelio asked, nodding out toward the city lights.

Teo pointed to Quetzlan's narrow beam.

"What about you?"

Aurelio leaned toward Teo, his shoulder pressing against his wing, and pointed in the opposite direction. San Fuego was closer and brighter, practically blazing as it shot up into the night sky.

"Man, I wanted to see the rest of the cities so bad," Teo said with a weak laugh.

"And now?" Aurelio asked, his eyes still locked on the light of his city's Sun Stone.

"Now, I think you've got to beat out Dezi to be Sunbearer," Teo said, nudging him with his elbow. "Then I can show you around Quetzlan."

Aurelio only hummed in response. For a little while, they sat in silence. Teo waited for Aurelio to say something, but his odd stillness made Teo wonder if maybe Aurelio was waiting for *him* to say something first.

Just be quiet, Teo told himself. *Don't ruin the moment.* But he couldn't help it. "So, do you think I'm a liar, too?"

Aurelio's eyebrows creased. "What, for what happened at dinner?" Teo nodded. "No, I don't think you're lying. Something does seem … off."

Silence fell between them again. Teo didn't want to push it, didn't want to feel the harsh sting of Aurelio's disbelief on top of everyone else's. But he also felt, deep down in his chest, that Aurelio would actually listen.

"You know, for a second I thought your sister was going to bash my skull in," Teo tried with a chuckle.

"For a second," Aurelio said, finally looking over at him, "So did I. She's not like that, though," he added, dark eyebrows bunching. "Auristela is competitive but she's not violent."

"Guess I'll have to take your word for it," Teo mumbled under his breath.

Aurelio nodded. "Yes. She's never done something like that before," he said, troubled. "She's been acting weird lately. Everyone has, to be honest."

"Just as a third-party outsider," Teo said, pressing his fingers to his chest, "all the Golds come off as very 'I'll do anything to win.'"

"We're competitive, sure, but even back at the Academy, it's more like friendly competition," Aurelio went on, idly toying with the strings on his hoodie. "We go hard but then after we're still friends, still joke around—"

"*You*, joke around?"

Aurelio gave him a withering look. "I'm serious. Usually it's just head-to-head and there isn't all this sabotage and . . . ruthlessness."

"Maybe the stress of the trials is getting to us," Teo suggested with a shrug, trying to convince himself more than anything because the other option was too terrifying. "The possibility of fame and glory or impending death doesn't exactly bring out the best in people." It certainly hadn't in him.

"Maybe," Aurelio conceded after a long pause, but he didn't seem convinced.

Aside from the obvious, there was something else that had happened in the fourth trial that was still bugging Teo.

"Before your sister destroyed the Sol Stone replica, she tried to get you to take it," Teo said. "Why didn't she just take it for herself?"

Aurelio held his breath and tipped his head to one side. "It's . . . complicated."

"I've got the time," Teo told him.

"Me and Auristela have always been really close."

"Well, you *are* twins."

Aurelio rolled his eyes. "It's more than that. We were mostly raised by our mortal dad because our mother was busy. I was so excited to start at the Academy back then," he said with a weak laugh.

A wistful grin rolled across Teo's lips. "I remember."

All the nights Teo and Aurelio had spent during holidays and events flooded Teo's head. How they'd pretend they were Heroes, fighting off villains and monsters in order to protect the people of Sol. Aurelio was always so excited, talking about what it'd be like at the Academy, the two of them together.

"But then I actually started school and it was nothing like I thought it would be," Aurelio went on, frowning down at his hands in his lap. "We didn't have our dad anymore, our siblings were all busy being Heroes, and the Lumbre priests weren't the warmest."

Teo could easily recall.

"My mom kept impressing on us the importance of being a *Gold* and how we should only be friends with *other* Golds, but only the strongest ones."

Aurelio turned to face him, and Teo caught himself holding his breath.

"I'm sorry for the way I treated you."

Teo's stomach sank. Hot shame flooded his cheeks as his shoulders crept up to his ears.

"It was a shitty thing to do," Aurelio said, refusing to look away. "You were so nice to me—the only person who tried to be my friend. I treated you horribly and I regret it every day."

Aurelio's sincerity was unsettling, and the pain of Aurelio ditching him all those years ago still ached. He wasn't sure if he was ready to forgive Aurelio just yet.

Aurelio gave him one more intent look and turned away, freeing Teo of his gaze. "It's funny," he said with a short mirthless laugh. "I spent my whole childhood looking forward to joining the Academy and training to be a Hero. I was so desperate to get my mother's attention, but when I finally did, it was nothing like I expected. And there was no one I could talk to about it, no one who would understand, anyway, except Auristela.

"That's why I'm so close with my sister," Aurelio continued, his coppery gaze sliding to Teo. "She's the only one I'm *allowed* to be close to. She's the only person I've ever really been able to rely on."

It sounded so awful and isolating.

"My sister has always been very ... protective."

"Yeah, I've noticed," Teo grumbled, rubbing the lump on the back of his head.

"Auristela and I are supposed to be model students, model *Heroes*. The best of the best. Constantly in training, constantly in competition. Our whole lives, it's been beaten into us that we need to be the best of the best—to be *exceptional*."

"And you've achieved that, haven't you?" Teo asked. "Niya says you and Auristela are the top-ranked students. And both of you were chosen to compete in the Sunbearer Trials," he pointed out. If this was Aurelio's attempt to make Teo feel sympathetic then he really didn't know his audience. "And what does that have to do with her smashing the Sol Stone?"

"Auristela wanted me to take the Sol Stone because she wanted me to win the trial," Aurelio said.

"Obviously she wants one of you to win," Teo said, waiting for some kind of revelation.

"No. She wants *me* to win. So, when I wouldn't take the Sol Stone, in a very poorly constructed plan, she decided if I wasn't going to take it, then it'd be best if *no one* had it, to help me get into first."

"But now Dezi's in first."

"Like I said, a very poorly constructed plan."

"Why does she want you to win so badly?"

"So she can prove to our mom that I'm not a failure."

He said it so plainly, at first Teo thought he'd heard him wrong. "*What?*" Teo said, a laugh jumping in his throat. "How the hell could she think *you* are a failure?" Surely this was some kind of joke. He was

Aurelio, the Golden Boy. How could anyone accuse him of being anything less than perfect?

"I'm not fireproof."

Aurelio turned to look at him, a crease between his brow like he wasn't sure how Teo was going to respond.

And Teo didn't even know *how* to respond. What Aurelio said didn't make sense.

Teo shook his head. "But you're the son of Lumbre," he said. "All children of Lumbre are fireproof, that's, like, your whole *thing*."

"Yeah, well, not me," Aurelio said gruffly, shifting uneasily where he sat. "I can manipulate fire, but my skin isn't fireproof," he explained. "My skin doesn't get damaged as quickly as a mortal's, but I can still feel it."

Aurelio pulled up the sleeves of his hoodie, revealing the ever-present golden armbands. He fiddled with the small clasps on his left arm and Teo's heart leapt into his throat.

He wanted to reach out and tell him to stop. Whatever Aurelio was about to show him, Teo knew he wasn't ready to see.

"As long as I don't handle fire for too long, it doesn't injure my skin."

With a small *click*, the armband opened up, revealing the marred skin beneath.

Teo sucked in a breath between his teeth.

Marbled scars encircled Aurelio's forearm. Some were darker brown, while others were bright red and shiny.

Teo leaned forward. They wrapped around in shapes Teo recognized but couldn't quite put his finger on.

"It was a matter of getting used to it," Aurelio said, his voice quiet as they sat next to each other, heads bowed over his arm. He flexed his fingers and patches of scar tissue pulled taut over muscle. "Resistance training, my mother called it," Aurelio murmured.

A sudden coldness struck Teo in his core. He recognized the shapes now.

Handprints. The same size but layered and in different stages of healing.

Teo clenched his jaw. Angry heat flooded his veins. If there was ever a reason to punch a god, this was it.

Aurelio was sitting there quietly, eyes downcast and scars laid bare.

Teo swallowed down the burning in his throat. He reached for Aurelio's arm but stopped himself short, fingers hovering.

"Does it hurt?" he asked, barely above a whisper.

That same bone-deep tired smile curled Aurelio's lips. "Every time."

Teo thought about every time he'd seen Aurelio touch fire. The gecko alebrije spitting fire at his hands. The wall of fire he'd thrown himself in front of to protect Teo. All of his people back in Quetzlan when the terrible fire had broken out in the panadería.

Aurelio could feel all of it, but he still went running into the flames.

"Auristela thinks all my problems will be solved if I become Sunbearer," he said, bringing Teo back to the matter at hand. "With that kind of title under my belt, maybe it would convince my mom to over-look my … shortcomings."

"*Shortcomings*," Teo echoed with a bitter laugh. Aurelio was the picture-perfect Gold, molded to be a Hero from his haircut to the clothes he wore—even to his photo-ready persona.

"Auristela was wrong to do what she did—"

"Destroying the stone or trying to bash my head in?"

Aurelio chose to ignore him. "But I understand why. When it comes down to it, Auristela is the most important thing to me, not titles." Aurelio locked the golden armband over his skin once again before looking up at Teo with a steady gaze. "I would do anything for my sis-ter, and she would do anything for me. I don't care about being named Sunbearer to impress my mother anymore. I just want both of us to make it through alive."

Aurelio was worried about Auristela coming in last.

They were both in similar situations, with people they cared about at the bottom of the rankings.

But someone had to die. Not just anyone—someone they *knew*. He hated to admit it, but Teo had actually grown to like some of the Golds. They were funny and they were just kids like him, not the supervillains he'd built them up to be his head. Dezi and Marino had saved his ass during the trials more than once. Auristela and Ocelo sucked, sure, but not enough to warrant him murdering them.

And if things continued the way they were now, it'd be Xio who was killed.

Teo was sickened by himself. He'd wanted to win for all the wrong reasons—not for some noble cause, but because he wanted to feel worthy. But it wasn't too late. There was still time to fix it.

Even if there was something interfering with the trials, manipulating people to act out and become violent, no one believed him, and he didn't know how to prove it. The reality of the situation was that they were stuck completing the final trial, no matter what. So, regardless of whatever else was going on, he had to figure out how to get through it alive, with Niya and Xio.

"I'll do whatever it takes to keep her safe," Aurelio told Teo, a fiery intensity behind his copper eyes.

Teo let out a forced laugh. "That's the fucked-up part, isn't it?" he said, looking back at the Sol Stone.

"What is?" Aurelio asked, looking between Teo and the stone.

The grin on Teo's lips was bitter. "That someone still has to die."

For a long moment, they were both silent.

Aurelio lifted his arm, pointing to a cluster of stars above them. "There they are," he said. "The Obsidians."

Teo squinted. "I was never good at identifying stars. They all look the same to me."

"It's not single stars," Aurelio explained, gesturing a little wider. "They're constellations. You see that bright cluster over to the left? That's the base of Chupacabra. And next to it, see that shape? Almost like an hourglass—that's Caos."

Teo thought he could make them out now. "What about Venganza?"

Aurelio's hand drifted to the right. "There. See? It looks like a goat head with horns. That's where Sol trapped them all among the stars."

"So, that's what we're fighting for, huh?" Teo asked. He couldn't help the bitterness that crept into his voice. "To keep away some big balls of light?"

But Aurelio shook his head. "They're much worse than that."

Silence fell between them again as they both gazed up into the night. Teo tried to imagine the Obsidians back before the war, when they were dioses as real as his mom or Luna. He couldn't picture it. The Obsidians were more like monsters in a scary story.

"I've been thinking about what you said the other night," Aurelio murmured.

"I say a lot of stuff," Teo said quietly. "You'll have to be more specific."

"About how, if being the sacrifice is such an honor, then it should be the winner of the trials."

Teo looked over at him, surprised. "Do you think I'm right?"

Aurelio shook his head, eyes heavy-lidded as he looked out across the sprawling darkness. "No." He let out a long sigh. "But I don't think you're wrong, either."

"Better than nothing," Teo joked, but there was a heavy weight draped across both of them.

"I don't…" Aurelio paused, his lips pinched together. Whatever he was trying to say, Teo could see it was difficult to express. "I don't know if I could do it."

Teo quirked an eyebrow.

"Make the sacrifice," Aurelio said. "Be Sunbearer. Even if it wasn't—even if I didn't know the person who had to die. Even though it has to be done. I don't know that I could take someone's life."

Tentatively, Teo leaned his shoulder against Aurelio's. He tensed but didn't pull away.

"I hope you don't have to," Teo said quietly.

Aurelio's shoulders slumped and he leaned into Teo, just a touch, the warmth of his skin spreading through Teo's side.

They fell into silence, staring up at the Sol Stone as it burned.

CHAPTER 23

The fifth trial wasn't until later that night. There was a lot of time to kill during the day, too much for Teo's comfort. Everyone was restless and unusually quiet. He was especially worried about Xio, who had dark circles under his eyes and refused to eat until Teo and Niya gently bullied him into getting down some bread and cheese.

At one point, Teo, Xio, and Niya were in the common room playing lotería and when he looked up, he realized most of the Golds were there, too.

Marino, Dezi, Atzi, and Xochi were half-heartedly playing pool, and someone said Ocelo had retreated to the training room. They weren't chattering and laughing like they usually did. Even Dezi, who was always smiling and so animated, propped himself up on his pool cue like he might fall asleep standing up at any minute.

Meanwhile, Aurelio and Auristela sat side by side on one of the couches that faced the large windows. They kept to themselves, but more than once Aurelio caught Teo's eye as he watched them from across the room.

The city below buzzed with activity as priests prepared for the night's festivities. The fifth and final trial began after sunset and the Sunbearer ceremony would happen at midnight.

As excitement thrummed through Sol Temple, the competitors silently ate lunch.

Teo wondered if they were all thinking the same thing—that in less than twelve hours, one of them would be named the Sunbearer.

And one of them would be dead.

Despite his restlessness, Teo was still surprised when the Sol priest came to gather them and he learned that the final trial would not take place in an arena at Sol Temple. Instead, they would be traveling to a different, undisclosed location.

In their uniforms, they followed Luna back to the docks. Sol priests paused in their preparations to cheer and wave at the competitors. Teo's breathing was loud in his own ears as he obediently walked the dirt paths until they were back by the docks.

Instead of the large boat they'd grown accustomed to, a fleet of trajineras waited for them. The competitors' priests were on their boats, a sea of colorful robes. Teo tried to spot the brilliant green and blue of the Quetzal, desperately searching for Huemac's face, but the small Jade trajinera was at the very back.

Luna instructed them to board the lead boat covered in the golden adornments of Sol. The table was laden with fruits, meats, and any freshly squeezed juice they could want. But when they sat down, no one touched it.

When they passed through the waterfalls, Teo had the brief, delirious hope that maybe they were going home to Quetzlan, but that was quickly dashed when their trajinera headed south. Teo had never traveled through these canals, and since he was shit at geography, he had no idea which unfamiliar cities their journey would take them through.

For each city they traveled through, people stood along canals and over bridges, cheering and celebrating as they passed. Gritos cut through the air and not even Auristela waved.

Teo wondered if these people understood what they were cheering for. This wasn't a silly parade celebrating a fun holiday—it was a funeral procession.

As the sun dipped lower in the sky, Niya's nerves finally kicked in. She started talking a mile a minute about absolutely nothing. No one said anything, instead letting Niya continue having conversations with herself for the rest of the trip. Even that was better than the heavy silence.

They traveled through one of the outermost cities as the sun set on its final day before being renewed.

It was a small and run-down city. Many of the buildings along the canal sat crooked with boarded-up windows. The farther they went, the more alert the Golds became. Dezi sat up straighter, eyes glued past the head of the boat. Ocelo's heavy brow pulled down over their jaguar eyes.

Suddenly, Niya stopped talking.

The trajinera had slowed to a stop at a rickety old dock. They were quite a ways from the nearest houses, and when Teo looked at what lay ahead, he at first only saw pitch-black night. But his eyes quickly adjusted, and when he looked up, he realized it was a mass of dark trees stretching far into the sky above.

"They're not serious," Xochi signed and said sharply, making Teo jump. Her hair whipped back and forth as she looked between the rest of the table and the trees. "They can't be serious!"

Over the sound of his suddenly thundering heart, short, shaky breaths caught Teo's attention and he realized Xio's dark eyes were huge as he stared unblinkingly at the looming jungle.

Auristela latched on to Aurelio's arm as she stared ahead at the jungle. Aurelio's mouth thinned to a hard line, his nostrils flaring.

For once in her life, Niya was speechless.

"Where are we?" Teo demanded, voice tight as adrenaline flooded his veins.

Aurelio was the one to answer. "Los Restos."

Every bit of warmth left in Teo's body was swallowed by icy fear.

From what Teo could remember from school, Los Restos was the wild southern jungle where the abandoned ruins of the betrayer gods now lay beyond the reach of Sol. After Venganza, Chupacabra, and Caos were locked up in their celestial prisons, the gods destroyed their cities and temples. Over time, nature had reclaimed the ruins and now dangerous animals and monsters roamed freely. Sometimes they broke into the borders of Reino del Sol, but such events were few and far between and swiftly handled by the Heroes. It was eerie, seeing how the jungle started where the outskirts of the city ended. Almost like an invisible barrier held the creeping roots and ferns back.

It started to rain. Not the soft, warm kind that Teo was used to during hurricane season, but the sharp, icy-cold kind that stung when it hit his skin. In the distance, he could hear a low growl of thunder as they followed Luna to the edge of the jungle; the silvery stars of her dress and streaks of her hair caught what little light they had to illuminate the way.

Waiting for them were ten raised wooden paths coated thickly with moss. They climbed rickety rope ladders up to platforms twenty or so feet above the ground. Each one was built with crisscrossing logs, and each platform extended outward, disappearing into the dense, dark forest before them.

For once, Fantasma's presence didn't give Teo comfort. Instead, she was an ominous reminder of the fate that awaited whoever ranked last.

"This trial requires you to follow a single path, but it is *not* a race," Diosa Luna said and signed as a priest held an umbrella over her. Her voice sounded strained and distant. "The deeper you get into the jungle, the stranger and more dangerous things you may see, and your paths will start to converge and cut into one another. The finish point of this trial is at the convergence of all paths. There will be a large platform with Sol's glyph waiting for you. Once you cross the finish line, you may not go back."

Teo tried to listen, but a deep quivering had taken hold of his spine, making it hard to concentrate. All he could think about was that if they were all split up, he, Xio, and Niya would somehow have to find one another.

"There are no rules for this trial. You must simply reach the end," Luna announced in a wavering voice. Teo had seen her be stoic and kind, and even harsh, but he had never once seen the diosa look frightened. It sent goose bumps skittering down his arms.

"The forests of Los Restos have been corrupted by the ancient power of the Obsidians, and their influence remains. Sol's light cannot reach you under the dark crowns of these trees. You are on your own, and you will be judged on how well you defend yourselves against the remnants of the Obsidians' power. We simply cannot know what obstacles lay ahead for you. You may use any means necessary to protect yourself. The only stipulation is that if you fall off the path, you won't be allowed to continue and your light will go out."

Light?

All at once, their uniforms lit up. The honeycomb webbing, stitching, and mesh panels were all illuminated with warm golden light—except for Teo's and Xio's, which glowed brilliant blue-green.

Diosa Luna's face faltered, just for a moment. She was looking at Xio with concern. She opened her mouth as if to speak, then paused. Her eyes broke away from him and scanned the rest of the competitors. When her silvery gaze met Teo's, she closed her mouth, and her expression hardened back into the still, round mask he was used to, though something about the set of her jaw was too tight.

"Competitors will be taken to their starting points and then we will begin," Diosa Luna instructed, and a line of Sol priests stepped forward to escort them.

Even after Teo reached the top of the platform, the rain continued to pour. Teo tracked where his friends ended up, which was easy to do in the dark with their illuminated uniforms.

Teo tried to ignore the shivers that kept sending his wings fluttering to shake the water from his feathers. Twenty feet up had seemed a lot lower when he was on the ground. The knotty wood beneath him was warped and slippery, but there was no railing or edge, just wet tree bark and moss and the inky blackness below him.

The familiar transparent barrier made of golden light separated him from the rest of the path, but beyond it, he could see the logs disappear into the depths of the jungle.

"Competitors, on your marks," Luna's voice boomed.

Teo turned to Xio and flashed him a thumbs-up. Xio returned it with a curt but shaky nod.

Mariachi's cornet sounded and Teo's watch shook at the same time the barrier disappeared.

As soon as Teo ran past the tree line, everything plunged into blackness, his suit the only source of light. The raised wooden path twisted left and right, making it impossible to see very far ahead. They were beneath the jungle canopy, which meant the heavy foliage blocked out the stars. The trees stood close together, leaning against one another, and branches tangling together like fingers.

Any hopes Teo had of using his wings to fly up and look for his friends were quickly dashed. The jungle was so densely packed that there was no way Teo could fly more than fifteen feet in the air without getting tangled up. Even then, his wings were sore from overuse, just like Aurelio had warned him, and Auristela's knees pinning them hadn't helped.

So it was back to old-school running.

And it was terrible.

Immediately, Teo got a stitch in his side, and every footfall jarred his aching shoulders. He stuck to the center of the path because if he got too close to the edge, the dark jungle below gave him vertigo. The canopy blocked out the direct rainfall, but the water also gathered on fronds and poured down on him in thick streams. In the dark, it was impossible to see wayward vines and branches protruding from the jungle, and Teo had to continuously catch his balance or risk faceplanting on the jungle floor.

It may have been wiser to take the path slow, to consider every step, but the sudden, oppressive feeling of loneliness in the dark trees urged him to go faster until he found his friends.

After what felt like ages, his path met with the one to his right. Teo slowed to a jog, straining his ears and eyes for anyone else. He heard movement within the trees, something heavy and inhuman. The icy raindrops pelted his skin and dripped into his eyes.

"Xio?" he shouted, hoping maybe they could find each other that way. He tried three more times, but the sound of rain crashing through leaves made it impossible to hear anything else.

He didn't understand how it could be raining like this. When Teo shielded his eyes with his hand and looked up, he swore it looked like rain clouds had gathered *under* the protective layer of the canopy.

Before he could make sense of it, Teo's scalp tingled and a strange metallic taste hit his tongue.

Light exploded at his feet a half second before a loud *crack* split through Teo's ears. Knocked onto his side, Teo quickly scrambled away from the now scorched and steaming log. When he looked up, he found Atzi had snuck up behind him.

She walked forward with determined strides, her hands twisting as thick rainclouds swirled obediently overhead. Something was off about the way she carried herself. Teo was about to call out when her mouth twisted into a very un-Atzi smirk. She held out her arm, poised to strike.

Shit, shit, shit!

He rushed to get to his feet, shoes sliding out from under him.

Atzi reached out and a bolt of lightning appeared, quivering between her hands. Teo managed to throw himself out of the way before she threw it like a spear. It struck the path where he'd just been, splintering the log.

Silvery light illuminated Atzi's frustrated face. With an angry shout, she chucked another lightning bolt.

Teo leapt, hot pain shooting through his shoulders as his wings got him over the bolt of lightning. It crashed uselessly into a tree.

"Come on, Teo!" she goaded. "Don't you remember the first trial, when I shot you out of the sky? Don't you want to get me back?"

There was something strange about her. He didn't know Atzi all that well, but in the short time they'd been traveling together, she had never been so antagonistic. Her focus was always intense but quiet.

"Or maybe you'd rather fight me," Atzi said, only it wasn't Atzi anymore. The facial features twisted and curved as the figure before Teo grew. Suddenly, it was Ocelo standing before him, pointed teeth flashing. "Let's go, Bird Boy."

The fake Ocelo bounded forward, claws out. Teo stumbled back, his ass slamming hard against the logs beneath him. Ocelo lunged again, and Teo rolled. Thinking fast, he kicked his leg out and, like Aurelio had done to him, swept Ocelo's legs out from under them.

"That all you got, Jade?" Ocelo taunted as they jumped to their feet. Though, Teo had to admit, it was a passable impression. This time, when they swung, their fist collided with Teo's jaw.

Teo's wings flailed as he was knocked down onto his side. He tasted blood in his mouth, but he was still standing. "That all *you* got?" he asked, spitting jade blood onto the ground as he struggled back onto his feet.

Ocelo's lips peeled back unnaturally from their teeth in a razor-sharp smile. "I could do this all day." They shifted again, this time growing almost double in size. Ocelo's smug expression melted into the angry sneer of Diosa Lumbre.

"You continue to be a disappointment," she said in a perfect imitation of the diosa's voice. Anger bubbled in his stomach. Lumbre's hands ignited into balls of flame.

There was no way this was the real goddess. This was clearly one of the tricks of Los Restos.

Lumbre flung her first fireball at his face. Teo swore his eyebrows singed off as he just barely dodged to safety.

It wasn't the real Diosa Lumbre, but that was definitely real fire.

The diosa laughed, something Teo couldn't recall ever hearing the real Lumbre do. It was a cruel sound. "Pitiful little Jade. I'll admit, I didn't think you'd make it this far. I was looking forward to watching my daughter destroy you."

She threw another blast of fire in Teo's direction. Sending a prayer to Sol, his mom, and any god that would listen, he clapped his wings together in front of him. The gust of wind he created was powerful enough to throw the flames back, but he wasn't sure he'd be able to pull that off a second time.

He had to get close, to take Lumbre out before she made more fire.

Using his wings again for an extra boost, Teo surged forward with his arms up. His elbow collided with the diosa's nose, knocking her back.

A thin stream of blood trailed down Lumbre's face when she looked up at him, but she was smiling. Her tongue peeked out of the corner of her mouth, licking the black ichor. "It's sad that that's the best you can do."

"Shut *up*!" Teo shouted. He charged forward again, this time aiming for the goddess's big, stupid mouth. Lumbre only laughed as he threw punch after punch, not even bothering to dodge out of the way.

What game was it playing? It could have knocked him off the logs easily with Atzi's lightning, or maimed him with Ocelo's claws. And Teo *knew* he didn't stand a chance against the real Lumbre. It was almost like it was throwing the fight, letting him get the hits in.

There are no rules for this trial, Luna had said. *You must simply reach the end.*

How much time had he wasted fighting this thing? There was no way he could defeat it. No matter how hard he hit, it always got back up, seemingly unfazed. The fight would never end.

Teo tried to think. What would Niya do? Or Aurelio? Did the Academy even bother giving lessons on fights you couldn't win?

Fights you can't win. Teo jolted with realization.

He let his fists fall to his side. Lumbre took the opportunity to shove him back, but she didn't even try to throw more fire. Teo grinned.

This was just like his favorite video game. Sometimes, to escape an enemy he couldn't beat, all he had to do was run out of range.

And so, Teo ran.

Lumbre didn't even bother running after him as he doubled back the way he'd come. All she did was shout, *"Weak!* Someone as cowardly as you could never be worthy of my son!"

Definitely not Lumbre, but just as bitchy.

He'd have to find another way forward—there had to be other paths. Everyone had run off in opposite directions, but their platforms had to converge at some point.

Teo pressed on. The only good thing about having to run so much was that he wasn't cold anymore. Yeah, maybe his exposed arms were numb at this point, but his core was warm and that kept him from shivering.

After rounding a couple more corners without incident, he almost didn't notice when the paths converged again. This time, there was already someone waiting up ahead.

Marino was on his knees at the edge of the platform, reaching down precariously into the darkness. He must have heard Teo's approach because his head snapped up with a panicked expression.

"Help me!" Marino demanded, arm continuing to stretch into the menacing dark. "We have to help him!"

Teo stepped forward, unsure what to expect, but all he saw was darkness.

"There's nothing there—"

"Dezi!" Marino screamed, ignoring him as he turned away again. His hands moved quickly as he signed something into the darkness. "He won't take my hand," Marino said, voice quaking. "Help me reach him!"

Marino's torso was practically over the ledge and he had no idea he was grasping at nothing.

Teo grabbed his shoulder, trying to pull him back. "Dezi isn't there, Marino!" He huffed with the effort of trying to haul the other boy's weight, but he refused to budge. "It's fucking Los Restos messing with us!"

Marino didn't want to budge. He kicked out, landing his foot right in Teo's stomach, but at least Teo had managed to pull him back from falling off and getting eliminated.

Another figure entered the clearing and Teo's stomach dropped, anticipating another trick. To his surprise, this time he did see Dezi. The boy was shaking his head as if trying to get rid of a vision before he noticed Marino and Teo.

Marino was already scrambling back to the edge.

"Marino, look!" Teo yelled, grabbing his leg.

Upon seeing this, Dezi's expression hardened, locking in on Teo.

Finally, Marino glanced back. When he saw Dezi—the real Dezi—his face crumpled in relief. He ran over and fell against Dezi's chest, grabbing him as if to make sure he was really there, not dangling over the edge about to be lost forever.

Startled, Dezi held him tight and pulled him away, putting himself between Teo and Marino.

Teo's heart sank. Everyone had people they wanted to protect.

He needed to find Xio. He had no idea what terrible illusions the younger boy had encountered, and he couldn't stand the thought of him facing them alone.

Finally, Marino and Dezi looked at Teo.

"I don't understand, I saw Dezi hanging from the edge—" Marino said and signed.

Dezi's eyes bulged, quickly looking between Marino and Teo.

"I've been seeing people, too," Teo said as he tried to catch his breath. Trying to keep a Gold from throwing himself over a ledge was a lot harder than it looked. "It's the temptations Luna warned us about. Whatever is still in this place, it's creating illusions to trick us."

Marino nodded solemnly, his hands moving as he relayed Teo's revelation to Dezi. A look of understanding spread across his face as his hands started moving, too.

"He saw things, too," Marino translated.

The boys looked at each other with such sadness and relief that Teo felt like he was intruding.

Teo looked away, surveying his options. There was one path that continued on into the jungle, and two that led back toward the starting points.

His heart thudded as he tried to figure out what to do. Shouldn't he have seen some sign of Xio by now? If he continued forward, he ran the risk of leaving Xio behind.

But if he went back to look for him, Xio could be up ahead and run into danger alone.

He didn't have the luxury of time to debate, so Teo followed his gut.

"Good luck," he said to Marino and Dezi, before he turned around and headed back down the path Dezi had taken.

Teo ran as fast as he could, hoping he hadn't made the completely wrong choice and wasn't doubling back for no reason. His chest heaved as he sucked in rainwater and salty sweat. This path was exactly the same as the one he'd started on, but this time he was able to ignore the familiar smells and whispers that tried to distract him from his mission. He raced as quickly as he could around the twisting bends, growing more unsure the farther he went.

"SON OF A BITCH!" a familiar voice rang out.

He skidded to a stop, stunned. "Niya?" he called out.

"Teo?"

"Are you all right?"

"Yeah, I'm just kinda freaked out!"

Her voice echoed, bouncing between the giant trees. He followed it down another fork in the path, finally coming upon Niya standing in the middle of a platform. When she saw him, her eyes lit up.

"Teo!" She moved forward to hug him but Teo took a step back.

"Say something that only Niya would know," he demanded. The words felt ridiculous leaving his mouth—it was something he would've seen in a movie but he didn't know how else to be sure it was really his best friend.

"What?" she asked, confusion furrowing her brow, nearly on the verge of tears.

"Tell me something that only Niya would know," Teo said. "To prove it's really you—"

"WHEN WE WERE TEN YOU ATE A ROLY-POLY AT THE MIDSUMMER FESTIVAL AND MADE ME LIE ABOUT IT!" she immediately listed, voice shaking and eyes glistening. "WHEN WE WERE THIRTEEN YOU GOT THAT HORRIBLE HAIRCUT AND MADE ME EDIT ALL YOUR INSTAGRAFÍA POSTS FOR A MONTH UNTIL IT GREW BACK IN! WHEN WE WERE FIFTEEN AT THE—"

"OKAY, OKAY!" Teo shouted back, cheeks burning. "Will you keep it down?!"

"Do you believe it's really me?" she asked, sniffling as she rubbed her nose off on the back of her hand.

"It better be, otherwise the real Niya is going to have to answer for sharing all of the most embarrassing moments of my tween years on television!"

Niya threw herself at Teo, capturing him in a backbreaking hug. It was a relief to be with Niya, but it was impossible to feel too at ease in this jungle.

"Have you been hearing things?" Niya asked, slowly composing herself.

Teo nodded. "Seeing things, too. People." He shuddered. "Diosa Lumbre."

"Gross."

He nodded again. "How are you doing?"

"I don't like being this high up! I like having my feet on solid ground!" Niya lamented, voice tight.

"Have you seen Xio?" Teo asked, turning in a slow circle as he tried to get his bearings.

"I haven't seen *shit*!" she replied. "It's dark as hell in here!"

Teo cursed under his breath. He was failing Xio already.

"Am I afraid of heights?"

"We need to find him," Teo announced. "I've been backtracking in case he's behind us."

Niya nodded firmly and fell in beside him as they continued back down the path.

Hundreds of terrible scenarios flashed through Teo's head, distracting him enough that when they rounded the next bend of the path, he barreled straight into someone. Teo clumsily tried to get back on his feet as quick as he could. He turned, ready to fight off whichever illusion he'd just careened into.

"Xio!" he practically cried in relief.

The younger boy was sitting on the wet log path. The illuminated lining of the hood pulled over his head revealed Xio's wide-eyed surprise.

"What are you doing here?" he asked, voice pitching as he shook his head in disbelief.

"Looking for you!" Niya rushed forward and dragged him to his feet. "We thought something might have happened to you!"

Teo looked at the boy closely. "Niya, how do we know it's really him?"

Xio's expression filled with confusion.

"Of course it's him. Look how sad he is!" she pointed out. "An illusion wouldn't just sit here looking helpless!"

He didn't know how to argue with that.

"What happened to you?" Teo asked.

"I—I got lost," Xio stammered, a flush blooming in his cheeks. "It's so dark out here—I ran as fast as I could—"

Bad luck really did follow him around.

"Doesn't matter now, we found you," Teo said, waving him off. "Come on, we need to hurry. This place is full of illusions, so don't trust everything you see or hear. I've already run into a few Golds, so we've got a lot of time to make up."

Xio nodded jerkily and did as he was told. He kept up, but Teo could hear his ragged breaths over their pounding feet. They adjusted their speed to keep pace with what Xio could manage.

They hit the first convergence, and by the time they hit the second, the rain had lightened to a drizzle. As they came down another twist, their path joined with another on the left up ahead. Teo had a brief moment of relief, that *finally* they were getting somewhere, when two figures in gold suits merged in front of them from the left path.

Auristela and Aurelio.

Immediately, Teo snatched the back of Xio's jacket, dragging him to a stop. Niya stopped with them. They crouched, ready to fight or something, but the twins didn't even glance back.

They looked a little worse for wear. Auristela's hair was out of its usual ponytail, flying behind her, and he couldn't be certain but Aurelio looked like he was running with a slight limp. Whatever, or whoever, had held them up hadn't been good news.

Teo nudged Xio forward. "*Quick, go, go, go!*" he said in a harsh whisper, not wanting to draw the twins' attention. Hopefully they'd be too focused on finishing the challenge to look back.

Aurelio and Auristela slowly pulled ahead, even with Aurelio's possible injury.

Before long, Teo could hear something up ahead. The path straightened out. Snatches of bright light sparked through the tunnel of tangled jungle. Suddenly, Teo could actually see the foliage around him, and it was terrifying. Gnarled black branches grew all around, sharp edges and obsidian crystals glinting dangerously.

Aurelio and Auristela ran faster, long shadows trailing behind them.

A noise grew louder, from faint murmuring to the loud chatter of crowds.

"I think we're almost at the end!" Teo told Xio, his arms and legs tingling with exhaustion. Xio only nodded in response.

All at once, the path opened up into one wide platform, just outside the tree line. Aurelio and Auristela ran out first and were met with an explosion of loud applause, momentarily startling them into stillness.

When Teo and Xio hit the platform, the crowd's clamor slammed to an abrupt, unnatural stop. Huge stands had been erected below and around the platform, packed tight with cheering priests and semidioses.

Sol's glyph stood in the center of the platform on a raised dais. A golden barrier like the one from the start of the trial surrounded the glyph. That must've been the finish point. Ocelo and Dezi stood inside the barrier, waiting.

Teo blinked and rubbed his eyes, hoping it was real.

As the three of them approached the center of the platform, the crowd roared to life again.

Aurelio and Auristela looked back, finally spotting Teo, Niya, and Xio.

He could've sworn he saw Aurelio's mouth start to quirk into a grin, but then he turned away and kept running. Auristela's gaze lingered longer, knocking her off pace a little as they neared the finish point.

There was a strange look on her face, but she snapped out of it when Aurelio turned and said something to her.

The sound of the crowd changed, warbling and growing higher and higher pitched.

Auristela shook her head and chased after him.

Then, the lights shut off, and they were plunged into blackness. Teo could hardly see where his feet were landing but it didn't matter. He could see their destination.

Aurelio and Auristela were only a few yards away from the finish, outlined by the dull glow of the glyph. The twins were going to beat them, but at least Teo knew he and his friends were going to complete the trial without getting disqualified. That had to count for something in the rankings, it *had to*.

"Come on, Xio!" he urged, tugging on his sleeve. "We're almost there!"

The barrier gleamed with golden light as Aurelio ran through.

Ocelo and Dezi greeted him with enthusiasm and claps on the back.

Teo saw the gleaming, brilliant smile on Aurelio's face for a short, sweet moment. Then his smile froze in place. His eyebrows bunched.

The sounds around them crackled back into reality, taking on the roaring cheers of the audience before melting into static, then eerie silence. The lights returned, so bright and searing that Teo's hand shot out to shield his eyes, slowing his steps.

Auristela hadn't followed her brother through. She stood a few feet from the final checkpoint, her back to Teo.

Aurelio looked to his sister and through the shimmering golden wall, Teo saw his lips move but couldn't hear what he was saying.

Auristela ignored him. Instead, she turned around. All of Auristela's attention locked on Teo and Xio. She stared at them, lips parted and head tilted to the side like she was listening for something.

A heavy weight dropped into the pit of Teo's stomach.

Auristela closed her eyes and took a slow, deep breath.

"*Wait.*" Teo shot out his arm, forcing Xio to slow down.

Xio looked up at him, confused. "What? What's wrong?"

When Auristela opened her eyes, they were black as coals, the skin around them darkened and webbed with black veins. Her nostrils flared and wet pieces of hair stuck to her cheeks. Her lips curled back over her perfect white teeth.

It was happening again. This time, Teo *knew* he wasn't imagining it.

Past her shoulder, Aurelio frantically looked between his sister and Teo. He pounded his fist on the barrier, producing little more than a dull *thud*. His mouth moved silently again. *Auristela.*

But Auristela didn't listen. Her skin flushed red and she thrust her hands out at her sides. Fire roared to life in her palms. Why was this happening *now*? It was almost over, they were almost done!

"RUN!" Teo grabbed Xio and roughly shoved him out of the way.

The light cut out around them once again.

A ball of fire illuminated the darkness, exploding between them. Auristela charged at Teo, ruthlessly throwing fire. He did his best to evade by spinning and dodging, but she was relentless. Gusts of heat prickled his skin as he tried to outrun her attacks, one after the other.

His body was already exhausted and every muscle screamed, but he couldn't stop, he couldn't even think past yelling at himself to move faster, to stay on his feet and keep her away from Xio, but in the darkness, he wasn't even sure where Xio was. There were too many sights and sounds and things trying to kill him. Earlier trials had been confusing, but this was a whole other beast.

It was pure chaos.

Auristela only grew more ferocious, grunting and seething as she threw volley after volley at Teo. A gust of wind from Teo's wings sent one of her fireballs careening on a curved path. It connected with one of the horizontal logs laid across the platform, the fire crackling as it took hold on the wood.

Teo looked back at Auristela. The skin around her eyes was bruised and sunken, the dark veins spreading across her face. She opened her mouth to speak but was cut off when the arena was bathed in obsidian darkness again. This time, the roaring sound of the crowd was distorted to a low, slow warbling that only made Teo's pulse beat faster.

He didn't have time to understand what was going on. All he could do was run. What Teo lacked in strength he made up for in speed. His legs were wobbly, barely propelling him forward, but he knew if he fell, it'd be over.

Auristela must've been feeling it, too. As Teo feinted to her right, Auristela stumbled. A shout tore out of her, loud even above the bellowing crowd. Teo looked back over his shoulder as she kicked her leg straight up. For a moment she looked like a ballet dancer, leg held high and foot perfectly pointed, before she struck her foot to the ground.

A crescent of flames fanned out with a *whoosh*, scorching the darkness and heading straight for Teo.

With every ounce of energy Teo had left, he pitched forward, jumped, and thrust his wings downward. Her flames took hold with an unnatural quickness, blackening a large swath of the wooden platform. Teo shot into the air and the fire washed over the logs below him like a wave, singeing off bark. When he tried to flap his wings to get higher, pain tore through his shoulders. His wings buckled and he crashed back onto the platform.

He rolled a few times, dangerously close to the edge. As he regained balance on his hands and knees, the sound melted into a low, thrumming buzz. It pounded in a steady rhythm, and the lights around them flickered in time. Teo desperately scrambled to get back onto his feet, but the world was flashing in and out of his sight and he couldn't get his legs to work. Auristela was quick, but beneath the now-strobing lights, Teo saw her move in slow motion

Auristela closed in on him, steam billowing off her skin. She raised both her hands over her head. A ball of fire ignited between them. The sound of the crowd cut off once more, but the flickering lights remained.

Teo's eyes widened. His pulse raced and his lungs burned.

"This is for my brother!" she snarled.

A strangled shout lodged in Teo's throat. He threw his arms over his head, waiting to be hit with excruciating pain—

"GET AWAY FROM HIM!"

A silver chain twisted around Auristela's wrists, binding them over her head.

There was only a split second when confusion split through her rage before Auristela was yanked off her feet and flung to the side.

Niya appeared next to Teo, the silver chain held in her fist. She turned to Teo, standing over him, muscles bulging under her lustrous skin.

"Did she get you?" Niya asked, her brow wrinkled as she frantically looked him over.

"Not yet," Teo croaked out, so happy to see her that he was on the verge of tears.

"We need to get to the finish!" Niya said, grabbing his arm and practically lifting him off the ground as she pulled him to his feet.

"Where's Xio?" he asked, adrenaline still rushing through him.

Movement at the corner of his eye caught Teo's attention.

"*Watch it!*" Niya dragged him out of the way as another ball of fire soared past, crashing into the stands behind them.

Something wasn't adding up. Auristela had been aggressive during the other trials, but this was on a whole other level. This was *vicious* and unrelenting, with no regard for others' safety. Regardless of how much she hated Teo, it didn't add up to the picture Aurelio had painted of his sister at all.

More than that, she was frenzied, like she couldn't control herself, and the flickering lights only made it harder to predict her movements. Behind her, more of the logs that made up the platform had turned to a deep black. They didn't look burnt and ashen, but glistened wetly. Something about this wasn't right, but with the pulsing lights and the distorted screams of the crowd, it was hard to get his head straight.

Auristela was back on her feet with renewed vigor. In one burst, her entire body became engulfed in flame. She drew in a deep breath and splayed hands on either side of her face as she puffed out her chest.

"GET DOWN!" Niya bellowed above the garbled sounds around them, dragging Teo back down to his knees.

A huge, round shield made of gold appeared on Niya's arm, protecting herself and Teo just as Auristela reared back to blow a stream of fire at them. Teo crouched behind Niya as the fire sprayed against the shield. Flames licked the edge of the shield, reaching for them. Obsidian logs sizzled and popped.

Niya held tight but the gold started to glisten and melt, unable to stand up to the intense heat.

Just when Teo thought they'd both be doused in liquid gold, Auristela ran out of breath.

In the time it took her to draw in a new one, Niya charged forward.

Like a human battering ram, Niya slammed her shield into Auristela, sending her flying back.

"Holy shit," Teo panted, struggling to get back on his feet. "Did you know she could do that?!"

"Do what, be a douchebag? Yeah, duh."

"No, become a *human fireball*."

Niya wiped the sweat from her brow. "I forgot!"

"You *forgot*?!"

"Why didn't she come after us?" Niya asked, brows furrowing.

Auristela wasn't looking at them anymore. Her gaze was locked on Xio, who was hovering at the edge of the platform.

"Xio!" Teo shouted.

Auristela looked at Teo. In between bright flashes of light, a smirk curled her lips.

"RUN!" Teo and Niya shouted at Xio.

He ran across a log that had been blackened by one of Auristela's fireballs. As though it were expecting him, the log disappeared at his touch. Xio yanked his foot out of the gaping hole, but as he continued toward the center of the platform, Auristela ran after him, with chunks of the platform blackening and disappearing in her wake.

Cautiously, Teo spread his wings, ignoring the sharp ache it caused, and relaxed them. He tried to survey the ruined platform to find a path, but the flashing lights and trembling debris made his eyes ache. There were more missing logs than remaining ones now, and it seemed like any step could bring the platform down around them.

Auristela kept moving, single-minded, leaping over logs as she went, creating huge holes open to the jungle far below and sending more long sections of logs askew. She danced around Xio, circling and cutting him off like a predator toying with its prey.

"AURISTELA!"

The shout came from behind them, hoarse and strangely muffled.

Aurelio stood with his body pressed flat against the invisible barrier, beating his fists against it and shouting more words that Teo couldn't make out.

A crack of splintering wood sounded. The platform was crumbling around them.

Teo turned back to Auristela just in time to see a log fall, the opposite end slamming up between her legs, taking her with it as the far end raised in the air. She grappled for a solid grip on the wood, barely hanging on.

Something changed in Auristela's eyes. The angry snarl on her face flashed to surprise. The fire engulfing her went out. The angry bruising and black veins were gone, leaving nothing but fear in her ember eyes. For the first time since they came upon her on the platform, it was as if she was finally seeing the scene clearly.

"Relio!" she cried, but it was too late. Her brother couldn't save her. Auristela scrambled to hang on, but her fingers slipped uselessly over the smooth, shimmering black log. She lost her grip and fell without another sound.

No one could do anything but watch as the golden light of her suit plummeted, faded, and blinked out.

Teo desperately searched the rubble and smoke for Xio.

He clung to the top of a log that was swaying back and forth, its balance at the other end precarious. It could turn over at any moment, or Xio could lose his grip. It was too far for him to jump. If he fell, he could land in one of the jagged holes across the platform, or a blazing fire, or straight over the edge.

But his uniform was still lit up. He hadn't lost the trial yet.

And Teo had wings. Without the jungle canopy overhead, he could use them.

With no time to second-guess, Teo launched himself into the air.

He knew it was going to hurt, but Teo realized midair that this wasn't going to work *at all*. With every flap of his wings, Teo wasn't sure he'd be able to do it again. Fireworks of pain shot across his back and deep into shoulders.

No. He could do it. He had to do it. He had to make it to Xio. One foot higher in the air, and then another.

"Come on!" he said, holding his arms out to Xio.

Xio shook his head, tightening his hold on the log. "I'll fall!"

Teo bit back a groan of frustration. He was bigger and stronger than Xio—he could get him, he could do it. Teo grabbed him around the waist and *pulled*, using the force of his flapping wings.

And then they were falling together. Teo threw out his wings to slow the fall and snagged the log again in his free arm, dangling with Xio in the other. His wings were useless now, stripped of every ounce of strength.

Fire ate up the log, getting closer. The wood groaned and cracked. Feral heat licked at Teo's fingertips.

What could he do? How could they get out of this?

"TEO!" Niya shouted, and he realized: He couldn't get out of this. But his friends could.

"Trust me, okay?" Teo said.

"No!" Xio said, arms pinwheeling to grab hold of something.

There was no time to talk him into it.

Teo loosened his grip on Xio. As Xio dropped, Teo kept his hand against Xio's body, feeling it pass over his chest, his armpit, his bicep, and finally his forearm, which Teo latched on to. He did his best to secure his sweaty grip on Xio's jacket.

They were fifty feet from the barrier around the finish point. Teo could make it fifty feet.

With all his strength, he gathered momentum, swinging Xio back and forth, and then finally let go. Even with Xio flailing and adding drag to his descent, Niya tracked him and was exactly where she needed to be to catch him when he fell back to the platform.

And, just like Teo hadn't dared to hope: She toppled backward, straight through the barrier past the finish point with Xio still in her grasp.

Teo closed his eyes and took a deep breath.

It had worked.

His friends were safe.

He could let go now.

As Teo fell and the lights on his suit went out, he prayed to Sol that it had been enough to keep Xio safe.

And then everything went dark.

The trial was over. Teo and the other competitors who had failed to complete it—Xochi, Atzi, Dezi, and Auristela—were brought back to the finish line for the rankings. Nearly half of the platform had been destroyed. Diosa Agua and Dios Tormentoso had doused the logs that had caught fire, leaving scorched wood and small wisps of smoke.

All the semidioses stood around as the rankings board was presented, their godly parents standing behind them. For once, the presence of his mom did nothing to console Teo. There was no excited chattering this time. Niya went to Teo's side immediately, tugging him into a tight, one-armed hug, and even she was silent. Teo leaned against her, his whole body quaking.

Xio stared up at him like he was still in shock over what had just transpired.

Hushed murmurs from the crowd pressed against them.

To the side, Auristela and Aurelio stood close together. It was like Auristela had turned into an entirely different person. The anger and ferocity driving her minutes before were gone. Her face was ashen as she kept her unblinking gaze on the rankings board. Her hair was a tangled mess, her shoulders tight as she pressed her elbows into her sides.

And then there was Aurelio. His jaw was clenched tight, coppery eyes wide as he clutched Auristela's hand with white knuckles. Teo could see the rapid rise and fall of his chest, his visible pulse as the tendons in his neck stood out. He stood still as a statue, not once looking anywhere but forward.

Teo felt like he was going to throw up and he couldn't stop shaking.

He didn't want the rankings to go up. He didn't want to see them. It didn't matter who became Sunbearer, because one of them was about to be sentenced to death, and another one was going to have to kill them.

He hated himself for even thinking, *Not Xio*, because none of them deserved to have their lives end. What other choice was there? Without sacrificing someone's life to keep the Sol Stone fueled, the world would end and all the people of Reino del Sol would be doomed.

How could Sol ever possibly decide whose life was worth sacrificing to save the rest of them?

As Diosa Luna stepped forward, Teo held his breath. When she spoke, her voice was quiet and resigned. "Sol has determined the rankings."

Teo glued his gaze to Xio's glyph at the very bottom, anxiously waiting as the other glyphs shifted positions, stone sliding against stone.

He squeezed his hands into fists, his fingernails biting into his palms. *Move*, he pleaded in his head. *Please, move.* His eyes stung from not blinking. Teo was ready to pass out when *finally*—

The jade glyph of Dios Mala Suerte moved up from last to ninth.

"YES!" Niya cried out, grabbing an absolutely shocked Xio.

Relief crashed into Teo so forcefully his knees buckled. He turned to his friends to celebrate, but suddenly the dais was filled with Sol priests in their white robes.

They converged around Aurelio and Auristela.

"Wait!" Aurelio's weak, broken voice stabbed into Teo's chest.

Panicked, he spun to the rankings.

Diosa Lumbre's fire glyph sat at the very bottom.

Sharp panic and terror grabbed Teo by the throat. *Aurelio?*

But no, it wasn't Aurelio's glyph, it was—

Auristela stepped away from her brother with her head held high, allowing the priests to bring her forward to Fantasma.

"*Auristela.*" The pain was audible in Aurelio's voice. He stepped forward, reaching for his sister, but Diosa Lumbre's hand shot out, gripping him by the shoulder. Aurelio winced but stopped, his fingers catching empty air. Stricken, Aurelio's chest heaved with shaky breaths.

Teo's heart sank. Because he'd saved Xio, Auristela had lost.

The stands broke out into thunderous applause. It was disorienting. Why were they cheering? Didn't they see what was happening? This wasn't a celebration, it was a condemnation.

Teo turned, searching for Niya, only to find himself suddenly surrounded by smiling priests. He stumbled back a step, bumping into his mom. Every fiber of his being screamed at him to run.

Diosa Luna stepped toward him, a calm smile on her face.

Teo instinctively leaned away.

"Congratulations, Teo," she said, but he didn't understand why.

Finally, he looked at the top of the rankings board.

There was a sudden, familiar shift of weight on Teo's head. He reached up and the cold prongs of the sunburst crown brushed against his fingertips.

Sol had chosen him as the Sunbearer.

It was like Teo didn't have control over his body anymore. The priests swept him forward to stand next to Auristela, facing the crowd, which erupted in roaring cheers.

Beside him, Auristela stood tall, staring straight ahead. Her face was wiped clear of emotions, but the delicate skin around her eyes was pinched. A tear slid down her cheek, leaving a trail on her soot-covered skin. Her amber eyes were hard and resolute, but below them, her jaw trembled.

It didn't feel real. This wasn't right. None of this was what he wanted.

"This decade's Sunbearer Trials are over," Luna announced to the crowd. "I am thrilled to present our honored sacrifice, Auristela, Daughter of Lumbre, and Teo, Son of Quetzal—our first Jade Sunbearer."

With that, Fantasma gently led Auristela away, surrounded by a group of Sol priests. Diosa Lumbre followed, not even sparing Aurelio a glance as she walked by, leaving him alone on the platform.

Teo froze in place. Quetzal raced forward, encircling him in a tight embrace. Past her shoulder, Niya watched Teo with no trace of triumph on her face. At her side, Xio stared up at Teo's crown.

"You did it, Teo!" his mom sang in his ear.

And she was right.

CHAPTER 24

The crowd was dispersing and it was time to head back to the trajin-eras. Aurelio had broken away from the group first, storming back through the jungle on the wooden paths.

"Aurelio, wait!" Teo tried to chase after him, the crown an awkward weight on his head.

Aurelio didn't slow down. Every muscle in his back strained under his skin, the tendons of his neck tightly corded.

Teo ran forward, catching hold of his wrist, the golden armband hot to the touch. "Relio!"

Aurelio violently wrenched himself free of Teo's grasp. He spun to face him and jabbed his finger in Teo's face. "DON'T!"

Teo stumbled back a step. He'd never heard Aurelio's voice like that.

Niya surged forward but Teo threw out his hand to stop her. He tried to swallow past the thickness in his throat. "I'm sorry—"

"She's all I have!" Aurelio tried to hold on to his anger, but his watery eyes betrayed him. "I *told you*—" His voice broke.

Teo saw his chin dimple for just a moment before Aurelio turned away, scrubbing his hands over his face.

They'd drawn an audience. The Golds grouped together, watching anxiously and whispering to one another. Xio slipped between Niya and Teo.

Teo could see the shift in Aurelio's face—anguish swallowed by wrath.

"I would've taken her place!" Aurelio insisted through clenched teeth.

"The trials don't work like that," Teo said.

"You let her fall, *knowing* she would come in last!" Aurelio accused, still not looking at him.

Teo flinched, his heart aching. He wanted to defend himself, but he couldn't. There was no easy answer. Someone had to be the sacrifice, they all knew that, there wasn't a choice. Without a sacrifice to refuel the Sun Stones, the world would literally end. No matter what happened, someone had to be killed.

That was what Aurelio had been saying the entire time, only now he was forced to confront it.

Aurelio's head was bowed as he walked away.

This time, Teo let him.

The steps of Sol Temple were lit by torches and full of semidioses and priests gathering for the Sunbearer ceremony. Separated from his friends, Teo felt like he was watching himself make the long walk to the top of the temple. He was completely untethered, surrounded by a sea of people all smiling and congratulating him.

He was led to Diosa Luna's office below the observatory. To the naked eye, the planets of the astronomical clock already appeared to be in perfect alignment, with midnight only a handful of moments away.

Tick, tock. Tick, tock.

Sol priests swarmed, pulling out Teo's regalia on a rack and speaking excitedly to one another. A gold basin was brought out and filled with warm water and bright flowers. Teo let them strip him out of his uniform, not even self-conscious because his body didn't feel like his own.

They methodically began the process of washing his skin with soft sponges until the mud and smell of burning wood was replaced by nicotiana, honeysuckle, and marigold.

As they worked, Teo stared at the murals painted along the walls, stopping at the final scene. Last time, Teo had been so distracted by the death in the mural where Sol lay dying, he hadn't paid much attention to the final image.

Sol shone in the sky above the people of Reino del Sol as they lived their lives in peace, protected by the sun's rays. Sol had given his life to protect his people, just like every sacrifice thereafter. But something didn't sit quite right with Teo. It kept poking at the back of his brain.

They used warm, fluffy towels to dry his skin and iridescent black curls. With numb fingers, Teo changed into fresh underclothes.

When it was time to get dressed in his regalia, a familiar voice spoke behind him.

"I will take it from here."

Huemac walked forward slowly. His bright blue robes shone in the sea of white and gold.

Teo exhaled a shuddering breath. "What are you doing here?" he asked, barely recognizing the dullness of his own voice.

Huemac clasped his hands in front of him, watching Teo carefully as he spoke. "It is my honor and responsibility as the Sunbearer's priest to ready him for the ceremony."

As the other priests filed out, Huemac helped Teo to change into his regalia in silence. His limbs were impossibly heavy and difficult to move, but Huemac was patient with him. The feathered cape was suffocating when Huemac draped it across his shoulders.

When Teo was dressed, Huemac circled him, making small adjustments.

"After they bring you up to the altar, Diosa Luna will present both of you to Sol," Huemac said, not looking Teo in the eye as he gently smoothed out the cape. "When the lights of the Sun Stones go out, that's when you must perform the sacrifice."

Teo swallowed past the rising bile in his throat but nodded.

"She will be laid on the table and you will be presented with the ceremonial blade," Huemac explained, like he wasn't walking Teo through the steps of murdering someone. "Her heart is in the center of her chest, slightly to the left of her breastbone. Angle the flat of the blade so it can easily slip between her ribs," Huemac continued.

"Push your weight into the handle. Firmly, Teo." Huemac retrieved the sunburst crown. "Release her quickly."

"Auristela."

Huemac paused, the crown hovering above Teo's head. Finally, his eyes dropped to meet Teo's.

"Auristela," he repeated. "Not *her*—Auristela."

Huemac's dark, tired eyes considered Teo for a moment. His features were smooth and expressionless. He gave Teo a smile that was little more than a grim twist of the mouth. "Auristela," Huemac agreed.

Finally, he placed the crown on Teo's head. The cool gold bit into his scalp as Huemac made the final adjustments. His hands came to rest on Teo's shoulders.

"I don't want this," Teo choked out.

Huemac's grip tightened. "I am so sorry, Teo," he said in a low tone, his head bowed so Teo couldn't see his face.

The pain in his voice made Teo's chest ache. He threw himself forward, clutching Huemac's robes as tightly as he could, his whole body quaking.

Huemac started, letting out a small sound of surprise. After a moment's hesitation, he wrapped his arms around Teo.

"I want to go home," Teo choked out against the priest's chest. "I want this all to be over."

"*Soon*," Huemac said, trying to sound reassuring.

But it wasn't true. First, he'd have to travel to all the other temples in Reino del Sol to bring them new Sun Stones. And for that to happen, he'd have to end another human's life.

How could the world continue normally after that?

✳

When Huemac led Teo up to the observatory, everyone was gathered around the Sol Stone, waiting. As Teo followed Huemac through the crowd, he felt like he was underwater—moving in slow motion, every sound muffled in his ears.

Heads turned to watch and they kept *smiling*. A sea of flashing teeth and hungry eyes.

When Huemac presented Teo to Diosa Luna, he almost latched on to the priest's arm and begged him to stay. He had spent so much energy proving himself, trying to compete with the Golds, only to feel just as small and helpless as he had during the trials.

Luna brought him forward to where the rest of the competitors stood around the Sol Stone, waiting. They were all in their regalia once again, a strange echo of their first night at Sol Temple.

Teo immediately sought out Aurelio. He stood rigid and still, his hands locked behind his back. He looked like he'd been through hell in the short time since they'd seen each other. His eyes were bloodshot and puffy and his posture sagged like gravity itself were trying to crush him.

"Come forward, Teo," Diosa Luna said with a warm smile.

She motioned for him to stand at the foot of the sacrificial slab. Overhead, the Sol Stone slowly spun and glowed like it always did. This close, Teo could easily hear its quiet humming. In every direction, the beams of the Sun Stones shot into the night sky, but even now as Teo watched, their lights were slowly fading.

"I present our Sunbearer." Luna motioned for him to face the crowd and when he did, they erupted into applause.

It was sickening.

Even Niya clapped, but she stood stick-straight, eyes wide and lips pressed into a tight line. At her side Xio watched Teo carefully, his brow furrowed and a calculating expression on his face.

Aurelio refused to look at Teo, and Teo couldn't blame him. Seeing Aurelio like this was bad enough. Teo didn't want to see the look in Aurelio's eyes if his glassy gaze landed on him.

The back of Teo's throat burned. He didn't want to be here. He didn't want to do this. This wasn't right.

There was movement from the crowd, quiet murmurs and shifting.

Auristela approached the Sol Stone. Fantasma stood dutifully at her side, flanked by Sol priests. She was in her fiery regalia, but this time she was covered in gold adornments and ornaments of Sol. Sunbursts hung from her ears, and chains draped across her shoulders and looped around her waist. As she walked with her head held high, gold bangles clinked together on her wrists and ankles.

Her steps were steady and determined as she approached the Sol Stone. Shoulders back and chin lifted, she didn't look at all like a sacrifice being led to her execution. Instead, Auristela looked fearless and ethereal, every bit the Gold Hero she was raised to be.

Teo felt like dirt beneath her feet.

"Many years ago, Sol saved our people with the ultimate gift of their sacrifice," Diosa Luna said. "Today we will honor their choice, renew their gift, and preserve the balance of this world. Sol chose ten worthy competitors for this year's Sunbearer Trials, and all of you played an important part in creating the future we step into today. Thank you for your brave and indomitable spirits. And we all thank Semidiosa Auristela for following in Sol's sacrifice."

Fantasma led Auristela to the sacrificial stone. The golden skulls it lay upon sparked in the firelight. The table itself was covered in bright orange marigold petals that smelled like sweet apples. Auristela's adornments clinked together as she lay down. Fantasma kneeled next to her side and took Auristela's hand in both of hers.

Luna brought Teo to stand beside her, like some kind of prince approaching a sleeping princess in a fucked-up fairy tale.

Auristela had closed her eyes, but not in a gentle way where Teo could maybe convince himself she was asleep. They were tightly squeezed shut, her lips pressed between her teeth as her chin wobbled. Her arms were pressed against her sides, every muscle in her body taut as she waited for Teo to end her life.

None of it felt real except for the heavy weight of the obsidian dagger Luna pressed into his grip. His hand shook. He tried to grasp it tighter.

The last few moments before midnight ticked away. In the darkness surrounding the temple, the Sun Stones faded to golden threads.

Teo's heart hammered in his throat, his breaths shallow and sharp.

He looked out, trying to find someone, *anyone* who could reassure him, but no one met his gaze. Niya had lowered her head. Xio's eyes were on his wrist where he clutched his bracelet in his hand.

The only one still watching was Aurelio.

While everyone else diverted their gaze, Aurelio refused to turn away. He looked on helplessly, the tight lines of his face betraying his anguish no matter how hard he tried to hide it as Diosa Lumbre towered behind him.

The Sun Stones flickered out of existence, plunging the world into night and allowing the stars to blaze overhead. Slowly, the light of the Sol Stone began to fade.

It was time. Auristela's heart needed to be pierced so her blood could replenish the Sol Stone before it went out.

Sweat prickled on his brow as Teo gripped the obsidian blade in his hands, poised above Auristela's heart, just like Huemac had told him.

He had to do it. He couldn't put it off any longer. This was his responsibility.

Silvery tears slipped from the corners of Auristela's eyes.

But Teo didn't *want* to do this. Something had been terribly wrong about the final trial, the way Auristela had acted and looked. Something wasn't right.

None of it was right. He didn't want to hurt Aurelio. He didn't want to kill anyone. He didn't want anyone, including Auristela, to have to die, and especially not by his hands. He couldn't.

"Now, Teo," Luna said, quiet but firm.

He wouldn't.

"I won't do it." The words flew out of his mouth, surprising Teo just as much as the people surrounding him.

For a moment, there was silence as no one moved and the Sol Stone continued to dim.

Teo lowered his hand from over Auristela's chest. Everyone jumped into action.

"Get the dagger!" Diosa Luna cried out. The Sol priests leapt into action, converging on Teo. He yanked the dagger from their desperate hands. His wings shot out, shoving a wave of them back.

"AURISTELA!" Aurelio shouted to his sister, who stared up at Teo, too stunned to move.

"*Teo*," came a voice beside him. Xio had snuck up around the priests somehow and was reaching up toward Teo's hand. "Give me the dagger!"

Another sea of priests swarmed forward. Xio flexed his hands, waiting. If Teo could fight off the priests, maybe Xio could take the dagger and run. Teo passed the dagger to the younger boy.

Above him, the last embers of light faded from deep within the Sol Stone, revealing the golden skull hidden inside.

Suddenly, Xio changed.

What had been an expression of desperation and fear morphed into something dark. For the first time since they'd met, Teo could see a resemblance between Xio and Mala Suerte.

"Xio?" Teo asked. Even the priests had stumbled to a stop, watching the two semidioses in confusion.

"It's too late," Xio said, clutching the obsidian dagger protectively against his chest. "The stone went out." He said it like he was *relieved*. A shuddering exhale rolled through Xio. His black eyes slid to Teo. "Sol can't help you now."

Xio raised the dagger to his opposite palm. As the blade pulled away, a trail of obsidian-black blood dripped to the ground.

Behind Teo, the priests gasped. For a moment, he forgot how to breathe.

Head tipped back, Xio stared up into the sky. "They're coming."

The world plunged into darkness.

CHAPTER 25

The ground shook, sending Teo sprawling onto his side. The sunburst crown skittered out of reach. Terror and pandemonium rippled through the onlookers. Suddenly, everything was illuminated with silvery light. Overhead, the stars turned blazing bright. At first, Teo thought they were growing bigger, but then he realized they were getting closer.

Stars rained down all around them. Their gorgeous, celestial bodies painted Reino del Sol in brilliant explosions of light. They crashed into the ancient buildings surrounding Sol Temple and dove into the waters of the canals.

Stone groaned and shifted, knocking people off their feet. Cracks and fissures opened up, dislodging huge chunks of the temple. Sol's glyph teetered, the large golden slab tipping toward the sacrificial table where Auristela still lay.

Teo struggled to his feet and ran forward, grabbing Auristela and dragging her to the floor.

The huge stone glyph fell onto the stone slab, cracking the table in half.

What had Xio done? What had *Teo* done?

Priests ran for cover while semidioses raced to help.

"Leave now!" Diosa Luna shouted as the confused crowd turned to a sea of panic. She tried to move, but her legs gave out. Face straining, she dropped to her knees. "Before they get here!"

But it was too late.

An inky blackness filled with glittering stars spilled from the night sky, pouring into the temple. Three towering figures rose from the ether, cloaked in black—a woman with the wolfish head of a chupacabra; a tall and slender being with midnight blue skin and a smooth, featureless face; and a man with a white goat's head, horizontal pupils, and a yellow smile.

Xio stood in the middle of it all. Gone was the fear and apprehension Teo was so used to seeing on Xio's face. Now, he looked relieved and triumphant.

"My, my, how time flies when you've been locked away for a few millennia," Venganza said as he stretched his taloned, knobby hands over his head. His goat eyes cut down to look at Xio. "Good job, my boy."

Teo sucked in a breath. *My boy?* Several things clicked into place at once—Xio's lacking any powers from Mala Suerte, how he kept failing in the trials, his black blood dripping from the cut on his palm.

Xio wasn't a Jade at all. He was an Obsidian.

"And look, they've thrown a welcome party for us!" Chupacabra said, her black lips peeling gleefully from her sharp teeth as people ran for cover.

"So many half gods for us to take under our wings, as well," Venganza added, his gaze drinking in the competitors. "You're the ones Sol deemed *worthy*, are you?"

Xochi dragged Atzi behind her. Marino stopped signing as he and Dezi gripped one another. Niya bared her teeth even though Teo could see the fear in her eyes.

Venganza chuckled. "How perfectly poetic."

"YOU WON'T TOUCH THEM!" Diose Guerrero roared. They raced forward, two large blades appearing in each of their hands.

"Calm down, kitty cat," Chupacabra said with a roll of her eyes.

With a flick of their wrist, Caos knocked Guerrero back with a ball of black ether. Walls like black fire encircled the semidioses, blocking the diose from reaching them.

"And where is the boy who made this all possible?" Venganza asked, eyes sweeping the crowd.

Teo couldn't move or speak, but he didn't need to. Venganza's smile widened unnaturally. "There he is." He bent down to get a better look at Teo.

Teo tried to scramble away, but he couldn't get his body to work. Venganza loomed over him, so large he could swallow Teo whole.

Venganza smiled widely as he peered down at Teo. "We owe you thanks, Son of Quetzal! I thought my son would fail us, but you handed him the solution." He laughed delightedly.

Teo looked to Xio, searching for some sort of answer or explanation, anything to dispute what Venganza was saying. But Xio's dark curls fell across his eyes. He wouldn't even look at Teo.

"Stay away from him," Diosa Luna spat as she struggled to get to her feet.

"You banished us and stripped us of our cities and titles," Venganza explained, so calm as the sky continued to rain down around them. "Our families were taken from us, so it's only fair that we take your most prized semidioses. Without Sol, you have no power over us, *Diosa*."

With fierce determination, Diosa Luna pulled herself to her feet and tried to step forward only to collapse back to her knees once again. The silver in her hair had faded to an ashy gray.

"Oh dear, you don't look so good, Luna," Chupacabra said, salivating.

"Remind me, Chupacabra, how does the moon live without the sun?" Venganza asked. He reached forward and plucked the Sol Stone from the ground. The light was quickly fading, the tiny sun flares shrinking. Usually too bright to look at, now Teo could see Sol's golden skull under the glass surface.

Diosa Luna's hand shot out. "Don't!"

Chupacabra threw her head back and howled with glee.

"Ah, that's right," Venganza purred, his eyes sliding to Diosa Luna. "She doesn't."

The light of the Sol Stone was finally eclipsed in black, the hot orange glow of the sun burning through the skull's eye sockets for a moment before dying completely.

Diosa Luna's eyes flew open. A small gasp burst past her lips. Luna's calm had collapsed into shock, fear, and, at the edges, rage.

"NO!" Teo cried out, lunging for her.

Teo's hand grasped hers, but it was cold and strange. Teo looked into Diosa Luna's glimmering eyes just as she disappeared into a burst of stars. Above them, Caos cackled into the night, the gales of their laughter turning to wind that scattered the silvery dust swirling around Teo.

Chupacabra yawned. "Should we head home then, Venganza?"

Venganza nodded and turned to Caos. "If you wouldn't mind, Caos?" he asked politely.

As Caos twisted their hands, a rift opened on the temple floor.

"And don't forget the kids," Venganza added with a dismissive flick of his wrist before he and Chupacabra sank into the ether.

Thick dark matter swirled with dizzying lights like a nebula, sucking in stones and marigold petals around it. A lurching, magnetic tug inched its way up Teo's body, swallowing and trapping his ankles.

Shouts filled the air. Teo latched on to a large chunk of solid stone among all the debris as the rift threatened to pull him in. He watched in horror as Ocelo fell into the darkness. Xochi held on to Atzi, but with nothing to cling to except each other, they were both swallowed up.

"TEO!" He turned to see Niya getting dragged toward the abyss. A shout tore through Teo's throat. There was no time to think.

He threw himself forward, using his wings to fight against the pull.

He grabbed Niya around the waist and only had a second of reprieve before they were both pulled toward the rift.

The sound of steel striking stone cut through Teo's ears.

Niya had conjured up two large spikes and sunk them into the stone floor, anchoring them. Her biceps bulged and her face contorted with pain as she held on as tightly as she could.

More bodies slid past them. First Dezi, whose hands scrambled for something to hold on to but slid uselessly across the floor. Teo saw his terrified face before he was devoured by the darkness.

Another body came sliding their way. It was Xio, eyebrows raised in surprise as the floor disappeared beneath him. Teo didn't think— he thrust out his arm, catching Xio by the sleeve before he fell into the pit.

"Argh!" Niya cried, straining to support all their weight while dangling from her spikes. Teo wasn't sure how long they'd last.

Xio was squirming in his grip, trying to break free.

"*Stop!*" Teo cried. Whatever was going on, Xio was clearly involved— but Teo had sworn to protect Xio during the trials, and now those same instincts took over. "Just stay still! Niya will get us out!"

"Don't you *get it*?!" Xio shouted. "I don't *need* your help, I don't want you to save me! I am Obsidian, and this is our revenge!"

With a final wrench, Xio slammed his small fist into Teo's chest, breaking free of him and falling into the dark. Above him, Niya cried out in dismay. Teo's head filled with static, unable to make sense of what had just happened.

"Relio!" Auristela screamed.

Teo looked down to find Aurelio and Auristela trapped a mere ten feet from the rift.

Auristela dangled from Aurelio's forearm as he desperately held on to the broken sacrificial table with the other. Sweat covered his skin, the tendons straining as the pull of the vortex tore at his grip. Aurelio's face was contorted as he tried to hang on, but Auristela's grip was inching down his arm.

He couldn't hold on much longer.

He needed help.

Teo rolled onto his side and quickly tried to gauge how far away Aurelio was. If he timed it right, he could get to him.

Niya must've realized what he was thinking. "*Teo, don't!*"

He let go. Teo angled his wings and, with the pull of the rift, slid diagonally across the floor. His stomach slammed into the slab of rock Aurelio hung from, knocking the wind out of him. His body curled around the stone, crushing his chest but keeping him from getting sucked into the abyss.

Aurelio was barely holding on. His fingers dug into a crack in the stone, gold blood trickling down his hand. Teo tried to grab Aurelio's hand, but it was just out of reach.

"Aurelio!"

With a jerk, Aurelio looked up. Shock and confusion flashed through the pain on his face.

"I'm slipping!" Auristela cried out.

Aurelio looked down. Auristela's hands slid down her brother's arm but he latched on to her wrist. Below her, the rift slowly started to shrink.

They just needed to hang on a little while longer.

Aurelio's attention was fully on his sister. His arms shook. His grip on the stone started to slip. "Don't let go!" he shouted, but she continued to slip until they only held on to each other by their fingertips.

Under them, more cracks formed in the stone table. It couldn't hold all three of them much longer. Teo knew it, Aurelio knew it, and so did Auristela.

Teo pressed his thighs against the stone, trying to get more leverage to stretch farther.

The rift continued to close.

He only needed a couple more inches—

But Auristela didn't allow it. Her eyes flicked to Teo. "Find us!" she shouted over the noise of panicked cries.

Aurelio shook his head fiercely, refusing to let go. A section of stone fell away. Teo dug deep and held on, every fiber of his muscles screaming.

Auristela ignited a fire in her hand.

Aurelio cried out in pain. He tried to hold on, to fight through it, but it was too much for him to handle. Auristela slipped through his fingers.

"NO!"

Aurelio let go of the stone and dove after his sister. Teo lurched forward and snatched Aurelio's hand, locking his grip around the other boy's wrist.

Auristela fell. She sucked in a breath, eyes wide and terrified, before she disappeared through the rift.

"STELA!" Aurelio's raw shout tore through his throat. "LET ME GO!"

He tried to wrench himself free, but Teo refused to let go. He squeezed his eyes shut and pressed his forehead against the stone slab. The muscles in his shoulders screamed as Aurelio thrashed, but still he hung on.

Slowly, the rift closed, plunging the world into stillness and night.

Teo and Aurelio slumped onto the ground. When Teo released his hand, Aurelio didn't move. His chest rose and fell with shuddering breaths, staring at where his sister and the others had disappeared.

Where was Niya?

Teo staggered to his feet and scanned the crowd. People darted back and forth with panicked voices. Huge chunks of the stone floor had been damaged or dislodged.

"Teo!"

In a flash of feathers and gold, Teo's mother found him and pulled him into a crushing embrace.

"Thank Sol you're all right!" she gasped as she ran her fingers through his hair, down his arms and across his chest.

"I'm all right," he heard himself tell her. "Where's Niya?" Teo asked, trying to look around his mother's huge wings.

He found her kneeling on the floor, curled in on herself as Dios Tierra tried pushing the hair that'd come loose from her braids out of her face.

Teo jogged over, panic climbing his throat. "Niya, are you okay?"

When she looked up, her nose and eyes were bright red, her chin dimpled.

"What's wrong?" He looked her over and didn't see any cuts or gold blood, but the pain written across her face looked excruciating.

Her face was pinched and streaked with fresh tears. Her hands were upturned in her lap, palms red and raw. "They're gone," she choked. "We couldn't save them."

She looked up at Teo with eyes full of an anguish he'd never seen before. "I wasn't strong enough."

Niya's face crumpled. Tierra pulled her tight to his chest.

CHAPTER 26

Teo tentatively approached Aurelio where he remained on the floor. "Aurelio—"

"I don't want to hear it," he growled, pushing himself onto his knees. He'd found the obsidian sacrificial dagger and held it in his palm.

"I'm sorry," Teo tried.

"*You're* sorry?" Aurelio said, finally looking at him.

"I—I did this," he stammered, barely able to wrap his mind around how thoroughly he had fucked up this time. "If I had just—"

"Killed her instead?" Aurelio gulped down air like he'd been punched in the chest. "No. You couldn't kill her. I should have known you couldn't. You're just too—" He shook his head. "You did what you thought was right," Aurelio managed. "*I'm* the one who left her behind."

For a long moment, Aurelio didn't say anything. He just sat on his knees, his arms wrapped around himself. His fingers were white from how hard they were pressing into his ribs, like he was holding himself together.

Teo stopped thinking and moved on instinct. He wrapped his arms around Aurelio and hugged him with everything he had. He wouldn't let Aurelio hold this alone.

It wasn't about fault or blame. It wasn't about the trials or the apocalypse. All that mattered right now was Aurelio's pain.

Aurelio's body went limp under the embrace. His arms wrapped around Teo, fists curling into feathers.

What happened next was a blur.

My fault. It's all my fault.

Niya was on high alert, her entire body at attention and their parents close behind. Teo realized they were still together because *she* had made it so, refusing to let the bustling crowd tear them apart. He wished he had enough left in him to feel good about that.

The gods gathered around Diosa Lumbre, who stood with her arms crossed, emanating barely contained rage. The observatory was full of more people than Teo could keep track of. Distantly, he realized Huemac must be among them, but he was too ashamed to seek him out.

"Settle down," Lumbre said, her voice low as her molten eyes scanned the crowd. When that didn't give her the desired effect, she tried again. "SETTLE DOWN."

That time, the room obeyed.

"We need a plan," the diosa declared, voice flat. If she had any ideas, she wasn't letting on.

"We *need* to know what happened," another voice cut in. On some level, Teo recognized it. Maize, maybe.

On Teo's other side, Aurelio radiated heat. Teo had never been more aware of the space between him and another person, but now those inches were screaming all the words Aurelio hadn't said.

Why did you stop me?

She's my sister.

You should have let me go.

"We need to get to the bottom of this," Lumbre agreed. Half the eyes in the room shot to Teo. The other half glanced around, probably seeking out Mala Suerte, but he was nowhere to be seen.

Niya's arm pressed closer to Teo's. He didn't feel particularly worthy of her protection, though. Not when the others were gone.

The room broke out into low murmurs again and Aurelio took the opportunity to step forward. Diosa Lumbre cut him a stern look and he stopped.

"Without the Sol Stone, the world will remain in perpetual night," Lumbre said, and all murmuring ceased. "The Obsidian dioses will continue to gain power until they are strong enough to destroy our world, and us along with it."

For a moment, the silence stretched on. Then it shattered. Everyone shouted all at once—some gods arguing over the best way to move forward, others already trying to leave for home to protect their people.

"What *happened*?"

"Where's Mala Suerte?"

"Did you see the boy's blood? It was *black*."

"Why didn't the Sunbearer finish the sacrifice?"

"Was this the Jades' plan all along?"

To the side, Tierra stood with his head bowed, the Sunbearer crown held in his gloved hands. "Hope is not yet lost."

Silence enveloped the room at the sound of the raspy, unfamiliar voice of the earth god.

"*Papi?*" Niya asked, incredulous.

"There may be a way to undo what has been done," Tierra continued. His voice was low and grating, like rock scratching against rock.

"Only Sol has the power to banish the Obsidians," Diosa Lumbre cut in, clearly annoyed by the dramatic interruption. "And Sol is dead."

"Not dead," Tierra corrected. "Just gone from this world. It is up to us to bring them back."

"Bring back Sol?" Quetzal echoed. Murmurs broke out once more among the crowd.

"I dispersed Sol's mortal remains in the form of Sun Stones," Tierra explained. "They cannot return to Reino del Sol in so many pieces. But if we were to put them back together again—"

"Then Sol could come back!" Niya exclaimed, clapping her hands together in excitement.

"You want to *remove* the Sun Stones from our temples?" Lumbre snarled disapprovingly.

"The Obsidians have already been freed," Aurelio said, stepping forward. "Without being refueled, the Sun Stones won't protect our cities much longer."

Lumbre shook her head. "We do not have time for Tierra's half-thought-out schemes. Sol cannot help us now; we must protect *ourselves.* Guerrero," she said, turning to the jaguar-headed god, who growled in agreement. "I hope these last centuries of peace have not made you soft. As of today, Reino del Sol is at war—"

"I will go after the Obsidians," Aurelio declared.

Lumbre shook her head, eyes cast down, like even now she was somehow still disappointed. "No."

"Yes," Aurelio pressed, loud enough to quiet the room. Now instead of arguing with one another, all eyes were turned on parent and child, diosa and semidiós. "I will go after the Obsidians and I will rescue the stolen semidioses."

A low hum of support traveled through the crowd. This was Aurelio after all, their Golden Boy.

"I will not send a child after gods," Lumbre spat.

Teo's mind snagged on her choice of words. *A child, not* my *child.* For a goddess of fire, Lumbre was as cold as ice.

"The dioses must remain here and protect the cities," Aurelio said. "I'm the only logical choice."

"The Obsidians weren't the only ones banished to the stars, boy," Lumbre hissed. "The celestial monsters were locked up with their masters. Without Sol, they've been set free to wreak havoc and destruction on our world. You couldn't *possibly* fathom the horrors that have been unleashed."

Teo's stomach gave a sick lurch. He'd learned about the celestials in school—deadly monsters the dioses had trapped in the cosmos as constellations. He remembered all the falling stars he'd seen crash back to the earth. Without Sol, they had been set free as well.

"I can do it," Aurelio insisted as he attempted to stand tall.

Diosa Lumbre let out a sharp, ugly laugh. "You will die."

"Then I will die protecting our people."

Teo reached out for Aurelio's arm. "Aurelio—"

Aurelio didn't even blink. "I'm going. No one in this room can stop me."

That time, Lumbre did not argue. Instead, she regarded Aurelio with cool detachment. "Then you will die a useless death."

The crowd's arguing started up again, and Lumbre struggled to regain control.

Teo watched Aurelio's expression tighten with resolve. He had no regard for himself or his safety. Brave, foolish Aurelio, who would set himself on fire to keep others warm.

Teo swallowed his fear. If Aurelio was risking his life to save their friends, then Teo would go, too. But before he could voice this decision, his mother's hand clamped down hard on his shoulder.

"Come with me," she whispered, gesturing for Aurelio to follow as well.

Quetzal led them through the crowd and down the steps to Diosa Luna's office. When Teo blinked, he could still see Luna's burst of stars spotted behind his eyes. There, then gone.

Xio did this. He betrayed us.

Amid all the arguing, some of the gods had snuck off to reconvene. Tierra and Fantasma stood at the center of the circle with Niya at their side.

"Dude," Niya said, spotting Aurelio. "Your mom *sucks*."

Teo silently agreed, but decided to keep that thought to himself.

"But it's okay," Niya continued, "because my dad and Fantasma totally have a plan!"

"The Obsidians breaking free was always a risk," Tierra said. Teo couldn't imagine ever getting used to the sound of that voice.

Teo's eyes drifted across the office, landing once more on the murals along the walls. His focus shifted from the scene of Sol's sacrifice to the image right beside it—the sun glyph in the sky above the rejoicing people of Reino del Sol. Sol had sacrificed themself to keep them all safe.

What had Xio done? What had *Teo* done?

"Lumbre will convince most of the Golds to focus on preparing for war. It's up to us to bring back Sol," Pan Dulce explained. She tapped her fingers against Luna's desk and the map carved into its surface.

"The refueling of the Sun Stones does not happen immediately once the sacrifice is complete," Tierra said. "Normally, it takes a fortnight to finish the ritual and replenish every stone."

Niya leaned in to whisper in Teo's ear. "What's a fortnight?"

"I don't fucking know," he whispered back.

"It's two weeks," Aurelio said.

"We must complete the reformation of Sol before the fortnight ends," Tierra continued. "In order to reach all the Sun Stones in time, we'll have to split up. One group to the north, another to the south, east, and west."

"And someone must go to Los Restos to retrieve the Sol Stone," Quetzal added gravely. "Now that the Obsidians are back, they'll be able to sense our presence if we get anywhere near their temples."

"*Our* presence," Opción emphasized, gaze locked on Teo, Aurelio, and Niya. "But not semidioses.'"

Quetzal's brows shot up. "You can't mean—"

"I already said I would go after the Obsidians, and free my sister and the others," Aurelio agreed. "I can retrieve the Sol Stone, too."

"*We* can retrieve the Sol Stone," Teo corrected. "I'm going with you."

Niya and Quetzal looked over at Teo, both of their expressions asking the same question: *Are you sure about this?*

Teo's heart swelled. These two women would defend him to the ends of the earth.

He nodded once.

Niya cracked her knuckles. "I'm going, too, then."

"The celestials are back. The sun has failed and the moon is dead. This is the *apocalypse*, not a field trip," Dios Tormentoso warned with a rumble.

Teo hadn't noticed the few Golds interspersed among the crowd. But there were Amor and Agua and Tormentoso. All parents whose children had been taken.

"Then they'll need all the help they can get," Diosa Amor said, stepping forward.

Amor held out her hand and a small vial filled with metallic red liquid swirled inside. "An Elixir of Charming," she said, handing it out for Aurelio. "Drink this and it will grant you the power of Soothe Speak for ten minutes. You can use it on humans or animals. A strong enough dose will even work on a god."

"Thank you," Aurelio said, taking the small bottle. If they needed to talk their way out of something, Aurelio was the last person Teo would put in charge, but that also meant he was the one out of the three of them who most needed the elixir.

"Take this, as well," Diosa Agua said, her voice as soft as water tumbling over rock. She summoned a crystal bottle full of clear liquid as she approached Aurelio. "It's a Decanter of Endless Water." When Aurelio's face pinched, Agua chuckled and added, "Even a boy of fire needs fresh water to survive."

"And this," Tormentoso added, producing a white drawstring bag about the size of Aurelio's fist. "My Bag of Winds."

Niya snorted, one hand shooting up to cover her mouth. Teo tried to cut her a look to say, *Be serious*, but as soon as he made eye contact, a laugh bucked in his chest.

Aurelio flicked them an annoyed glance, but Teo could've sworn he caught an amused grin under Tormentoso's cloudy beard.

Tierra stepped forward next. He pulled off one of his gloves, revealing his sinewy scarlet-red hand and a gray metal bracelet around his wrist. When he touched it, it turned into a ball, which he held out for his daughter to take.

"Papi!" Niya gasped. "Your Unbreakable Blade?!"

Tierra nodded.

A massive, lethal-looking, nearly black blade sprang to life in her hand. "This is the *only* unbreakable metal in the world!" Niya explained as she gingerly brushed her fingers along the flat side of the short sword. "It can only be forged in the fires of La Cumbre, and only a child of Tierra can transform it." Niya jutted out her bottom lip as she looked up at her dad. "Thank you!"

She threw herself at him, squeezing him in a tight hug. Tierra affectionately leaned his cheek against the top of her head, running his fingers over her braid with his ungloved hand.

"Take this as well," Diosa Primavera insisted, pushing a brilliant green stone into her hand. "It's a Gem of Regeneration. Drop it into water and use it to douse a wound or drink to heal."

"Oh, hell *yes*," Niya said, holding her gifts from the gods. "I can strike down somebody with this and then bring them back to life!"

"It doesn't work *that* well!" a very startled Primavera rushed to add.

And then it was just Teo. The Golds exchanged looks, unsure what to do with him.

"You have me," his mom said. With a quick tug, she pulled one of her brilliant blue-green feathers from her hair and laid it in Teo's palm. "*Always*," Quetzal added with a reassuring smile. "When you've gotten the Sol Stone, use this to summon us and we'll arrive with the Sun Stones to perform the ritual and resurrect Sol."

Teo took the feather and ran his fingers along its edge. In the dim light, the bright green feather sparked with flashes of blue and gold. He wasn't alone. He had Niya and Aurelio at his side, and Mom and all the dioses at his back. He could fix this. They would fix this.

There was a shuffling of bodies and suddenly Fantasma appeared, pushing her way through the group. She walked right up to Teo and pulled something from the sleeve of her dress.

It was a plain tapered candle that was already halfway burned through. Fantasma delicately placed it in Teo's hand with the other gift.

"Thanks, Fantasma," he said with a weak smile.

She beamed up at him proudly.

Compared to Aurelio's and Niya's gifts, Teo's feather and used candle looked incredibly unimpressive, but he pretended to be excited anyway.

The gods dissolved into urgent chatter, filing out of Luna's office as they strategized the best ways to protect their home cities and gather all the Sun Stones.

The trio stopped when they reached the door to Luna's office. Standing there expectantly were Lumbre and Guerrero, disapproving looks on their faces.

"The gods are splitting into factions," Guerrero observed. "Horrible strategy in a time of war."

"And you," Lumbre said, eyes only for her son. "You're siding with the Jades on this?"

Aurelio nodded.

"Then here," the diosa said, a circlet seemingly made out of burning coals appearing in her hands. "A Scorching Circlet," she said as Aurelio, reluctantly, took it. "When worn, it will amplify your fire powers," Lumbre told him.

Aurelio nodded as he turned it over in his hands.

Of course, the diosa couldn't leave it at that. "It might make you almost as powerful as your sister."

Aurelio winced.

"What a dick," Teo said, because he couldn't help himself.

Niya snorted.

Lumbre's blistering eyes burned into him but Teo just scowled back.

"Have my Ring of Shielding," Diose Guerrero said as they slipped a gold band from their middle finger and handed it to Niya. "All you have to do is throw up your hand and it will summon my shield."

Niya gave it a try. She momentarily stumbled under the weight as a heavy shield materialized on her arm, covered in leather with Guerrero's snarling head branded on the front.

"Oh my *gods*," Niya breathed, pulling out the Unbreakable Blade so she stood there with sword and shield. "It's totally over for those bitches!"

Lumbre looked unimpressed but Guerrero chuckled approvingly.

"Wait, why are you even helping us?" Niya asked bluntly. With a flick of her wrists, the shiny weapons returned to their mundane forms. "Our parents are going *against* your orders."

Guerrero and Lumbre exchanged a look. Guerrero replied, "We, too, want our children home."

With that, the two Golds turned on their heels and stalked away, mixing back into the crowd of gods and priests scrambling about.

"So, what's the plan?" Niya asked, now that they were alone.

"Try to undo the apocalypse, I guess." Teo shrugged.

Aurelio let out a mirthless laugh. "You make it sound so easy."

Teo bumped him with his shoulder. "You have to admit—an end-of-the-world road trip does sound kind of fun."

Aurelio grinned. It was a tired grin, but a grin nonetheless.

"Shit." Niya huffed a heavy sigh. "We're gonna need a bigger bag of candy."

TO BE CONTINUED.

ACKNOWLEDGMENTS

This book was conceptualized and written during quarantine and an ongoing global pandemic. Without these important people in my life, Teo's story would've never taken flight.

The first person I want to thank is Max—my sounding board, my voice of reason, and the one who always re-centers me when I get overwhelmed by life. I know I say this a lot, but I would literally be lost without your beautiful brain and warm companionship!

Alex—your voice and sense of humor echoes throughout this entire story. Thank you for all the brainstorming, ranting, terrible jokes, and the many late nights that turned into early mornings. At this point, I owe you royalties! Or at the very least, a series of fun vacations.

Jennifer March Soloway—you are the best agent anyone could ask for! Thank you so much for all of your support and encouragement, especially when I'm feeling panicked or down on myself. You give the best pep talks and always know how to make me feel better. Thank you for being my guide on this wild journey!

Mars Lauderbaugh—my *amazing* cover artist! I can't believe we started with Oikawa fanart, and now you've done my second book cover! You have no idea how much your art brings to my stories. Working on characters has turned into a collaboration and it's the highlight of my entire writing process!

Mik—you've been such a constant and reliable writing partner. I've gone through every step of this book while being on video chat with you. Your company has been such a comfort while trying to survive the apocalypse. Thank you so much for all the laughs.

Anda—you always make sure I'm taking care of myself, and you bully me into getting my shit together when I cease being a functional human toward the end of a deadline.

Ezrael—your ability to see the emotional core of a story is a gift. You have one of the kindest hearts I've had the pleasure of being around. Thank you so much for always pushing me to dig deeper.

My *amazing* friends Austin, Bird, Katie, Raviv, Samantha, and Teddy. You are the best cheerleaders and I can't tell you how much it means to have you all in my life. Whenever I need help figuring out a problem in a book, or I'm too nervous to go to an event by myself, y'all always step in. You can't fathom how much that means to me.

It truly takes a village to create a book, and I have the actual *best team* of creative professionals supporting me!

First and foremost, I'd like to thank my incredible editor, Holly West. You are the real reason I have the career of my dreams, doing what I love. Thank you for taking a chance on me and continuing to do so with every wild book idea I come up with. I am so lucky to have an editor who totally gets me, my humor, and the stories I'm trying to tell. I owe you everything!

Thank you to my publisher, Jean Feiwel, for believing in me. Hana Tzou and Oliver Wehner, my early readers who gave very helpful feedback when this book was still a whole mess. Thank you to Arik Hardin for juggling and coordinating the many steps it took to turn this idea into a novel. A big shout-out to my copyeditor, Melanie Sanders, for going through over four hundred pages of my word vomit and making it intelligible.

Thank you so much to Liz Dresner, Trisha Previte, and L. Whitt for giving me such a *stunning* cover and interior design! And big shout-out to Raymond E. Colón for handling production. It's everything I could've asked for and more!

My wonderful friend and publicist, Kelsey Marrujo, who has been with me since *Cemetery Boys* and continues to be a huge support. My marketing genius, Teresa Ferraiolo, who always takes my wild ideas and big dreams and makes them into reality. I owe so much to my subrights team, Kristin Dulaney, Jordan Winch, and Kaitlin Loss. One of the most exciting things about being an author is seeing all the different languages my books get translated into, and how far my stories travel!

An absolutely critical stage of the editing process for me is getting authenticity and sensitivity readers. They provide crucial feedback when I'm including characters in my stories outside of my lived experience, but they also catch anything harmful that may have slipped my eye. This even includes characters who share my own identities, because you never know if something you've internalized will make it onto the page.

Melissa Vera from Salt & Sage Books and Johanie Martinez-Cools—thank you so much for reading *The Sunbearer Trials* and providing such thoughtful feedback. Anna-Marie McLemore—I admire you so much. You were one of the first authors I met and have been such a kind and giving friend through all of this.

Most importantly, I want to thank my family. Mom, Christine, Chris, Grammy, and Gramps. Thank you for always being there and believing in me.

Last, but certainly not least, I want to thank Bo Burnham for getting me through 2021. I spent countless hours alone in an abandoned office building listening to *Inside* while working on this book. Enough hours that I was in the top 2 percent of your listeners in my Spotify Wrapped, but we don't have the time to unpack all that right now. Thank you for making the pandemic feel a little less lonely.

Thank you for reading this Feiwel & Friends book. The
friends who made THE SUNBEARER TRIALS possible are:

JEAN FEIWEL, *Publisher*
LIZ SZABLA, *Associate Publisher*
RICH DEAS, *Senior Creative Director*
HOLLY WEST, *Senior Editor*
ANNA ROBERTO, *Senior Editor*
KAT BRZOZOWSKI, *Senior Editor*
DAWN RYAN, *Executive Managing Editor*
RAYMOND ERNESTO COLÓN, *Director of Production*
EMILY SETTLE, *Associate Editor*
ERIN SIU, *Associate Editor*
FOYINSI ADEGBONMIRE, *Associate Editor*
RACHEL DIEBEL, *Assistant Editor*
ARIK HARDIN, *Assistant Managing Editor*

Follow us on Facebook or visit us online at mackids.com.
Our books are friends for life.